MARKS OF IDENTITY

JUAN GOYTISOLO

Translated from the Spanish
by Gregory Rabassa

SERPENT'S TAIL

With thanks to Kathy Acker, Mark Ainley, Martin Chalmers, Bob Lumley, Enrico Palandri, Kate Pullinger, Antonio Sanchez for their advice and assistance.

British Library Cataloguing in Publication Data
Goytisolo, Juan, *1931–*
Marks of identity
I. Title II. Señas de identidad. *English*
863'.64[F]
ISBN 1-85242-134-7

First published 1966 as *Señas de Identidad* by Editorial Joaquín Mortiz, Mexico.

First published in English by Grove Press, New York.

This edition first published 1988 by Serpent's Tail, Unit 4, Blackstock Mews, London N4

Printed in Great Britain by WBC Print (Bristol) Ltd.

FOR MONIQUE, ALWAYS

Yesterday has gone; Tomorrow has not come.
FRANCISCO DE QUEVEDO

Let's be sure about it, I said to myself; where
is the cemetery? Outside or inside? . . . The cemetery
is inside Madrid. Madrid is the cemetery.
MARIANO JOSÉ DE LARRA

Better yet destruction, fire.
LUIS CERNUDA

I

"Established in Paris comfortably established in Paris with more years of residence in France than in Spain with more French habits than Spanish ones including even the classic one of living with the daughter of a well-known exile a regular resident of the *Ville Lumière* and an episodic visitor to his homeland in order to bear Parisian witness to aspects of Spanish life that might serve to *épater le bourgeois* an expert in that vast European geography that is traditionally hostile to our values and also present in his intineraries the well-known hand of the great bearded saint of that ex-paradise of a Caribbean island transformed today by work and the grace of Reds semi-Reds and useful idiots into a silent and lugubrious floating concentration camp evading the realities of the moment with an easy comfortable and advantageous non-conformity showing himself with prudent niceties and calculated tactics in all the social circles of the Boeotian world beyond El Ferol in order to gain for us the forgiveness and pardon of the malicious critics beyond the Pyrenees at the same time that the sum of our authentic cinematographic values remains the object of wishful ignorance bolted doors and a conspiracy of silence such are the characteristics of the individual in question and his contacts and coordinates abroad raised to the level of official photographer for *France Presse* and announced beyond our borders with the bass drum and cymbals of that international and well-worn repertory of noise and show with which anything from far or near that smells anti-Spanish is always greeted in certain circles for having filmed a brief documentary that was defective and dull in its planning horribly put together and without photographic grace or poetry a fact that does not startle those of us accustomed as we are to acts and attitudes whose sad reiteration reveals the impotent hatred of our adversaries no matter what the Regime in our homeland since the Counter-Reformation up till the present Spain has suffered under the most unjust irritating and intolerable attacks that any nation could receive attacks which systematically and periodically emerge from the crafty hole of lies resentment ill-intentioned and tendentious information everything that implies an attack against the sovereign decision of a country to govern itself in its own way without outside interference or arbitrary impositions and if these attacks are irritating when they come from a foreign hand they only deserve a sneer when they are the work of a fellow countryman ready to sink his turbine into the sewer with the idea of making himself a famous little person by aligning himself with political positions of which we have had our fill of knowledge at a time like this which is so suspiciously exhausted by restless disagreements it is exceedingly simple to turn out scenes of the poor suburbs nor does one even have to bother to make them real a few extras dressed as policemen can beat a worker strip a little boy cover him with coal dust and seat him on a pile of manure this is within the reach of any careless person but one who does it reveals such moral taste that it is best not to mention him even though all we need is a preposition and two nouns for an all-out attack an artful insult vituperation opprobrium and mocking all lit up by the livid lights of a lie there can be no freedom or leeway or any tolerance which would be criminal that there does exist misery and grief in Spain no one can deny taking pictures of miserable huts is a common thing not only in the civilized countries of Europe but also in the golden land of the United States finding some skinny child with his belly swollen is not hard either in any country no matter how high its standard of living when the gangsters of the camera decide to photograph it and reveal the defects of human society to a foreign public made up of intellectuals and snobs but it is not right or honest to see with only one eye one cannot refuse to see the whole understand only the part of course there is hunger drought and lack of housing in the marrow of all these scenes of Murcia and Andalusia but there is also something that the affected little big shot from Paris has forgotten and that something is hope more than any-where else one must look at these century-old poor regions with clear eyes and an open heart without harboring the stupid idea of transposing their secret through a fleeting and hazy vision more worthy of a second-rate Mérimée than that of the heir of a wealthy and respectable family whose father was basely murdered by the Red hordes a fine child with all of his pleasures and whims taken care of with a Christian education in an old religious institution under the tutelage and protection of irreproachable and worthy men what is essential we repeat is to go down on one's knees before this broad and arid panorama look up at the sky in an attempt to keep the cloud there and scratch in the earth to find the redeeming spring any other way would be walking blindly wrapped up in the dazzling dust storms of the Yeste mountains living in a dramatic and inconsolable Polyphemus complex bearing witness with the pimples of one's soul insisting on being a know-it-all in mourning and a mendacious pimp . . ."

That was how they were talking about you when the incident of the documentary became known, in cafés and gatherings, meetings and parties, the self-satisfied men and women with whom a laughable decree of fate had awarded you at birth as fellow countrymen: dim childhood friends, innocuous schoolmates, female relatives with cold and severe looks, virtuous and sad acquaintances, all entrenched in their impregnable class privileges, conspicuous and right-thinking members of an autumnal and doddering world which they had given to you, without asking your permission, with religion, morals, and laws made to its measure: a promiscuous and hollow order from which you tried to escape, confident, like so many others, of a regenerating change and cathartic which, because of mysterious imponderables, had not come about and, after long years in exile, there you were again, in the painful and affectionate landscape of your childhood, deprived even of the bitter consolation of alcohol, while the eucalyptus trees in the garden aired their green branches and changeable and flighty clouds floated toward the sun like somber swans, feeling yourself less the prodigal son who humbles his brow before his father than the criminal who furtively returns to the scene of his crime, while the Voices—the congenital evil and frustration of your caste joined in one chorus—treacherously continued their dull singsong whispering in your ear: "you who have been one of us and have broken with us have the right to many things and it is not hard for us to see that you have the right to think that your country is living a really atrocious existence we are sorry for your error but who has put up any gates in the fields Andalusian farmers are the only ones who allow themselves that luxury and that is where those solitary isolated gates come from ones that seem neither to close nor to open outside of that exception which is like poetic license no one is obliging you to pass through the arch go ahead then with your ideas about politics and the other realities of Spain go right ahead too if it pleases you with your annoyances and mortifications concerning the racial qualities of our breed who is stopping you we know that you are a Barcelonan in spite of your Asturian name but Asturian or Barcelonan supposing that Barcelona does not inspire any emotion in you or the land of Asturias raise any warm feeling in your soul turn your back on all of us and look toward other horizons why must you contradict a spontaneous movement of your soul if some feeling carries you along pathways of such indescribable sadness after all you will not be the first Spaniard to stop loving his country but why come back then it would be better for you to stay away and renounce us once and for all think about it you still have time our firmness is unmovable and none of your efforts will succeed in undermining it we are made of stone and we will remain stone why do you blindly seek disaster forget about us and we will forget about you your birth was a mistake bear with it"

You had been asleep and as soon as you opened your eyes you sat up. The clock showed ten minutes to seven. On the marble table there was a bottle of wine and on the porch you could hear the first notes of Mozart's *Requiem,* majestic and grave. You looked for Dolores, but Dolores was not there. You could have drunk some Fefiñanes, cool and yellow, just the right thing to moisten your lips and you did not decide. The clouds had gone away while you were asleep and the sun was burning up the late sky. Leaning on the railing you contemplated the domesticated hills girded with vines and carob trees, the birds splitting the thin transparency of the air, the distant sea with muffled waves, softened and embellished by the distance. All you had to do was turn your head and take in with one glance the slim cypresses in the garden, the conclave of sparrows perched on the boughs of the cedar tree, the toys forgotten by Dolores's nieces and nephews when they went off after some new and absurd distraction. (You remembered their winged appearance the night before, solemnly dressed up in two chasubles they had got from the chapel when the servant girl had been careless for a moment, delicate and agile, slightly sacrilegious, with dissipated and smiling faces that had filled you with rapture.)

Within just an hour Dolores would come with the drops prescribed by Dr. d'Asnières, would take a laconic look at the bottle immersed in the bucket and, lying on the bench in the summerhouse, the two of you would wait for the fateful horn that regularly announced the arrival of visitors, the feared intrusion of strange people into that analgesic and tender backwater of peace. Then it would no longer be possible for you to appreciate the swift and fresh abundance of air among the pines or lose yourself to the point of vertigo in the difficult geometry of the constellations, wrapped up once more in the mesh of a dialogue which would oppress and asphyxiate you, the prisoner of a character who was not you, mixed up with him and supplanted by him. But for the moment and leaving the garden, you still could, if you felt like it, wander around at your leisure beside the pond, smell the sober dense perfume of the rosemary patch, spy on the mute entreaty of the recently uncorked cork trees. Go through the inside of the house, inhabited now by the severe and rigorous voice of the *Dies irae* and one by one dig out of your dusty memory the singular and irregular elements which made up the mythical decoration of your childhood, the huge porch, the dark dining room, the old and musty rooms. Go up into the moth-eaten attic and examine the battered cupboards, the lame chairs, the foggy and fantasmal mirrors. Lean over looking at the old prints with ebony frames which had fascinated you so much as a child and whose resuscitated inscriptions had been engraved in your inner world forever: "*Valenciennes prise d'assaut, et sauvée du pillage par la clémence du Roy le 16 Mars 1677,*" "*Panorama della città di Roma,*" "*Vue de la Ville et du Chateau de Dinant sur la Meuse, assiégée par les Français le 22 May et prise le 29 du même mois en l'année 1675, acreve et fortifiée depuis de plusieurs travaux.*" In the stern study presided over by the portrait of your great-grandfather you could open one of the desk drawers, with the bundles of family correspondence arranged by date and for a few minutes, if you wanted to, dive into the disheveled and anachronistic universe of your forebears: letters from slaves on the vanished plantation of Cruces, asking for the blessing of "massah," the remote master—your responsibility in the slow succession of generations—the very one who turned them down and threw them out; post cards from some aunt, dead now and a very saintly death no doubt, written in French with the unmistakable fine hand of the pupils of Sagrado Corazón—"*Nous avons célébré la fête de l'Immaculée et nous avons fait une procession très jolie mais comme il faisait un peu froid et il y avait quelques enfants enrhumés nous n'avons pu mettre la robe blanche*"—the same Sacred Heart, an organ like the one in an anatomical drawing, arteries and veins, auricles and ventricles, reproduced in various sizes and honeyed poses in all of the bedrooms of the house; receipts for the closing of accounts from banks in Havana, New York, and Paris, before the Spanish-Yankee War and the breakup of the family. In one of those drawers you could even thumb through four bunches of envelopes written with a hesitant and clumsy hand, as you did the day you came back, and discover once more with repeated surprise that you were the author: letters sent from the boarding school where part of your youth had been uselessly consumed, during the opaque and ominous years following the death of your mother; psychograms drawn up for your family—"Nervous temperament and great self-esteem. Somewhat withdrawn from his schoolmates, has relationships only with a certain few. Average religiosity and piety. Rarely plays games at recess time."—from forgotten teachers with illegible signatures; the annual school bulletin where you had found your grades in courses during the school year 1945–46—"Religion A–, Philisophy C+ Latin B, Greek A–, Literature B–, History and Geography A, Mathematics C, Science D, Medal of Honor, Gold"—and even a surprising synoptic table of the Angelic Hosts and Orders, copied in your hand twenty times in a notebook, headed by a finely written notation in green ink: "For having distracted the class during the lesson"—convincing documentary proofs of the picturesque and loquacious child that you had been and in whom today's adult was hard to recognize, suspended as you were in an uncertain present, lacking a past as well as a future, with that desolate and intimate certainty of knowing that you had come back not because things had changed and your expatriation had had meaning, but because little by little you had exhausted your reserves of patience, and, in a word, you were afraid of dying. That was how your thoughts were going, all by yourself, as the afternoon used up its splendor in an ostentatious burst of fireworks and the light slowly left the clearings in the woods spread out at your feet, before you finally decided to take a cold sip of Fefiñanes, lazily light up a cigarette, cross the porch which was being shaken by the chorus of the *Benedictus* and poke around the shelves of the massive library for the photograph album which might help you recover the lost key to your childhood and your youth. You could go back to the garden and settle down with it at the marble table, breathing in the ancient and musty aroma of its pages; observe in peaceful relaxation the sleepless countryside, the malleable sky and sea, the red and dying sun: the family specters lay there for you, one after the other, immobilized in dull and yellowed photos, as if in concerted and tedious repetitions of a disappointing scene and your brief and now distant history was being reborn along with them, the link in an uninterrupted chain of mediocrity and conformity—adventure and pillage would have been better—the unconscious and culpable fruit of their quiet and idle lives, their stunted existence, calamitous and useless.

A pompous conference room with a broad table surrounded by empty heavy chairs and a portrait of Alfonso XIII on the wall; a picture of the steamship "Flora," property of that prosperous and magnificent family; hazy post cards of Cienfuegos with its deserted squares, white churches, and royal palms elegantly placed about as in the ingenuous décor of a theater; a railroad station with unnecessary and ornamental dead tracks and a multicolored group of Cuban peasants leaning on the platform; the cane train from the plantation, where one could read the inscription *Mendiola y Montalvo,* it was the grinding season; a view of the plantation buildings, with the mill, the sheds, and an oblong square, clear and clean; the fire-path of palm trees leading to the country house of his great-grandfather; the evaporating pans, the cauldrons, and other equipment through which the cane juice would pass to be clarified, strained, and reach its proper level of sweetness; and, perpetuated in gestures and expressions that still endured, their bodies having already disintegrated after more than a century, Álvaro could make out his exemplary and dominant great-grandfather along with his ungainly and inconsistent offspring. A poor *hidalgo* from the Asturian provinces, astute businessman, speculator, and slave-trader, with a cruel and haughty look, thin lips and a mustache curling up in the shape of a crank handle, he seemed to be conjecturing about the fallibility and insignificance of the descendants who once he was dead would govern his empire and who in the studied arrangement done by E. Cotera, photographer, Santa Isabel 45, Cienfuegos, were straight and stiff as they faced the lens; somewhat apart from him, the sad reproduction and copy of the resigned and mute great-grandmother, firmly dressed in mourning, the deceived and unhappy wife—supplanted in bed by Negro slave women—with no other refuge except the melancholy practice of a consoling religion and the care of sons brought up according to the norms and precepts of a tyrannical, austere, and inflexible moral code. These same sons, twenty-five years later, fat and bald, prematurely aged, as if crushed by the weight of their enormous responsibilities, heirs to the fortune if not the talents, virtuous and selfish, devout and miserly: Álvaro's grandfather and the unending procession of uncles photographed in Havana, New York, and Switzerland before the sudden liquidation of the plantation and the breakup of the family, a consequence of the war with the United States and the loss of the colonies. His elegant grandfather, wearing his proverbial straw hat, beside the absurd and extensive Moorish chalet in Barcelona, established now in Spain with his wife and children, chauffeur and gardener, summerhouse and horse-drawn carriage and—since his Negro slaves had lamentably been freed—some poor natives of the country for his use alone, a pretext of charitable deeds, meritorious works and indulgences, a guarantee of God's merciful pardon in this life and eternal salvation in the other. Years later, with Álvaro's father dressed up like a little English sailor, an innocuous collection of children, the ambiguous mixture of rich orphans and frightened princes: the stigmas and scars which came from the disorderly and irregular life of his great-grandfather could be seen on the children's faces—like old people pickled in alcohol, Álvaro thought—which the anonymous photographer had caught with the refined malice of a Goya facing the progeny of Charles IV and María Luisa; a degenerate race of future embittered old maids and—with the exception of Álvaro's father—gentleman parasites as useless as they were decorative. Two pages farther on—after the obligatory exchange of pictures with the Mendiolas still living in Cuba—groups of school children in a compact discipline of hazy faces and blind looks which brought back the uniformly gray times which Álvaro remembered well: seven years of secondary school in a religious institution, by means of which his mother first and then the family council had tried to break his rebellious streak and bind him in the rigid corset of certain principles, morals, and rules which were the principles, morals, and rules of his ignorant and hated social class; those had been years of repentance and sin, sperm and confession, attempts at reform and renewed doubts, stubbornly spent in the invocation of a deaf god—emptied some centuries before of his pristine and original content—up until the moment when life had imposed its ordinances and the precarious and costly edifice tumbled down like a house of cards. Partial views—July 1918—of the recently acquired farm, with conceited young people—aunts and uncles—indolently distributed about a garden decorated then with pots of morning-glories, round wicker chairs, and a strange rustic observatory with a straw roof where Uncle Eulogio had set up a wild-looking portable telescope. That last photo taken before he had been born clearly reproduced the hives on his mother's property in Yeste, an oven for drying rosemary, a snapshot of the neighboring communal farm of La Graya. Álvaro's father figured in all of them, disdainful and distant, conscious perhaps of the stupid and empty social comedy that he represented, sensing perhaps—Álvaro would say to himself—the vengeful platoon of rebellious peasants and the quick rifles that would cut short his life. An obscure feeling of intimate and pleasant profanation accompanied the slow turning of those pages which brought back a dead and vanished past, a round of people identifiable only by the merciful inscription of a name and date, which saved them, therefore—for how long?—from irrevocable and lasting oblivion; and, as in the splendid and familiar great mansion of the Country Club which Álvaro had visited on his trip to Cuba—transformed by the Revolution into a modest school for art teachers, with photographs of Castro and Lenin hung mockingly on the walls—the posthumous rancor against this stupid breed and its presumptuous respectability that fed itself on that silent and tranquil hecatomb. By a wild irony of fate it depended on him—who was keeping him from erasing the inscriptions, capriciously tearing up the pages?—that the very memory of their existence might also not be lost along with the good and the evil they had done during their lifetimes—the painful carnival masquerades of the album would then dissolve into the nothingness from which they had sprung without necessity and to which they had reasonably and justly returned.

You had searched for it without avail among the shelves in the library, among the numerous pious and instructive readings that your uncles had: *Enlighted Youth, or Virtues and Vices,* by Madame Dufresnoy; *The Kingdom of Heaven,* by Doña Ana María Paulín y de la Peña, Baroness of Cortés; *The Novena of the Most Blessed Sacrament; The Devotions of Saint Joseph; Manual for Pilgrims to Rome; The History of Christianity in Japan; A Course in Apologetics, or The Rational Exposition of the Faith,* by Father Gualterio Devivier; *The Yearbook of Mary,* or *The True Servant of the Blessed Virgin.* . . . The book Señorita Lourdes was holding in the picture dated May 1936—shoes, stockings, hat, skirt, and blouse all black, a book that even after twenty-five years would still have the same subtle smell of incense and naphthalene and whose contents the beautiful child that you once had been—prettily resting your curly hair on a soft cushion—had seemed to absorb with great pleasure and joy, was not there, obviously lost, like so many others, during the hectic days of the revolution and the war, your father dead and the house requisitioned, the surly country shaken by a hollow and delirious crisis, the death rattle of an agony that had been prolonged over centuries on end. And sitting in the garden, cloaked and protected by Mozart's serene music, you were reliving the scene that had been rescued by the neutral and objective lens of the photographer: the dead nursemaid and the devout child, as if both had been conceived in a soft and extravagant dream, shown in a playground full of nurses and children, aged gentlemen and imperturbable ladies, four months, you were startled to think, before the vaunted February elections and the fateful victory of the Popular Front. Señorita Lourdes's swooning hands prevented you from deciphering the title of the book and your bright face was putting forth a bastard feeling of envy and admiration.

You could remember your immense disappointment at not finding it and the sterile visit to the bookstore that specialized in religious books the day you first went to Barcelona when, facing a pale, monkish-looking girl, you had asked her for *Stories of Child Martyrs,* which Señorita Lourdes had given to you on your seventh birthday—the book you kept by your pillow during the distant and shady days that preceded the outbreak of the war.

"Is it a collection of biographies?"

"Yes."

"We have a life of Saint Mary Goretti with colored illustrations. Would you like to look at it? . . . It would be very good for a present. It's sold a lot of copies this year."

"No, that's not the one. It's an older book . . . I remember that there was a drawing of Saint Tarsitius on the cover."

"Can you remember the author's name?"

"No."

"We have this *Lives of Child Saints* for less. Paperbound. Thirty-five pesetas."

"May I look at it?"

The clerk handed him a medium-sized book whose cover showed an Infant Jesus (blond) embracing a child saint (blond) under the approving glance of two chubby angels (blond), carefully reduced by the artist to pink- and fat-cheeked heads adorned with wings.

"These are the lives of child saints," the clerk said. "We sell a good many of them."

"The one I'm looking for is about child martyrs."

"Some of them were martyrs, too," the girl insisted.

You had been taken unexpectedly by the fear that she would think you were a sadist and had covered the cost of the thirty-five peseta book, rejoicing at her chaste expression of suspicion, with the same stimulating itch you had had when you were sixteen—when you had come out of the dirty little kiosk on Atarazanas with an obscene photograph in your pocket and had run to find some refuge where you could look at it and enjoy yourself all alone as you stared at the glacial and depressing image. On your way back to the country you had examined the book, written in approximately the same language as Señorita Lourdes's, and the past had erupted in you in an unforeseen way, turning your book into the lost book, your voice into the flutey voice of the nursemaid.

" 'The Prefect, blinded by such a glorious profession of faith and filled with hatred for Christians and turning his wrath on the beautiful Virgin, ordered her bound and led off to prison to be cruelly lashed.' . . . Are you listening, Álvaro?"

"Yes, Señorita Lourdes."

" 'He then decreed that she be tortured in every possible way.

She was stretched out on the rack and her flesh was barbarously torn away with iron hooks. The torturers applied burning fagots to her chest and sides. They threw her into a vat of quicklime to induce unbearable burning in her insides; they sprinkled her with molten lead and gloated as they martyrized her senses. But the greater the fury of the Prefect and the torturers, so was the perseverance, strength, and joy of the Saint, from whose lips there poured forth praise and thanksgiving to the Lord.' . . . Are you paying attention, Álvaro?"

"Yes, Señorita Lourdes."

"Listen carefully, the story isn't over. . . . 'The headstrong Prefect, in an attempt to satisfy his diabolical thirst for vengeance, ordered the Saint tied to a wooden cross and her body roasted with flaming torches. At the moment she gave up her soul to God there was seen to fly out of her mouth a pure white dove which ascended to heaven, the symbol of her virginal spirit which was going up to receive its martyr's crown. Another miracle occurred, witnessed by many people, as the heavens covered the naked body of the Saint with a mantle of snow so that it would not be the object of the pagans' unworthy eyes.' . . . Are you crying, child?"

"Yes, Señorita Lourdes."

"Are you suffering because of the terrible pains of the Saint?"

"Yes, Señorita Lourdes."

"Would you be ready to die like her and bless the Lord for every one of your tortures?"

"Yes, Señorita Lourdes."

Yours was a mediocre universe, you were thinking, that of a healthy, spoiled, and idle child, the inhabitant of an ordered world, without risk or the possibility of heroism; crushed by the weight of so many children destined at an early age for death and eternal glory—Agnes, Tarsitius, Pancratius, Agapitis, Pelagius, Lucy, and others more recent in time and no less miraculous, like Saint Magdalen Sophia Barat, Saint Dominic Savio, or Alexander the Acolyte—without even perceiving in your life any of the forewarning signs that invariably point out to pious souls the presence of an angel of God in the world and which, in Señorita Lourdes's reader, would usually manifest themselves from the very birth of the future saint: celestial visitors, apparitions of the Infant Jesus between two pitchers of Sèvres china, unjust persecutions, painful illnesses, fragile health.

" 'Miracles of God also appeared during the life of this Saint who passed so quickly through our vale of exile. Even during the time he was in Murialdo and Castelnuovo, a mysterious youth—certainly a heavenly inhabitant in human form—had carried him in his lifetime on one certain occasion so that he would not tire himself on the road. Later on a no less mysterious lady—the Blessed Virgin herself?—accompanied him from Castelnuovo to Mondonio, disappearing quite suddenly. . . .' "

You had innocently tried to imitate the expressions on the faces of the martyrs as they had been drawn in the book, with a crown of sainthood miraculously held above their blond angelic heads, looking at yourself for hours on end in the bathroom mirror and wondering with anguish whether dark and healthy children like you could still aspire to the favor and protection of the heavenly powers, lulled by the pleasant voice of Señorita Lourdes who, with her glasses lowered on her nose, always seemed to be astutely spying at the emotions painted on your face.

" 'The little girl was known for her piety and good heart at an early age. When she cried she could only be consoled when the names of Jesus and Mary were pronounced. As soon as she began to move her lips, those sweet names were the first that she learned to babble. She was seen many times with her little hands lifted up to heaven and with her eyes in prayer, lost in tender love. From her earliest infancy, she showed an enchanting and ardent devotion for the Holy Sacrament. She would often disappear from home to prostrate herself before the Sanctuary. They would find her there, smiling and as if in ecstasy, respectfully motionless and carried away by love. In spite of her early years she already understood and she meditated profoundly on the infinite worth of the treasure kept behind that modest little door.' "

Jealous, you were amazed at the synchronized precision of those elevated lives, in such cruel contrast with the routine and emptiness for your own, dreaming—for lack of the longed-for apparition—about the grave illness that would put you to the test or about the coveted and spectacular martyrdom.

"Don't any of you go out into the street," your mother said some weeks later. "Yesterday they asked about him again and I've seen them go by in trucks. . . . It looks as if they're going to burn the churches. . . ."

And even though your existence had not changed on the surface—regular meals, reading, walks with Señorita Lourdes—in the serious and worried looks of the adults you had sensed the intrusion of a new and disturbing factor about which they never spoke in front of you and which, in your absence, brought on dark conferences with your uncles, the secret of which you tried to decipher in vain by pretending sometimes you were asleep or making believe that you were involved in your geography puzzle.

"We'll have to hide the chalice in the attic . . ."

"And what if the farmers turn us in? We can't take a chance on . . ."

"The best thing would be to leave at night."

"With the roadblocks?" It was Uncle César's voice: "You're out of your head."

"I'll take the child. A woman by herself . . ."

The urgent ringing of the bell had interrupted the conversation and, hours later, when Señorita Lourdes was serving you your usual cup of chocolate and cookies, your mother had dried her tears with a handkerchief and, from your modest seven-year-old level, you felt obliged to intervene.

"Mama."

"Sweet."

"Are you crying because Daddy's not home?"

"Yes, child."

"Why is he taking so long in coming back?"

"He's at the house in Albacete. . . . He has a lot of work to do."

"Who were those men who were asking about him?"

"Nobody. Some friends."

Your mother still did not know what had happened in Yeste—the official notification of his death was received a year later—but her tears had confirmed your suspicions that something—what?—was going on behind the scenes, happenings that for some dark reason the adults were making an effort to hide. . . . Señorita Lourdes was the first to reveal the secret to you.

One night she had knelt down with you in front of the little toy altar where you often celebrated mass, imitating the looks and gestures of the real officiants, and she had said with emphasis: "Help us during these difficult days, oh Lord. Do not let the Godless ones stain the soul of this child and turn him into a slave of Satan."

"What's going on, Señorita Lourdes?" you had asked her.

"Nothing, my prince, nothing."

"Yes it is. I know that something's going on. And I've seen the trucks full of men from the window. . . . Are they really bad men?"

"I can't tell you anything, my prince. Not a single word."

"Yes you can, Señorita Lourdes. Please tell me."

"No, my sweet. You're still a child. I promised your mother."

"Tell me, Señorita Lourdes. I swear I won't tell anyone."

"No, no. I don't want to make you suffer. You're too young to understand. . . ."

"Please. I'm older now. I won't tell anyone."

"Oh, my prince, my poor prince."

"If the bad men come I'll pray to the Virgin and they won't be able to hurt us."

"Your mama told me not to."

"Please, Señorita Lourdes."

"I can't, my child."

"The Infant Jesus will tell me."

You had put your hands together, just as they did in the illustrations in the book, and when her weak resistance was overcome, Señorita Lourdes had drawn you to her with sobs and had announced to you with a quavering voice the arrival of the Anti-Christ. The poorly dressed men crowded into the trucks that were driving by beneath your window were special envoys of the devil, hardened agents of the Evil One. The fabulous world of persecutions and tortures, of executioners who slavered like wolves over the naked bodies of their victims had caught you up in a sea of happiness and anxiety, still incredulous before the glow and magnitude of your dream so quickly and unexpectedly brought to realization.

"I'm not afraid to die, Señorita Lourdes." It was a sentence you had learned from the book.

"No, no, oh Lord. Don't take the life of an innocent little angel."

"What do a few years of life matter if I lose my soul?"

"Lord, do not listen to the voice of this child. Think of the grief of his mother."

"I will call on the sweet name of Mary and the bad men will repent."

The expedition was decided upon then and there. Exultant and vibrant with enthusiasm, Señorita Lourdes was weeping in front of the little altar, she embraced you, she begged for God's forgiveness. Her waxy parchment face seemed to have come back to life, with two rosettes on her cheeks and a clear and almost adolescent gleam in her eye, you finally felt like an inhabitant of the world described in the book, included at long last among the band of martyrs. With Señorita Lourdes's ecstatic approval you had knelt down beside the purple-painted sanctuary with the tiny toy chalice in your hands, savoring within your realm the sublime instant, living in anticipation your glorious life as a saint haloed with divine light, pictured in future books with a radiant and volatile little crown.

"My God, my God, forgive me," moaned Señorita Lourdes. "Soften the terrible Calvary of his mother. Give her the strength to bear this test."

"Why don't we tell her to come with us?" you had suggested.

"No, my prince, she wouldn't be able to bear it."

"I'll pray for her."

"Angel of my soul. . . . Pray for me too."

That night neither of you had slept, you clutching the ciborium like Saint Tarsitius, she kneeling before the Infant Jesus, begging God's absolution and repenting for her sins. After your mother's nightly kiss when you went to bed—after some whispering and get-togethers which were no longer an enigma for you—you had taken one last look at Señorita Lourdes's book—"with the nails they held forth they nailed him to the wall in the form of a cross and they gouged open his veins to collect his blood . . ."—enjoying the somber descriptions with an almost terrifying pleasure, indifferent to the sirens and horns announcing the passage of the men along the street, repeating over and over again like a sleepwalker: "This is my last day."

At nine o'clock your mother had brought you your breakfast tray. Señorita Lourdes had dressed you in a shirt, pants, socks, and sandals which were all white and had hung a relic of the Holy Cross around your neck which you kissed many times, almost in ecstasy, while she combed your curls and moistened your temples with cologne. Uncle César was to come for your mother and he arrived at the house with his eyes wide with terror, tieless and hatless, grotesquely masquerading as a poor man—a clouded memory associated in your recollection with the smiling little man who, weeks later, had dressed himself up as a priest right in front of you and had said mass in the living room without anyone's becoming indignant at the deceit—he said that he was going on his vacation in the mountains and that he would send you a pretty post card. You only half believed him and you watched him walk away so you could make the agreed-on signal to Señorita Lourdes and slip out too. Outside the sirens were howling.

"My sweet, my prince. . . . Will you be able to keep a stiff upper lip?"

"Yes."

"Will you resist the threats and tortures?"

"Yes."

"Oh my sweet, my poor sweet. . . . Repeat after me: Lord Jesus . . ."

"Lord Jesus . . ."

"True God and true man . . ."

"True God and true man . . ."

Barcelona at that time was not a prosperous and flourishing city of over a million pompous corpses, satisfied with their condition, and the look of the men who were guarding their recently recovered dignity in improvised barricades and roadblocks and raised their fists with pride was easy for you to reconstruct thanks to the documentaries and flashbacks from the *cinémathèque* on the rue d'Ulm: a long blank smile, long sideburns and heavy beards, red kerchiefs tied around their necks, blue cotton coveralls and the tilted militiaman's cap, workers, peasants, small farmers; the rough and rustic virility of a people come to life as adults and put aside again, in the midst of the indifference of others, by their traditional tenacious enemies; the therapeutic maleness and roughness which months before you had found among the Negroes and mulattoes of Havana as you were being pursued by an adolescent love which was like the omen of the fainting spell on the Boulevard Richard Lenoir and your irrevocable down-payment existence.

". . . the resurrection of the flesh . . ."

"the eternal life . . ."

"the eternal life . . ."

"Amen."

With the help of your later memory of the *cinémathèque* you were also able to imagine the strange appearance of the streets of Barcelona during the revolutionary days of 1936, gathering empty existences like that into a story woven together exclusively from scattered and truncated elements: a city deserted by aristocrats and businessmen, priests and playboys, ladies and fops, while multitudes of living prisoners invaded the center like a warlike and sullen army, miraculously sprouting forth from the bowels of some neighborhood cemetery. The houses looked dirty and ragged, with flags and slogans on the balconies and on the walls and, among the anguished clamor of the sirens which cut the hot and humid air, groups of the curious were examining the impact of bullets and were mockingly studying the livid glow of the fires.

The parish churches of Sarriá and Bonanova were burning, the convents of the Reparadora and Josephine Sisters and, holding tight to Señorita Lourdes's bony hand, you went on to your place of martyrdom dressed in white and with the precious relic hanging around your neck, invoking now and again with holiness the sweet names of Jesus and Mary. By your side, Señorita Lourdes had ostentatiously unfurled her lace mantilla and was reading prayers and maxims aloud from a book bound in velvet and with metal corners.

"Soul of Christ, sanctify me . . . Body of Christ, save me . . . Blood of Christ, transport me . . ."

For the moment you were thinking more about your appearance than anything else, waiting for the grandoise instant when the weightless crown would descend upon you, trying to console yourself with the idea that after you were dead your curls would become blond, fully identified with the images of Agnes and Tarsitius, Pelagius and Pancratius, Eulalia and Dominguito del Val . . .

"Halt! Where are you going?"

A bad man, bearded and poorly dressed, had stepped in front of you, putting his naked arms up with his hands on his hips.

"To the one and only true church founded by Our Lord Jesus Christ," Señorita Lourdes said in one breath.

"Can't you see that it's on fire?"

"God's mercy will protect us from the flames."

Other men dressed like the first one had come up to you and were looking at you both—you seemed to remember it all—with a mixture of humor and curiosity.

"Look at the pair of them," one said in Catalan.

"Sacred Heart of Jesus, I trust in You," you managed to say.

"What did you say, kid?"

"Leave them alone. They're cracked."

"God's will be done."

"Come on, move along," the first man said.

"The Church is the House of God. He will take us in His arms."

"Don't get excited, lady. The chapel's on fire. We have orders not to let anyone pass."

"Forward," said Señorita Lourdes.

"Didn't I tell you they're a couple of nuts?"

"Take it easy."

"Passion of Christ, comfort me. . . . Oh, hear me, good Jesus."

"You go right back home," the man said. "If you want to pray nobody's going to stop you there."

"Lord Jesus, my life."

"Come on, let's go. We don't want any trouble with women and children."

The grappling that followed came back very confused in your memory and you could not remember for sure whether Señorita Lourdes had attacked them (as you had imagined on occasion) or whether, quite simply, the anarchists had seized her by the sleeve when, dragging you along, she had tried to run toward the church (a much more plausible hypothesis).

"We're martyrs, we're martyrs," you were repeating in vain.

The return home, escorted by two gunmen of the FAI, was very sad. Weeping, without the weightless crown, your white suit soiled, you meditated bitterly about the unquestionable failure of your career as a budding saint. Señorita Lourdes, having got over her crisis of tears, seemed to be worried with good reason about how your mother was going to take it.

"It was a mad thing to do," she moaned. "She'll never forgive me."

That afternoon the tray of chocolate and cookies was waiting for you again and your mother did not speak to Señorita Lourdes except to scold her and criticize her giddiness and exaltation in harsh tones.

"As if times were not bad enough as they are. . . . As if I don't have enough to bear already . . ."

Señorita Lourdes wept in silence and a few days later she disappeared from the house for good. Your mother opened the window of her room wide and all she said was that the room smelled bad.

Such was your only sincere entry into the world of piety and as long as the war lasted, in refuge with your mother and your aunts and uncles in the south of France, you never again thought about martyrs or your little altar. When the Nationalists won and society took you back, your educators used fear to impose a superstitious and masochistic cult on you, one from which—having faced the realities of life—you were quick to free yourself. Since then, Christ had left you and you lived in peace without him, at least until that day (because you would not go ahead and face up to the inevitable conquest) you would fall down lifeless as you did on the Boulevard Richard Lenoir and, as you were deprived of your consciousness and your faculties, your vicars would pounce on you with oils and ghostly crucifixes and take charge of your body with impunity—it was all ready to fall apart, food for worms—so they could exhibit it later on for the four winds to see in the name of honor and prestige, crown and scepter of your ambitious and proud caste.

Mozart's *Requiem* had stopped and the half-light had softly shaded off the outline of things, the fresh breath of the wind was dying little by little and in the rural sunset a silence was bearing down, interrupted only by the song of the crickets and the sonorous croaking of some frog or other—"We are not to blame we didn't really know anything so sure that in 1939 we would join the Falange or the Requetés in great numbers and dress our daughters as Morning Stars or Daisies and our sons as Arrows or Pelayos but we were doing it out of pure patriotism the logical reaction against the dreary disorder that had gone on before disorders that even today no man of good will can deny if there was any mistake it came from an excess of love of country and in most cases our political involvement was brief just enough time to organize things a little after that terrible and useless struggle which was to cost us so much blood of one against the other and when the first ephemeral enthusiasm had passed we retreated to a prudent and disreet life entirely devoted to family and business believing firmly in the idyllic picture painted for us in the newspapers convinced that Hitler's victory would inaugurate an age of peace progress and prosperity for all nations without thinking about the other side of the coin about his profound pride and his disdain for the spiritual and earthly values that the Catholic Church defended an excusable mistake if one keeps in mind that since our fratricidal war was over we were thinking most of all about the economic future of the country about repairing buildings and factories encouraging business and developing industry so that work and bread could be furnished the millions and millions of indigent fellow countrymen many of whom it must be said in all truth had fought on our side or had left widows and children when they fell with the innocent idea that the professional politicians would resolve things in due time and would re-establish the monarchy when called for a liberal monarchy with legislatures and chambers attent upon the common good and free enterprise awake to the distributive justice advised in the papal encyclicals completely alien to the abuses of a repression whose existence we were unaware of trusting ingenuously in the uprightness and civic virtue of the men who ruled the destiny of the country sacrificing themselves too when circumstances called for it submissive as we all were to such an extreme rationing that its very rigor often obliged us to evade it not for ourselves ever ready loyally to serve the overriding interests of our country but because of our poor children reduced to eating a scanty ration of four ounces of daily bread while the fortunate possessors of a third-class ration card would get a pound not to mention the scarcity of other products which much to our distress we had to acquire by means of shady deals just like everybody else who was in need but obviously it is only a matter of venial sins practically insignificant and it is hard to find a just man whatever his social origins might be free enough himself of any blame to cast the first stone restoring national parties enthroning the Bourbons again today it seems the opportune solution to us considering the hostile groupings of totalitarian regimes and the Red subversion that threatens us these five years of Spanish post-war have been equally hard on all of us as much for the winners as for the losers for the rich as for the poor therefore today we have imposed the malleable and just formula the opening of the dialogue pacts which respect people and goods the erasure of the old and a healthy new ledger as a prelude to spiritual peace and the long-sought handclasp . . ."—In what obscure corner of his adolescent memory had the sardonic recollection of those Voices come to roost? Was an anodynic image all he needed to pull himself out of his forgetfulness and impose the light upon him in all of its rawness? What demon, hidden like a patient beast in its lair, was threatening to jump, quick to the clawing attack, at the fleeting stimulus of a gray and innocuous card?

By means of the photograph taken in the garden some months before his mother's death. Álvaro was able to recall the jingle of conversations during that memorable autumn of 1944 and give a proper name to the distant faces that in a grave and studied pose made up the withered family council: the aquiline nose and petulant lips of his most pious Aunt Mercedes, abandoned by her bridegroom at the foot of the altar and, ever since, the dedicated enemy of men and the pleasures of the flesh; the watery look of Uncle César, veiled by his incredibly thick glasses, swallowed up in the lethargy of a home life without history, with two marriageable daughters—future old maids—and a snuffed-out son predestined for the priesthood; Cousin Jorge with his recently awarded bachelor's degree and a career marked out as a young Tax Assessor, corruptible and worldly; and, in a corner of the photograph and dominating the others with his look of an absent and inaccessible deity, Uncle Eulogio, who had one hand resting on Álvaro's shoulder and was severely staring at the lens with his deep black eyes, which were shining and inspired. "Europe is done for, my boy. The West has entered its stage of biological decadence and no surgical operation can save it. It's the life cycle: youth, maturity, agony, death. . . . It has been our lot to be present at its death rattle. . . . Like Rome at the death of Theodosius and Byzantium before the dynasty of the Constantines. . . ."

Through the musty pages of the album Uncle Eulogio, with his mysterious scientific baggage, seemed at times like a visitor to the shady coffee plantations of Nicaragua or an unexpected guest of the Mendiolas living in Cuba. In his youth he had given himself over heart and soul to the study and plotting of the stars and among the moths and cobwebs of the attic, slashed by the dusty rays of light that crept in through the shutters, one could still find some vestige of his first and forgotten passion: some broken and useless lens, a faded map of the moon, a drawing of the northern constellations. Later on, troubled by new worries, he had abandoned astronomy for astrology, passing thereafter almost without transition to the Occult Sciences and Rational Religions finally to emerge—and after an unfortunate series of operations on the stock exchange—with bonds and shares of Russian railways, acquired before the war of 1914, notes on the Shanghai Streetcar Company, and a good chunk of Nicaragua Coast Company bonds, anticipating barely by a few months the war in China and the collapse of the world coffee market in 1924—into a period which covered his adulthood and the threshold of his prolonged old age.

Some faded pictures from the period showed the image of a young man with mustache and sideburns, tormented and firm, who was regarding Keyserling with a somber air, leaning against the pillows of a plush sofa: a racist and music lover at the same time, he seemed to be meditating, among other things, about Spengler's catastrophic predictions while abandoning himself with obvious beatitude to the melodic chords—*The Ride of the Valkyries,* Álvaro said to himself—coming out of an antiquated phonograph with a speaker that looked like an ear trumpet.

The Spanish Civil War had caught him in Havana and on that very July 18, 1936, at exactly seven o'clock in the evening local time, Uncle Eulogio offered his services as a volunteer to the Consul of His Majesty King Victor Emmanuel III, without taking into account his advanced age or his precarious state of health. Signor Romano Balbo, who was a friend of the elder Mendiola, succeeded in dissuading him from his proposal and sent him back to his startled family—in whose company he remained until the end of hostilities. Back in Barcelona, white-haired and shrunken from illness, Uncle Eulogio divided his time between reading the Espasa encyclopedia and a new and devouring enthusiasm for crossword puzzles. Unlike his brothers, he had never believed in the triumph of the Nazis and every day when he arose he would thumb through the newspapers—*La Vanguardia, El Diario de Barcelona,* and the *Correo Catalán*—with a skeptical expression.

"Whoever wins," he would say to Álvaro, "it will be the same result. Europe is bleeding herself while Asia is sharpening her teeth."

"Germany can't lose," Uncle César maintained.

"Comfort, the easy life, is degenerating the race. . . . The birth rate is dropping. . . . In Siberia Kirghiz women bear their children on horseback."

"With their secret weapons. . . ."

"No army will be able to hold back the avalanche. . . . Just like the fifth century and the invasion of the Huns and the Ostrogoths."

During the melancholy weeks that preceded the death of his mother, Álvaro had restlessly followed the slow but continuous erosion of the German positions on the eastern front. Uncles and cousins had established themselves in the apartment waiting for the end, and in the nightmares of his dozing and moments of insomnia the harsh and admonitory phrases of his Uncle Eulogio took on a tangible and anxious precision. When his mother was dead, his uncles had taken him for a rest to the inherited paternal farm and, suddenly—like a projection of his entertaining realm of anxiety and fear—historical events began taking place.

The Allied landings in Normandy, the fall of Paris, the Red Army's advance into Poland and Rumania all confirmed, point by point, the pessimistic predictions of Uncle Eulogio and even Uncle César, an admiring reader of *Mein Kampf* and the passionate herald of a German victory, seemed humble and subdued and with a mournful voice evoked the eventuality of an agreement with Churchill to hold back the irresistible advance of the Russians. Day after day, on his schoolboy map of the world, Álvaro would examine with concern the frightening red stain which was avidly extending its tentacles across an exhausted Europe. The abstract fear of war had become transformed little by little into care and concern for his own personal future, what better prey to search for than he, young Álvaro, scion of a virtuous and right-thinking family, the weak heir of a delicate and doddering world? Would the ones who had murdered his father pardon him? Wouldn't they, rather, reserve for him the horrible fate of Uncle Lucas and Cousin Sergio?

Uncle Eulogio had loaned him copies of *The Decline of the West* and *The Twilight of the White Nations* and during the summer and fall of 1944 Álvaro had read and reread them without cease, fascinated by the inevitable character of evil, unprotected as he was and without any weapons to combat it. Ruined, exhausted, divided, the European nations could not compete in extension and population with the fierce and warlike components of the Soviet bloc. When the moment of truth came, the masses would refuse to take up their rifles against the invaders: communists, socialists too, Uncle Eulogio would say, and who can predict about democrats and liberals. The precarious balance was finally being upset in favor of the East. With their first push the barbarians would be at the Pyrenees.

Those months were ones of alarm and unrest, doubt and fright, through which Álvaro had lived in tow behind Uncle Eulogio and his reading while life around him continued on, confident and happy to all appearances, far removed from the threatening and brutal hour of the German defeat. On Sundays and holidays his uncle would be waiting for him at the door of his boarding school and, rejecting the tempting distractions of his age, Álvaro would willingly retire to the apartment to meditate with oppressive lucidity on the weakness of the West—the product of a comfortable and soft life—and about his own—increased in part by his frequent and refined masturbation—comparing the low birth rate in France—despite the tremendous advances in obstetrics—to the rapid multiplication of the Kirghiz people, with their women who give birth on horseback and whose basic food, according to Uncle Eulogio, consisted of several daily pounds of raw meat, a substance rich in calories and vital humors, the origin and source of their voracious urge for expansion and their immoderate warlike appetites. More than once, his uncle's old and self-abnegating maid—less self-abnegating, however, his Aunt Mercedes would remind them, than that other legendary maid, because when she had died after an existence of privation and work, she had left the entire amount of her savings to that scornful grandfather of his who had exploited her during her lifetime—would shout out in her sleep, "Sir, sir, the Kirghiz are coming!" and Álvaro would wake up in the white and ghostly dormitory at his school with his forehead breaking out in sweat and his pulse irregular, giving thanks to God for the beneficial presence of his fellow students who were snoring in beds just like his, safe for the moment—for how long?—from the Kirghiz and their women who gave birth on horseback, as he repeated a thousand times over "Lord do not forsake me" until fatigue became stronger than he and sleep mercifully overcame him.

"*Mene, tekel, upharsin,*" Uncle Eulogio pronounced when the news of Hitler's suicide was broadcast.

"The Americans are not blind," Uncle César would say without great conviction. "If we bring back the king and re-establish political parties. . . ."

"I'm already old and life hasn't much to give me any more. But you, my poor Álvaro, what will become of you?"

An unreasonable fear had slyly infiltrated his veins, translated into the hermetic and hard face of the Kirghiz reproduced in a colored picture in his Human Geography book, and hasty plans for flight to safe and remote countries were taking on the sweet consistency of a possible lifesaver, a tiny buoy to which he could cling on the day of the shipwreck and the sinking.

"In your place, I would go to a peaceful place like Cuba," Uncle Eulogio would say. "There's no danger of revolution or wars there. Cousin Ernesto is very wealthy and he could get you started.

Only in his last letter he says that he has sent Juan Carlos to the United States for an engineering degree. . . . And Adelaidita is a very pretty charmer, blossoming out, as they say. Did I show you the clipping of her in her evening dress in *El Diario de la Marina?*"

The cold sweats and palpitations gave way then to soothing dreams of happiness and euphoria in a paradise island, far from the Kirghiz and their women, in the shelter of pleasant and friendly relatives, the ageless guarantee of a serene and lasting order of things. The big house on Punta Gorda in Cienfuegos, the plantation at Cruces, the tobacco-colored photographs were a cool oasis of calm and good fortune, pleasure and repose, which his uncle waved before his eyes like an astonishing mirage, comfortably resting in his leather easy chair with his hand on the *Geography of Cuba* which Cousin Ernesto had sent from Havana some weeks back.

"Besides, the climate is magnificent, very good for rheumatism and gout. Listen to this: 'Cuba's location in the semi-tropical zone and the pleasant activity of the trade winds make our winters quite mild. According to Koppen's well-known climatological scale, Cuba has a warm savanna climate without any winter, a condition symbolized in terse scientific abbreviation by the letters AW' . . ."

Other times during those Sunday get-togethers interrupted only by the fleeting appearance of the old maidservant with a teapot and two porcelain china cups, Uncle Eulogio's fantasy would pour out in the direction of other points on the terrestrial globe, just as far away from Europe and therefore safe.

"And if you don't want the Caribbean, you can go grow coffee in Kenya or Angola. A while back I was reading an article by a missionary priest that was very interesting. The Negroes there are very peaceful; they live on wild herbs and flowers and obey and respect white people. The priest says that he has had to scold them many times because the poor unfortunates wanted to make a god out of him. . . ."

For months and months Álvaro had received these scientific explanations and chats like spring rain until, first because of summer and then because of his absorbing passion in Jerónimo, the wonderful meetings became less frequent. In the fall his uncle's health took a turn for the worse and during his rare protocol visits to the apartment, he would find Eulogio withdrawn and taciturn, peeping out of the corner of his eye at the coming and going—with mysterious potions and draughts—of the old maid-servant. The last time Álvaro had seen his uncle free, the latter had looked at him firmly and ordered him to: "Go away, leave me alone." Around Christmas time Aunt Mercedes gave him the brief news that because of medical reasons he had been put into a sanitarium.

At the end of that time Álvaro still had a friendly and tender memory of their strange and luminous friendship and during his trip to Cuba after the victory of Fidel Castro's revolution, he had often thought about it, still smiling, trying to imagine Uncle Eulogio's reaction if he were still alive to the expropriation and the flight of the Mendiolas to Miami and the Negro uprisings and killings of missionaries in Angola and Kenya. As for Uncle César, after the first shock of terror had passed, he had imitated the actions of other members of his class, helping swell the ranks during the period of the sterile closing of the frontier and the hypocritical withdrawal of embassies from around the man who had been, was, and would be the best defender of their real interests. Years later —separated already from the family by a barrier infinitely stronger than the casual and always doubtful ties of blood—Álvaro had seen his uncle's picture in the paper in the midst of a group of the faithful who were cheering the passing of the Benefactor during one of his sporadic visits to Barcelona. That last image he had of him was still enough to convince him, however, that simple logic and common sense should have brought him in 1962, as it did so many others, without any break or contradiction and through the efforts and bounty of the tourist business and the economic revival, to the defense of European and liberal values, prudent, very prudent, keeping in mind the sad day when the Benefactor would no longer be around and once more, just as in that desolate winter of 1945, they would have need of a king—a decorative and showy item in exchange.

The light went on unexpectedly. Night had fallen without your noticing and, still sitting in the garden, you could not make out the versatile flight of the swallows or the reddish fringe of the sunset along the wavy profile of the mountains. The family album was still in your hands, useless now in the shadows and when you got up you poured yourself another glass of Fefiñanes and drank it down in one gulp. The first stars were being painted above the tile roof and the weathercock could just barely be seen in proud silhouette against the dark sky. Dolores had appeared at the porch gate. A pair of green stretch pants molded her slim adolescent behind. She was coming toward you with a lighted cigarette between the index and middle fingers of her right hand and, just as you had predicted, she took a furtive glance at the level of the bottle of Fefiñanes, but her face did not reveal any sentiment except pure unmoved approval. Her friendly and propitious lips were smiling slightly and her free hand traced a sober greeting and stopped on top of yours. Like a sleepwalker, you heard her talk about the dinner preparations, remind you about the time for the drops prescribed by Dr. d'Asnières, become interested in the contents of the album. When your looks met for a few instants they revived the previous sweet impression of play and complicity: an illusory belief in a moral unity that neither time nor human decay could destroy. The wind could be heard in the branches of the eucalyptus trees again and it wafted a slow freshness across your face, flighty and caressing. A while later the girl appeared with the glass of water and your drops and after her Dolores's nieces and nephews burst happily into the garden. The porch was inviting you with its comfortable sofas and the insidious nostalgia of Mozart's *Requiem*. You drank down the mixture in one gulp. Holding each other around the waist you walked toward the house while the servant girl picked up the ice bucket, the glasses, the bottle of Fefiñanes and, with a pained shout, called the children to the kitchen. Dolores put the record back on the turntable. The chords of the *Introitus* imperiously annulled the silence and leaning back on the sofa you opened up the album again.

The picture had been taken by Cousin Jorge with the latest model Leica that his parents had given him for the five honor grades he had received in his first year at the university and Jerónimo was in it, just the way you remembered him eighteen years later: feline look, black eyebrows, thick lips, slim and robust body under the miserable clothes that covered it. The grape baskets that he had carried were lined up empty by the wine press and a dog of unknown identity was jumping around him with his tongue hanging out, in humble and graceful adoration. Uncle César was nibbling at a bunch of grapes, disguised in white as was the fashion of the time. The rest of the retinue must have been guests of Jorge, who knows, or simply bystanders or neighbors. The dense light of September made the distances hazy in the picture. It was grape-harvest time.

While you were away at boarding school he had appeared one afternoon on the farm looking for work from the farmers and, although suspicious in general of migrant workers, old Xoaquim had taken him on. He said his name was Jerónimo López—he had neither pass nor papers, only the endorsement of a parish priest unknown in the region—day laborer by profession, unmarried, thirty-two years old. He was strong and dark and spoke with a marked southern accent.

If his personality aroused natural reserve, the unaccustomed seriousness and scruple that he put into his work had immediately brought him everybody's liking. When you arrived around the end of June—your fifth year of secondary school was over—Xoaquim was already inviting him to his table and treating him like one of his sons. Jerónimo did not have much to say, he always slept in the stables, and on Sundays, instead of going to the cafés as custom demanded, he would stay home loafing about or would go off lazily into the woods. If he ever went to town it was just to pick up a week's supply of tobacco and return immediately afterward.

Since you were absorbed in your deep reflections, the fruit of an assiduous reading of Spengler and your visits to Uncle Eulogio's apartment, you had seen him there without noticing, in the company of other workers, a sash of black cloth around his waist and his rustic straw hat on, his bare feet planted on the ground, whipping up the colt during the harvest chores. You had probably opened the window of your room, attracted by the familiar noise of the threshing and you looked at the piles of unthreshed blond wheat on the threshing floor, the graceful merry-go-round of man and horse, the beautiful and ancient task of separating the grain from the chaff, winnowing it with sharp and slender pitchforks. In those days life was passing peacefully and deceitfully before your eyes like the colored pictures projected by a magic lantern, secretly undermined at its base by the subterranean enemy who sooner or later was going to destroy it all. Were you aware of his real presence then? Or did you consider him just one more element, empty and null, of the suggestive and artful picture?

Some days later you saw him again, still barefoot and with a hoe on his shoulder, going through the garden toward the vegetable patch while you were arguing with your cousins over the daily croquet game and one of them was accusing Jorge of dragging his mallet after the ball, anachronistic all of them, you think now, like the grave personages in the album, photographed fifty years ago, just as decadent and ornamental. He said good afternoon to all of you, briefly touching the brim of his hat with his hand, and he was eclipsed by the cork trees, leaving you all behind, you remembered, in the limbo of a time without limits, in the useless nothingness you all inhabited.

"I don't like that man, not one bit," Aunt Mercedes said, interrupting her embroidery for a few seconds. "What do you think, César?"

"Me?"

Your uncle took his eyes off his magazine—*Life en Español,* no doubt, since *Signal* had not come out yet.

"Why ask me?"

"Nobody knows him in town. He arrived here without any papers, according to what they say."

"Xoaquim is happy with him. He doesn't talk back and he does his work well. Besides he brought a recommendation from a priest. . . ."

"If he's such a good Catholic, why doesn't he go to mass?"

"How should I know? Should we make him go?"

"Have you talked about him to Mossén Pere?"

"Look, Mercedes. The important thing is that he does what he's told and does his job. I don't want to be more of a Papist than the Pope."

The following Sunday, with her mantilla and her breviary in her hands, in the rig that was taking you to church, Aunt Mercedes took the offensive again.

"Did you notice, César?"

"No."

"The Andalusian."

"What about him?"

"The way he said hello to us on the road. . . ."

"Perfectly normal, just like the rest of the farmhands."

"Yes, but I'm not so sure about it. That man has something working in his brain."

"What do you know about it."

"I've got a good sense of smell. There's a certain challenge in his look. . . ."

"You're imagining things, Mercedes."

"I'm willing to bet he's tied up with the underground."

The word rolled around in your motionless existence, round and hard like a stone, raising in its path an avalanche of emotions which the real world had abolished, confronting you, defenseless, with your own persistent nightmare. Could he be the assassin you had feared so many times? The executioner who would coldly kill you when the time was ripe? Could that be the new farmhand? In a progressive sort of way his copper face had supplanted the hazy and distant face of the Kirghiz that came to you at night, plunging you into a quivering sea of hypothesis and conjecture. The man who passed by you every morning and smiled at you was your enemy. One day he would come into your room with a knife and kill you. Did you believe it? It seemed difficult to believe.

Doubt was getting the better of you—a lack of confidence in your world and its celebrated values. From then on you had got into the habit of spying on Jerónimo. You would lie in wait for him, hidden, when he went down to irrigate the plots alongside the ditch and you would walk furtively behind him, trying to walk in his tracks on the Sundays when he had no work and was apparently idle and would suddenly disappear into the woods. You hid it from everybody, taking pleasure in the secretive game, already an accomplice of his in the eyes of your people, having more and more doubts about his role as executioner and the historical necessity of the crime.

How long had your cleverness and his benevolence lasted? It was impossible for him not to have noticed that you were spying on his every step in such a way that for several days in a row he had turned his head quickly and had discovered you hidden in ambush in the thickets, ironic and compassionate at the same time. Maybe he found pleasure just like you in slowly prolonging the web of intimacies and secrets which held you together. He was content to smile and without pretext or reason to justify your mute presence near him, you would backtrack, hoping for some opportunity when, like a jealous lover or a thief, you could spy on him again.

Who broke the chain, he or you? It was both of you, really, the day when you ran into him by chance in the chestnut grove and he said good morning to you. He laid down his hoe and took a pack of tobacco out of his sash and skillfully rolled two cigarettes, the first for you.

"Who gave you that medallion?" he asked.

Confused, you fingered Aunt Mercedes's gold chain and, to get out of your difficulty, explained that it was a miraculous medal, specially blessed.

"Who by?" Jerónimo asked.

You did not even know and even though you knew his interest was slight, you told him about the legend of the two travelers struck by lightning on a mountain—one was killed and the other saved, thanks to a medallion of the Virgin.

"That's funny," Jerónimo said, "just the opposite happened in my village."

He had lit your cigarette with his flint and he was looking at you with an uncertain look.

"Shall I tell you about it?"

"Yes," you said.

"These two fellows were out walking, a storm came up and the one with the medallion on got it."

"Why?"

"Precious metals attract lightning," he replied. "Didn't you know that?"

Xoaquim's sons were coming along the road back from the fields and Jerónimo winked and, as was his custom, greeted them by lifting his hand up to the brim of his hat. The emotion of the meeting, his sudden use of the familiar form of address, the disconcerting story about the two friends were still milling around in your head when, days later, and not wearing your medallion, you came across him again.

Was that too—can you remember?—pure chance: night had come on and when you were bothered by mosquitoes you had wandered uselessly from one room to another, pursued in all of them by their buzzing until, telling yourself at last that you would go out and sleep on the ground, you opened the porch gate and went out into the garden. The clouds were covering the sky and in a few minutes it began to drizzle. Fatigue had put your muscles to sleep and you went slowly toward the haymow beside the horse barn.

The door was ajar and you pushed it open. With your back to the slight nocturnal light you went forward, feeling through the hay, looking for the right place to improvise a bed. Suddenly the brutal light illuminated you.

"Oh, is that you?"

Jerónimo was holding the lantern over you, and even though his appearance had been sudden and you were still blinking, you still had time to see the butt of a revolver showing from beneath the sash around his waist. In one second your entire universe had become doubtful. Jerónimo was looking at you calmly and he took his time as he rolled a cigarette.

"You gave me quite a start, boy!"

"I couldn't sleep," you babbled. "The mosquitoes . . ."

"They leave me alone out here. Come on, lie down here. I'll give you my blanket if you want. . . ."

"No."

"Prop up your head and you'll sleep better."

That was all there was to it—or at least that was how you remembered it—no question from you, no explanation about the revolver from him, your friendship already arranged, happy as accomplices.

From then on you could get up at midnight, go through the ghostly hallway, tiptoe by your Uncle César's bedroom, open the lock on the porch gate, scurry quietly through the garden, stop in front of the haymow and hurt your knuckles on the door, whisper your name as a password, find him there.

Jerónimo would greet you with a smile, light his cigarette, give you his blanket, turn out the light. Talking, what they meant by talking, you didn't do much talking. What was there in common between the two of you? Just the friendly intimate address and the smile, the open gesture and the animal agreement, something beyond words. Did he trust you? Of course. More than once you put out your arm while you were asleep and you felt with thanks the benevolent bulge of the revolver at his waist.

Once he showed you a photograph—the first night you went out to the haymow and did not find him and you had waited, tired from the cold, until the break of dawn. He came out of the woods, scurrying like a shadow and finding you awake had run his hand through your hair.

You were looking at the dark-haired girl hugging the child, and Jerónimo had commented: "My wife and boy."

"Where are they?"

"Away."

"Won't you ever see them again?"

"Maybe at the end of the year."

Several times during that hot August and the grape-gathering season you went out to the haymow at night and you found it empty. Jerónimo would come back out of the woods at dawn and since you were resting then, he would wash his face and go off to work with the other farmhands.

It was around the beginning of October—you remembered it well: just before your classes were about to start and the family was ready to go back to Barcelona—that you waited for him in vain and he did not return. You went back to your room stiff with cold, with an anxiety and torment that you would not recognize until much later, already in love with Dolores, a love conceived in the studio on rue Vieille du Temple, anxiety over love and fortune and your having been deprived of both with yourself to blame during one of those mutilated and ragged years that later on would be called the Years of Peace.

Xoaquim could not understand what had happened—Jerónimo had gone away without collecting his wages—and when the Civil Guard came down the road one night and asked about him, your heart became a crazy organ that suddenly seemed to break away from you and your ears were buzzing as if somebody had put the iridescent mother-of-pearl of a seashell to them.

That was how you found out—listening to them talk to Xoaquim, Uncle César, and your exultant Aunt Mercedes—that his name was not really Jerónimo; that he had crossed the Pyrenees clandestinely at the head of a band of exiles and that he was—they had proof—one of the leaders of the underground in the region.

"He's a very dangerous person," the sergeant of the Civil Guard said. "Last night we came across him several miles from here when he was on his way to meet his people in the hills and in the exchange of fire we wounded one of them."

How sad the return to school—to the austere and creolined hallways; how cold and sterile was your universe of sin and repentance, prayer and pupil desk, study and worship: dim stations of the cross, always the same—rancor slowly mounted in your breast—until the university and emancipation.

You had never heard anything more about Jerónimo. Maybe he had crossed the border again, his generous attempt to no avail; maybe, you thought more often, with a flutter in your heart that had persisted after so long a time, he was lying in a nameless grave in some corner of your—your?—Spanish geography. You told yourself then that your homeland was quite base and deaf if as you were inclined to believe sometimes his rich offering had been useless. But no, you were delirious, that cannot be the end, and—waiting for a country that would see better times—you should understand and make the others understand that Jerónimo, or whatever his name was, the one who had awakened your moral sensibility with his pure conduct, had died for each and every one of you, as you knew—with such pain, my God, such shame—that he had died, in the same way, for you.

His mother's family did not figure in the album. By virtue of some strict and selective criterion someone had eliminated from its pages that other bourgeois line, more cultivated and sensitive than the Mendiolas, equally as unjustifiable as the latter through the decadence and insignificance of its products. The adventurous spirit of his entrepreneur great-grandfather had never come to nest in it to revive it with his wild thirst for splendor and rapine. Its original sap had little by little been reduced and undermined, one might say, by an acute and critical intelligence, doubtful of its own truth and reasons, incredulous of its mission and duties. Its leaves had been swept away one by one, its branches were sterile, Álvaro was the last bloom on the condemned and sickly tree, hanging by the beat of a fragile heart, at the mercy of the illness that might strike it down into oblivion with one breath. It was enough, however, to get up from the sofa, abandon for a few minutes the *Rex tremendae majestatis,* go through the crooked hallway where the elves of his childhood universe had lived and come into the stern colonial dining room and look at the oil painting presiding over the mournful meeting of overstuffed chairs in between the absurd and pompous bronze lamp and the sleepy piano that held the score of *The Turkish March:* two dreamy and absent blue eyes; an ancient beauty that had evaporated along with the perfume from an old open vial; a silk shawl over her rebellious hair, still golden and abundant. In a corner of the picture, under the illegible signature of the artist, a name and a date: María Canals, 1911.

When Álvaro had come to know her, in the obscure prehistory of his memory, time had altered her features in a marked way:

her skin was withered, her lips anemic, her hair was white and she always kept it in a graceful lace net. It was already the middle of the thirties and his maternal grandmother was sixty-eight at the time. Only her eyes, intact and as clear as in her remote childhood, had not grown old.

Their common past consisted of images of a big house, a run-down English garden and a tennis court overgrown with grass. Álvaro would wander along the twisting paths dressed up as a little sailor and the mythological Señorita Lourdes would instruct him in the delicate sensibility of plants and urge him to greet them with affection and tenderness. Flowers, she would say, were delicate and susceptible just like people, and children's caresses and care brought them intense joy and satisfaction. With the fervor of a catecumen, Álvaro would run from one flower to another, depositing on all of them kisses that were modest and pure, soothing and restoring, alleviating sufferings and sorrows in turn, sowing good, recognition, and happiness in a rapid and fruitful apostolate. And the lilacs? The lilacs too, my prince. And the hydrangeas? The hydrangeas too. When I kissed this flower it broke, Álvaro would say, did I hurt it? No, my prince, if you didn't mean to it wasn't your fault. And the little birds, are they good too? Yes, my prince. Then why do they peck the flowers? (His incipient and fickle dialectic stopped there.)

His grandmother would be waiting for them in the summer-house in the garden and as a recompense, after each one of his visits, a precious object carefully kept in a metal box which Doña María would lock up immediately after would go to enrich his private property, some colored picture, stamp, sketch, or decalcomania. At dusk his parents would come to pick him up in the buggy (or in the recently acquired DKW) and his grandmother would go out to the curb with them and wave good-by with her handkerchief (sitting on his mother's lap, Álvaro would throw kisses to her).

There was a parenthesis of several years. The storm of the civil war had furiously shaken up those lazy and inert existences and so many characters and groups in the medieval world of his family had suddenly disappeared, as if swallowed up through a trapdoor. Without getting upset, Álvaro had been present at their sudden eclipses, and once set up in his life as an emigrant orphan, he vegetated in the pleasant hot season of the Midi; secretly happy about the providential conflict that was freeing him (until when?) from the troublesome obligation of school (a monotonous round of stations that were all alike in the embryonic recollection of his still confused memory).

It was afterward, peace having been happily re-established, the frozen social levels conforming once more to a severe and immutable order, back in Barcelona with the prerogatives and rights that corresponded to his worthy caste (private school and abundant food, wealth and virtue harmoniously joined together under the imperious divine patronage): his mother had come to pick him up after class and had gone with him in a rented car to a town on the outskirts (it was autumn, it was a gray day and the wind was undressing the trees).

"We're going to see Grandmother," she said.

"Where is she?"

"In a house in the country, a half hour from here. You'll see: it's the house of some nice nuns who are taking care of her and helping her."

"What's wrong?"

"She's not well. During the war she suffered very much and now she has to rest, understand? . . . She's lost her memory and she doesn't remember many things. . . ."

"Why?"

"Because she's very old now and she's suffered very much. . . . Do you remember her?"

"A little," Álvaro said. "She used to live in Pedralbes."

"Well, when you see her, if she doesn't recognize you, don't pay any attention to her. . . . The poor thing has suffered so much."

"What should I say to her?"

"Don't say anything. If she speaks to you, answer her. If not, smile at her and go play in the garden."

"What about you? Does she recognize you?"

"It depends on the days. . . . The poor thing lives in a world of her own and she's not aware of things. . . . She's happy in her own way."

The car had stopped in front of an iron grating with bars shaped like lances and when they got out Álvaro intensely examined the wall surrounding the place which was crowned with a ridge of broken glass and pieces of broken bottles. His mother rang the bell at the doorway and a nun opened the latch and immediately closed it again, locking it with a padlock.

"Good afternoon, Sister. Have you met my son?"

"No, I haven't. He's quite a young man. How old is he?"

"Ten."

"What year in school is he?"

"First year of secondary school," he said.

He came to a halt. Sixty feet away a blond woman was roaming along the edge of a lawn on the arm of a nun. When she saw them, she looked at them and burst into a fit of quivering and fleeting laughter, like a quick arpeggio.

"Come, come, don't be a child," Álvaro had heard as they went away. "Where do you want to go?"

"Mama," he whispered. "Did you see that?"

"And how is my mother?"

"Oh, she's always happy and in good spirits. If only they were all like her. . . ."

"Mama."

"Has her temperature gone down?"

"It was just a cold. A draft she caught in the garden."

"Mama."

"Hush. What did the doctor say?"

"Normal. Sister Ángeles will show you his report later." The nun was walking slowly and she pointed at the somber baroque building: "Yesterday she tried playing the piano. . . . A piece of music that your sister used to like. . . . She said: 'My youngest daughter used to play it every day and she wrote some poetry about this piece. . . .' "

"Yes, Ravel's *Pavan for a Dead Princess*. . . ."

"I don't know. A very pretty piece, with great feeling. . . . I don't know very much about music, but I stopped to listen and I was really moved. . . . She was at the piano for over an hour and then she ate very well at lunch."

"Where is she now? In the dining room?"

"No, she's probably walking in the garden."

They went on through a clump of horse-chestnut trees and his mother and the nun were carrying on an incomprehensible conversation, purposely at a distance from him. The layout and the leafiness of the garden brought back to Álvaro the paths, plots, arbors, and steps of the fabulous mansion in Pedralbes and the memory of his distant visits with Señorita Lourdes (the drive in the carriage from Bonanova, the lace net over his grandmother's white hair, the hidden surprises in the inaccessible metal box) flourished suddenly in his memory simultaneously with the appearance of an old cadaverous-looking woman, dressed in a coarse apron, who was coming toward them, majestic, unreal, and looking like a sleepwalker in the midst of autumn's vegetable desolation. (Questions crowded into his mind: who is she? how old is she? why is she dressed like that?) Her eyes were blue, just like the transparent blue in the painting and the wind was stirring up her hair through the openings in her net.

They were painful moments, during which Álvaro had held his breath, imploring God that the wandering shadow would recognize him as belonging to her, would recover her pure and remote gifts, would miraculously rejoin life. Her wandering sweet smile had made him build up hopes right to the point where their eyes crossed and her pupils seemed to go right through him as if to scrutinize some object located behind him. Almost at once his grandmother tilted her head and after an exploratory and interminable circular glance, looked away and turned her back, denying him and denying her past, as if it did not exist or had ever existed, cutting off all links between them, absorbed, alienated, fugitive.

Ever since that date (October, 1939?) Álvaro had learned to recognize the limits of his condition and even without formulating it with clarity (that would come much later), he knew that everything, including himself, was not definitive and lasting as he had confidently believed up until then, having based his opinion on the continuity of his universe that had been reconstituted after the terrors and frights of the war, but that it was changeable, precarious, governed by a biological cycle against which will and virtue were powerless, everything exposed to chance, everything fortuitous, hopelessly promised to death, transitory, fleeting, everything in its dotage.

Some years later, while still an adolescent and preparing to matriculate in the university as a first-year law student, you had examined the family album, not with the present idea of recuperating lost time and making a balance of your existences (the necessary balancing of the books, just as with your great-grandfather's ledgers) but with the somewhat illusory hope of guessing by those means the uncertain and problematic coordinates of your unique future (somewhat like the augur who finds recognitions in the entrails of his victims or the customer who sits before the fortune-teller's cards). The rebellion hoarded up day by day against the fate which they had generously offered you by means of a silly ejaculation, was searching for its explanation at that time and its roots in the hated family tree. It was not possible, you said to yourself, that such a vivid and intense feeling, such a deep and bribe-free anomaly could rise up out of nothingness and thrive entirely in the air like an unrooted orchid. An anonymous member of your lineage had experimented before you perhaps, had transmitted them intact to you at the cost of dark years of compromise and dissimilation. What was maturing in you and giving forth no fruit could feel it germinating inside of itself, terrified, like a cancer that grows and strengthens itself in the midst of the blindness and the ignorance of others. That impulse, obscure and luminous at the same time, had hidden in it something like a grace perhaps, perhaps like a shame, sacrificing, in any case, its true imperative to the stupid and inconsistent approval of the clan. You, his heir, had managed to cut the bonds in time without managing to free yourself completely because of it. Family, social class, community, land: your life could not be anything else (you subsequently found out) except a slow and difficult road of breaking and dispossession.

Since the family tree had been definitively established (the paternal branch, with its wild and holy people, the maternal one, with its psychopaths and illuminati), you had done research on your fated predecessors, tracing in their lives the buried track that would lead you groping toward the truth. The material at your disposal was scarce: the photograph album, a few letters and personal objects, remote anecdotes heard during your forgotten childhood. The maternal family (almost extinct now) could still afford you some slight fervor, thanks to the total absence of any real elements, an exciting game of hypotheses and conjectures. Like the transcription of Erik Satie's *Gymnopedies*, the property of your late Aunt Gertrudis, which you discovered in your mother's storeroom one day and a post card sent by your aunt showing the ruins at Taormina with the thin columns rising up under an exaggeratedly blue sky (the only memories of her that had come down to you) had been enough to reconstruct a personality that was without doubt shy and sensitive, soft and melancholy (the younger sister of your mother, Aunt Gertrudis died of a heart attack during a theatrical performance soon after your birth); or the library of your Great-Uncle Néstor (idolatrized by your maternal grandmother and kept in silence by the rest of your relatives) in which you had found copies of Baudelaire and Verlaine, Clarín and Larra that later on would feed your non-conformism, his anarchic and violent temperament, euphoric and depressive: the strange blend (according to witnesses) of a revolutionary and a dandy, a Catalan heir and a vagabond (Great-Uncle Néstor had squandered a fortune at Monte Carlo, he lived in sin with a tumultuous Irish poetess and as a Catalan Separatist had worked for the Sinn Fein uprising and had committed suicide at the age of thirty-five in a Swiss sanitarium, hanging himself from the window of his room with his own scarf).

Dimly at that time, more clearly later on, you had looked for enough stimulation in his deflection to continue firmly on your road. The remote mutilations inflicted on your body out of racial pride by some fellow countrymen perverted by their dogmas and those others, more recent, the work of your great-grandfather the trader (slave women offered up for his whim and pleasure, men reduced to the miserable condition of tools) you assumed, upon your flesh and spirit as the necessary harvest (expiation perhaps) of the crudest and most boorish seeds that they had sown in life. Thanks to the usual damned pariahs (Gypsies, Arabs, brusque instinctive Negroes), you had managed to meld within yourself for a few moments the lost and ancient unity toward which your rebellious impulse tended, above precepts and laws, with irreducible nostalgia. Only in this way, completing in this way, purging in this way, were you able to restore the innocence of your common past and face up to your solitary destiny. Appeased, submissive, lucid, conscious living at last, in abrupt and regenerating challenge amidst the fatuous and complacent multitude of corpses.

Soul of Christ, sanctify me.
Body of Christ, save me.
Blood of Christ, transport me.
Water of the Side of Christ, wash me.
Passion of Christ, comfort me.
Oh, sweet Jesus, hear me.
Hide me inside your wounds.
Do not let me stray from You.

Defend me from the evil enemy.
At the hour of death beckon me
and have me come unto You;
So that I may praise You with your
saints, now and forever. Amen.

The sixth year of secondary school, section B, forty adolescents dressed in knickers, ties, and starched collars, tightly lined up shoulder to shoulder alongside the pompous large neo-Gothic windows of the ancient school building. In a corner of the photograph, somewhat away from Álvaro, the severe and circumspect figure of the Reverend Father Confessor.

"Father, I accuse myself of having sinned three times against the Sixth Commandment."

"In thought or in action, my son?"

"Both ways."

"Alone or with someone else?"

"A friend showed me a magazine with women and I bought it from him."

"Did you look at it with him?"

"Yes."

"Did you touch each other?"

"No. When he left I sinned by myself."

"Did you know that you were committing a serious error?"

"Yes."

"Among all of the sins that is the one that most offends God and the Holy Spirit. Were you sincerely repentant?"

"Yes, Father."

"Have you destroyed the magazine?"

"No, not yet."

"Destroy it, and in the future avoid dangerous contacts, which are the favorite weapon of the devil to catch the unwary. . . ."

"Yes, Father."

"Every day for a week when you get up and go to bed you will recite an Our Father and three Hail Marys."

"Yes, Father."

"Go now, God be with you."

Physical and moral consequences of the impure act. The classification of the celestial hierarchies with the specific attributes of each of them. Ticino, *Trebia,* Thrasimene, *Canas.* Pichincha, Chimborazo, and Cotopaxi. Newton's binomial theorem. Oviparous, viviparous, oviviparous. *Barbara, celare, darii, ferio.* The formula for bicarbonate of soda. Pythagoras's theorem.

. . . Opportune and diaphanous, the chorus of the *Lacrimosa dies illa* harmoniously unfolded its structure, erasing with one breath the vestiges of his past domination.

Who the devil had put that picture in the album? Dolores followed the direction of your glance and was also looking at it.

It was just a clipping, no label or explanation, as if the very eloquence of it had precluded any necessity for commentary. A man lying on his back—dead? wounded?—by the edge of the sidewalk—a killing? an accident?—in the midst of the impassive curiosity of some other men—probably compatriots of his. A typical picture of our times without distinction of grade or latitude, divulged every day by all of them in their newspapers and magazines, movies and television.

It was not the first time that you had looked at a document like that and by the call of your profession you yourself had taken several when you were working as a photographer for *France Presse,* but there was something now that you did not know then and, in some dark way, had joined you to the anodynic image mislaid in the pages of the album: a diffuse restlessness as far as your personal destiny was concerned and something like a deep and painful instinct of solidarity.

It was exactly five months ago, on a harsh March day that you had got off the huge roller coaster in the carnival set up in the Place de la Bastille and went staggering off toward the Boulevard Richard Lenoir with an empty head and a hollow heart, mentally counting—you remembered—the number of steps you were taking. . . .

It was easy for you to reconstruct what had happened then, making the details of the photograph fit the circumstances: your blind look, your livid face, your garish and unimportant fall—the unconscious protagonist of the gratuitous spectacle you were offering the men and women who were casually walking by. Just as in the clipping, they had looked imperturbably and passively at you, their looks fastened on the defenseless animal that was panting at their feet, waiting for the arrival of the ambulance or the patrol wagon, so they could sneak off with that blessed French prudence of not seeing themselves obliged to give testimony. Some of them, perhaps, had come up to you and had felt you cautiously with the tips of their shoes.

An efficient and cold civilization, skilled in the modern media of propaganda enough to consider time as a set of ciphers and man as a tool for work—the only civilization plausible today, you said, with bitterness, however—had reduced you to this: to a common and laughable incident in the everyday of men and women strolling along the Boulevard Richard Lenoir, happy at feeling out of harm's way, tranquil and sure of themselves, with selfish disdain painted on their faces and in their chests a forceful *Moi je m'en fou.*

That would be your future and, as you calibrated it, you admired the dash and valor of those who without waiting their turn would voluntarily face the black mouth of the sudden shotgun or revolver—and even those who even though they lacked what the others had, would make up for it with a bottle of brandy and once drunk, would absorb the ominous tube of veronal.

A new Lazarus, you came to life again in an immense ward in the Saint-Antoine Hospital and, just as now, Dolores was next to you and she was smiling at you tenderly.

The headlights unexpectedly lit up the ragged trunks of the eucalyptus trees and the sharp silhouette of the cypresses, rescuing them for a few moments in a silent wave from the thick darkness into which they had been sunk. Álvaro went to the porch gate and with a sigh, Dolores lifted the arm of the phonograph.

The gray Dauphine had traced a semicircle of yellow light before coming to a halt beside the observatory and almost simultaneously the four doors opened and Ricardo and Artigas got out along with two blond girls who looked like foreigners, dressed in checkered shirts and levis.

"Hi," Ricardo said. "Are we late?"

"If instead of being Jews, the Chosen People had been Spaniards, we'd still be waiting for the coming of Christ," Dolores answered.

"We're thirsty as hell," Artigas said. "Got anything to drink?"

Dolores and Álvaro shook hands with the girls. They blinked, looking at the garden, and muttered something unintelligible.

"We found them coming out of Cadaqués. They'd pulled off the road and they ended up sleeping with us."

"They're Danes," Artigas explained. "Danish very sexy beautiful women," he said in English.

"They can't speak a word of Spanish," Ricardo said. "I curse them out and they don't have the slightest notion of what I'm saying."

The two girls were smiling in unison, perfectly adapted to the new situation. When they went onto the porch their eyes converged on the pile of records next to the phonograph.

"Put on a cha-cha-cha for them and let's see if they can wiggle their asses," Ricardo said.

"Don't they have any baggage?" Dolores asked.

"They've come to live off the traditional hospitality of the Spanish people."

"They arrived at Port Bou without money or anything," Artigas said. "They're genuine consumer goods."

Dolores went away for a minute to inspect the dinner preparations and immediately afterward the serving girl appeared with the bottles and ice.

"Shall I make you a Daiquiri?" Álvaro proposed.

"Native claret for me," Ricardo said. "Perelada or something like it."

"Do you want a drink?"

"Thank you very much." (Both in English.)

"Speaking of Daiquiris, do you know who wrote to me?" Artigas dropped onto the sofa and stroked the leg of one of the Danish girls. "Enrique himself."

Dolores came back with the glasses and exchanged a very brief look at Álvaro. The girls were carefully examining the labels on the records. Artigas took out a wrinkled envelope from his pocket and showed it off triumphantly.

"Shall I read it to you?"

"Thank you no," Dolores said.

"Just a paragraph, listen to this: 'I've been following happenings in the newspapers and I think my presence is needed there more than here. If you think it advisable, let me know and I'll make arrangements to come.' "

There was a pause. Dolores calmly lit a cigarette.

"What happenings is he talking about?" Ricardo said. "Hasn't he got his countries mixed up?"

"He probably thinks this is the Congo," Artigas suggested.

"The poor guy is getting more and more out of touch with things. What do you figure?"

"If he comes here all that will happen is that he'll die of fright."

"Or he'll screw some French girl one lousy time and be happy."

"People aren't afraid to say they're right-wingers any more," Artigas explained. "The other day I saw Paco in the Stork Club and he told me: 'I'm a monarchist and a conservative'. . . ."

"Don't tell me," Álvaro smiled. "What's he doing now?"

"Living off his income and drinking whisky, what else do you expect him to be doing?"

The Danish girls had found a Ray Charles record and were looking at Dolores as they conferred about deciding whether to intrude on the phonograph.

II

Take your foot and cover over the many mouths of an ant hill that had been patiently constructed grain by grain on harsh and sandy soil and visit the spot next day: there it will be again, complex and flourishing, the image of the collective instinct of the hard-working and stubborn community that inhabits it, just as the natural habitat of the Spaniard, that ancestral and always slandered hut made out of sticks and tin, condemned to disappear now that you are what they call Europeans and the tourist trade obliges you to freshen up the façade by the expeditious and slightly brutal means, one must admit, brought on by modern, powerful, and well-organized neo-capitalism, is swept away one day from Barceloneta and Somorrostro, Pueblo Seco and La Verneda, only to surge up again, flourishing and healthy, in Casa Antúnez or in the free port, the symbolic expression of your primitive and genuine tribal structure.

You were looking at that vagabond kingdom made up of huts and shacks, so like the one you had filmed some time back (a kingdom destroyed by decree later on along with the presentation of comfortable and clean quarters to its uncouth and suspicious inhabitants) and the indignation that had come over you in time past now seemed as odd as the well-known look of its inhabitants (small and thin, dark and tight). You were surprised (you really were) at the obstinacy and pigheadedness with which they were trying to cling to a life whose premises they never doubted, as if the aim of it (you told yourself) was to be born, grow, multiply, and die with the mute resignation of animals, oh, Spanish people (you would invoke them), crude community, rustic flock, forged upon the cold and barren steppe (yours and your fellow countrymen's).

Ricardo had parked the SEAT by the last stop of the streetcar line and when you got out you examined the half-naked children running along the esplanade and the old people sitting next to the first row of shacks. Were they the same ones as before, or were they new people? Age-old Andalusian poverty had become familiar terrain in which to expand there: a woman dressed in mourning was carrying a jug on her head and even the mangy dog swishing flies with his tail seemed to be the exact replica of another one that could be seen a thousand times in southern villages. At the edge of the cemetery the shacks proliferated like a closely planted crop of mushrooms. You began to count them (something like a person counting sheep), but boredom got the better of you. One hundred, two hundred? From your place of observation (or was it an effect of the light?), the last huts blended in with the first stones of the cemetery, as if the borderline between the two worlds had suddenly been erased. Poor peasants and rich Barcelonans, the sleeping dead and the dead who were awake: the difference between the two had been reduced to a simple matter of horizontal position.

Without saying anything, you both walked toward the stairway that led to the cemetery gate. Around you several stalls that had natural and artificial flowers displayed bouquets of roses, carnations, everlasting, anemones. A woman dressed in black was haggling with one of the vendors over the price of a wreath and, without knowing why, you remembered the little old man who years before, at sunset on a melancholy All Souls' Day, had furtively picked up a bouquet left by others on a gravestone and, after a quick and cautious look around, had placed it in his own niche before the faded photograph of some dear relative. Ricardo was looking distractedly at the slabs of jasper and alabaster and he said: "We've still got an hour before they get here."

"It's all right," you said. "Let's walk around a little."

It was the cemetery where your family was buried, and when you were young, you had gone to visit it along with your aunts and uncles, the day your mother was buried and on the anniversaries of her death, secretly fascinated by the underground part of that tomb where a place had been reserved for you from the very moment of your birth, already aware when you were sixteen that unless you cut the bonds in time, you were going to give back to that earth the scattered elements of your body in an obscene symbiosis with other members of your line who were disintegrating there in the nothingness of their absurd periplus *per omnia secula seculorum.*

By the cemetery gate several funeral processions were awaiting their turn with a general mixture of apathy, resignation, and impatience. The hearses were parked beside the flower beds and a chaplain was going from one group to another shaking hands and pausing beside the coffins to say a prayer. None of Ayuso's former students had arrived yet. While you wandered through the gardens, the cemetery workers were talking to one of the families there and when the consultation was over, the procession of relatives and friends began moving again.

The procession strung out slowly along the main drive and you both walked behind it toward the upper part of the cemetery. The niches were on the left-hand side of the road, with their epitaphs, inscriptions, photographs, wreaths. As the road climbed, you could make out the graves at the foot of the hill, guarded by the dark green of the cypresses and, in the distance, the turbulent blue sea, the derrick and the lighthouse on the jetty, the ships anchored at the mouth of the harbor, waiting for the pilot's clearance to unload. The honeyed summer sun seemed to be taking its time in setting, but the force of the wind was predicting a downpour. Sporadic clouds hung over the fortress of Montjuich, the advance picket of a dark and menacing army, as they took up strategic positions in a skittish sky that was transparent and colorless. A hoopoe flew by rapidly, skimming the tombs, and went over to perch lightly on the frontispiece of a mausoleum. The sounds of the city rose up from the flatlands like the tired panting of an animal.

The cemetery had been conceived originally as a peaceful and sleepy provincial town with gardens and avenues, squares and boulevards, niches for the lower and middle classes and sumptuous mausoleums for aristocrats and the wealthy. Opened during the time of Barcelona's development and expansion, when the confines of the old cemetery had been found to be completely inadequate, the diverse architectural styles and decorative fashions stood side by side there with a profuse and motley sense of aggressiveness: tombstones in the shape of crosses, wreaths, garlands, *Pietàs* and archangels; marble mausoleums inspired by some medieval mortuary monument; neo-Gothic chapels with stained-glass windows, apse, nave, and transept scrupulously reproduced in miniature; Greek temples in imitation of the Parthenon of Athens;

extravagant Egyptian structures with sphinxes, colossi, litters, and mummies, as if made to order for a production of *Aida,* following one after another before the eyes of a visitor as the synthesis and prolongation of the economic adventures of their owners, names famous in the private Catalonian Gotha, businessmen, bankers, and industrialists who had made fortunes in Cuba and the Philippines, autonomists and defenders of economic protectionism, a sturdy bourgeois caste (later titled), the pillar of the stock exchange, the textile industry, and overseas trade, your caste (yes, yours) in spite of your efforts to get away, unless (or was it just another useless rebellion?) you stood up to fate with resolution and voluntarily cut off the allotted time.

The spirit which had made the city grow and flourish could be seen there, you said to yourself, with a coherence that was foreign to and immune from death, as if the deceased dignitaries of cotton, silk, and knitted fabrics had wanted to perpetuate in the unreality of nothingness the norms and principles (pragmatism, *bon seny*) that had oriented their lives. Those pompous mausoleums were an exact response to the rustic and uncultured taste of their proprietors, like the chalets or summer towers built in Lloret or Sitges (perhaps the work of the same architect), both the product of an anachronistic system of paternalistic and family-run businesses, quietly being undermined over the years not only by the struggles and demands of the workers (now put down with rifle butts), but also (which was much more serious) by the imperatives and exigencies of modern State capitalism. The tombs did not seem to be aware of it, however, and with touching innocence were still on display, their owners dead now, with their belvederes and cupolas, bay windows and balustrades, all of them laid out as if it were a question of real dwellings, ridiculous comfort and luxury that the old and brittle bones they sheltered would never enjoy.

Twelve years before, in the basement bar off the courtyard of the Faculty of Letters, across from the chapel door, Álvaro had noticed the presence of a boy his age, dressed with affected carelessness, who seemed to be moving about in a ghostly universe, going forward groping among the groups of students like a sleepwalker in a sudden and obstinate nightmare. At the table where he was studying his history lesson, Ricardo and Artigas were arguing with the then brilliant delegate of their class to the SEU, Enrique López. Antonio was sitting farther back in the room with two law students, also in Professor Ayuso's class. The boy stumbled past them and searched in vain for an empty spot among the benches on the side. His air was growing stranger and stranger, and glances were converging on him with growing disapproval. At one point, he stumbled against a chair, he was about to lose his balance and to avoid falling, he grabbed the shoulder of a young man with glasses. His clear eyes scrutinized the scene around him as he stoically retreated toward the door and disappeared in the direction of the washrooms until he was out of range of Álvaro's field of vision, at the very spot where, years later, Artigas had lit the fuse of a bomb and calmly went up the stairs, anticipating the explosion by a few seconds.

"What's wrong with him?"

"Couldn't you tell?"

"I didn't notice."

"He's gassed."

"Who is he?"

"A kook. His parents are filthy rich."

"What's he studying?"

"Nothing. He drives around in his car and writes poetry."

"I never saw him before."

"He doesn't come here very much. If you want to meet him you'll have to go to the bars and the whorehouses."

It was around the beginning of November, and Álvaro had been vegetating for a few weeks in the company of timid and bored university students, part of the compact mass of scholars who, after class, would argue about the lectures and review them together.

Enrique was one of the top students, but unlike the others his activity was not limited to the strict cultivation of his own subjects, and he often took pleasure in going on in his fine baritone voice about sports, history, literature.

"Are you familiar with José Antonio's speeches?" he had asked Álvaro.

"No."

"Read them, then. You won't be wasting your time."

"I'm not interested in politics."

"Even if you're not interested. His theory about the modern State, Unions, getting beyond the class struggle. . . . It's something great. . . . The only serious answer in Europe to Lenin's challenge."

Enrique spoke with expansive eloquence about Ramiro Ledesma, Hedilla, Pradera, the *sinarquistas*. Tall, robust, with harmonious features, when he spoke in public he would let a lock of blond hair fall down over his forehead and he would toss it back with an energetic fling of his head, the instinctive wisdom of a public speaker. His dialectics did not exclude the use of his fists, and in the university they were still commenting with admiration about the fight he had put up against four student Don Juans, whom he had attacked like a bull, knocking down three of them in turn, and finally tossing the fourth into the pool in the courtyard. His fellow students from the Colegio San Ignacio recalled the times when, dressed in his blue shirt and red beret, he would drill the youthful legions of the Falange, marking time with a precocious and elegant militarism and saluting stiffly in the Hitlerian manner. Others affirmed that they had seen him in 1943 at the head of a group of demonstrators who had set fire to the screen of a Barcelona movie theater that had showed an English war picture for the first time. When he was fourteen, the military defeat of Germany had plunged him into the depths of despair and he wept for many hours locked up in his room as he listened to the overture to Wagner's *Götterdâmmerung*. Since then, Enrique had dedicated his efforts to the restoration of José Antonio's original doctrine, and when he entered the university he became active in the small but working nucleus of discontented Falangists.

"If Ramiro Ledesma were only alive . . ."

"Dead or alive, things would still be the same," Antonio affirmed.

"That's a lie," Enrique interrupted peremptorily. "The leaders we have today are the ones who betrayed the Revolution."

A few days later Álvaro had seen the boy in the bar again. He was sitting at a corner table and seemed absorbed in a book. When Enrique arrived and began to raise his voice, the boy put his book down and lit a cigarette with trembling fingers.

"Did you hear Ayuso's lecture?" Antonio asked as the waiter brought their food. "A real blast."

"Against what?"

"Against what else? Haven't you ever heard him talk about the old laws? Periods of freedom and tyranny? . . . Well, the man hasn't got any hair on his tongue."

"This guy, at least, isn't afraid to say what he thinks," Enrique said. "The ones that make me sick are the lukewarm ones."

"Ayuso has never been lukewarm," Antonio said. "He was in jail for two years after the war, did you know that?"

"When I come across a Red, I like him to show his face," Enrique said with vehemence. "With Ayuso you know what you're dealing with, but some of the others . . ."

"What others?"

"Why mention names? We took the chestnuts out of the fire for them, and now they're passing themselves off as liberals."

"They're a bunch of blowhards."

"Democracy's the worst plague that can happen to a country."

The boy was listening to the conversation and was smiling ironically. When the waiter came back with the tray, he asked for a double gin.

"You'll get drunk again. . . ."

"From what a person has to listen to here, it's better to be drunk."

Enrique stood up and faced him. Ricardo had tried to hold him back in vain.

"Would you please repeat what you said?"

"I said that in order to listen to what you're saying it's best to get drunk or put cotton in your ears," the boy replied in a natural way.

Enrique made a move as if to attack, but he held himself back. His cheeks had suddenly turned red.

"If you're a man, you'll come out into the courtyard with me."

"I'm not a man."

"What are you then, a woman?"

"I'm nothing, and neither are you. But you think you're somebody."

Antonio and Ricardo had intervened and held Enrique back.

"Don't pay any attention to him. He's drunk."

"Oh, let him hit me. . . . Can't you see that he'll feel much more of a man for it afterward?"

"You shut up or . . ."

"The only thing I won't forgive you for is using the familiar form with me."

The arrival of a group of professors in the bar put an end to the incident. Little by little, the students went out into the courtyard and Enrique did the same, followed by his companions. Álvaro had decided to play truant, and when he got up to pay, the boy stopped reading his book again and their looks crossed for a few seconds.

"Your friend's an imbecile."

"He's not my friend."

"So much the better for you. Every time I come here, I find him preaching, as if he were strolling through the world carrying a portable platform. . . . Can't he keep quiet for just a minute?"

"He's really not a bad guy," Álvaro said.

"People like him make me sick. . . . Preparing themselves, preparing themselves the whole damned day long. . . What for? I ask myself. . . . Then they end up as shopkeepers and dedicate their lives to cheating the public."

"What about you? What are you studying?"

"Nothing. Nothing is worth the effort in this country. . . . But since my father wanted me to go to school, I went. . . . But I don't do any studying."

"What Faculty are you in?"

"I don't know." The boy put his hand in his pocket and poked inside his wallet. "It must be written on the receipt, I don't remember. . . . When I got to the window, I tossed a coin."

"And what came up?"

"Look. Here it is. Law," he smiled. "A pettifogger, as they say. . . . Frankly, I'd prefer sticking on stamps in a post office. What are you drinking?"

"I'm not thirsty, thanks."

"It's not a very inviting place, of course," he admitted. "I've got my car parked upstairs. . . . Do you want to take a ride?"

The road rose in a zigzag along the side of the mountain and at a bend you stopped to take a look down at the countryside. The oil tanks in Campsa were shining in the sunlight and thick, tangled clouds were sailing out to sea toward the horizon. The freighters were quietly waiting on the other side of the breakwater. Beyond the sheds and warehouses of the free port, the sea was making its biting attack with monotonous regularity. From the shacks of Casa Antúnez piercing and turbulent voices were rising. At one end of the terrace, two cypresses, straight as sentinels, were keeping watch, solitary and serious, over the slow decomposition of the bodies.

You continued on up the drive. Niches were slowly replacing the mausoleums, like the sockets of a gigantic beehive. It was the newest part of the cemetery, and the utilitarian concept of modern urban civilization had been crystallized there in a more common and simpler architectural formula, related in a certain way to the schemes of Le Corbusier. At the top of the hill, the vegetation disappeared—cypresses, willows, palm trees, pines—and only the roadways, traced out in crossings and squares—grass, rosemary, prickly pears, agaves—added a plain touch of color. The niches were lined up in compact blocks, like the blocks of houses built in a row for bureaucrats and office workers, just as dehumanized and antiseptic, with their marble slabs that shook like windows, their open tombs like empty buildings under construction, their naked and uniform sidewalks and streets, their traffic lights set up on every corner: the protected dwellings of Madrid or *H.L.M.* in Paris, why not supermarkets, movies, drugstores, cafeterias, neon signs? A desolate impression came over the visitor to that (involuntary?) parody of the industrial world. Cement and stone. Not a single flower or bird. You, the living-dead, and nothing else.

The car was an MG convertible, a rather old model. Sergio had helped you open the door and when you got in he took away a wrinkled brassiere that was on the seat.

"Last night I took a whore for a ride along the Diagonal, and when she got dressed she forgot it in the car. I noticed it driving down here this morning. She had magnificent teats. . . . Oh, the poor girl crawled upstairs on her hands and knees."

"Why?" you asked.

"Because she couldn't make it standing up. Me either, if you have to know. . . . I haven't got the slightest idea how I got back home. Ana woke me up and gave me a bath."

"Did you drive when you were drunk?"

"I drive when I'm drunk practically every night. It's habit for me. Ana used to worry at first, but now she leaves me alone."

"Have you ever had an accident?"

"Never. Alcohol works just the opposite on me. My reflexes are better. . . . The only thing that really knocks me out is anise."

"And your father, what does he say?"

"My old man is an ass. Life for him is reduced to a question of arithmetic. A house isn't a house, it's a budget; a field isn't a field, it's so many acres; when he looks at the ocean he dreams about turning it into oil. . . . He thinks he's very clever because he makes a lot of money and the people who work for him take off their hats when they pass him. . . . Ana's quite different, fortunately."

"What does your father do?"

"He exports and imports oranges and things like that. . . . Something appealing, just imagine. . . . Cacao from the Galapagos Islands and flour to make hosts out of. . . . The damned fool thinks that I'll take over the business later on. Let him dream, if he wants to. . . . Someday, when he least expects, I'll wake him out of his fright."

"And your mother?"

"Ana is stupendous. Repressed and insecure, but stupendous. What I don't understand is how she puts up with a cretin like him. . . ."

Sergio was driving fast, dodging through the traffic on Las Rondas, and suddenly he turned down the Calle de la Cera, in the direction of Hospital.

"Do you like the Barrio Chino?" he asked.

"I've never been there."

"I go there everyday. The only place in Barcelona you can find interesting people. . . . Whores, pickpockets, fairies. . . . The rest aren't people, they're mollusks."

Through the window of the MG you had looked out for the first time at the dirty and ragged city, at the façades of the threadbare houses with the rags of their occupants being aired on the balconies. The comfort of the fifties was still not evident in the slums and, having stolen away from the delicate and invigorating atmosphere of the residential sections, you had the feeling that you had plunged into a different world, deeper and denser, the feeling that your lungs were not getting enough oxygen, fearful and uncertain, like a domestic animal suddenly dragged out into the normal daily element around him. Gloomy bars like dens of thieves, dark and evil-smelling coffee shops, dirty dives with blankets for doors and drinks of doubtful origin followed one after the other along the miserable streets, and on the corners women of unclassifiable origin and profession were selling black-market bread, American cigarettes, lighters, bundles which at the slightest alarm they would hide in their skirts, down their necks, in their garters, with a bold and perpendicular challenge to the rules of modesty and hygiene. In shops and grocery stores an age-old filth seemed to have accumulated on the strange products of Iberian underdevelopment: pots of olives, boiled chick peas and string beans, great, greasy Manchegan cheese, ponderous and round. All proliferating in that splendid cultural stew, the very Spanish Corte de Milagros—the only lasting and authentic court in your maimed and astounding history—was exhibiting its vices and defects in the midst of the general indifference of the tribe: twisted arms, stumps, sores, eyes veiled like blind mirrors, all placing you in contact, after nineteen years of vacuous existence, with the true structure of a society to which you belonged without being aware of it, a parallel and inverse excrescence, all of that, to your own parasitic caste—voracious, tentacular, madreporic.

You stopped on the Calle San Rafael, Sergio had shown you a shopwindow that had a rich variety of contraceptives and offered you a small box with the Mona Lisa on it. Your inexperience and innocence revived in him the natural prurience of someone in the know, and while you headed toward the Robadors brothels, he filled you in on his experiences.

"The best whores are the cheapest ones. The other day I was with a six-peseta one. Toothless, mangy, a real model for Solana."

"Did you go to bed with her?"

"I asked her to get undressed and wash herself in the bidet. Something extraordinary, I swear to you. I tried to make a sketch of her, but she balked. She said to me: 'Hey, you, you devil! What do you think this is, the Academy of Fine Arts?' "

"What did you do then?"

"I gave her five *duros* and took off."

"You didn't touch her?"

"I didn't touch her."

"Didn't she get mad?"

"Get mad? . . . She was relieved. Just imagine, a hundred times a day. No matter how easygoing they are, nobody can take that."

(When, a few days before, you had set foot in Barcelona after seven years' absence, you minutely retraced Sergio's itinerary, trying to relive the emotions it had inspired in you that first time. The setting was just about the same: the houses of prostitution were shut down, but in the bars that had replaced them, the women were actively continuing their business; the hovels and dives were the same as before, and there were the ever-present bootblacks and beggars. But you had changed, and your youthful exuberance had been succeeded by a melancholy attitude of detachment. The neighborhood continued on in its gloomy existence, alien to you and the lust for life of your young years. You vaguely remembered the festival of the Octave of Corpus Christi—the year 1956, months after Sergio's death—when you had photographed the procession on the Calle Guardia: Roman gladiators wearing Catalonian peasant sandals, an adolescent Saint Eulalia who was chewing gum, the round yawn of a priest, an atrocious choir of little vampires dressed as altar boys; behind them, under the legendary sign that announced "Madame's Rooms," the little girls who had made their first communion went by disguised as little angels with wings and white tunics, and they seemed to be heading toward the *meublé* with the mystical compunction of some of De Sade's adolescents on their way to a sacrilegious, demented, fabulous orgy. A forgetfulness thicker than the one that covered other moments of your past had justly shrouded over that period of your life. The only visible proof, the photographs, the only thing that had survived; but how could you use elements like that to reconstruct those months, so decisive for you, of that friendship between you that had been abolished?)

After a tour through the neighborhood, Sergio took you to one of the bars and you both sat down in the company of two women. Your friend moved in that environment as if he had always thrived there, and you were jealous in your admiration of his impertinence, his youth, his daring. The prostitutes treated him like one of the family and, at one point, you remembered, he went off to chat with a man, and he bought a small envelope from him which he immediately stuck into his pocket.

"Do you like pot?"

"What is it?"

"A plant."

"Is it a drug?"

"Yes."

"I never tried it."

"If you come to my studio, we'll smoke some."

You did not go to his studio that day, and you did not smoke any pot (the fact was, according to what you found out later, that Sergio did not smoke it either: he limited himself to breathing in the smoke and exhaling it right away, without ever letting it reach his lungs). Something had happened that was of great importance to you, even though you had tried to hide it at the time. One of the women had proposed that you go with her and you agreed, afraid that they would recognize you as a virgin, not knowing either (which strengthened your boldness) whether it was possible to make love at one in the afternoon (up until then you had thought that it was the exclusive privilege of darkness, possible only along with harmonious music of a flute and on the oriental sofas of Pierre Louÿs's conquering courtesans). The room was still and stuffy. The bed dirty. The clothes closet depressing. You got undressed, trembling, not daring to look at her body, ashamed as you were of your own, marveling when you finally discovered that the rubbing of her expert fingers was making a man of you, even though you were lying clumsily on top of her and, even more clumsily, penetrating her (still guided by her hand), your cheeks were burning, the cheekbones red, the two of you were fused together until the twitching pleasure brought you back to life after those endless seconds of forgetfulness, of death. When you sat up in bed, you examined yourself in the mirror and your reaction was, quite simply, one of surprise.

Could this be the deep love you had looked forward to since childhood?

A funeral procession had unexpectedly come along the drive and had stopped beside a cluster of niches, three hundred feet from where you were. Several priests were in the group, and while the undertakers unloaded the coffin, you observed their witchcraft with lush disbelief. The ritual farce—invented by others and mechanically repeated by them there—pursued your fellow countrymen right down to their last redoubt. Vicars of an aphasic and null god were living—were prospering—from the costs of fear and abandonment, like sumptuous and voracious vultures. The rebellion of your youth had returned intact and, as you thought about Professor Ayuso's posthumous fate, you felt like vomiting.

"Are you tired?" Ricardo asked.

"I'm not used to climbing."

The two of you went back by taking a shortcut down the

stairs. The panorama was magnificent again (the agitated and metallic sea, the sheds and warehouses of La Campsa, the open beach) during the descent (your heart was pounding and you should walk more slowly), and you amused yourself by looking at the epitaphs on the stones: "WHAT YOU ARE, I HAVE BEEN, WHAT I AM, YOU SHALL BE." "THE LORD MY GOD WILL RECEIVE HIS SERVANT IN PARADISE." "HE IS NOT DEAD, HE IS SLEEPING." "MERCIFUL GOD, HAVE PITY ON THIS POOR SINNER." Invocations, prayers, advice, sayings, the vain decoys of immortality.

Such a strange religion, your people's, you were thinking, and so strange what it tells—a god cheated by the fiasco of his own creation to such a degree that he feels obliged to descend to earth to correct and fulfill it; with the well-known results: was it not another obvious failure? What moral lesson can be deduced from a rocambolesque fable like that?

Niches with vases, wreaths, laurels. The dim photograph of a gentleman ceremoniously dressed in a cutaway coat. An allegory of death carved in alabaster on the base of a column topped by a Virgin Mary. A tomb decorated like an Egyptian sarcophagus. A wrathful and solemn angel, standing straight like the Statue of Liberty in New York.

Violent, oppressive, the sky was blending its dark emptiness in with the sterile environment of the headstones spread about on the grass. A willow was trembling in a faint, and the grim menace of the clouds seemed to be closing in over it. Some leaves flew through the air, a kind of omen in anticipation of autumn. Into the deep substratum of the hill, through the porous ground, death was sifting (imposing) its hollow evidence, its cheap apotheosis, its base and inert victory.

"FORGETFULNESS SHALL NOT TRIUMPH EVEN THOUGH IT STEALS OUR LOVED ONES FROM US. THE BONDS OF TRUE LOVE SHALL NEVER BE BROKEN."

Ricardo was looking at you with surprise, and you suddenly came out of the depressing reality of that overwhelming Spanish summer of 1963, coming to in the Southwest cemetery of Barcelona, thinking out loud, alone, amidst the desolation of the crosses.

In his restless sleep of the night before, after Antonio had come to the country, Álvaro had tried to bring back from his memory the intimate and remote face of the professor. Discontinuous and fleeting, his memory had been limited to tracing an unconnected series of gestures and expressions that it had intercepted separately during its biweekly exposure in his classes. Ayuso was walking hunched over, he climbed unhurriedly up on the platform, he rapped his knuckles on the table to let them know that they could be seated. Most times his look was friendly and timid; sometimes it was severe and distant. The professor spoke with a measured voice, emphasizing what he thought was important with a particular and thicker intonation as he would drum nervously on the arms of the chair or let the bridge of his glasses slide down the slim ridge of his nose. Facing him were four hundred students, listening and writing as they leaned over the dirty desks of the lecture room.

Álvaro also had a hazy recollection of the only time he had seen him in private (his admiration for him would not come until much later, when he was already settled in Paris, based on the disturbances at the university in 1956 and the brave and firm position that the professor had taken at the time in defense of his students). Ayuso lived modestly (of that he was sure), and a picturesque housekeeper (tyrannical, without doubt) had served Antonio, Ricardo, and him a cup of coffee sweetened with saccharine. In the apartment there were dark drapes, old furniture, a bookcase that extended along a narrow hallway, and a pampered Caravaggio reproduction. The desk was covered with folders and books, and on one corner of the table there was an old photograph of Américo Castro with an affectionate dedication. The visit had lasted several hours, but in spite of all his efforts, Álvaro had not been able to dust off in his memory the exact theme of the conversation. Ayuso was smoking one cigarette after another, sitting opposite them, and a black cat had stretched out voluptuously across his legs and remained motionless in his lap, proud and slim like a heraldic figure. (Thirteen years had passed since the visit, and his minute reconstruction stopped there.)

That autumn (1950) Álvaro had registered for the seminar in political science and had regularly attended Ayuso's lectures on the history of medieval juridical institutions. Antonio, Enrique, and Ricardo were also in the class, and arguments often broke out over the course and the professor's ideas. Álvaro would listen to them without understanding, convinced that politics was something for imbeciles, completely absorbed in his discovery of the

Barrio Chino and the reading of the books loaned to him by Sergio. Liberated from the busybody eye of Aunt Mercedes, he was savoring the idleness of university life with an invigorating feeling of independence from the social circles where he had been vegetating until then—inert, indecisive, restrained.

"When you graduate, what do you intend doing?" Antonio asked him.

"What about you?"

"Me, exams."

"For what?"

"Diplomatic service."

The idea had seduced him, but Sergio immediately took it upon himself to knock it down, affirming that the mission of a diplomat consisted, above all else, in smiling, kissing ladies' hands, and knowing how to peel an orange well.

"Congenital idiots. Congenital and polyglot. It's better writing toothpaste ads for the papers."

Sergio had suddenly appeared once when they were coming out of the seminar and had joined the group of students who were arguing in the bar about the theories of the physiocrats.

"Your friends bore me," he said to Álvaro. "Always so serious, as if they'd just come from bowing their heads at a funeral, talking about Adam Smith and social classes. . . . Every time I have a glass of vermouth in front of them, they look at me as if they wanted to say: you're getting drunk while laborers are working twelve hours a day for thirty-six pesetas and seventeen per cent of the children in Andalusia have tuberculosis, aren't you ashamed? . . . Well, no, I'm not ashamed. Who do they think they are? The redeemers of humanity?" He had a tired expression as he spoke, and he shrugged his shoulders. "On the other side, the workers, what are they? *Des bourgeois qui n'ont pas réussi*. Workers or bourgeois, anyone who works is a shit."

They had left the university and were slowly walking toward the MG. The other students had already scattered.

"I know what you're thinking: that if I weren't rich, I wouldn't be talking like this. Maybe it's true. Money makes things easy, and I'm not to blame if my father didn't withdraw in time and if Ana didn't think of douching herself. . . . But listen to me closely; even if I had been born poor, I don't think I would have worked either. If you're that unlucky, why play the fool to boot?"

There was a girl in the front seat, somewhat younger than they, thin, dark, with bright blue eyes.

"This is Elena," Sergio said simply.

Álvaro had put out his hand to her, but she was content to put hers together and salute like a boxer after winning a fight.

"How do you do."

The MG took off at full speed. From the back seat Álvaro was looking at the back of the girl's shapely neck, shaved, like a small boy's.

"Where are we going?" Elena asked.

"I've got a bottle of cognac at home," Álvaro said.

"I want to see some respectable people," Elena said. "Ladies from Catholic Action and all that. . . . Where can we find some?"

"In polite places."

"Let's go to some polite place."

"Shall we pick up Pepe?"

"If you want to."

"Who's Pepe?" Álvaro asked.

"A bootblack. He lost his hair from a dose of syphilis and he looks like Frankenstein."

"He can sing boleros, too," Elena said.

They went down Las Rondas, and when they reached the Paralelo, they turned down Conde de Asalto. Sergio parked on the corner of San Ramón and blew the horn. A bald head immediately emerged from the door of the bar.

"Hurry up. Come on with us."

"My guitar's inside."

"It's O.K. Leave the guitar."

Álvaro moved over to make room. The bootblack had a cross-eyed look, and when he smiled, he showed his clean bare gums.

"We're taking you to the Salón Rosa," Sergio said.

"I'm not dressed."

"It's O.K. You go in with us and nobody'll say anything."

It had been a stormy afternoon. In the Salón Rosa, the ladies (hats with artificial flowers, painted faces, flabby chins that would suddenly puff up as pastry was swallowed greedily) had grown restless when they spotted the invasion of the quartet (the bootblack was wearing a raging yellow visor cap) and as soon as the drinks were served, Sergio cut a lock of hair from Elena with a pair of pocket scissors, cut the Vienna bread that the waiter had brought in two, sprinkled it with salt and, surrounded by the mute hostility of the public (ceremonious parrots, contemplative owls, magpies ennobled by some pontifical title: a real aviary), he put the lock of hair inside and proceeded to eat the sandwich, swearing (to all who wanted to listen) that he had never tasted anything better in his life. Then Pepe started to sing the bolero entitled "Tu cintura es flexible como un flan de aguacate" (Your waist is as pliable as an avocado pudding), but the headwaiter stopped him.

"You're all anti-Semites," Elena accused in a harsh voice.

They left, insulted and with great dignity, and they strolled through the downtown section for a while, escorted by the bootblack's frightful voice (as he finally rendered "Tu cintura es flexible como un flan de aguacate" without benefit of accompaniment). Sergio would climb up a gaslight pole to light Elena's cigarettes and, when they got to the car, he proposed that they empty a bottle of pernod among the four of them.

"Then we can go back to the Salón Rosa and vomit."

"Forget about them," Elena said. "Why don't we go to a bar where there are some girls?"

"To Sans? Or Casa Valero?"

"Wherever you want."

They started up again (after brief visits to several bars), and when they got out at the Montjuich stadium, Álvaro discovered that he was drunk. The air was thick and cottony. His head was spinning.

"What's the matter?"

"I don't feel well."

"Change your drink. If you mix them it's much better."

They had gone into a cheap dive and Sergio ordered double rums. The tables were filled with Andalusians. Álvaro had downed two glasses without taking a breath and, through a thick veil of fog, he was following the argument Sergio was having with an individual who looked like a Gypsy. The bootblack had intervened and was trying to separate them.

"His laugh is bothering me," Sergio was saying.

"Leave them alone, can't you see they're having a good time?"

"They've got no right to have a good time."

"You cut out provoking us, mister."

"It's our duty to provoke. Life is one big provocation. . . . Sixty centuries ago Assyrian poets . . ."

From then on the memory was horribly confusing. Álvaro had the impression of having been thrown violently out of the dive and, when he came to, he was in a bar in El Borne, surrounded by strangers. Elena and Sergio were sound asleep at the next table. The bootblack had mysteriously gone into eclipse.

"Quina castanya jove. . . . ¿Voleu una mica de café?"

It was light out on the street. The sky was purple and Álvaro pointed at it.

"What's that? The northern lights?"

"It's dawn," the man said laconically.

The questions came to his brain, new at the time, familiar later on: how? where? when?, and the disgust and depression and the nausea, as old as the world (it could have been a night like that, and you would no longer have existed: fifteen miles out on the Valencia highway the MG had passed the DKW, license B-64841, blind on the curve known as the Coix lookout at the precise moment that the Ford, license B-83525, was advancing swiftly in the opposite direction, obliging him to accelerate in order to avoid the collision and sending him first to the right and then to the left on the bridge that led down from that spot on the outskirts of Garraf. Out of control, the MG had broken through the wire mesh fence strung out between the posts and had gone hurtling over the 150-foot drop, turning end over end twice before it bounced off the cliff and sank out of sight into the sea).

The sun had suddenly gone into hiding and from the landing of the stairs you watched the rapid flight of a tern that was skimming, slashing the curly surface of the sea, accompanied by the fine spray. Hundreds of gray gulls were swarming about the sewer openings. The clouds were coming together over you, clumsy and muddy-colored. The wind was shaking the hoods of the cypresses and transmitting a winged tremor to the tiny leaves of the willows. Everything was saying that a storm was imminent.

"What time is it?"

"Five o'clock."

"They ought to be getting here."

While you were passing through the residential and aristocratic section—"modern" or Gaudí mausoleums; the hybrid cross between a tomb and a summerhouse—you cast your eyes around for the tomb of the Mendiolas—an exact and prim copy, you remembered, of the pretentious Duomo of Milan. For the space of a few minutes, you went back in vain over the silent walks, plagued by the hazy memory of your bygone visits: Aunt Mercedes severely dressed in mourning and Uncle César with his hat and his glasses and between the pair of them, you, indifferent and alien to the ceremony you were taking part in, conscious of the gratuity of the gesture that was unilateral and without recourse, changed by ancestral custom into a strictly social and worldly rite.

What obstacle had come between you and your mother? Even though it had often come up, the question caught you off guard, and you did not know what to answer. Like two parallel lines, her existence and yours had never crossed, and on occasion you felt retrospective sorrow for the adventure that had not been lived, for the meeting that had never come to pass. Her modesty and your reserve had kept you both at a distance, and as you approached the border line of your fifteenth birthday, you had not been able (or had not known how) to invent friendship. Now (distant from her in time and memory) it was too late. Except for exceptional moments (and becoming rarer and rarer) her image (clear blue eyes, broad forehead, straight nose, congealed in some photograph) had deserted your memory forever.

From the balcony on the Calle de la Piedad, lying down on Sergio's reading couch, you were taking in a somber and rhythmical sight, the memory of which (even after your many trips) is always vivid in your mind: the apse of the cathedral with its massive and elegant towers; the enigmatic gargoyles carved in the form of griffins or hippocampi; the flat terraces darkened by the patina of time; the palisades of buttresses and windows; the harmonious and austere line of the central nave; the corner of the Calle de los Condes. On the couch, in exemplary disorder, your friend's bedside books: Blake, De Quincey, Lautréamont, Gérard de Nerval. At dusk the greenish light of the tulip tree was filling the room with an ambiguous glow. Old period furniture, etchings, pieces of sculpture took on a new dimension (a sudden fervor), something like contact with their original and native element. The rugs cushioned the sound of walking, and in the silence of certain streets where there was no traffic, the conversations took on a tone of complicity, the phrases a more subtle structure, the questions an equivocal, thick, and caressing flight. Ana was accustomed to lying with her back to the light and, in spite of it, during the bleak winter sunsets, her intense eyes were shining, soothing and autonomous.

The first day that Sergio took you to his house, he had introduced the two of you in a casual way, and Ana had held your hand in hers for a few moments, as if she had wanted to use osmosis to transmit some secret, private, and unique message: "Oh, for heaven's sake, don't call me ma'am or address me formally. . . . Even though I could be your mother, I still like to flirt. I like people to appreciate me for what I am, not as anybody's mother or wife. I always tell my husband: we're married, but you're one person and I'm another, different. . . . Call me Ana and use the familiar form. . . . We'll never be friends if you don't."

A few days before (the sun was shining, the children were feeding the pigeons, the policeman was strolling along in his gaudy uniform, and the whole city was offering a radiant look of happiness to the unwary), you had parked your car on the glowing Avenida de la Catedral just like one of the millions of tourists who had been swooping down on the lethargic and lazy country for some weeks already, and you had scrutinized with astonishment the wavy and agile movements of the sardana dancers in front of the portico, enthralled, you might say, by the skillful, clear, and vibrant voice of the female tenor who was singing nothing less than "La Santa Espina" (the same "Santa Espina" that was fused in your memory with the odyssey of the defense of the popular republic that had been filmed by Ivens and narrated by Hemingway) before you decided to go past the walls of the Casa del Arcediano and the chapel of Santa Lucía and up the Calle del Obispo by the Santa Eulalia and La Piedad doors and finally come to the apse, stopping by the Calle de los Condes entrance which was being photographed (in that thirsty summer of 1963) by a sinister group of bare-chested and hirsute Germans. You turned your head around and looked up at the row of balconies on the fifth floor. In what had been Sergio's room the drawn blinds were discoloring the façade of the building, withered and bleary. The apartment seemed to be closed up for good, and you continued your sentimental journey through the neighborhood and decided not to question the doorman. (I wonder what became of Ana?)

"Sergio has spoken so much about you that it's really as if we already knew each other."

The three of you were sitting, you remembered, on the Moorish sofas in the studio. The afternoon was growing late and the sun was now tinting the sturdy towers of the belfries.

"How did you make out in Robadors?"

The question took you by surprise, and you blushed.

"I told Ana that we went whoring," Sergio said.

"My son and I have no secrets between us," Ana explained in a soft voice. "Did you have fun with your partner?"

"I can barely remember."

"A good-looking boy like you must count your exploits by the dozen, I imagine."

"Not Álvaro," Sergio said. "He's very timid, even though you wouldn't think it to look at him. . . ."

For the first time in your life you had the feeling that you were going around naked. Ana laughed across from you, showing her white teeth.

"Are you surprised at my talking to you like that?" she said. "What did you think I was, a typical Spanish mother?"

"I don't know," you babbled.

"I've been like that all my life. Lots of times I've tried to change my ways, imitating other people, but I haven't been able to. My husband always says: if you were any different, I don't think I'd be in love with you."

"Dad is a fool."

"You know I don't like you to talk that way about your father," Ana protested. "My husband is completely different from me, and he doesn't understand certain things, but he's a good and loyal man. He's really worth a lot more than I am," she added with a persuasive tone.

"The world is full of meek people who are good and loyal," Sergio cut her off.

(The conversation was repeated many afternoons; Ana's defense of her husband and the son's attacks, harsher and harsher. . . . Ana would raise her voice, feign indignation, and end up confessing with resignation: "He's terrible. Ever since he was a child, I've tried to erase myself so that he would love his father and not notice the difference between the two of us. But he's like me. Hypocrisy disgusts him.")

Thanks to them, you had learned to love your city (a surprising thing in a difficult character like yours, this love maintained over the years for some places and streets that had only been discovered on the borderline of your youth, in a city where you had been born by chance, as they say, and whose beautiful language had always been profoundly strange to you in spite of all your efforts. Until then your knowledge of the city had been reduced to a few spacious and sad districts, monotonous and pompous, built after the walls had been torn down and that prodigious industrial growth had been brought about by an upright and business-like bourgeois race whose frightful artistic taste was only comparable in intensity, you used to say, to their immeasurable and insatiable zeal for wealth: the mediocre chalets of San Gervasio, the stuffy apartments of Gracia, the sordid and small-town piety of Sarriá, the laughable luxury of Bonanova and Pedralbes, independent nuclei in their day, gobbled up a century ago by the land-surveying, geometrical delirium of Cerdá (the compact blocks of houses that turned the flatland into squares, the streets perfectly parallel like a well-ruled musical staff). The Barcelona that they had shown you began down below the cathedral, and the light that bathed its houses you had never discovered anywhere in your travels: it was the light that shone along the Calle Montcada, with its palaces that belonged to rich and ennobled merchants, the neighborhood of the church of Santa María del Mar, the Calle Carders, with its admirable romanesque chapel, the Paseo del Borne. With instinctive wisdom, Ana guided you through a labyrinth of narrow streets where the lye ran down from the balconies, the cats sniffed around in garbage cans, and the color of the sun could be sensed on top of the tile roofs. Barrel shops, nineteenth-century pharmacies, herb stores, cork articles were fearlessly resisting the passage of time, awaiting perhaps, you would say to yourself, the future challenge which, by dint of and thanks to tourism and the rise of middle culture, would some day soon transform their anachronism into an exciting and profitable novelty.

At other times Ana would let the two of you go by yourselves to the Barrio Chino, and she would lie distractedly in wait in the small parlor for your return, lighting one cigarette with the butt of another. Before you left, she had given Sergio some money for you to go to a brothel and when you came back she would scrutinize your faces anxiously for the recent vestiges of passion.

"Tell me," she would say. "How did it go today?"

Sergio would talk about the afternoon's erotic incidents, and Ana would laugh quietly and demand details.

"I know very well that these are not things a mother should know," she would excuse herself. "But what do you want me to do? I'm incorrigibly curious. We women live under oppression in Spain. If I were a man, I'd be able to go to the whorehouse with you and nobody would care."

"Why don't you try to find a lover?" Sergio asked.

"And you, Álvaro," she would ask. "What did you do this time?"

(Ana had gradually broken down your resistance and after a few sessions, you were talking to her just as crudely as her son. She would look at you with her glowing eyes, and her harmonious face seemed to contract with attention as she listened to you pour out the details. "I would have enjoyed being a man," she would say.)

In the strict selection of your memory, certain scenes would emerge with greater precision than others, and that first year at the university was almost reduced in your memory to the company of Ana and her son, the nocturnal strolls through the Barrio Gótico, the languid conversations of accomplices in the apartment on the Calle Piedad.

On one occasion, weeks before your break with Sergio, Ana had undressed to take a bath and had asked you to shut your eyes.

"Promise me that you won't peek," she begged. "If there's anything I can't bear it's being caught in the nude."

You had turned your head modestly, shut your eyes on the backs of the books lined up across the shelves, and you suddenly felt the close and licentious presence of Sergio as he lay next to you.

"Look at her. Do you like her?"

You risked a glance at the bathroom door: Ana had her completely naked back turned toward you and you studied, upset, the ample line of her hips, her soft back, her slim and graceful legs (her face appeared several times in your dreams that night, passionate and cool, restorative and healing. When you woke up, the excitement had not abated and with your mind fixed on the quiet provocation of her thighs, you closed your eyes halfway as your body, face down, independent of your will, parodied the nervous motions of coitus. Pleasure finally came, short as a shiver, and you dragged yourself off to the washbasin like a sleepwalker, turning your back on the damp stain which, like a brusque condensation of the absurd, was inaugurating a new day, unjustifiable and monotonous like all the others).

"Why don't you go to bed with her?" Sergio insisted.

"Leave me alone."

"I'd like to see you cuckold my father."

(When, a few days later, during your friend's absence, the two of you had finally kissed, your face was burning up. Ana had put her juicy tongue between your lips, and its elemental and magnetic contact had filled you with happiness. You attempted the gesture of pushing her down, but she resisted firmly. "No, no," she said. "Let's keep on being friends.")

From that day on (for no precise reason), your relationship with Sergio had deteriorated. Was he jealous of your intimacy with his mother? Or, with his irrational rich boy's whims, had he just grown tired of you? The twelve years that had passed would not let you clear up the question in any definitive way. What was certain was that all day long your friend had begun to treat you with coolness, and underneath his habitual mask of cynicism you guessed (you sensed) the larval existence of some mortal wound.

"Do you know Elena?" Ana had asked you.

"Yes."

"What do you think of her?"

"I don't know. I've only seen her a couple of times."

"Do you all go out together often?"

"Oh, no." Her face had changed and you were trying to undo your mistake. "Sergio and I find her boring."

(As your friend grew distant and forgot his dates with you, Ana had made an effort to draw you out about the girl: what's she like? what is she studying? do you think she's really intelligent? Sergio took pleasure in making the two of you suffer and on more than one occasion you had waited until dawn for him in the apartment while Ana fidgeted impatiently in the easy chair and crushed Elena with the weight of her accusations and attacks: "She's an adventuress and a schemer, what interest can he find in going out with her?" "I don't know." "You, you've seen her, be sincere, is she as attractive as he claims she is?" And when her son would come in drunk, she would fight with him and shout at him as if it were her lover.)

"Why did you talk to her about Elena?" your friend had asked you.

"She asked me about her."

"And you answered her. . . . Don't you realize that she's crazy and capable of doing something wild?"

"I didn't know that. . . ."

"I thought that at your age you would have learned how to keep your mouth shut."

You stopped seeing each other and, unknown to him, Ana would call you every day, confiding endlessly in you her fears about a hypothetical wedding, informing you as she did that your friend never came home to sleep: "What do you think I ought to do? . . . He's discovered that I can't live without him, and he's having fun playing games with me. Yesterday he only came by to ask me for money, and he wouldn't even let me kiss him. . . ." That spring you had seen each other once in a while in secret, and Ana's eyes would be red from weeping and she seemed to have suddenly grown older. As for Sergio, he had stopped showing any signs of life, and the only time you ran into him he was drunk and he mockingly called you "Mama's crying-towel."

"Go to hell," you said to him.

(His end was unexpected, wild, lamentable. His meteoric (and deceptive) youthful rebellion had suddenly disappeared; he gave up alcohol and deserted Elena (today the upright mother of a family, no doubt) in order to contract matrimony with the very rich and conventional Susú Dalmases. He put on fifty pounds and devoted himself to the purchase of German patents and the breeding of Persian cats. According to what Álvaro could find out, he had sold his splendid library to a junk dealer and was seen regularly in the grandstand of the Club de Fútbol Barcelona. He was rising in aristocratic circles, and his name figured among those of the Civic Commission in charge of organizing the triumphal reception for the Blue Division prisoners sent home by the Russians. He died physically in September, 1955, on the Garraf coast, in a spectacular automobile accident.)

The stairway opened on the main drive of the cemetery and as you both approached the registry, you spotted Artigas's car parked beside some trellises. Antonio was waiting too, with his hands dug deep into his pockets, a little apart from the other members of the entourage. Ayuso's former students had gathered around the hearse with the family and members of the faculty—it was a small, black truck without a cross, flowers, or wreaths—and you scrutinized those solemn faces, vainly trying to give them names. Most of them had been in classes later than yours, and the few fellow students of your age were looking at you in turn out of the corner of their eyes—as if they knew all about your background—undecided whether to shake hands with you or not.

After a voluntary exile of ten years you were back among your people, and the country was just the same as when you had gone away, stubbornly resisting the change in direction that your friends and you had tried to impose on it. The professor had gathered you all around him, just as in the old days, and the presence of all of you was taking on in your eyes the pure meaning of a profession of faith. Nevertheless, you said to yourself, Ayuso's burial was the burial of all of you; his death was the end of the illusions of your extended youth. You remembered that beautiful time when recently freed from the tutelage of your family, you had met your companions in the classrooms of the university. And there you were again—except for Sergio and Enrique—overloaded with plans that had never been, aged by years that had not been, and the man who had said at that time, "I don't care if I die, as long as I live to see the fall of the Regime" had died, lonely and obscure, deprived of the consolation of his last and irreducible hope.

A dark fear had quietly crept into your blood and as the delegation stepped off with long strides toward the plots of the outlawed civil cemetery, a flash of lightning suddenly colored the countryside and almost immediately, before the birds took off in terrified flight, softly, very softly, the rain began to drizzle down.

Toward the end of the winter of 1951—it was already in March—Álvaro had got on the Number 64 streetcar that he always took to go back to his apartment on the Calle Muntaner, and the vehicle's deplorable state of abandonment and neglect suddenly attracted his attention. He was holding in his hands the *Manual of Political Economy* that Antonio had advised him to read, and while for the nth time he reviewed the theory of income from land tenure, the broken glass in the windows and the cold air that poured through them suddenly made him think of his late Uncle Eulogio and his habitual diatribes against the *Compañía de Tranvías de Barcelona.* Could they possibly be that negligent? he thought.

The next day, returning from a stormy session with Ana—it was dinner time and he was waiting for his uncles' weekly visit—the spectacle had been repeated in an alarming way: Number 58 looked terribly shabby and every windowpane, without exception, was broken. There were few passengers: a little man with a square mustache who was engrossed in reading his newspaper, a severe and imperious dowager, two nuns whose round faces emerged from their starched white hoods like two Astorga butter buns. On the platform, the conductor was smoking with a surly expression on his face, and Álvaro thought he could read furtive signs of hostility on the faces of pedestrians.

"Why did you take the streetcar? You ought to be ashamed of yourself."

When he got off on the Vía Augusta, a woman dressed in mourning had faced him, and Álvaro looked in amazement at her angry eyes; her expression of thick and restrained rage.

"I'm sorry," he said. "I didn't know that. . . ."

A Number 23 was coming in the opposite direction, just as windowless, and two women went over to the stop to head off two young men who were going to get on.

"What's going on?"

"People are boycotting the trolleys in protest against the fare rise."

"What happened to all the windows?"

"There hasn't been a single one left whole since yesterday. People throw stones at them and break them."

The appearance of a touch of anarchy in the widespread monotony of the life of the city called for a real celebration. Álvaro joyfully examined the uninviting succession of shabby streetcars, happy to know that underneath his people's veneer of resignation and conformity, there was a mute rebelliousness that still throbbed. Sometimes, during their agitated drives, Sergio had told him about his ideas for social provocation which were summed up in the motto "Oppress the Poor and Defraud the Worker through his

Wages" and, with Elena's agreement, they had decided to drive through the poorer sections of the city with the top down on the MG and use a thousand-peseta note to light a cigarette with in the presence of beggars. When he got home he telephoned Sergio and suggested they take part in the boycott.

"We can load the car with paving stones and bombard the streetcars."

"You're an idiot. That was O.K. before, when the people were behaving like sheep. . . . Elena and I will never imitate the rabble."

"What do you suggest doing, then?"

"The real provocation is to be a scab and insult people on foot."

His biting tone left no room for an answer, and Álvaro hung up feeling humiliated. Uncle César had come to dinner, along with Jorge and the girl cousins, and during the solemn and boring period after dinner, the conversation revolved around the transportation problem.

"The people are playing into the hands of the Communists. For a week now, I've left my car in the garage, and I take the streetcar to the office in order to set an example."

"Pepín Soler makes his employees show him their ticket stubs," Jorge said. "And anyone who doesn't have one, zip, out the door."

"The Mateus are doing the same thing at their factory."

It was Sunday, and that afternoon Álvaro stayed home shut up in his apartment preparing his lessons. When he woke up at his usual time on Monday, the twelfth, the old servant was terrified when she brought him his coffee.

"Oh, sir, it's the Revolution."

"What's happening?"

"Everybody's out on strike. People are stoning the streetcars, and they say a lot of people have been killed."

He was excited when he got out on the street. The country was still alive in spite of its apparent drowsiness, and the same men and women, resurrected from July of 1936, had invaded the beautiful sidewalks of the city with a rough and warning resolve. Shops, pharmacies, bars were closed, and detachments of shock police stationed at strategic points seemed overwhelmed by the uprising, unable, one might say, to keep order any more.

At the end of the period Álvaro had a hazy recollection of the episode (streetcars overturned, demonstrations in the street, the police attacking, cars set on fire). His consciousness was still in the dark (this he discovered much later), and it had prevented him from grasping the importance of what might have been (and doubtless was for many others in a country that had been deprived of the harsh and savage taste of freedom over the years) one of the most beautiful days of his life. Twelve years had passed since that date without the occasion's having been repeated, and often (during one of those somber crises that he regularly went through) Álvaro would be afraid that he would die without having enjoyed once more (even if only for a few brief hours) that miraculous and unusual fruit (in Spain, at least) which, because of a youthful lack of consciousness, he had not appreciated at the time.

Since the nation had been launched (that was what they said) along the path of spectacular progress, would he disappear before he could see the end of that misty and lamentable deception?

The procession moved along at a rapid pace toward the cemetery exit and, some thirty yards away from the fence, it made a right turn in the direction of the section set aside for Protestants. The tombstones were resting on the ground, elegantly adorned with flowers and little gardens, and as you went up the path that led toward the last plots—the drizzle was wetting your face and you were panting—you stopped to rest and you looked at the inscriptions for those there, lonely like you—who had chosen to die far from their countries and their people—the alert and secret accomplice of their changeable fate, embarking with them, you meditated, upon a like and irrevocable adventure.

"MAY SHE BE WITH US FOREVER," "SEIN LEBEN WAR LIEBE, GUETE UND STETE HILFSBEREITSCHAFT," "THE RIGHTEOUS SHALL BE HELD IN EVERLASTING REMEMBRANCE." An epitaph in Cyrillic characters. Rustic and retiring to the end, a world cut off from the Hispanic community by a hermetic and incomprehensible form of writing, what wandering fellow countryman, you wondered, had taken down his last desolate message? You were thinking about the Spanish tombstones in the Père Lachaise cemetery and the memory of your visit there with Dolores, filled with anguish: liberals exiled by one of the many authoritarian regimes that in an endemic way had governed your decrepit country, cruelly deprived of their own land by the very same fellow countrymen who had made you hate it, were lying there, like shoots amputated from the native trunk, while the perennial defenders of reaso (reason?) by armed force were living and flourishing, exploiting for themselves and their fauna power and riches, flattery and honors under the pretext of preserving (that was what they said) the unity and the fierce independence of the tribe. Drives, statues, ceremonies, mausoleums, all immortalized their hateful slander and solemn and expiatory masses assured them, beyond earthly glory, the benefits of eternal happiness.

The civic awakening of March, 1951, worked the miracle of shaking them out of their torpor. Ayuso had abandoned his classrooms to demonstrate his solidarity with the strikers, and Antonio and Enrique were arguing passionately in the bar and had stopped just short of blows. His break with Sergio had come about, and Álvaro was once more attending to his affairs and had accepted with satisfaction Ricardo's idea of getting in touch with a lawyer, an old friend of the latter's family, the ex-director, he said, of the dissolved Estat Catalá party.

It was a fifth floor on the Rambla de Cataluña: slow elevator, dark stairway, a pervasive smell of cooking rose up from the apartments below. Inside, an extensive law library, a showcase with incunabula and rare editions, Japanese vases, family portraits, a dusty Roman bust made of stucco. The carpet was threadbare and in order to hide its bald spots, someone had put a monumental copper brazier on top. The ancient maid had withdrawn behind the drapes and, after a few minutes' wait, the lawyer had appeared, wrapped in a checkered dressing gown, his feet in fur-lined slippers, his face alert, his eyes awake behind the thick lenses of his glasses. He had come over to Ricardo with an expression that was cordial and reserved at the same time, as if the harshness of the times, Álvaro said to himself, was impelling him toward a strict, cautious, and prudent discipline in the presence of strangers.

"Com ancu, minyó?"

"Very well, thank you, and how are you?"

"If they hadn't told me your name, I wouldn't have recognized you. You're all grown up. And your parents, how are they?"

"Very well, thank you." Álvaro had also stood up, and Ricardo turned toward him with a smile. "I'd like to introduce a friend of mine from the University, Álvaro Mendiola, you can trust him completely."

"How do you do," Álvaro said in Spanish.

The man nodded without blinking. There was a silence for a few seconds.

"My friend isn't Catalan," Ricardo explained. "His family originally came from Asturias."

"Asturias . . ." the man said, switching to Spanish from Catalan. "I was there many years ago with my wife. We both have wonderful memories of the place."

"Actually, I was born in Barcelona," Álvaro said.

"Are you by any chance a relative of a certain Lucas Mendiola who was active in the stock market before the war?"

"He was my uncle."

"Yes, I know how the poor fellow died. . . . What times, good Lord. . . . Would you care for some coffee?"

Comfortably seated on the plush sofa, they had listened to him discourse for an hour on the perspectives of the British labor movement and the latest action of American labor unions who were condemning all totalitarianisms without exception (he winked in a knowing way). Communist regimes and all the others, he added with a caressing voice. This was an extremely significant event, but, on the other hand, he had it on good authority that pressures were being brought from London and Paris, in accord with Spaak, to work out a common policy with respect to (another wink) you know who. The situation was very fluid and full of surprises. Had they heard about the conversation between the Nuncio and the British ambassador? A trustworthy person had been present, and, so it seemed, the ambassador had been firm. Besides, the commercial deficit was growing and private American banking circles were not so well-disposed, as they had been last fall, to extend the necessary credits, especially, he said, after the Secretary of State's trip to Europe. The ambassador in Washington had met with the Foreign Aid Committee of the House of Representatives and his reception, according to United Press (another wink), was glacial. As for the rumors of a rapprochement with Paris, it was a pure and simple invention of the Ministry. The French government had moved perceptibly from a friendly position to one that had a shade of opposition and was ambiguous in appearance but, in practice, was discreet and efficient. Did they know what

Auriol had said to the secretary-general of the PSOE? Very ingenious, and the allusion to the fable of La Fontaine was perfectly clear. It had stung them in Madrid, and it was rumored that the general (you know the one I mean) had threatened to increase his help to the Moroccan nationalists and had ended up swallowing his words after a good dose of bicarbonate. Although the picture had been shaky around the beginning of the year, the outlook for spring was, therefore (except for the unexpected, so frequent, alas, in the merry world of politics), frankly very hopeful. Especially if one kept in mind that the personal physician of the general in question had dined with a professor from the university (I'm sorry I can't give you his name, I promised to keep it secret), and the rumor of a stomach ulcer was confirmed. Evidently the surgeons advised an operation, and a specialist had come from London expressly for that purpose. Something very delicate, no doubt. Who knows (another wink) but that it might be cancerous in origin. The fake rumors going around Madrid concerning this show perfectly how precarious and uncertain the situation is.

"What do you think about what's been going on lately?" Ricardo had ventured.

The lawyer took off his glasses, breathed on the lenses, and leisurely cleaned them with his handkerchief. His expression, Álvaro seemed to remember, was ponderous and grave, careful and circumspect.

"The demonstrations evidently have some importance. They've shown democrats all over the world what the real feelings of the people are. From that point of view, I can't help but consider them positive. Which doesn't imply unrestricted approval, and I'm speaking now as a private citizen, with respect to their timing."

"Mendiola and I were thinking that . . ."

"The acts of violence that have taken place along with the civic protest have had a bad effect among our friends. Disorder, and that's a lesson I learned during our civil war, is always unprofitable. The people confuse the wheat with the chaff and tend to make hurried and abusive generalizations. Did you see the editorial in the *New York Herald-Tribune?*"

"No."

"I advise you both to read it. If I had a copy available I'd give it to you. Unfortunately, I loaned it to a colleague and as usual in such cases, he hasn't given it back," he noted with a smile. "It's a very balanced article that puts things in their proper place. The writer maintains, and I'll try to sum up his thoughts without deforming them, that the Democratic adminstration from now on should lay out a spare policy adapted to the Spanish situation, without worrying about pressures from the military sector or from Cardinal Spellman's friends. It would avoid, on the one side, and to my way of thinking this is the most solid argument the author puts forth, the current tactical disparity among Western foreign ministries, and at the same time it would be an effective weapon against the general already mentioned if, as everything seems to be pointing that way, he plans to exploit what has happened in Barcelona as a reason for raising the Communist bogey and thus consolidate the positions he has acquired in the Pentagon. To sum up: the protest, as far as the author of the piece is concerned, is a two-edged sword that can easily be turned against the very ones using it if they don't show greater sense and sanity in the future. According to what I've been told, and I heard this from someone who works in the American consulate, the Secretary of State himself read the editorial before it was published and gave it the green light."

"At the university they've handed out fliers calling for a strike . . ." Ricardo started to say.

"I know, I know. Every group without exception sends me its propaganda, and the police let it through, even though my mail is censored, but I get it all the same. As I said to the inspector the last time he came to question me: if it's so much work for you to read those things, why don't you just save them for me to read?"

"It's set for Monday the twenty-sixth," Álvaro said.

"Yes, I can recognize the message. The author of it obviously doesn't know his Catalan grammar. Do you have a copy with you?"

"No."

"That's too bad. The last paragraph is absolutely confusing. When I read it, I could swear that whoever wrote it was not a Catalonian."

"There are only five days left," Álvaro insisted.

"That's true, the time is short and, as usual, our friends have gone ahead with too much haste. . . . Their good faith is beyond question, of course, but here among ourselves, do you think it will be very effective?"

The lawyer took a pipe out of his desk and filled the bowl with tobacco. He looked for a match, lit it, and made a tuft of smoke.

"In my opinion, and I'm being sincere, it won't be. The situation isn't ripe, and by mobilizing their forces ahead of time, the opposition runs the risk of *perdre le soufflé,* as the French say." He made a vague gesture with his arms. "Oh, I know very well that youth, by definition, is impulsive and generous, but in politics, my friends, these qualities are quite often self-defeating. Politics calls for a great deal of practice and, in the end, the one who is strongest doesn't win, it's the one who can hold out the longest."

There was a pause. The maid appeared opportunely with a tray and took away the three empty cups.

"Would you like a glass of cognac?" he asked in Catalan.

"No, thank you."

"So, what do you think we can do?"

The lawyer was smoking with an absorbed expression on his face. The small bronze statues lined up along the mantelpiece seemed to be waiting for his answer, and Álvaro turned his glance toward the stucco Roman bust, the exact replica, he suddenly recalled, of the one that years back had dominated his Uncle Eulogio's gloomy study.

"My friends," he said in a slow voice, "the person talking to you is one who has known your restlessness, and he is in complete sympathy with it, my friends," he repeated. "If some advice can be offered to you by someone who, in his youth, committed the same mistakes that tempt you today, this advice would be: don't be hasty, don't ruin your chances. Politics is a slippery business, and anyone who takes a risk in it without taking precautions, will fall down never to rise again. The strike you're telling me about is premature and therefore useless. Let others burn their bridges behind them, but keep yourselves in readiness, like a force in reserve. . . . Must we stand with our arms folded? you'll ask me. . . . Not as simple as all that. The truth can always be found along some proper middle path. There are actions that seem to be minute but whose continuity assures them of greater effectiveness in the long run than others that at first blush are more spectacular. This kind of discreet and prolonged action is the best course for young men with a future like yourselves. Make your presence known, state your positions, but don't use bombast and haste to dull the natural process of ripening," the lawyer paused for a moment and cleaned his glasses again. "Do you know Nuria Orsavinyá?"

"No."

"Go see her. She's the widow of Pere Orsavinyá, the one who was the friend and collaborator of Companys. . . . Next week is her seventy-fifth birthday, and a group of close friends has organized a small party in her honor. Casals promised to send us a message, and we'll read congratulations from many exiles in France and Mexico. The plan for the strike is absurd, believe me. . . . It would be better for you to get together with us. The Bonet house is large enough, and the owner would be glad to have you. It's the twenty-third, at seven o'clock. You must know the house. . . . The one with the fir trees, at the end of the Paseo Bonanova. . . . Don't waste any more time on it and make up your minds. . . . Their sherry is famous. . . . I'll introduce you to other young people of your age. You'll be quite at home there."

From the appeased earth an elemental and dense breath was rising; hanging back from the main body of the group, you waited a moment to drink in its aroma. Coming after the sultriness of the morning, the wind was blowing in a furtive and caressing way. Meteoric clouds were scurrying off toward the southeast. Antonio was waiting for you at the foot of the stairs and when you reached him, he pointed at two individuals, unknown to you, who were going along with the group at a slight distance from the others.

"Police," he said simply.

"How do you know?"

"I saw them once when I was at Police Headquarters. The bald one punched me in the stomach."

"What are they doing here? Are they afraid he'll rise from the dead?"

"This morning an inspector came to my apartment with an injunction against speeches. . . . He said that if there were any incidents, I'd be held responsible."

"Why you?"

"That's what I asked him."

"What did he say?"

"The usual cliché. . . . An ounce of prevention is worth a pound of cure."

So, you were thinking, Ayuso has lived through difficult years with dignity, exile, jail, persecution, ostracism, voluntary forgetfulness, armed only with the truth of his words, never backing down in the struggle, and it all ended like this, covered with earth, cement, and bricks, in their custody, a defenseless body at last, in their hands once and for all.

You went trembling up the stairs. From up above you could take in the gardens of the Protestant cemetery all wrapped up in grass and, farther off, the orchards and rushes of the flatlands, gray and stumpy in the drizzle. The procession had come to the civil part, profaned in rage by the followers of order in the orgy of blood that had followed their victory after three years of dirty war, and as you made an effort to hide your emotion, you let your eyes glean among the niches that had escaped their destructive fury, lost in the midst of stones and niches of the imposed Catholic rite. From the epitaphs covered with a thick lime make-up, there stood out the flourishing and laughable (pathetic) messages of brotherhood and hope that Spaniards of some vague future would perhaps decipher with surprise (if the Kingdom of Twenty-Five Years of Peace lasted), just as present-day historians and scholars do as they reconstitute medieval palimpsests: HE LIVED AS A RATIONAL AND PERFECTIBLE MAN WHO DIED WITH THE SINGLE HOPE OF A LUMINOUS AND PROGRESSIVE HEREAFTER; Stars of David, theosophical inscriptions, the remains of some old masonic inscription; THE SYNDICALIST ATHENEUM IN MEMORY OF ITS COMRADE AGUSTÍN GIBAHELL, FEBRUARY 1, 1933, the portrait of a pilot in the air force of the Republic, dead in battle a few days after the military uprising; one in Catalan TO SALVADÓ, SEGUÍ, MURDERED ON MARCH 10, 1923, AT THE AGE OF 36, HIS COMRADES. You went over to the stone, decorated with artificial flowers and a wreath of everlasting, and you examined the image of the hapless Noi de Sucre, the legendary defender of the Barcelona working class, cut down by bullets in the cowardly ambush by gunmen of the Patronal. The photograph showed him from the chest up, dressed in a black jacket and a white silk scarf, with the melancholy expression, you thought, of a veteran composer of tangos. What mysterious fate had preserved his memory from the intense and nocturnal clandestine forces?

The employees of the funeral parlor were carefully looking for the niche among the faded numbers along the wall and, with your elbows on the railing of the stairs, you observed the unusual decoration that was offered to your eyes by the terrace directly below: three large stones, gray in color, parallel and anonymous, on which a hand that cared had deposited bouquets of wild flowers, roughly held in place by some small stones. The rain that was slipping across the naked surfaces added to the picture a surreptitious note of unreality.

Who were those dead, and what remote curse were they expiating? Antonio was also looking, confused, and someone behind you both whispered in Catalan:

"It's where Ferrer Guardia, Durruti, and Ascaso are."

"What about Companys?" Antonio asked.

"Companys is farther up."

You turned your head so that your friends in the spectacle would not see your waxen face. So, you thought, wrath had followed them to their graves, defeat and the monstrous price they paid was worth nothing to them, the battle against their memory continued, their unknown death was an everyday thing. Physical disappearance was merely the first step. The guardian angels of the secular orders were there to watch over the careful compliance with the rules: wrapped in obscurity and silence, the professor would descend to the depths of forgetfulness, mocked and drained by the same fellow countrymen who had tenaciously persecuted and humiliated him in life. The gravediggers put the casket into the open jaws of the wall and, like his underground brothers in the outlawed civil cemetery, he would be erased forever from history and memory for having espoused, as you were espousing, the rigorous and strict nobility of man.

It was still raining when, withdrawn and silent, you all abandoned the enclosure of your secret and clandestine comrades—the leafy harvest of anonymous dead without crosses, without flowers, without wreaths. You walked slowly down the moss-grown stairs and, as on the Boulevard Richard Lenoir six months before, your heart was beating out of time.

III

Don't ever forget it: in the province of Albacete, along route 3212, some ten miles from Elche de la Sierra, between the intersection with the Alcaraz highway and the turn-off that leads to the Fuensanta reservoir, standing on the right hand side of the road in the midst of a desert-like and arid countryside, there is a stone cross resting on a rough-hewn base.

R. I. P.

FIVE SPANISH

GENTLEMEN

WERE MURDERED

HERE BY THE

RED RABBLE OF YESTE

A REMEMBRANCE AND A PRA

YER FOR THEIR SOULS.

Coming from long plains of La Mancha, on the other side of the wheat fields and farm plots of the monotonous Albacete countryside, white clay and rocky ground succeed each other as far as the eye can see under the desolate glow of the sun. Steep paths mark the frequent locations of beehives and at intervals a traveler can make out some herd of goats along with its small shepherd, just like the conventional cork figures of a Christmas crèche. There is scarcely any vegetation—rosemary and thyme bushes, dry and drooping patches of esparto grass—and in August—along those dusty roads, still unknown to tourists—the soil burns and the air is thin, completely alien to life, inert stone, empty sky, pure motionless heat.

The first and only time that you visited the region, you had parked the car beside the ditch and, up on the crest of the hill, you silently contemplated the memorial cross, the naked and eroded summits, the shapeless and colorless mountains. In 1936 your father and four strangers—their names and surnames were also chiseled on the stone—had fallen there, cut down by the bullets of a platoon of militiamen, and you tried in vain to reconstruct the scene as you fixed your gaze on the last sight their eyes had seen before the sound of the rifles and the traditional *coup de grâce:* a cluster of hives, a fallen-down shack, the twisted trunk of a tree. It was early in August—the fifth, according to documents discovered later on—and the surroundings, you said to yourself, must have been more or less the same as what you were looking at then: the barren plain, lethargic in the sun, the cloudless sky, the ocher hills that were steaming like loaves just taken from the oven. A snake may have been prudently sticking its head out from among the stones, and the thick buzzing of the locusts rose up from the earth like a complaint.

You leaned over, you remembered, and you ran your hand over the wrinkled surface of the schists with the absurd hope of taking a further step toward a knowledge of the events, investigating the marks and traces like a diligent apprentice of Sherlock Holmes. It had rained a lot since the day of the execution (even on that baked and greedy steppe), and the bloodstains (if there had been any) and the impact and splinters of the bullets (how could they be found after twenty-two years on that bare and stony ground?) were already part of the geological structure of the terrain, joined forever to the earth and integrated in it, free, for almost a quarter of a century, of their original meaning and guilt.

Time had gradually erased the vestiges of the event (as if it had never happened, you thought) and, every so often, the memorial stone seemed like a mirage to you (the sudden product of your confused imagination). Other acts of violence, other deaths had disappeared without leaving a trace, and the organized and somnolent life of the tribe went on insatiably along its course. Your father's executioners were also rotting in the common grave in the village cemetery, and no stone requested a remembrance or a prayer for them. Some were remembered, and others were forgotten, shot during the summer of 1936 and the spring of 1939, all of them, executioners and victims alike, were links in the repressive chain that had had its beginnings months before the war, caused by the killings that had taken place in Yeste during the Popular Front regime.

On the way back to the farm—after the bitterness of Ayuso's burial and the aimless drive through Montjuich—the scene of the shooting had come gradually into your memory, interspersed with numerous images and impressions of your trip to Yeste the year you photographed the bull run and when you had been interrogated by the Civil Guard. The events were juxtaposed in your memory like geological strata that had been dislocated by a sudden cataclysm and, slouching on the couch on the porch—it was still raining outside on the ground that was intoxicated with the water—you were examining the mixture of papers and documents in the folder—old newspapers, photographs, programs—in one last and desperate attempt to find the coordinates of your strayed identity. Photostats Enrique had made in the Barcelona newspaper library, clippings from *ABC, El Diluvio, Solidaridad Obrera, La Vanguardia* that referred to the events of May, 1936, were piling up in a heterogeneous mixture along with prints of the bull-running you had taken in August of 1958. With the help of both elements, you were still unable to reconstruct the incidents and imagine the situations, dive into the past and emerge in the present, pass from evocation to conjecture, shuffle the real in with what had been dreamed. In spite of your efforts at synthesis, the diverse elements of history were decomposing like the colors of a bright ray that was refracted in a prism and, by virtue of a strange development, you were there beside the slow parade, participant and spectator, witness, accomplice, and protagonist all at the same time in that remote and obsessive drama.

They would gather under the shade of the plane trees along the walk, beyond the groups of onlookers who, with that unanimous look of people in the know, were lazily assaying the skill and prowess of the bowlers during those very French, interminable, and summer games of *pétanque*.

They were a dozen bourgeois families who had fled from the terror and disorder of the Republican zone and had taken refuge in the peaceful environment of a small spa in the Midi as they awaited the outcome of the struggle that their countrymen on both sides were vigorously engaged in among themselves in the Peninsula. Uncle César, his late wife, Aunt Mercedes, and Álvaro's mother brought them (him, Jorge, the two girl cousins) there in the afternoon to gather at the foot of the equestrian statue of Marshal Lyautey, along with the families of their other playmates: Mr. and Mrs. Durán (Pablito's parents), the parents of Luisito and Rosario Comín, Conchita Soler and her daughter Cuqui, Doña Engracia (Esteban's mother), and other gentlemen and ladies whose names Álvaro had forgotten: the women were wearing old summer clothes that had been adapted to the style of the time; the men wore pleated jackets of white linen and Maurice Chevalier hats. While the children ran among the slides and swings of the playground, the adults would settle down on the flowery terrace of the Café de la Poste and, over a cup of chocolate and cookies or weak tea with milk (because the times were bad and they had to watch what they spent), would talk mournfully about the news and communiqués coming from the Headquarters of the Generalissimo, about the latest crimes of the Communists and the victorious advance of the Nationalist army.

For several hours French and Spanish children would play separately from one another under condescending and kind eyes of a mustached *gardien de la paix.* Álvaro and his friends had worked out an adventure novel about the criminal activities of the one designated as the Red Spy, and the pursuit and punishment of the guilty party, carefully worked out in different versions every day, made up the group's main distraction during that languid and hot summer of 1937. At dusk, the older people would go back home and, still excited by the episodes of the capture, Álvaro and his cousins would return, heads down, to the old and somber mansion on the Avenue Thermale: a two-story house with a tile roof and a glass marquee in the shape of a kepi located in the rear of a melancholy and damp English garden.

When dinner was over, his mother and aunts would clear the table (the budget did not allow for servants) and would lock up the canned goods and packaged food that prosperous Uncle Ernesto regularly sent from Cuba. It was time for the rosary led by the harsh voice of Aunt Mercedes (piety and narrowness where before there had been splendor and rapine): the litanies followed one after the other, broken by the short, soft sounds of *Ora pro nobis,* until the liberating finale of the special prayer for the return of his father (missing in Yeste a year before), which announced the yearned-for moment of crossing one's self and slipping out at a run into the garden.

His mother and his aunts and uncles would go to listen to the news bulletins from Radio Burgos at Madame Delmont's and, settled into some beautific island, Álvaro would listen to them talking in French about the fall of Badajoz and the surrender of Santander, the air raids on Madrid, and the generous help of the Italians. *"Mussolini est un homme étonnant,"* Madame Delmont would say, fanning herself. *"Il porte le génie sur son visage. Ça fait longtemps que je le dis. Il va nous sauver tous de la pourriture démocratique."*

It was she—the afternoon they received the official news from the Red Cross and Álvaro's mother had fainted—who came to get him in the playground in the park and hugged him, weeping. The spy hunt had been in its final phase, and Álvaro was looking in irritation at the scarlet and tearful face of the woman without grasping the full meaning of what had happened. Fellow countrymen and foreigners, old and young, were looking on silently at that unusual scene: Madame Delmont's theatrical fuss and the expression of surprise on the face of the seven-year-old child whom—it seemed impossible in *la belle France:* the sun was shining and the birds were even singing—tragedy had unexpectedly struck. *"Mon Dieu, pauvre petit. Les Rouges ont assassiné son papa."*

You continued on in the direction of Yeste. Past the memorial cross the terrain rose and the road was rough. Route 3212 goes up, goes down, twists, hugs the cliffs along the mountain, emerges dizzily above the plain. The esparto fields alternate with clean white clay, bordered in stretches by an occasional grove of live-oak trees. Junipers, mastics, rosemary, thyme grow as best they can on the infertile plain. A few miles beyond, schists and rocks disappeared, and the highway suddenly opens up.

You still had several snapshots taken with the Linhof: yellow wheat fields, rose and ocher hills, white shacks, the greedy path of an irrigation canal marked out by fruit trees. Beyond the naked and formless vista of the plateau, the unexpected variety of colors had pleased and captivated your eyes. The traveler discovers a pitted expanse, burned by the perennial caress of the sun. The State forest preserves begin a little farther on, and the vegetation becomes richer in a sudden sort of way. There are trees, woods, thickets, groves. On the opposite slope the green climbs up and progressively covers the mountain until it comes to the crowning apotheosis of the pines.

The road goes perpendicularly across the valley, and as it goes up the slope, it passes next to the walls of a farmhouse alongside the family property that your mother had got rid of right after the Civil War. A hundred feet or so farther on one comes to a crossroad, and Dolores, Antonio, and you took the turn to the left that leads to the Fuensanta reservoir road.

The woods crown the crest of the hills, and, at times, one can make out the blue surface of the reservoir through the branches of the pines. The outsider feels a sensation of strangeness, as if he had suddenly been transplanted beside an alpine lake. The way is lined with some country houses built in the style of the thirties, surrounded by gardens with rosebushes, oleanders, mimosas, and bougainvillaeas. It is what used to be the residential area for the engineers and technicians who built the dam, and ordinarily not a soul is to be seen. The houses look uninhabited, and when you passed by them, you remembered a documentary whose title and author you had forgotten that you had seen on the program of a cinémathèque in Paris about a colonial city in the Middle East that had been evacuated during a typhus epidemic. Like a challenge to the imagination, a light plume of smoke was coming out of one chimney. At the side of the road there are rows of thujas and cypresses and, at a bend, a chapel built in the same architectural style as the chalets. You wanted to go inside, but it was locked. The highway descends some more for a quarter of a mile in the shade of the pines and, announced by a long, dull sound, the wall of the dam suddenly appears.

You parked the car at the end of the path, and you all leaned over the wall, over the two-hundred-foot drop where the falling water was breaking up into the colors of the spectrum in the sunlight, like a winged and fluttering rainbow. Seen close up, the waters of the reservoir have a dull green shade. The wall of the dam, the huts, the whole countryside seemed completely deserted. On the right-hand side there was a tunnel dug out of the cliff, and you all went over without paying any attention to the no trespassing sign. On the walls there were erased inscriptions that you vainly tried to decipher. With your backs to the falls, the silence was complete. Having avoided space and time, you were walking in the shadows like sleepwalkers. At the other end of the tunnel the light suddenly hurt your eyes.

You came out onto the flat. At the edge of the dam there is a building without doors or windows, and a man in his fifties was going about his work. The view there embraced a great extension of the lake. Beaches, cliffs, promontories, small islands can be seen. In the distance, the water gradually takes on a bluish tint, and on the opposite shore the pine trees grow dark and wild.

"Good morning. Are you the caretaker?"

"Yes, sir."

"We're visiting around here." Antonio took out a pack of cigarettes and offered them around. "Much work?"

"Not very much," the man replied.

"My friends and I were looking for the transformer. . . ."

"You're wasting your time. Everything's dead around here."

"There isn't any transformer?"

"No, sir. When the work was going on they planned to put one in, but the war came, and they abandoned the project."

"What's the dam used for, then?"

"Irrigation. All the water for the Segura flatlands comes from here."

"It's strange that they don't use the water power the way they do at other dams," Antonio said. "Is there always plenty of water?"

"Always. More in winter than in summer, but, all in all, there's always water."

"It's strange," Antonio repeated.

"Nobody bothers about it."

"They're building reservoirs in other places," Dolores observed.

"Yes, but they didn't build this one." The man averted his eyes.

"No?"

"No. This one was built during the Republic."

There was a pause. The caretaker was smoking with an absorbed expression, and he pointed vaguely at the dam.

"You're too young to remember, but I do," he had turned his back on you with an instinctive gesture, and all at once he added, "This reservoir cost a lot of lives."

"During the war?"

"During the war, and before. . . . Have you been in Yeste?"

"We're going there from here."

"Are you going to see the running of the bulls?"

"We didn't know there was a running. We heard about it in Elche. Just by chance."

"You young people find your fun any way you can," the man said. "In my day we were cut from a different cloth."

"Were you in the war?" Dolores asked.

"The war and what came after. . . . Three years in the trenches, four in a camp."

"Do you think they'll talk to us about it in Yeste?"

"About what?"

"About thirty-six."

The man dug his hands into his pockets, and with a glance he took in the deserted dam, the thick vegetation of the hills.

"If you want to talk about bulls and runnings, everything you want to know. . . . But about the other business, no. . . . Some because they don't know anything, others because they're afraid. No one will tell you a word."

The news had reached the most distant places: there was work to be had in Yeste. Advised by relatives and friends, men arrive en masse from Madrid, Barcelona, France, Morocco. Messages and letters spoke of high wages, guaranteed employment for many months. After dark years of narrowness and penury, an era of progress and well-being suddenly seemed to be opening up. When the work on the dam had begun, some two thousand emigrés had returned to the town.

Engineers and technicians were going over the municipal boundary lines with stakes and plans, taking soundings and diggings, having mysterious conferences with the powers that be. At first, the men who floated the pine logs along the meanderings of the Segura had looked with skepticism at that group of citizens armed with theodolites and a new planimetrical instrument who were patiently measuring the gorges and narrows of the river as it went through the gaps in the mountain. Isolated in those remote regions by geography, they had learned from childhood to look upon people sent from the capital with mistrust: priests, tax collectors, Civil Guards, appraisers. What did they care about the topographers' plans? Armed with their boat hooks, they had gone about their work without bothering to find out what was behind the visit. Simple common sense told them that this arrival could not mean anything good. Were they plotting, maybe, as in times past, to take away their communal woods and property? The overthrow of the king had not changed things. The central power was still making its presence felt entirely through the use of anathemas and commands and, as if by chance, the interests behind one or the other always were for the benefit of the local *caciques,* the political bosses.

As the measurements progressed, the favorable rumors from people in the know began to take on consistency, and the wariness of the natives gave way to surprise. After so many centuries of having been forgotten, the Republic, was it going to remember them? It was hard to believe. And yet, the authorities affirmed that it was so. It was a question, they explained, of damming the waters of the Tus and the Segura so as to guarantee irrigation for the truck farms of Murcia during dry spells. An undertaking in the national interest that would be profitable for everybody. While the work went on, there would be no unemployment in Yeste, and the economy of the town would improve measurably.

There were gatherings, meetings, debates, discussions. The loggers who floated lumber along the river, the farmers who worked the land along the banks had timidly brought up their objections to the government commission. They were rough backwoods people—most of them illiterate—who lived in refuge in their huts and shacks in the hills the same as when their ancestors who belonged to the Military Order of Saint James had defended the frontiers of the kingdom against Moorish raids. Woodcutters from Orcera and Siles, beekeepers from Molinicos and Riópar, charcoal burners from Létur and Bonanche, rosemary distillers from Jartos had come down in bands from their redoubts and were silently gathering before the members of the Commission in their sandals and caps, corduroy pants and vests, raising their hands and clearing their throats at great length when the question period began.

"My brother and I bring pine logs down the river. When the work is over, will we still be able to stay in business?"

"You can bring them along the road."

"And us?"

"You just work on the dam and don't worry about what happens afterward," the spokesman for the Commission expressed himself with a persuasive voice. "That's what we're here for. To take care of your future. The Ministry of Public Works has on file a series of projects for reconversion and will implement them at the opportune moment."

"And those of us who farm the bottom lands? At the town hall they told me that they'll be flooded."

"We'll set up new irrigation sections in the communal lands. Everybody will be indemnified."

"My village is twenty miles away, and there's no bus line. How will I be able to get home at night?"

"For those who live far away we've arranged to build a series of barracks, where they'll be able to sleep and cook. People from Yeste will be transported free of charge in trucks of the organization."

"In case of an accident, who'll pay us?"

"All workers will come under the social legislation approved by the Labor Ministry."

"What about meals?"

"The organization will set up a commissary and canteen for you."

"How long will the work last?"

"Approximately eighteen months."

The answers of the spokesman warmed the chilly atmosphere of the hall, dissolved doubts and suspicions, pacified their spirits once and for all. When the question period was over, the men left town satisfied. The days of endemic unemployment were over, the man-killing wages of the bosses, the hard necessity of leaving town to earn a few chick peas. Humiliations, misery, injustice were behind them; the eternal round of seasons that were all alike.

Imagine them as they leave along paths and trails, climbing up steep mountain roads, climbing up the heights of their cliffs: they are the ones, your fellow countrymen, the same ones who one oppressive August day will point their rifles at your father in the place where today the sinister memorial cross rises. Happy at finally being able to sell their poor workmen's strength. Unaware that the curtain has just gone up and, for them just as for you, the staging of a drama written in blood, sweat, and tears is beginning: your common destiny as Spaniards, laughable and somber.

You were all sitting on the porch, and the needle was transmitting Kathleen Ferrier's serene lament as she interpreted Mahler's *Kinder-Totenlieder*. Antonio had gone into the kitchen to make himself a Cuba Libre. It was still raining outside.

"Do you remember what we did?" Dolores asked.

'No."

"Coming back from the dam, we went by a beach and I wanted to go swimming nude."

"It's possible."

"We'd gone without talking for several hours because the night before you'd refused to make love with me. Your wonderful Jumilla had aroused me, and when we went to bed, you gave me a quick refusal."

"You've got a good memory. That's just how it was."

"You said to me: 'If you're so eager, go down into the street and find yourself a man.' "

"That's just what you did, didn't you?"

"I was ready for it. I got dressed, I went down onto the Paseo de Albacete, and I began to make eyes at everyone around." Dolores had snuggled up against you, and she ran her hand through your hair. "Within five minutes all traffic came to a stop."

"Don't exaggerate."

"I'm not. The men were looking at me like dogs, and I got frightened. I've never been able to adjust to the underdevelopment of the Spanish."

"What did you do?"

"I ran back to the hotel, and I drank another bottle of Jumilla."

You both laughed at the same time. The night before—before you had gone to the professor's burial—you and she had made love as you had in the old days, and when you felt the beat of your own heart as you ran your tongue across Dolores's soft stomach, her firm thighs, her hidden and moist sex, you thought about the fateful news of the slide in La Bastille and the tragicomic episode of the death of President Fallères in the arms of his mistress. Was not an orgasm a small death perhaps?

Antonio had come back with his Cuba Libre, and he settled down on a cushion on the floor. His appearance closed the parenthesis of your personal interlude and, accompanied by the silken voice of the contralto, you fell to dreaming again as your vision wandered off into the colored photographs of the dam that you yourself had taken years ago as you had leaned over the tripod of the Linhof.

The work began within the time that had been forecast. While a first brigade of workers proceeded to open a side ditch for drainage, the drillers were opening holes in the rocky mass of the river bed, and after a few weeks they blew it all up with dynamite. The barbarous noise of the explosions made the narrow passes vibrate as it was theatrically multiplied by an angry echo. The pines that were rooted on the edge of the cut shook, and a movement of panic scattered the wild animals of the woods. Wild boars, foxes, squirrels, and hares ran away to hide in more remote places. Hawks and blackbirds took nest in the shadows on the other side of the mountains. At bends in the river and in irrigation ditches in the lowlands, hundreds of silvery trout were floating along lifeless, victims of the brutal cataclysm.

With the terrain cleared, an army of workers, assistants, technicians, masons had filled up the holes opened by the drills with heavy blocks of reinforced concrete. The men were coming and going, working on the scaffolding and the machine realm—a choral orchestration of harsh and unpleasant noises—had eclipsed for good the cooing of the doves, the sharp song of the hoopoes, the clear, cool sound of the water. Trucks, cranes, drills, stone drills were dully buzzing from morning to night. The height of the retaining wall reached a level of twenty, thirty, forty yards. The workers looked at their own work with startled eyes.

The harsh winter months passed, and with spring the countryside seemed to have become young again. An exuberant and vigorous sap was injecting new life into the pines of the forest, and gaudy, weightless birds cut cautiously across the reservoir and continued their lazy flight up toward the mountain tops. The sun was shining like a golden ember. Up above the naked green of the woodlands, the sky was transparent and blue.

The light aroused the workers on the dawn shift. Teams of them worked ceaselessly under the foreman's watchful eyes. The level of the dammed waters was rising and, along with it, the dizzying height of the dam. The men's meals and wages were the subject of laborious arguments with the representatives of the Commission, and strikes broke out, along with demonstrations of protest led by Socialists and Communists. And, all the same, there were numerous accidents (the life of a poor Spaniard is not worth very much): the victim's body, dressed in his work clothes (his street clothes could be used by the family) would be laid out for twenty-four hours in the project chapel before being transferred (gratis) to the village cemetery. In such cases, widow and children would receive a small indemnity.

When the work was finished, the water had already obliterated the highway bridge (Public Works had built others, sixty yards upstream), the gardens along the banks of the Tus and the Segura, the houses and the cisterns, the ruins of the old olive-oil mill. The opening ceremony was attended by the Minister and the provincial deputies (the political boss himself among them). There were speeches, toasts, and cheers for the Republic, the workers ate at the expense of the project, and bartenders in the canteens poured out wine and brandy without moderation. According to reliable witnesses, the important people were sent on their way with strong applause.

In accordance with the promise of the spokesmen, the landowners on the bottom lands had been indemnified by the Government, and loggers, farmers, charcoal burners, woodcutters had gone back home confidently to wait.

It was the year of our Lord nineteen hundred and thirty-four.

Twenty-four years later—in the midst of the Quarter Century of Peace and Prosperity—you had looked across the still surface of the reservoir at the thick pine groves on the mountainside, the columns of smoke from the ovens where rosemary was distilled, the bald spots and clearings in the woods that showed the faraway existence of some lonely charcoal shack. The road adapts itself to the whimsical waves of the terrain and, as you got closer to Yeste, a confused emotion that you had anticipated took control of you.

The sun was dehumanizing the inert countryside, and the elemental song of the locusts at intervals would drown out the monotonous drone of the motor. Small, tangled clouds were floating over the ocher fields of the Tus valley. There were farmhouses with their walls in ruins, and numerous clusters of decrepit hives lined up in the middle of a sunny spot. At the entrance to town, you paused for a few minutes at the communal cemetery. Hateful and vengeful epitaphs reminded the visitor of the executions of the summer of 1936. The mausoleum where your father's remains had reposed before they were transferred to the Barcelona Southwest cemetery rose up among the wild grass at the foot of a pointed and graceful cypress. When you identified it, you thanked your mother for the sobriety of the inscription. On the other hand, there was no stone to recall the victims of the shootings of May 29, the list of whom—published on the front page of *Solidaridad Obrera* of June 3, 1936—you have before you in a photostat:

Jesús Marín González
Justo Marín Rodríguez, Secretary of the Socialist Youth Organization
Andrés Martínez Muñoz, 40, Town Manager of Yeste
Nicolás García Blázquez
José Antonio García
Jacinto García Bueno, 25, Secretary of People's House
Antonio Muñoz
Manuel Barba Rodríguez
José Antonio Ruiz
Miguel Galera Fousladi, of Boche
Fernando Martínez, of La Graya
Antonio *"el Gilo"*
Jesús "the Stocking," of Yeste
Balbino, of La Graya
"The Moth," of Yeste
"Juan *"el Bochocho,"* 60
Two other unidentified corpses.

Those shot in the spring of 1939—the Red cancer finally having been extirpated from the country—had also evaporated without leaving a trace.

Not dead, nonexistent. Denied by God and by men. Conceived —it could be said—in a fallacious, poorly drawn, remote dream.

The period of waiting stretched out over eighteen months. Little by little the men had used up their skimpy savings and, while the Government studied (that was what it said) an ambitious plan for hydraulic projects and the transfer of those in need to Hellín, loggers, farmers, charcoal burners, woodcutters saw themselves obliged to go into debt again. The technicians talked about clearing, leveling, and banking the hillsides, about building irrigation ditches by taking advantage of the differences in level of the Tus. The transportation of pines by road turned out to be ruinous. At irregular intervals, the government press would promise immediate solutions. When the economic crisis came, the new Ministry filed the projects away. One after the other, the Commissions went back to Madrid. At the beginning of 1936 there were more than two thousand unemployed families in Yeste.

Properly indemnified for his flooded lands (the sum awarded, it was rumored, was far greater than the actual value), the local boss was idle because of it. One fine day, thumbing through the provincial information bulletin, the town discovered that the municipal government had sold to him, by unanimous vote of the council, almost all of the communal woodlands. The men who burned charcoal in the nearby communal lands were ordered by the public authorities to leave at once. There were protests, immediately muffled by the arrival of reinforcements of the Civil Guard. When the announcement of the February elections was made, the boss made it known through his agents and spokesmen that, because of the higher interests of the nation, he would run for re-election as a candidate for Deputy. The social situation in the town was explosive.

The election campaign was violent and, in spite of pressures and threats, the Popular Front won a majority in town. When the news of its victory in the principal cities of Spain became known, masses of men gathered under the balconies of the Town Hall and applauded the winners. (One of your earliest memories of childhood—or was it a later creation of your imagination on the basis of an anecdote that was so often repeated in the family?—you went to mass with your people, and as you come out, you all walk over to the district polling place. At the door, a man hands your father some pieces of paper. Aunt Mercedes crosses herself and says very loudly: "For you? Never!" The story was doubtless true, but you could not vouch for yourself as a witness.)

Although the new municipal government had named a Commission to deal with the reactivation of the plans for irrigation and to reduce the unemployment problem, the people in the capital were taking things calmly: it was necessary to be a little patient, they exhorted, the Popular Front was facing much more urgent questions, everything would be arranged in due time. Day after day the workers would come down from the hills, to look for work and would return home empty-handed. No store would extend them credit. Hunger was threatening hundreds of families.

Three months of waiting and fine words went by. But the workers could wait no longer. Hunger did not know and had no reason to know patience. If the Popular Front would not resolve their situation, they would resolve it themselves (that was what your fellow countrymen were like).

In the middle of May, loggers, farmers, charcoal burners, woodcutters went into the boss's woods and began to cut trees.

It had stopped raining. You got up, you took the bottle of Fefiñanes and filled your glass to the brim. Dolores was carefully examining the papers in the folders and showed you a printed sheet that had miraculously come through unharmed from the inspection and confiscation of your belongings by the conscientious sergeant of the Civil Guard. It had the sketch of a bull traced across it lightly in black ink, and you settled down on the arm of the sofa to read it.

MUNICIPAL GOVERNMENT OF YESTE—
OFFICIAL FESTIVAL PROGRAM

20th

5 P.M.
Grand Opening of the Festival—Children's Parade
Brass Band and Parade of *Gigantes* and *Cabezudos*

21st

7 A.M.
Floreada Diana by the Brass Band
5 P.M.
Public Festivities at the Fairgrounds
8 P.M.
Band Concert in the bandstand on the square
11 P.M.
Verbenas

22nd

7 A.M.
The Brass Band will parade through the main streets of the town playing *Alegres Dianas*.

10 A.M.
Solemn Religious Ceremony and Procession in honor of the Most Holy Christ of the Consolation

5 P.M.
Public Contests, with grand prizes

8 P.M.
Concert, in the park

9:30 P.M.
Burning of the Great Castle of Fireworks, under the auspices of the Pirotécnica Zaragozana Company

11 P.M.
Verbenas Populares

23rd

6 A.M.
Grand Diana

7 A.M.
Procession in honor of the Most Holy Virgin of Sorrows,
Holy Rosary followed by *Holy Mass*

11 A.M.
Traditional Running, with animals supplied by the accredited breeder Don Samuel Flores

5 P.M.
Grandiosa Novillada, details of which will be announced in special programs

11 P.M.
Sensacional Verbena with the Grand Finale of the Festival

"What day did we get there?" Antonio asked.

"The twenty-second. It was the day before the running, remember?"

"What I'll never forget is getting back to the inn, the Civil Guards," Dolores said. "People were looking at us as if we were Martians."

"The funny part came afterward," you said.

"When they grabbed me in Barcelona, the documentary came up again," Antonio said.

"If they were trying to make me famous, they succeeded."

"I wonder what happened to the films."

"They have them filed away in Madrid."

"Don't drink any more," Dolores said.
"Let's go back to Yeste," you replied.

There was a lot of movement on the edge of town: teams of mules, wagons, motorcycles, horses. The crowd was spilling over onto the roadway, and the car slowly made its way through, the object of surprise and curiosity on the part of the onlookers. There was unusual activity all along the way. Young men were building barriers across the intersections, townspeople were decorating their balconies with flags and bunting. From time to time the quick and lively roll of a drum could be heard. Before you reached the square, a constable had made you go back, and you parked in an alley a few feet away from the inn.

The sun was beating down on the rustic buildings along the main street. Dolores's stretch pants drew shameless looks from the men, silent and envious reprobation from the women. The people took you for foreigners, and some noticed your 16 mm camera with suspicion and hostility. You took some shots of the preparations for the running, an old woman riding a donkey, the corner of a building with the sign: "Calle de Norberto Puche Fernández, killed in action in Russia." The children followed close behind you, sticking like shadows, and with shrill voices they asked you if you worked for the Nodo.

You tried to visit the castle where they had held your father, but it was closed. The watchman had gone off with the keys, and nobody knew where he lived. For a while you wandered through alleys and narrow streets, looking in vain for the foundations of the ancestral house that your mother had inherited from a great-uncle in the distant and for you mysterious days of her admirable beauty and youth (the house where your father had probably been arrested in 1936, caught there by the military uprising and the popular mobilization in defense of the Republic). Sold for sentimental reasons a few months after Franco's victory, it had evidently changed hands several times before being finally torn down by its last owner (a businessman who had grown rich on the black market). Your mother kept a snapshot of it on her dresser next to the post card dated July 12 that her husband had sent her from Yeste. ("The trip was fine and I arrived in good shape. The situation is calm. Tomorrow I see the representatives of the Agency. Plan to return Sunday. Love," or something like that); but the photograph and the post card had disappeared after her death and your searches and inquiries afterward had been fruitless. Mutilated and imperfect, your recent history was already being lost in the moving sands of conjecture.

You all went to the inn to have a drink. Cattle dealers, retailers, traveling salesmen, farmers from the neighboring communal lands were eating, drinking, smoking, arguing in a small and noisy room in the midst of smells from an active and rustic kitchen: loaves of bread, roast ribs, chick-pea soup, thick red wine. At the bar, a man in his thirties kept staring at you all.

"Are you from Madrid?'

"No, Barcelona."

"Bullfight writers?"

"Just fans."

You invited him to your table, and you talked about bulls. He explained that he was a bus driver, that he was on vacation in town, that his family was in Catalonia.

"Are you from Yeste?"

"You might say so," he smiled. "From a village called La Graya."

Your heart gave a turn. Even though you were trying to hide it, you brought the conversation around to the subject of the reservoir, to what had happened on the communal lands before the Civil War.

"Wasn't there an uprising there?"

"Yes, sir. Actually, on the road between Yeste and La Graya, a mile and a half from here. If you want to see the place I can take you there."

"Agreed," you said.

You went back to the car with him, and you drove through the town, wounded at that hour by the hot laziness of siesta time. The whitewashed houses were reverberating, there were strings of peppers and ears of corn on most of the balconies. When you got out into the open country, the pines suddenly covered the top of the hill. The road looked down on the blue surface of the Fuensanta reservoir, the green depression of the Segura valley, the fields of the bottom lands that stretched out like different-colored remnants. Little by little, the town grew smaller, huddling below the bulk of the castle, and a stranger looks with astonishment at the dark curtains of its walls, with the towers, machicolations, loopholes—all in the form of the inexorable geometry that the past had conceived, like a splendorous challenge, now just a slab of stone, enduring and inert, covering over the fate of its resigned inhabitants.

"It's there, at that bend in the road."

You put on the brakes alongside the ditch, and you got out with your 16 mm camera. The light dominated the empty countryside, the locusts were buzzing in the olive trees, nauseous from so much sun. From town—as you found out later—a Civil Guard—the sharp eye of your people's order—was watching you with his binoculars.

The farm was called La Umbría, and it belonged to the communal lands of La Graya. Communal property since time immemorial, it had slowly passed into the hands of the political boss during the period when his figureheads in the Yeste town hall did his bidding and ever since, the men who had habitually burned charcoal there saw themselves with the hopeless choice of unemployment or emigration. The work on the dam had relieved their situation momentarily. When the dam was opened, there was a period of hope that had been fed in part by the boss's defeat in the February elections and the renewed promises of help from the leaders of the Popular Front. The members of the Agency were trying hard, unsuccessfully, to overcome the resistance of provincial authorities. Driven to distraction, their patience now exhausted, the inhabitants of La Graya went into the woods of La Umbría and began cutting trees.

The decision was taken unanimously. Men, women, old people, children had gathered together before the quarters of the forest rangers, armed with sickles, sticks, axes, crooks, boat hooks.

"We're going to burn charcoal in La Umbría."

"You know very well that Don Edmundo has forbidden it," the chief ranger was standing in the doorway with his shotgun slung over his shoulder.

"Don Edmundo's got nothing to do with it. These woods are communal property. From now on we're going to make charcoal out of the pines and plant the flatlands."

"Have you told Don Edmundo about it?"

"We're telling you."

"If you don't have any authorization . . ."

"We authorize ourselves. That's why we came to talk to you.

We've all made up our minds. We want to know whose side you're on."

The forest ranger had looked at the resolute and bold faces of his fellow countrymen. Some of them were gripping their weapons menacingly.

"If that's the way you feel . . ."

"We're not asking for anything that doesn't belong to us."

"When Don Edmundo finds out . . ."

"Leave Don Edmundo out of it. These woods have always been part of the communal lands. If he says anything to you, tell him to deal with us."

"I wash my hands of it."

"We've got nothing against you or your men. If the old man gets tough, we'll go to the mayor."

"You're looking for trouble. Don Edmundo has better connections than you."

"Don't worry about that. That's our lookout."

"Do whatever you want to. I've done my duty by warning you."

That same day the inhabitants of La Graya climbed up the hill and began to clear the woods and set up their ovens. The echo of the axes rang out like music in the happy valley. Months and months of enforced unemployment had accumulated an energy that was being vented gaily, accompanied by shouts and songs, the ancestral and primitive ballad of men accustomed for centuries to a harsh and free existence, to a savage and unconquerable individualism. The pines fell, the saws hummed, the picks and shovels were active around the newly cut stumps. Women and children from the community joined in the chore with enthusiasm: they cleared out the underbrush in the woods, they trimmed branches, they made cones of wood which, under a slow fire, would turn into charcoal. In the forest clearings, hoes and scrapers were vigorously scratching the soil, primitive plows removed the surface of the ground, agile and flying hands threw handfuls of seed into the furrows. It was a race against the clock. Dogs went back and forth with their tongues hanging out and looked on in their skinniness at the harmonious work of the community.

For two weeks the sun propitiously watched over the regained union of man and countryside, the selfless task of the mountain people, the beautiful and wise discipline of the tools in the hands of the woodcutters. Its rays poured down rapidly through the foliage of the trees, lighting on the opulent baskets of charcoal, wounding the mossy stones on the river bank, shimmering fleetingly on the edge of an ax. The smoke from the ovens rose up toward the sky, peaceful and thin. The peace of work that was useful and profitable for all seemed to have become established forever in the valley when, at sunset on the twenty-eighth day of May, without the previous knowledge of the mayor of Yeste, ten pairs of the Worthies, led by a sergeant and a staff sergeant, appeared around a bend in the road and undertook the military occupation of the communal lands of La Graya.

Olive groves, fields of corn and barely, a culvert, no memorial stone.

"I was very small when the shooting took place," the bus driver said. "But if you want to know what happened, I know someone who was there. His name is Arturo."

"Does he live in Yeste?"

"Yes, sir. He used to work for the Agency people. After the war he was sentenced to death, but they pardoned him. When he got out he didn't look like the same man. Now he repairs wagons."

You all went back to town after a quick visit to the communal lands in the Segura valley: La Graya, La Donar, Los Paules. The sun was about to go down behind the hills and the crowds were invading the streets again. The bus driver led you up a steep slope to the repairman's house. A woman was waiting in the doorway. She explained in a soft voice that her husband had just gone out.

"You might find him at the fair," she said. "If you want to leave a message . . ."

"It's not necessary," the driver said. "These people wanted to talk to him."

"Ask in Morillo's bar. He usually stops by there around this time."

You scrutinized the town from one end to the other. Shepherds from Arroyo Frío and Peñarrubia, beekeepers from Raspilla and Llano de la Torre, farmhands from Tus and Moropeche, peasants from Rala and El Arguellite were flowing through the fairgrounds in compact and sweaty squadrons, stopping to have some fun at the tavern doors, besieging the stands where fritters and French fries were sold, consuming immense tubs of cottage cheese by the spoonful. The young girls were walking arm in arm, smiling and merry, pretending to flee from the compliments of the men, swaying their bodies with the precious virginity in retreat and defended like a shrine. You stopped to have a drink in a shack. Dolores tried her luck at the wheel of fortune, Antonio tested his marksmanship and got a bag of candy as a prize. You were in the Spain of the Taifas, petrified and unmoving in the slow passage of the centuries (massive tourism had not yet arrived, nor the Development Plan of your celebrated technocrats) and, as you drink (now) a cold sip of Fefiñanes, you try to delimit and encircle the motley and excessively fussy image of the town during a holiday (occupied by its own inhabitants and hundreds of outsiders) with the cruel and lucid vision of your double experience as a Spaniard and as an emigré, with thirty-two years of national history (not lived) that was hidden in back of you by sleight of hand.

The darkness hides the picturesque poverty of the place and the lights from the fair weakly illuminate a livid and disconsolate countryside. . . .

You drank another sip of Fefiñanes.

Look at them: they are the children of the heroes of Guadalajara and Belchite, Brunete and Gandesa. They were moving about bare-chested, in groups and clusters, with crooks and fifes, leather pouches of wine and tambourines, going down the middle of the street and bothering the passers-by with more shouts and noise than a wagon on a rocky road, all of them animated (it could be said) by a demanding and imperious ideal (freedom? dignity? or the simple exhibition *ad absurdum* of some twenty-odd years not of peace, but of lethargy, not of order, but of sleep, torpor instead of life? . . . Hold on, don't talk nonsense), a real popular army (it could be said) equidistant between the current flock of the Beatles and the revolutionary militiamen of 1936.

The apprentice bullfighters are killing time at the drink stand over a jug of spring water. The public surrounds with admiration that group of determined and anonymous adolescents who risk their bodies every day for a handful of *reales*. Grown men, gray-haired heads of families lavish them with expert advice, slapping them lovingly on the back, offering a modest round of tobacco. Hearing them speak, one would take them all for rivals of Arruza or Manolete (at the moment of truth, perhaps some of them had fought under Líster or Durruti). The scrub bullfighters listened to them in silence, with sleepless eyes, still stupefied by heat and fatigue. Most of them travel on foot, sleep in the open, follow as best they can the difficult rounds of the runnings. (Lietor, Aina, Elche, Peñascosa, Ferez, Letur, Molinicos, Bogarra, Paterna, Socovos . . .)

"Do you remember Arturo?" Dolores asked.

You had finally found him in a bar on the square when the fireworks castle was ignited, all of you deafened by the noise of the explosions, the town bathed in a lavish light of sparks.

"These people wanted to meet you," the bus driver said.

The man was looking at you with an attentive expression. He was tall and thin, with a narrow nose and very lively dark eyes in the middle of his tired face.

"Why, yes, I went through all of that," there were many people around you, and he changed his voice perceptibly. "If you want, some other time . . ."

"We're leaving tomorrow," you said.

"Come by and see me after the bullfight. We'll be more comfortable in my house. My wife will make you a cup of coffee."

You didn't see him again. When you kept the date the following day, Arturo was not at home. When you got back to the inn, a sergeant of the Civil Guard was waiting for you.

You poured yourself another glass of Fefiñanes.

"Don't drink any more," Dolores begged.

Toward the end of the afternoon, eight pairs of Guards had come in among the huts of La Umbría with rifles slung over their shoulders. In the pine grove a dense silence reigned, accented by the counterpoint of the boots on the stones in the clearing. Warned by their families, most of the men had taken refuge in the woods. The column of Civil Guards advanced cautiously, as if fearing an ambush. The three-cornered hats were shining brightly in the midst of the thick growth. When the Guards came out into the clearing, they spread out into strategic guerrilla positions and the corporal warily examined the yellowish pine stumps, the clean and plowed flatland, the smoldering of the charcoal ovens, the cones and bundles of wood ready to be carried over. Six woodcutters were still in their places, indifferent, as if alien to the sudden presence.

"Who's in charge here?"

There was a pause. The men went on with their work without changing expression. The corporal took a few steps forward and planted himself in front of the most robust man.

"I asked who was in charge here."

"I heard you."

"I'm waiting for an answer."

"Nobody's in charge here."

"Nobody?"

"No, sir."

"It doesn't make any difference. You can answer for the rest."

"One's just the same as the next," the man replied. "We're all equal."

"Who gave you permission to burn charcoal?"

"The woods belong to the communal lands."

"We'll see about that," the corporal was looking over the ovens, the ricks of wood, the newly planted ground. "Have you talked to the owner?"

"We told the people at the Agency."

"The Agency's got nothing to do with it. I want to know if you've got Don Edmundo's permission."

"No, sir."

"Well, then, you better get off of here right now and on the double."

"I already told you that the woods belong to the communal lands. If you don't have a written order from the mayor . . ."

"You shut your face and do as I say."

"First show me the order."

"The order?" The movement of his arm was quick. The man took the blow without blinking. "There's the order."

"My friends and I won't leave."

"If you don't go peacefully, you'll leave by force."

An hour later, in the community, witnesses had described the scene. The rain of insults, kicks, blows with rifle butts. The beating of the fallen men. The violent extinction of the ovens. The enraged trampling of the planted fields.

The six prisoners had passed through the streets of the village on their way to the barracks with their hands tied. The Civil Guards took off their capes and three-cornered hats and sat down to eat by candlelight. Shielded by the darkness, the inhabitants milled around outside. Wives came to ask about their husbands, they argued and shouted at the Guards. The excitement had increased with the spreading of the rumor that the prisoners were being mistreated. Several groups came to the door of the small barracks and argued heatedly with the sentries. The Guards inside came out with their guns, and the crowd drew back. On orders from the staff sergeant, the Guards withdrew into the barracks. According to later testimony by one of the Guards, a ringleader was stirring up the crowd for a lynching.

The people of La Graya sent emissaries to the mayor of Yeste, to the president and members of the Agency, to the inhabitants of the nearby communities. All had spent the night on watch, by the reflected light of the moon, spying on the movements and voices of the Civil Guards barricaded in the barracks. Along mountain roads and paths, guiding themselves by the stars, loggers, peasants, charcoal burners, woodcutters converged punctually to give help. The whole region was on foot and on guard.

The harsh crow of the rooster had anticipated dawn by a few minutes. Almost immediately, the colors of the day began to break.

Purple, yellow, red, like the colors of the Republic, Friday, May 29, was dawning.

The curtain was about to rise on the drama. You had engraved in your memory the harsh setting of the mountains of Yeste, the twenty-two Civil Guards stationed in the community of La Graya, the arrested charcoal burners accused of cutting down trees, the silent crowd of peasants gathered together there to show their solidarity with the prisoners and, like an expert who moves the threads of the plot, you, Álvaro Mendiola, habitual expatriate, married, thirty-two years old, no known profession—because it is neither a trade nor a profession, rather a torture and a punishment, to live, see, annotate, portray everything that happens in your mother country—were recalling with fascination that remote and irrevocable past that was unfolding before you, thinking a thousand and one times: if it were only possible to go back, if things had happened differently, if by some miracle you could modify the outcome. . . . You were daydreaming about a real Spain, about fellow countrymen raised to the dignity of people with a human existence maintained in the face of the voracious enemies of life. . . . You felt like an orator, and you were haranguing them drunkenly from a ragged platform with the miserable eloquence of a talkative demagogue: You have always been waiting for your chance. Now it is before you. Do not let it go by. Death does not matter. A few seconds—a few brief seconds—of freedom are worth—we know now—a whole eternity of centuries.

When the column leaves the barracks, it is eight o'clock in the morning. The woodcutters walk tied together and, wrapped in their capes and wearing their three-cornered hats, the Guards carry their rifles at the ready. The people waited expectantly for a moment, and as the string of prisoners follows the wood road along the river in the direction of the jail in Yeste, they escort it at a prudent distance. The men are armed with axes, sticks, boat hooks. The terrain is lonely and rugged, and the rumor is going around that in order to teach them a lesson, the Civil Guards plan to invoke the law of "shot while trying to escape."

The two delegations advance separately, sixty feet from one another. The silence is absolute. The sun is already crowning the crest of the mountains, and the partridges fly up in fright. At bends in the road groups of peasants appear. Without a word, they watch the string of prisoners, and they join the column of their neighbors. There are ten, twenty, forty, a hundred of them. From the neighboring communities they appear along paths and trails with their work tools tied to their waists. The women come too, hard of face and hostile. A boy aims his sling at the Guard leading the column: the stone brushes him, missing the target, and the boy immediately disappears into the underbrush.

In a clearing in the woods, four members of the Agency come forward to parley with the Guards. It is nine o'clock in the morning, and the string of prisoners is still three miles from Yeste. The people come close to listen to the argument, and when they see themselves encircled, the Civil Guards cock their rifles. Insults rain down on them. The men from the Agency intervene, exhorting the peasants to be calm. Under his jet black three-cornered hat, the sergeant is perspiring abundantly.

"If they take one step closer, I'll open fire," he says.

"Obey him," the people from the Agency order.

The peasants draw back, but they do not disperse. New groups come pell-mell down the sides of the hill, stop at the edge of the road and enlarge the torrent of peasants. The people from the

Agency are asking for the provisional freedom of the prisoners. The sergeant will not give in. With a checkered handkerchief he wipes away the sweat that is running down his face. The peasants shake their rustic weapons. There is still a good hour of road left and, to the naked eye, the besiegers already number more than four hundred.

Little by little, the procession attracts the beekeepers from Boche, the woodcutters from Jartos, the charcoal burners from Rala. The string of prisoners leaves the wood road that runs beside the Segura and winds slowly up the mountain along a rough wagon road. With every step more men appear, as if they had burst forth out of the ground. The sun begins to beat down, Guards and prisoners are panting. The people from the Agency have sent a messenger to town and announce that their president and the mayor are going to meet with the lieutenant of the Civil Guard. The peasants are skeptical and, animated by the continuous arrival of reinforcements, they again close in on the Guards.

It is ten o'clock in the morning when, huddled at the foot of the castle like a frightened flock about its shepherd, the first houses of Yeste can be seen. The woods open up at intervals and, below the road, the pine grove gives way to an olive grove planted with barley. At the turn, armed in the same way with their tools, three hundred people await the arrival of the procession. The sergeant silently observes the ever-growing legion of those who are following and the compact mass of those who are waiting. He mechanically unbuttons the chin strap of his hat and wipes away the sweat with his hand. Voices and shouts are coming from all sides. The peasants of Yeste are blocking the road with their bodies.

"Clear the way!"

Nobody obeys. A thousand men surround the column of Civil Guards. The sun is burning the angry faces of the peasants, making the bolts, rear sights, and mouths of the rifles flash, shining playfully and mischievously on the patent leather of the twenty-odd three-cornered hats.

"Clear the way!"

Unexpectedly the crowd comes together, draws back, opens the way for a pair of Guards who have been sent from town. The sergeant confers with them, and the members of the Agency come over to argue. According to what they tell them, their president has promised to bring the prisoners in person before the justice of the peace in exchange for their immediate release, and the lieutenant has given orders to free them. A great noise accompanies the news of the victory. The sergeant obeys and, while the Civil Guards are untying the prisoners, friends and relatives run forward to embrace them, peasants and Guards get mixed up together, and there is an exchange of insults that soon degenerates into a fight. The members of the Agency try to intervene in vain. The Guards see themselves overwhelmed by the crowd and, suddenly, they throw back their capes and raise their rifles to their faces.

When the shots ring out, it is ten-thirty in the morning. A stork is floating voluptuously through the air and, alarmed by the sound of the shooting, it cuts rapidly through the sky and takes refuge in the belfry of the church in Yeste.

The slow tolling of the bells at eleven o'clock. The crowd waits patiently. Balconies, doorways, windows, ledges are jammed. There is no more room on the parapets and platforms. On the roofs, shinnied up lampposts, climbing up the strangest places, there are clusters of youths and grown men who maintain an impossible balance, just like tightrope walkers. For months and months they have been waiting for this moment, the needed recuperation from the starvation wages, the desired and fierce challenge to the brutality of fate. The sun is beating down on them, and they bear it stolidly. Some cover the tops of their heads with handkerchiefs, the women protect themselves with faded umbrellas. The more impatient ones stroll through the square armed with their canes and their oak staffs, ready, it could be said, for any eventuality. The same communion in the face of danger unites all of them, and you are the only one left out, the foreigner who is looking on and filming them.

Improvised safety abutments stick out at the mouths of the alleys, made of trucks, fences, palisades. Farmers stretch strings of firecrackers between balconies and lampposts and some light rockets and sparklers that twist wildly before exploding. In the center the second-rate bullfighters wait for the chance to show off with their improvised *muletas,* their dirty and tattered capes. Heaped up behind the wheels of the wagons or underneath the backs of the trucks, the women shriek. Emissaries sent from the corral announce the imminent arrival of the drovers. There are false alarms, shouts, shoving, tripping. The air is getting warmer, the crowds mill around, the temperature grows red.

When the animals come out of the alley, the people on foot run away. The *novillo,* the young bull, is small and black and runs along escorted by half a dozen tame bulls who noisily shake their bells. The ox-drivers come behind and, while two bullfighters hold a cape between them, they beat the hocks of the oxen that hang back. The young bull seems startled by the spectacle, he sniffs the ground with his snout, he cannot decide whether to attack or not, he consults the oxen with his gaze. A man runs rapidly past him and gives him a whack on the rump. The animal lows, turns halfway around, tries to gore him. The people applaud. The bullfighters stir up the bull, they advance step by step with great solemnity, but the sudden movement of the oxen scatters them. The young men relieve them with their jackets and greasy aprons. As soon as the animals advance, they open a path through the distinguished audience. There is a shout, the group breaks up and disperses. Everyone escapes as best he can, slipping into the jammed doorways, climbing up the grating on the windows, clambering up toward the balconies and cornices, breaking their behinds to flee from the bull. Suddenly the young bull and the oxen turn around and head uphill, preceded by the beating of the cowbells and the running of the young men, the barbarous howl—a hybrid mixture of terror and ecstasy—of the aroused multitude. The people on foot go into the doorways, cling to the human clusters in the windows, flatten out motionless against the ground. The farmhands grip their forks, sticks, stakes and as soon as the animals go by, they run after them and beat them savagely on the back, the rear, the hocks, the flanks. In a few seconds the street is empty of people. A steer rings his bells at a careless person, tramples him without touching him with his horns, continues his mad run in the midst of the ringing bells, disappears with the others out of your field of vision.

Rescue this image from forgetfulness: the gathering is silently lying in wait at the intersection and two men appear in a doorway with a red flag. Its color stands out intensely in the ocher dust, contrasts with the gleaming white walls. The flame of the sun seems to make it even brighter as it waves and vibrates in the air as if it were the effect of a mirage. It is the shout of ancient and muffled freedom, of the old days when the hopes of your people were summed up in their elemental and beautiful symbol. You were present, hallucinated, at this unusual unfurling after so many years that had simply been and had not been lived, empty and deprived of their substance, with the same feeling you had in the cinémathèque during the documentaries of the Civil War by Ivens and Karmen: the defense of Madrid, the battle of the Jarama, the moving chords of *La Santa Espina.* The two men walked with the flag to the applause of the crowd and the blood was buzzing in your temples. Blinded by the thick and obscene sun, drunk and delirious, you had greeted the miraculous appearance of the symbol with tears in your eyes, having lost all control over yourself, murmuring, with so much love, my God, so much sweetness: "Oh, my redeemed people. . . ."

No, it was not a red flag, it was a bullfight cape. You had served yourself another glass of Fefiñanes and you drank it down in one swallow.

From the platform where you are filming the running, you watch the return of the young bull with the steers and the drovers. The two men drop the red cape and scurry away. The cattle are in the small square again. The spectacle is repeated and, to liven it up, the master of ceremonies lights the string of firecrackers. When the firecrackers explode, the bursts follow each other like the rattle of a machine gun, the air fills with smoke, children put their hands over their ears, women shout hysterically. The animals run in disorder and, with startling agility, a young man ties one end of the string between the horns of the young bull. When it is lit, the animal becomes startled, turns on himself like a top, charges, tries to shake off the string as he dodges and thrusts his horns upward, provoking delight and excitement on the part of the crowd. Some firecrackers explode on the hero's back, singe his shirt, blood dampens the shreds of cloth. The young man disdains the solicitude of those who want to help him and plants himself opposite the bull again, gripping a stake. The detonations continue on without interruption.

When the roll of film is over, a generalized smell of powder, sweat, and blood floats sharply over the square.

Made up from the double and contradictory version of those who took part in the event, here is the informative synthesis published afterward in impartial newspapers.

When the first shots ring out, there is a movement of panic. The peasants try to grab the rifles away from the Guards and they attack them with their sickles and knives. While the main body of the crowd breaks up, the more audacious men struggle with the Civil Guards and join in a violent hand-to-hand battle with them. A peasant manages to get the gun away from one of the detachment and fires at him. The Guard, Pedro Domínguez Requena, raises his hands to his cartridge belts and takes them off soaked in blood. When he falls, a peasant sinks a peavey into his throat. The delegate from the Yeste town hall, Andrés Martínez Muñoz, first assistant to the mayor and head of the employment office, uselessly begs for a cease fire. The staff sergeant fires at him point-blank, saying: "That's for you and your Agency!" Fallen to the ground, he begs for his life to be spared in the name of his children, and the sergeant finishes him off with three shots. "Don't worry about this one," he shouts, "he won't recover." Two other men are lying on the ground, one of them has his head opened up. In order to shoot more freely, some of the troops are using their pistols. A group of three manages to get away from the peasants and scales the hill while the hand-to-hand fighting continues on the road. The wounded drag themselves away as best they can and their blood trickles out on the dust. A peasant throws himself on top of a Guard, waving an ax. Another soldier shoots him at close range and the peasant falls down dead. The three Civil Guards have entrenched themselves behind a rock and they spray the road with their rifles. The peasants who are still there flee downhill through the barley fields in the direction of the olive grove. A detachment of the Guard goes to town for help. The Civil Guards are masters of the day and, ignoring the wounded and dying, they begin to pursue the fugitives. Dozens of men are running down the slope, completely in the open. The shots come one after another, like a string of firecrackers. Three peasants take refuge in a culvert where there is barely room for one man and the Guards go over to the mouth, kill two and seriously wound the third. In another drain they find a peasant who has been wounded twice. The man shouts at them and begs them to kill him. One of the Civil Guards shoots him twice, in the arm and in the leg. "There you are!" he shouts. "It'll take longer that way."

When the reporters reach the place, a few hours after the shooting, pools of blood can still be seen at the mouth of the drain. In the other culvert there is a brackish flow, several yards in length. Among the brambles, a new beret, a handkerchief, and several pieces of cloth that are stained red reveal the efforts of the victims to stop their bleeding. Four bodies lie forgotten in the middle of the field. A woman weeps as she kneels next to one of the bodies. The man wounded in the arm and leg is still dying, losing blood and spitting up. The sun is shining down implacably and ants and flies are fighting over the unexpected banquet under the ominous presence of the vultures, who are gliding over the olive groves in tenacious and concentric circles.

Caps, berets, corduroy pants, blouses, aprons, kerchiefs knotted around the neck, dirty vests, sandals: young men, adults, children climb up on the horizontal boards of the platforms beside the gate where the young bull is boxed in. It is an elemental and rough audience, without tourists who read Hemingway, dandies with Cordovan hats and Havana cigars, beauties of the bull ring with combs and shawls, frigid Anglo-Saxon women in search of crude and primitive emotions. To give spice to the moment, the young men slowly sharpen their stakes. Others raise their arms to drink down a stream of the rich wine of the province. The flow enters through a mouth opened with geometric precision and sometimes the drinker makes arabesques and filigrees that arouse the admiration of the gathering. The wine pouches pass from hand to hand and, during the round, the vendors of beer and soft drinks hawk their merchandise. The bullfighters wait for the appearance of the animal, executing parlor passes with their capes and adopting disdainful and virile positions in imitation of their famous fellows.

Unfortunately for them, their posturing does not stand up for long: when the bull gate is opened, the young bull comes charging out and their stamp of master bullfighters seems suddenly to melt away under the pitiless heat of the sun. The beast charges, tears a red cape with an upward flick of his horns, gores the boards of the barrier with rage, attacks the blows and pokes given him from atop the palisade with surprise. As he approaches them, the men squeeze together and help each other, drawn into a tentacular and polychrome mass. Those on the lower boards cling to those above as best they can and where they can, and the human clusters hang over the horns of the animal like the condemned souls over the flames of hell in the illustrations by Gustave Doré for *The Divine Comedy*. On the other side of the barriers, the women are crowded together, standing, squatting, sitting on the ground, their faces altered with pleasure, insulting the bull, egging the men on with their shrieks.

The lens of the camera slowly captures the incidents and rites of the death of the animal: the unsuccessful passes of the journeyman bullfighters, the whacks with sticks of the drovers, the happy ecstasy of the public. As soon as the bull turns around, the young men run to beat him, the spectators throw stones at him, a farmhand pulls him furiously by the tail. The blows rain down on him without sparing any part: horns, nape of the neck, fat of the neck, back, stomach, hocks. Custom forbids killing him with one thrust: the game must be prolonged up to the limit, his death throes must be drunk down to the dregs. The head drover tries to get a loop around his horns, but the animal is wary, retreats, backs his rump into the door of the bullpen. Several times the man throws the lasso without success. The bull is drooling and blood is coming out of his mouth. Taking on courage, the bullfighters challenge him with their red capes. As the animal will not move, the public bombards him with all manner of projectiles. An individual appears in a small door behind him and gives him a deep cut at the base of the tail with a butcher knife. The blood bubbles out and the beast lows in pain. The gathering awards the audacity and ingenuity of the artist with applause. The head drover tries the loop again, but the noose slips off the horns. The attempts are repeated, and the men crowded up against the grating nearby beat the animal with their whips to make him go away. The bull humbles his head, scratches the ground with his snout, walks a few steps, digs his hooves into the soil, bends his legs, kneels, sits down, gets up, falls down again, vomits more blood.

His impotence enlivens the joy of the crowd. Reduced, the beast witnesses his own downfall, as if in a violent and overwhelming nightmare. The farmhands immediately punish the bull with vigor, pull on the rope to tie it to a lamppost, a gray-haired man passes next to him and sinks a pick into his rump. As dozens of hands hold the end of the rope, the crowd gets down off the stand. Some young men grab the tail of the beast and pull on it with so much force that, half cut off already by the slash of the knife, it comes completely off. The young bull does not seem to feel this new disaster and he looks at that thick human stew with his bloodshot eyes . . .

Mercifully, the reel of film ends here.

Where are you, what stratum of memory importunes you? Violence engenders new violence, brutal images cross. . . . These happenings take place a mile from Yeste and between eleven o'clock and noon. Yet, there is testimony about people wounded in the town and during the afternoon. A woman who is ordered to halt, they make her lie down on the ground and they open fire on her. . . . She staggers, she kneels, she falls down again amidst insults, punches, blows with sticks. . . . A worker is coming home at ten o'clock at night when the town presents a completely normal look and yet, without any warning at all, he is wounded by a shot. . . . A thick forest of legs surrounds him and gives him angry kicks. . . . Nicolás García Blázquez, who goes out on orders of the mayor to pick up the bodies of the victims, is obliged to get out of his truck because he is wearing a red shirt, and he dies from the shots he receives. . . . After the butcher has slashed his neck with his knife, the young men pile on top of the body, touch it, handle it as if it were a relic and triumphantly exhibit their handkerchiefs stained with blood. . . . The man lying in the olive grove, wounded in the arm and leg, is he still dying?

"Your papers, please."

Dolores has gone to bed and the bottle of Fefiñanes is empty. The wind is whistling evasively among the branches of the eucalyptus trees. You get up and put the *Kinder-Totenlieder* on the phonograph again.

At 5 P.M. *Grand Opening of the Festival—Children's Parade* your papers *Brass Band and Parade of "Gigantes" and* what authorization do you have to live abroad *"Cabezudos"* when was the last time you entered Spain *the 21st at 7* A.M. *"Floreada Diana"* how long have you been living in Paris *by the Brass Band* why have you come to town *at 5 P.M. Public Festivities at the Fairgrounds* does this movie camera belong to you can you tell us why since you've been here you've been in contact with *at 8 P.M. Band Concert in the bandstand on the square* only the running what were you doing yesterday on the La Graya road you stopped where *at 11 P.M. "Verbenas"* trustworthy people heard you talking to Arturo about the Republic and the war don't you know what kind of person he is you can't make me believe that a fellow on file all over the district for his dislike of *the 22nd at 7 A.M. the Brass Band will parade through the main streets of the town playing "Alegres Dianas"* we've followed every step you've taken since you came to town and we know just who you've had contact with *at 10 A.M. Solemn Religious Ceremony and Procession* right now where are you coming from you can explain to me what interest you have in visiting a person who has on his conscience *in honor of the Most Holy Christ of the Consolation* do you have permission to take movies we don't know what you have photographed or with what intention you've taken pictures until higher Authorities decide in the case we will be obliged to *Most Holy Christ of the Consolation* confiscate your camera and films *of the Consolation* you can continue on your trip if you want on the condition that you present yourselves *Con-so-la-tion* whenever the Authorities think it necessary.

When Antonio decides to go to bed in turn, you decide to go out into the garden. The sky has cleared and the stars slip out of the chaos of the night and are twinkling in the darkness like embers. The wind livens them up and seems to be making them shine more brightly. The eucalyptus trees are drying their light leaves and the coolness of the air clears your head.

For a few minutes you lean on the banister of the lookout. Sea and sky come together off there on the marine horizon. The last lights of the village have gone out, one after the other. An intact silence cloaks the sleeping countryside. The only consciousness of what is around you, you keep watch, evoke, imagine, become delirious.

The headlights of the car sweep along the cobblestones of the road and with a flash light up the men of the FAI who are barring the way with their revolvers and rifles.

"Halt! Hands up!"

The old Ford brakes hard a few yards from the roadblock. The lanterns shine on the worried face of the driver. Next to him, another man of mature age is also blinking.

"Why didn't you stop sooner?"

"We didn't see you," the chauffeur stammers.

"Come on, get out, both of you. . . . Your cards."

The driver lowers his right hand and brings it to his pants pocket. Without saying a word, the leader of the patrol hits him with the butt of his revolver. Surprised, the man groans and staggers.

"You be quiet, you hear?"

The leader takes the two wallets, takes out the documents, shows them to a young man wearing a leather apron.

"What does it say here?"

"Lucas Mendiola Orbaneja. . . ."

"Profession?"

"Exchange and stockbroker."

The young man reads it off like a schoolchild. One of his comrades, in the meantime, examines the inside of the vehicle and struggles with the handle on the trunk.

"Hey, look here," he says. "Something's moving."

The people from the roadblock come over to look. Hands in the air, the men are trembling like quicksilver.

"What the hell have you got in there?"

"Frogs."

"There's a frog for you, you bourgeois bastard."

The shot catches him in the middle of the chest. Uncle Lucas falls down like a puppet, with an expression of infinite and irrevocable astonishment.

His companion falls to his knees next to him. The muscles of his cheeks titillate with panic.

"Don't kill me, please don't. I swear it's the truth."

One of the members of the patrol throws the bag onto the ground and unties it with a tug. In the mocking light of the lantern, dozens and dozens of frogs emerge suddenly and with clumsy and laughable agility, jump over the still-warm body of your uncle along the road that is stained with blood.

How many times, when your mother was alive and the family conclave would gather in the shade of the eucalyptus trees, had you heard the tale of Uncle Lucas's lamentable end, the victim of his insatiable gluttony and his extravagant gourmet urges, the same day, no less—oh, wonderful historical intuition of your breed—as the popular assault on Police Headquarters and the stormy uprising and the capture of General Goded. Miraculously rescued, thanks to the skill and valor of a handful of men who were determined to stop the sovietization of Spain by the international conspiracy of Freemasons and Jews, you were listening, trembling with horror, to the stories of murder and arson, torture and Chekas, while Pepín Soler, the fat and fiftyish witness of the crime, fondled once more the scene of your uncle's death and, without losing a stitch in the sewing destined for the mission pickaninnies, Aunt Mercedes remembered with her sorrowful voice the disappearance of your cousin Sergio. (Dressed in white from head to toe, with a soft hat and a silk tie, he had had the vanity to parade in public his figure of a dandy during the days when the red and black flag of the FAI was being flown from balconies, carried around on the sides of taxis, colored the façades of buildings, and men and youths, vengeful and arisen from no one knew where, were arrogantly displaying their red kerchiefs, their crude ammunition belts, their variegated dress of militiamen. The trucks were leaving for the front, loaded with volunteers, and the driver of one of them—you imagined him with a beard and mustache, just like the newsreels you had seen in Paris—had stopped beside him.

"Hey, pretty boy!"

"Me?"

"Yes, you. . . . Tell me, where are you going all dressed up like that?"

"Taking a walk."

"Oh, you like to take the air?"

"Yes, sir."

"Well, come on, climb up here in the truck with us and we'll take you along."

Cousin Sergio had obeyed under the threat of the revolver and he left for the front with the people in the truck. Nothing was ever heard of him again. His mother, the cousin of Agustín, Eulogio, Mercedes, and César, had moved heaven and earth to find out where he was. In all probability he had died in the trenches, the victim of a Nationalist artillery bombardment. He was only seventeen years old.)

What had happened to your father?

When the war was over and you were settled in Barcelona, the family had completed the necessary investigations for the identification of the body and, in the presence of your mother and aunts and uncles, his mortal remains were discreetly exhumed from the cemetery in Yeste. The components of the patrol who had taken him for a ride had disappeared, some dead, others in exile, and the already ancient history of his last days remained wrapped in a cloak of mist from which no one, no doubt, would be able to rescue it.

Without documents, without proofs, without witnesses, you were able to embellish in comfort the pomp of his arrest in the demolished maternal house, the probable confrontation with the victims of the events of May 29, the lonely wait for death behind the naked walls of the castle. Imprisoned with the other landowners and the former puppets of the political boss, had he finally rebelled? His stern and sad face, marked since childhood by the stigmata of a rigid puritanical upbringing at times seemed to cover a secret torment, a tenacious and buried doubt that had perhaps flowered in moments like that and would impose itself like a sudden piece of evidence, sweeping away in one wave beliefs and dogmas, laws and principles, all of that arduous and precarious sand castle built by others and where he lived in resignation. Photographs usually showed him withdrawn and taciturn, as if scourged in his insides by an ominous and warning premonition. Had he thought about you, the delicate child, abandoned forever into the hands of women? about the abnegated wife with whom he had shared ten useless years of peace and lies? about the god of his people, remote and mute, absent and problematic? A nullified and absurd dead person like all those of his band (who had defeated whom? whom did that cruel and infanticidal victory honor?), you imagined, with slow and horrible precision, the dry sound of the steps along the corridors of the castle, the last cup of coffee, drunk with cautious sips, the brief and harsh sentence of the local Committee (the just paying for sinners); his exit between two armed peasants, the vengeful insults of the people, getting into the back of the truck under shoves and blows . . .

The landscape of the Yeste mountains is beautiful in August. Provincial route 3212 winds through stands of timber, dominates the blue waters of the Fuensanta dam, goes down, runs along the bank, climbs again, leaves the pine trees behind, crosses the plain. Rocky ground begins a little beyond and the vegetation gradually disappears. White clay succeeds esparto fields. The sun flames down, white and colorless. All life is extinguished.

The memorial cross rises up at a harsh turn in the road and, when he gets out of the truck, your father looks out over the same panorama that you are looking at: in the foreground, beehives, a shack in ruins, the twisted trunk of a tree; farther on, the plain lulled by the sun, the cloudless sky, the hills steaming like loaves just taken from the oven. Perhaps a snake prudently sticks his head out from among the stones. The deep buzzing of the locusts rises from the ground like a complaint. The platoon is opposite him and one prisoner urinates from fear as the patrol leader raises his arm and the peasants aim their rifles . . .

How can it be explained? Often, in phases of depression and anguish (so frequent in you), the death of that unknown person (your father) and the material impossibility of your meeting (except for the accidental and gratuitous link of his fatherhood) gnaw at you inside like the image of a lost chance, the weight of an undone thing, the specter of a treacherous and incurable nostalgia. You think that in a different country, in a different age, the common history of the two of you would have been something else and, more or less, you would have come to understand each other. Now your communion is reduced to this strict and irreplaceable instant. With the dark muzzles of the rifles before you, you try in vain to capture time.

The volley rang out sharply.

For the period of three years a wind of madness had blown across the skin of the bull—that is what some people call your barren and bare ancestral home, the ambit of your present conglomeration of petty kingdoms—completing the destructive work carried on over the centuries with tenacity and patience by your illustrious ancestors. Possessed by dark and inconfessable instincts, at once the incubus and succubus of their hateful appetites and dreams, they had proceeded with order and detail toward the cruel and inexorable self-pruning, toward the expulsion and extermination of their inner demons, without stopping for a reason or consideration of any kind, destroying in turn, on the altars of an impossible exorcism, commerce, industry, science, art. Crushed, swept away, conjured up a thousand times, the ghost was always reborn with aleatory labels and along with it the tenacious drive to suppress it, to go down one more step in the scale of barbarism, happy, your people, to affirm before the world their grim conception of the country as a hard and resistant cliff against which the agitated sea of all histories fruitlessly breaks and dies.

When you were a child, you had been present at the spectacle of the demented and fratricidal struggle without understanding it, terrified at first by the crimes and atrocities of the ones, indignant later on because of those (carefully whitewashed) committed by the others, before you really came to realize that all of them (those of the vanquished as well as those of the victors, those that were justified, as well as those that could not be) obeyed the laws of the same clinical cycle in which the frenzy and madness of the crises would be followed by long periods of calm, stupefaction, and drowsiness. . . .

Under cover of the noisy wave of tourists which, like manna from heaven, was falling on the sleepy and lazy country in this burning summer of 1963 (the radio had exultantly announced the entry of a hundred thousand vehicles across the border at Perthus during the last weekend: Frenchmen, Swiss, Belgians, Dutchmen, Germans, Englishmen, Scandinavians who were coming to see bullfights; drink Manzanilla; lie in the sun like saurians; eat pizza and hot dogs in garish cafés baptized with Iberian and traditional names like Westminster, Orly, Saint-Trop, Whisky Club, L'Imprevu, Old England, and others; they finally initiate the Spanish people in the indispensable exercise of industrial and economic values, converting them all at once, by means of the proverbial radicalism you all had, into a fertile and rich nursery of climbing vines and sausages) you were thinking (your drunkenness already dissolved) about Ayuso and your father, about the people who died uselessly between 1936 and 1939, about that bitter generation of yours, condemned to grow old without youth or responsibilities. Leaning on the railing of the lookout, you were able to catch the distant echo of the caravan of cars which, like a river, was flowing day and night along the coastal highway, to sink back into the quiet and silence of the familiar garden, dust off in your memory some tardy recollection, meditate while you were still on time.

You knew that when you died the past would die out with you. It depended on you, only on you, to save it from disaster.

In the small spa in the Midi, it was a cold spring and the children who were romping in the playground, beyond the grove of plane trees, were still dressed for winter, bundled up in coats, mufflers, and gloves. For two years, Álvaro and his friends had wandered freely through the streets, continuously at war with the band of French children who would come to challenge them after class with stones and slingshots. A weak attempt at scholarship brought about by Álvaro's mother had, to his relief, run up against the absolute disapproval of Madame Delmont: "*À l'école laïque? Vous êtes folle. Un athée, un mauvais patriote, voilà ce qu'ils feront de lui. Si vous ne pouvez pas lui payer le Collège du Saint-Esprit autant qu'il n'apprenne rien . . . Ah, si Mussolini était là.*" And Uncle César and Aunt Mercedes had abounded with their arguments and healthy reflections about the dangers of bilingualism and the final and imminent end of the civil war that was a deliverance.

During the last months, Álvaro had been present at the get-togethers of the Spanish colony that inevitably followed the publication of each important piece of news: the breakthrough on the Ebro front, the liberation of Barcelona, the breakup of the Republican army (fifteen years later, in the cinémathèque on the rue d'Ulm, Álvaro had looked with emotion at the painful images of the defeat, the caravan of thousands, men, women, children, old people who, with their miserable belongings on their backs, were fleeing on foot toward the border at Perthus, a massive exodus that could only be compared in numbers with the present movement in the opposite direction of tourists of all ages and countries who, with their automobiles, trailers, and baggage racks, seemed to be running away from some silent and tranquil hecatomb along the same cliffs, by the same trees, the same countryside that had been the setting of the great cataclysm of February 1939). Little by little, the members of the colony had returned to Spain when the road was opened to Irún, and Mr. and Mrs. Durán, the parents of Luisito and Rosario Comín, and others whose names Álvaro could not remember, were waiting in San Sebastián, Burgos, or Salamanca for the epilogue of the tragedy. From there they had sent the Mendiolas Carlist berets, Falangist caps, and even a blue shirt with the yoke and arrows embroidered in red which Uncle César had appropriated for himself and which he often wore in public, at Sunday mass or on the flower-filled terrace of the Café de la Poste. On the advice of the uncle, the women knitted for the soldiers and regularly sent their sweaters, windbreakers, and socks to some grateful Spaniards (or Italians), who would respond with pretty post cards and romantic letters, destined, no doubt, to build up the enthusiasm and beatitude of their foster mothers (Aunt Mercedes had kept the photograph of her protegé, the engineer Sandro Rossi, on her night table until the fateful date of Badoglio's proclamation and Italy's cowardly and treasonous surrender to the Allies).

The day of the last communiqué from the Burgos Headquarters, Álvaro and his cousins were running through Doña Engracia's garden while the adults uncorked bottles of champagne in the living room and, after the toasts, they listened with religious attention to a recording of the voice of the Caudillo. Inspired by the excitement of their elders, the children were playing, for the nth time, the capture of the Red Spy, they flew kites, they threw stones at the cat, and when they had exhausted the repertory of their games, they invented a peepee-shooting contest, standing in a row and aiming at the hedge of thujas at an official distance of twelve feet. Somebody (Jorge?) was winning when, warned no doubt by one of the girl cousins, Conchita Soler came out shouting into the garden (at that very moment in Madrid, a delirious crowd was welcoming the conquering army).

"Children! What are you doing there, exposing yourselves now that our side has won?"

You turned your back on the sea. The darkness palliated the familiar arrangement of the trees in the garden—the winged leafiness of the eucalyptus trees, the graceful tremor of the cypresses —cloaking the entire countryside under its broad and diffuse shadow. Temporarily invisible, life was throbbing nonetheless, diminished and faint. The wind was blowing, impregnated with vegetable smells. From time to time a breath of breeze would detach an ephemeral necklace of raindrops from the already gorged leaves. Sharpening your ears, you were able to make out the distant croaking of the frogs, the mechanical spring of the crickets being sprung, the whole mysterious net of complicities and plots of the subtle nocturnal universe. Alone in the middle of the chaos, the lamp on the porch was propitiously keeping watch over the sleep of the community.

You went back into the house, you put the papers back into

the folder, you turned out the light. The old clock on the wall struck the hour while you stepped along through the half-light. You were thirsty, you opened another bottle of wine, you drank half of it down in one swallow. You wanted to forget the passage of the day, reality, memories, mirages. Going over to Dolores's bed, listening to her breathing, touching her body, slipping your lips across her stomach, going down to her sex, lingering there, looking for a refuge, losing yourself in its depths, paying back your maternal and fetal prehistory.

Oh, you said to yourself, if only you had never come out.

IV

Your efforts at reconstruction and synthesis had run up against a serious obstacle. Thanks to the documents and proofs stored away in the folders, you were able to dust off in your memory happenings and incidents that in the past you might have considered lost and which, once rescued from forgetfulness by these means, were able to shed light not only on your own biography, but also on certain obscure and revealing facets of life in Spain (the personal and the collective, the public and the private, joined together harmoniously both the inner search and the outside evidence, the intimate understanding of yourself and the growth of civic awareness in the Taifa kingdoms), but because of your voluntary exile in Paris and your vagabond existence in Europe, that previous communion had dissolved, and when you had been uprooted from your uninviting native soil (the cradle of heroes and *conquistadores,* saints and visionaries, madmen and inquisitors: the whole Iberian fauna), your own adventures and those of your country had taken divergent directions: you went one way, the bonds that had once linked you to your tribe having been broken, drunk and astonished at that new and incredible freedom of yours; along the other way, your country and that group of friends who were persevering in their noble efforts to change it, paying with their persons the cost that from indifference or cowardice you had refused to pay, coming to their maturity at the price of indispensable mistakes, they were adults, with the concise tempering that you did not have: the harsh experience of jail that you had never known; a strict awareness of the limits of the alienated dignity that you all had. With an empty memory after ten years of exile, how could you reconstruct that lost unity without doing it mischief?

Since then (mark the date well: October, 1952) the alien story of your friends became juxtaposed to your own and in order to grasp them both at the same time, it was necessary for you to alternate the facts: shuffling them as if it were a question of two different decks of cards, putting what had been lived side by side with what had been heard (Barcelona and Paris, Paris and Águilas), without ever getting them to meld completely. The surveillance record of the Regional Social Investigation Brigade (given to Antonio by his defense attorney after the trial), the transcript and records of the Arraignment Court that had heard the case, the associations of ideas and memories that had not yet been filtered through the demanding sieve of memory (belonging to different periods, with no common denominator) interpolated in a chaotic way Antonio's story of his arrest and imprisonment (all put together again later on by you with Dolores's help). Submitting to the demanding canons of reality, your imagination compensated for it by slowly putting situations together, polishing the edges of dialogues, tying up loose ends and filling holes, skillfully manipulating its effect as a catalyst.

In the clear, bright summertime (the sunlight on the pool full of vegetable smells, the fresh and golden garden, the porch piled with cushions and a motley stack of mixed-up record jackets), the three of you together, just as on the night before, continued the elliptical and twisting conversation while the sun spread with equal justice its tint upon the vineyards and the pines, the cork trees and the olives. Bands of sparrows were tearing up a thin, smooth sky that was light in its transparency. The soft, thick hills gave you protection from the mad caravan of vehicles that ran along the coast and in the unaccustomed silence of the place, as in olden days, mistress and owner, the word was queen.

File 61. Report—Aware of certain symptoms of new Communist activities and bearing in mind reports of the presence in Barcelona of certain elements of the Party who have come to guide and build up their organization and convert it into the guiding force of the underground PSUC according to the directives of the Central Committee located in countries on the other side of the Iron Curtain, the Chief of Police has given instructions that vigilance be strengthened and the head of the Regional Social Investigation Brigade see to it that the Second Group of said organization, under the command of Inspector Florencio Ruiz García and composed of agents Eloy Sánchez Romero, Mariano Domínguez Soto, Juan Domingo Anechina, Francisco Parra Morlans, Eleuterio Cortés Sánchez, José Luis Martínez Solsona, Eduardo García Barrios, Mamerto Cuixart López, Mariano Fernández Sierra, Máximo Olmos Martín, Enrique Gutiérrez Badosa, and Dámaso Santos Morube, with the help of Aurelio Gómez García as secretary, take the necessary steps for vigilance and surveillance to make an attempt to localize the elements that have infiltrated from abroad as well as their activities, operations, contacts, and travels.

It had been a long time since he had set foot there. During the last two years, preparing for the entrance examinations, he had spent the summer abroad perfecting his languages and, just having been admitted to the school, he was preparing to visit his mother a little before the Christmas holidays, the police came to his boardinghouse at six in the morning and after turning his room upside-down and confiscating all of his books, took him in handcuffs to a cell at Headquarters and from there—seventy-two hours later—to the block for political prisoners in the Modelo jail: eighteen months of forced repose and solitude, dreaming awake in his cell and wandering tirelessly around the courtyard, his ear intent on the sounds outside—the voice of a woman calling her child, the familiar sound of a streetcar—until the secret trial of the sixteen who were indicted and the unexpected establishment of a residence. The long imprisonment had caught him unawares: during his period of detention the village had become his only point of reference, changed into an arduous, difficult, unobtainable objective. To his heart's content, he remembered the pugnacious sun, the quiet blue sea, the reflection of the light on the whitewashed houses. His childhood on the docks and the fishermen's wharf, waiting for the men to come back. In his free time he would go on a trawler to El Hornillo. The judge's decision had suddenly destroyed that impassioned expectation as that refuge he had dreamed of so many times became a place of punishment. Twice frustrated in his desire to get out into the world, as he approached the village in the uncomfortable bus, he was thinking, with growing restlessness, about his mother and the crumbling of her illusions about his future: about his arrival, not as a brilliant student in diplomatic school—an image that she innocently associated with the latest model Cadillac belonging to the Consul General of Spain in Alexandria that Don Carlos Aguilera would use to visit his family during his yearly leave—but as a prisoner sentenced to three years in jail who was coming to serve the last part of his sentence under the escort of a pair of Civil Guards.

After his first moment of euphoria—seeing Ricardo, Paco, Artigas, and other friends in his group, the nervous preparation for the trip, the farewell walk along the Ramblas—his excitation had slowly declined and there were the demands and formalities at each stage—the obligatory appearance before the authorities in Valencia, Alicante, Murcia—had pushed him gradually toward a pitiful state of resignation, fatigue, and restlessness. In Lorca, the Civil Guard sergeant had read and reread his itinerary, scrutinizing it with quiet suspicion and with a sudden burst of mistrust, unforeseen in his program, had decided to turn him over to the care of two policemen—an Andalusian peasant and an aging Galician—who stayed by his side, dozing, looking at the deserted countryside, with their three-cornered patent-leather hats and their carbines between their legs. The bus bounced along the ruts of a road he knew by heart, one which in the half-awake moments of his cell he had enjoyed conjuring up in all of its details: the mountain tops washed and sculptured by erosion, salt flats speckled with live oaks and dwarf fig trees, dry gullies with oleanders and pitas on their edges, prickly-pear hedges, white farmhouses. The last time he had been there—during the filming of the 16 mm documentary on emigration—Dolores was driving the Dauphine while Álvaro filmed through the window the parched grain fields, the dry olive groves, the huts abandoned by their inhabitants, the ruined cisterns, and catch-buckets of rainwater. After crossing the Mazarrón, the view clears up. The sleepwalking work of many generations has carefully banked the side of the hills and from sustaining wall to sustaining wall one can see almond and olive trees surrounded by circles of steep terraces. As the level of the land descends, the fields become green again and take on life. The young men from a nearby farm were digging around in an orange grove. Farther on there were maturing arbors and gardens planted with tomatoes and lettuce. When the sea finally came into view, he suddenly understood the deep reasons behind that pilgrimage into the past to the mythical and fabulous scenery of his childhood: the town came up, miraculously white in the bright, clear atmosphere, and on the left the mountains showed their bulky forms against a quiet sky, speckled here and there by cottony ox drool; the sea was an intense blue below the almost vertical Cope escarpment and the little island of El Fraile stuck out its ponderous rump, half-hidden behind the nearby plume of the palm trees. When his friends had come to film the documentary, he remembered that they had parked their car on top of a rise and, taking in the African countryside—pitas, prickly pears, water wheels, mills—that extends out to the salt marshes of San Juan de los Terreros, Álvaro had lit a cigarette and, facing him suddenly, had exclaimed: "What kind of a country were you born in, you peasant? Among a tribe of Tuaregs?"

The bus made a straight line across the planted fields and when it went over the level crossing, the irregular beating of his heart surprised him. A woman on a donkey was protecting herself from the sun with a faded umbrella, a few dozen children were running around half-naked through the streets and throwing stones at a dog they were chasing. Almost immediately, the driver turned to the right toward the Almería road. Despite the heat, people were taking their ease on the sidewalk and the usual loafers were grouped together outside the bars. When it reached the crossroads, the bus slowed down and came to a complete stop, and Antonio got out with his suitcase along with the Civil Guards. The old gasoline pump had been turned into a service station, a blond girl was smoking as she leaned on the fender of a convertible. The clusters of onlookers had stopped their conversations and were examining them in silence.

"Let's go," the Galician said.

Escorted by the three-cornered hats, Antonio set off for the small barracks. He could feel the looks of the village fixed on him and with a distressed feeling of guilt, he thought about the inevitable meeting with his mother.

Surveillance report. Sat., Nov. 2, 1960—At about 11:15 A.M *agents detailed to search out and observe undercover Communist activities spot, on the Avenida José Antonio, in this capital, a person between 45 and 50, about 5′ 6″ tall, well built, broad shoulders, swinging walk, brown hair, high forehead, bald spot, long face with massive features. He goes toward the Calle Entenza carrying an average-sized package. We shall call him Gorilla. He goes into the Pereda automobile-repair shop at number 81 on the above-mentioned street. Reappears after a few minutes with an individual we shall call Blue and goes to the Pichi bar, located on the corner of Diputación. Leave bar, Blue goes back to garage and at 12:55* P.M. *Gorilla goes to newsstand on José Antonio across from the Rex movie. Makes contact with two people. They give him a light-brown suitcase and go with him to Mariola bar on corner of Diputación and Rocafort. Gorilla takes suitcase after a few minutes and goes to Blue's garage, leaves it with him, walks to bus stop, finds out that buses do not stop there because of repair work, continues on along Calle Sepúlveda to Muntaner; at corner of Ronda San Antonio takes taxi and goes to 51 Calle Almansa in Las Roquetas district. Goes into house mentioned above and surveillance is maintained.*

Meanwhile the two people who gave him the suitcase and stayed in Mariola bar come out a few minutes later, get into SEAT 600, license B-143271, and are lost. Car is located later at end of Calle Calabria on sidewalk on even-numbered side beside a wall. The two subjects given code names of Blondy and Boy, have following marks of identification: Boy about 30, 5′ 7″, average complexion, brown hair; Blondy about 40, 5′ 8″, blond hair, short and clean, ruddy complexion, foreign-looking. Shortly after ascertained that SEAT 600 registered at Traffic Police Headquarters under name of Enrique Casanova Miret, 32, lawyer, resident of Barcelona, 101 Calle Londres, no previous record. One called Blue 5′ 9″, strong, long face, straight hair, dressed in coveralls. As he walks does not swing one arm all the way out.

Getting back to Gorilla: not observed coming out of Calle Almansa because it is a dangerous place to approach too closely when on surveillance. But he was picked up later, around 6:15 P.M.*, in neighborhood of Blue's garage in company of another individual we shall call Gypsy, about the same age as Gorilla, little taller, thin, black hair, Gypsy look about him. Both enter Blue's garage and, not finding him there, walk to 145 Consejo de Ciento, a new cement-colored building. Wait in lobby for a while, disappear for a time, come down to lobby again. Around 7:15* P.M. *come out, accompanied by Blue. Three go to Pichi bar and stay there 25 minutes. Go back to Blue's garage and leave him there. Gypsy and Gorilla go to the bus stop on Avenida José Antonio, wait for bus, but since they are late take taxi to 51 Al-*

mansa, which they still have not left even though surveillance is continued until dawn.

They have been identified today: Blue is Enrique Medina Soto, resident of Barcelona, 145 Consejo de Ciento; record of having supported the Agrupación Guerrillera de Cataluña; arrested in 1948, imprisoned in Ocaña and Burgos prisons; released in 1956 and given complete freedom on Oct. 3 of same year; took up residence in Barcelona and again made contact with elements of the PSUC, as reported in investigations undertaken concerning Miguel Prieto Vernet in 1958. The one called Gypsy is Manuel Morera Torres, resident of Barcelona, 51 Calle Almansa; sentenced in 1946 in Madrid for underground organization, spent seven years in Ocaña and El Dueso; released in 1953, settled in Barcelona in 1954.

On your first and only visit to the place, you had parked the car at the corner and his mother had come out to greet you, conscious of her importance. Dolores was wearing very tight dungarees and a small boy pointed at her and said: "There's a Frenchwoman with Antonio."

It was the early part of August, 1958, and the village was having a festival. His mother had worked hard to prepare a *gazpacho,* which was one of her specialties, and when you finished dinner there were stars in the sky. After the drowsiness of the dog days, the breeze revived you. For a few minutes you all went through the alleys of the village that were cloaked in the darkness of the night. From the esplanade along the docks could be heard the confused hum of music that was being interrupted by the rasping voice of an announcer and the wild gallop of an outdoor showing of a movie, *Helen and the Sioux,* with the unmistakable accent of Madrilenian dubbing. The rhythmic breath of the festival was filling the air with a penetrating and subtle feeling of life. The people who lived on the hill were coming down in small groups to the center of town, and as you reached the square the picture suddenly changed. Palm trees and fig trees seemed greener than usual under the spotlights, and a stream of people overflowed the sidewalks onto the streets like a Sundayed-up and happy army suddenly abandoned by their officers.

At the entrance to the fair, the authorities had raised a triumphal arch. The noise and the confusion grew as you approached the dock. The vital forces were killing time in the musty salons of the Casino, and with the imaginary camera of an Eisenstein, you looked over those fat old men who were ensconced in their armchairs (in close symbiosis with them) and, big-bellied and motionless like Buddhas, were spying on the comings and goings of the young girls.

On the left, on a stage decorated in the form of a shell, some musicians dressed in blue jackets and red bow ties were playing a mawkish bolero. A few couples were lazing their way through the steps on the street to the envious curiosity of the onlookers who pressed up against the fence. It was the dance of the dandies, five *duros* a head, and Antonio told you about the time when, without a penny in his pocket, with the other children his own age, he had gone up to spy, fascinated by the spectacle of a universe (for him then) that was velvety and soft, remote and inaccessible.

On the right, another orchestra was giving vent to its enthusiasm as it played (magnificently according to Dolores) a cha-cha-cha. The dubbed-in Madrid voice was having a dramatic dialogue with Helen, surrounded by a band of Sioux (the seats of the outdoor movie were next to the fair, and the volume of the sound was positively terrifying). Constancio's bar was filled. You all went in and Antonio introduced you to his friends. When you left, you seem to remember, you were a little drunk.

It was the same old conversation about sex and the hard life of a professional man over a glass of beer and a plate of olives that you would come to recognize later, as the filming of the documentary went on, until you could not stand it any more. In your first contact with the South, the rude and rustic vitality of those men had captivated you (to the point of bothering Dolores) and, brought back to life by Antonio's recent experience (which he had told you in detail), the memory of your baptismal stay in the village was being reborn out of forgetfulness like a phoenix, dense, blinding, brilliant. When they found out where you lived, the fishermen wanted to know if you had any influential friends abroad and, superstitiously, they asked you to write down their addresses.

"If I got the chance, I'd follow you wherever you wanted. Anyone who can get me out of here will get a kiss from me, yes: right down to the soles of his shoes."

"In order to live in this town, you've got to take on two jobs and wag your tail when the big shots go by."

"Ten people have already left from my neighborhood alone."

"We Spaniards always go along like snails and carry our houses with us."

(Your ear would soon become accustomed to the litany, but not your heart. Conscious of the impossibility of personally resolving their problems, when you heard them, you still felt, in spite of ominous custom, the confused sensation, it might be said, of a spurious and surreptitious blame.)

When you all got up the next day, the esplanade was empty. The dominating southern light controlled the blue and motionless sea like a puppet, the eroded naked mountains, the sky as smooth as a wall. Antonio was waiting for you in Constancio's bar and, taking along your new 16 mm Pathé, you all went out to the tuna fishery to film.

Sun., Nov. 3—At 8:45 A.M. *Gorilla and Gypsy leave latter's house and take bus to end of Calle Mallorca, near the Sagrada Familia. In lobby of number 530 make contact with individual we shall call Ramallets. Three go to Compostela bar and have coffee. Ramallets returns home. Gypsy and Gorilla take streetcar to MZA station. Gorilla takes train for Mataró, Gypsy takes bus to 390 Sicilia and does not come out until lunch time. At 2:30 returns home, picks up wife, and they go to bar. Meanwhile Gorilla gets off at Ocata-Teyá station, slips through one of the exits to the street, starts to look for a certain house. Backtracks and asks a woman. Goes down to highway, goes on to Masnou, goes up Calle General Goded and rings bell at number 71, where he stays for more than two hours. Comes out at 2* P.M.*, takes train back to Barcelona; across from station takes bus to Las Roquetas and at 2:55* P.M. *enters 51 Almanza, Gypsy's home. Ramallets identified as Ismael Rodríguez Cepeda, resident of Barcelona, 530 Calle Mallorca, ground floor. Person at 71 General Goded, Masnou, identified as Lucía Soler Villafranca, no previous record.*

Mon., Nov. 4—At 8 A.M. *Gypsy leaves home for work. It is supposed that Gorilla has stayed behind because he has not been seen all morning. Appears at 2:35* P.M. *and takes a bus to 63 Calle Ausias March, offices of La Catalana Transport. Goes into nearby bar, back to office, and across from streetcar stop makes contact with short, fat individual, gray-haired, broad face, jovial smile. Chats with him for five minutes and they separate. Gorilla goes to MZA station, goes to waiting room, looks at schedules. At 3:45* P.M., *Lucía Soler Villafranca, whom we shall call Grackle, arrives. They go to Plaza Palacio and take bus to Urquinaona, get out at corner of Ausias March, go up Bruch, and stop in front of number 23. Go in at 4:30* P.M. *and ten minutes later come out accompanied by dark woman dressed in black, same height as Gorilla, average weight. They go to loby of 35 Bailén, come out immediately and leave the woman. Gorilla and Grackle walk to Avenida José Antonio and are lost on Lauria. At 6* P.M. *Gorilla is picked up again with Gypsy in Pichi bar. Go to Blue's garage, pick up suitcase Gorilla left on Sat., and at 7:20* P.M. *Gorilla and Gypsy take taxi to Gypsy's.*

Subject Gorilla spoke to across from La Catalana Transport and whom we shall call Nikita, identified as Ramiro Sauret Gómez, 40 Calle Princesa, Barcelona. Before war belonged to CNT and during Crusade was director of Control Committee of said Union. Later joined CP, having been jailed in Valencia by followers of Casado; arrested on 4/16/39, he was sentenced to 12 years and was released after 3 and a half. Freed again, made new connections with underground CP, and in March, 1944, sentenced to 20 years as organizing secretary of PSUC. On May 5, 1959, first reported to this Brigade as a released prisoner from the Burgos penitentiary, the position he is in at present time.

"Let's see if I can make things clear. You played a game and you lost. . . . You're in our hands and we can do anything we want with you. . . . Even kill you. . . . You wouldn't be the first to disappear. . . ." The man was gazing at him, almost tenderly: "I know what's going on in your mind. . . . 'I have to be strong. . . . Not talk. . . . Not tell on my friends.' " . . . He stretched out a hairy white hand to him and let it run lovingly along his shoulder: "Don't be foolish, everybody talks here. Some sooner, others later. . . . The wise ones without our having to touch a hair on their heads and the stupid ones with wet towels or electricity. . . . Let's see whether you're going to be wise or whether you're going to play tough. . . . In either case, you'll end up talking."

Suddenly, to his great relief, he was in the courtyard of the jail, among the common criminals. The inspector had disappeared and the other inmates were playing soccer with a ball made out of rags. Almost immediately, the guard gathered them together for roll call. It was meal time and his companions were beating their spoons on their aluminum plates. He was waiting to hear his name so that he could answer "present," but the shout was strangled in his throat.

During the first months after his arrest, his dreams invariably dealt with his life as a free citizen—casual walks, uncrowded places, open spaces—as if rejecting completely the reality of prison, his subconscious clinging blindly to a previous existence that could deny it all and make it go away. But after a time his imprisonment had infiltrated into his nights until it took them over completely and reduced the variety of his landscapes to one monotonous and obsessive setting: the yard, his cell, the lock-up at Headquarters. If he dreamed about his town, it was a town with barbed wire; if he saw his mother, she was a prisoner. The judge's decision had not yet trickled into his subconscious. By virtue of a process that was the opposite of his arrest, exile to his native region was a curtain of smoke that hid a deeper reality: whether he liked it or not, his environment would still be imprisonment.

Fermín was waiting for him in Constancio's bar, leaning on the counter. His old soccer teammate from childhood had put on a little weight since Antonio had seen him last, and he was smiling at him in a friendly way.

"Welcome home, Lenin. As soon as I heard you were out, I ran over here. . . . How are you feeling?"

"All fucked up but happy," Antonio said.

"Well, take some advice from me. From now on forget about what you did and stay here with us. You won't get into any more trouble that way. We'll take care of you here in town."

"How's your job?"

"I quit the one I had before, didn't they tell you? Last year I went into business for myself. . . . A repair shop for cars and motorcycles. I'll show you later on."

"Congratulations."

"I've got two assistants and the three of us have a pretty good deal. During the summer I close at midnight and there still isn't enough time. Things aren't the way they used to be. There are more cars every day, and every mother's son wants his motorcycle. If you don't have the money to buy one outright, you pay for it on time."

They were sitting by the window, facing the dock, and Constancio brought three cups of coffee. Fermín was a wide-awake boy, with political restlessness and for some time his one idea had been to leave for France. When they had been filming the documentary on emigration, Álvaro had given him his address in Paris and, as usual, had promised to find work for him.

"How are your friends?" he suddenly asked, guessing his thoughts. "Did they finish the movie?"

"I don't know," Antonio answered. "The day before yesterday I saw Ricardo in Barcelona and he didn't say anything. . . . Dolores is still in Paris and I think that Álvaro went to Cuba."

Contrary to what he supposed, Fermín did not make any comment. His eyes were glowing like coals.

"Do you remember when we used to play soccer, the afternoon we beat the Vera team and we had to fight our way off the field with our bare fists? . . . Ángel made the winning goal with a penalty shot one minute before the end of the game. . . ."

"Those were the good old days," Antonio said. "What became of all the others?"

"Ángel took off for Germany and in five years he put together a half-million pesetas. . . . A big shot, how about that? This spring he showed up in a Volkswagen and he spent twenty thousand *duros* just for repairs on his family's house. If you want to, we can go visit Pulpí some day on my motorcycle. He's a good egg. We'll have a good time."

"I strung along with him to Barcelona and from there he took off for abroad," Constancio explained. "Now he exports tomatoes."

"If there's a touch of rain, he lines his pockets," Fermín said.

"What about Lucio?"

"He practically never sticks his nose in town." Constancio's wife was speaking with her musical voice. "He's so involved in his engagement that his friends never see him any more. When he shows up once in a while on Sunday it's just to come and go."

The lieutenant had warned him about former prisoners, and Antonio asked about Rojas.

"He's around," Fermín said. "Only yesterday I ran into him at the dance."

Constancio got up to wait on a customer. Since Fermín was silent, Antonio went on: "Haven't they bothered him any more?"

"This is a small town and everybody knows where he stands. Even if he wanted to do anything, he couldn't."

"Does he work at the tuna fishery?"

"No, now he goes trawling on the 'Joven Carlos.' But he can't support his family with what he makes."

"Fishing isn't a trade any more," the woman said.

"That fellow will go to bed some fine day and we won't see him again. . . . His sister-in-law told me that he was getting his papers in order so he could leave."

An American-make car was slowly crossing the esplanade of the dock. A man in a blue uniform was at the wheel and piled into the back Antonio could make out two blond girls and a flock of small children wearing cowboy hats. After tracing a silent semicircle, the car stopped in front of the movie theater. Without paying any attention to the chauffeur who had jumped out with his cap in his hand to open the door for them, the children were looking out the windows at the posters. Their pale and bland faces immediately showed a lively annoyance. After a few moments, with the same gentleness with which it had stopped—docile as a domestic animal—the vehicle started up again and went out of sight in a cloud of dust.

"That's Don Carlos Aguilera's Cadillac," Constancio's wife said. "His family arrived from Egypt the day before yesterday."

There was a pause. The policemen had come to have a drink with the harbor pilot and Fermín exchanged a knowing wink with Antonio and got up.

"Let's go," he said.

After a quick peep, the sun had gone behind the clouds and toward the island of El Fraile the darkness was thicker than ever.

"Where to? The beach pavilion?"

Fermín was leading him by the elbow and he stopped to light a cigarette.

"It's usually dead around there in the morning," he answered. "Besides, they've got new people working there. Don Gonzalo brought the new bartender and his assistant from Madrid."

Antonio remembered Lolita, the year he had invited her to the processions in Lorca and on the way back to town, he had parked Álvaro's car beside an olive grove and lain down with her in the dew. He asked what had become of her.

"Dámaso's daughter?"

"Yes."

"She got knocked up and had to get married in a hurry so the kid would have a father."

"Who's her husband?"

"A guy who eats and shuts up and minds his own business. The tricky girl is still making out with the other one, and he, just as if nothing . . . Are you interested in seeing her?"

"No," he said. "I was just curious."

"I remember there was a time when she was making eyes at you. She was a model girl then. Not any more. She's got a lot fatter and she doesn't bother with make-up any more. Someday she'll take off for Barcelona and become a whore there."

"What about Arturo's daughter?"

"She had a fight with her boy friend and left town." Fermín was walking thoughtfully. "Things have changed a lot. None of the chicks my age are worth anything any more. . . . Almost all of them are married and have kids and have begun to look like their mothers. And the young ones I like find me boring and would rather live it up with twenty-year-old guys who smoke light tobacco and know how to dance the Madison. . . ."

"We're out of date," Antonio said.

"Yes, and what's even worse, things go along by themselves, just as if you and I didn't exist. When you were in the pokey, lots of times I used to think: when Antonio gets out, he's going to find everything changed. The country has changed and doesn't need us, have you noticed?"

"I had lots of time to think in jail," he replied.

"The best ones go to Germany and the ones who are left, what's the use of talking about them. Some a little more, others a little less, they just drag along. . . . People think they're breathing and in reality they're still just going through the motions."

To console him, he talked to him about the people who made the revolution and lost the war and since then have lived condemned to the sterile remembrances of their youth, but Fermín would not let himself be convinced:

"We're worse off than they are. At least they had a youth, as you called it. We didn't even have that. We prepared ourselves for something and nothing happened. We're growing old without ever having had any responsibilities, understand?"

They had reached the square and Fermín stopped and pointed at the groups of idlers who were chatting on the terrace of the bar.

"Most of them were Republicans and changed their stripes after the war. Then they became Falangists and when things got ugly, they tore up their cards. Now they're busy selling beach land to Germans. Whatever happens, they'll always stay on top, just like oil."

"Do you feel like some coffee?"

"Here?" Fermín smiled bitterly. "It's easy to see that you're from out of town. . . . Important people don't go to these places any more, didn't you know?"

"Where do they go?"

"Two coffeehouses opened up this summer, with music and uniformed waitresses who can say thank you in French. According to what I hear, Don Gonzalo put up the money. . . . Come on, the more elegant one is close by."

"Show me the garage first," Antonio said.

He went along with him toward the market, while Fermín let out his rage against the village establishment. At the first corner there was a sign with his friend's name and as they turned the corner, Antonio spotted a redheaded boy squatting in the middle of the sidewalk and carefully examining an automobile tire. Inside the place another boy was going about with a screwdriver and a pair of pliers.

"Anything new?" Fermín asked.

"Manolo came for the points," the redhead replied. "He said he'd be back this afternoon."

Antonio came in to take a look at the spare parts and Fermín brought him up to date on the various aspects of the business. The purchase price had been put up by the savings bank, thanks to a letter of recommendation from the mayor and for a few minutes he was talking like an expert in credit, interest, and loans.

"The day you least expect," he concluded, laughing waggishly, "you'll see me sitting in the salons of the club with the young swells."

"You have to put on a few more pounds for that," Antonio answered.

Fermín wanted to show him the new coffee shop, but he used the pretext of a date and left him. The storm clouds were coming together over the mountains, dark and ponderous, and from time to time a sudden flash of lightning would theatrically light up the countryside, a few seconds before the distant and intermittent rumble of thunder. Solitude closed in around him again, the same as during the worst moments of his imprisonment, and the imprecise limits of his freedom suddenly seemed crueler to him than the bars of his cell. By taking him away from the comfortable Manicheism of prison, exile was placing him in the malleable and ambiguous universe. In the future he would be able to wander through the town, get drunk in the taverns, dive into the sea like any other mother's son, and, nonetheless, in his deepest part, still feel himself captive, insensible to the mirage of that gratuitous and unexpected fate.

The pleasure boats were softly rocking and he immediately recognized Don Gonzalo's yacht. The fog was enveloping the island of El Fraile and foreshortening the miserable shanties of La Punta. The gulls were flying low, dropping into the water in search of a catch, breaking up into the air again, dropping down again. At the end of the sea wall a man was looking at the sea, absorbed, and before he was able to tell why, his heart gave a turn.

Many years before—fifteen, twenty?—Antonio had gone to the jetty to catch sea urchins and he noticed in the distance, with his back toward him, the silhouette of a hunched-over and poor individual who, like a scarecrow, was looking at the skyline as his jacket and baggy pants were flapping wildly in the wind. His lonely, unprotected state had made such an impression on Antonio that as he got closer, he had the innocent thought: "If that man were my father, I'd commit suicide."

It was his first experience of moral grief, the initial link in a long series. That night, reviewing the list of his father's humiliations since his release from the concentration camp—the silent rancor of his mother, the useless search for a job, the admonitory urge to avoid his neighbor's look—he cried, as he pressed his face against the pillow, and the open wound had never healed. The mutual shame of his meeting rose up from the year that Uncle Gabriel had paid his tuition to a boarding school in Murcia. Antonio had not committed suicide as he said, but some weeks after the walk along the breakwater, his father disappeared forever. One night his mother and he had waited in vain for him to come home for dinner. It was Antonio who had found him the next day, his jacket and pants fluttering, swinging slightly in the air, hanging from a beam.

Tues., Nov. 5—Gorilla leaves at 2:30 P.M. *to meet Gypsy and they take bus to Plaza Palacio. Go into a bar, Gorilla goes to MZA station, buys ticket, returns to bar and, not finding Gypsy, retraces his steps. At 4* P.M. *takes train on platform no. 1. Arrives Mataró 4:40* P.M., *goes to center of town, stops by newsstand on Avenida Clavé, and makes contact with man inside; speaks with him and few minutes later another individual appears who greets Gorilla warmly. The one in the stand will be called K1 and the other K2. Gorilla and K2 have coffee in La Maresma bar, leave, stop at another stand. K2 goes inside with great confidence and chats with woman running it, introduces her to Gorilla. Around 6:45* P.M. *latter leaves K2, turns down a street and K2 follows at about 60 ft. with a bag that looks like canvas, both finally going into 12 General Aranda, ground floor. At 7:20* P.M., *woman in second newsstand closes it, goes to butcher, and also goes to above address. As the place offered no suitable conditions for surveillance, it was lifted.*

Wed., Nov. 6—At 4:15 P.M. *Gorilla arrives MZA station coming from Mataró. Takes streetcar, goes to Blue's garage, reappears with latter and they go to El Pichi. Blue comes and goes between bar and garage five times. At 6:50* P.M., *Gorilla leaves and goes to Calle Viladomat. Meets Nikita at 7:05* P.M., *walk together, talk, stop at two bars on Avenida Mistral. At corner of Borrell and Floridablanca, Nikita takes some papers from his wallet and after they read them, Gorilla takes them. Separate on corner of Urgel and José Antonio and Gorilla takes taxi to Gypsy's house where he enters at 8:30* P.M.

K1 identified as Jorge Todó Salichs, sentenced on 5/4/46 to six years in jail for underground activities; released in 1949 and resident of Mataró, 36 Calle Cabrera. K2 is Damián Roig Pujol, on file as Communist sympathizer since strike of April 1951; during current year has made two trips to France. Residence, 12 General Aranda, ground floor.

Thurs., Nov. 7—Gorilla leaves Gypsy's at 3 P.M., *takes train for Masnou, goes to Grackle's house, and comes out immediately; returns to highway and meets her in door of nearby bakery; they walk and talk together, say good-by, and Gorilla goes along Calle Manila to private house where a gray Peugeot 403, license 9089 MG 75, is parked. After 10 minutes in house, comes out alone, takes train back to Barcelona. Meets Gypsy on the Paralelo and they go to look for Blue. Do not find him in garage, go to El*

Pichi and Blue joins them. At 7 P.M. *Blue leaves them; other two go to Gypsy's house and no longer seen.*

Owner of car is Theo Batet Juanico, 35 Calle Manila, Masnou, a person who has come from France, works at Hidrocarburos del Norte, S. A. *Speaks perfect Spanish. During our Crusade was pilot lieutenant in Red air force. On 2/4/58 declared at Spanish Consulate in Paris that before war lived in Barcelona and wanted to return to visit relatives, permission granted 5/24/58.*

Fri., Nov. 8—Gypsy and Gorilla leave at 2:30 P.M. *and agents lose sight of latter at 4:30* P.M. *on Calle Pelayo.*

Sat., Nov. 9—At 6:15 P.M. *Gorilla spotted again with suitcase near Blue's garage. Takes taxi and lost in traffic soon after, not seen all day despite surveillance at stations in case he planned to leave Barcelona. In view of fact that he does not arrive, surveillance lifted on Calle Almansa at 2:30* A.M. *Sunday.*

Sun., Nov. 10—Gypsy spotted at 9:15 A.M. *and at 10* A.M. *enters El Pichi bar. Gorilla arrives a little later, talks with him for a few minutes, and leaves by himself. At door of Mariola bar, an individual we shall call Shoes is waiting for him, about 50, 5′ 7″, light-brown hair, steel-rimmed Truman-type glasses, suede jacket, gray pants, expensive black shoes; a little knock-kneed. They go to Escocés bar, on Calle Rocafort. Talk for 20 minutes and separate on corner of Entenza and José Antonio, Gorilla acting as if Shoes did not know city well. After passing several corners, Shoes takes taxi to Aragon station and buys ticket to Saragossa on 12:30* P.M. *train.*

Gorilla goes into bar on the corner of José Antonio and Rocafort and about two minutes later Gypsy arrives with small package. Wait for a while, walk around the block, come back to bar. Continue on down Rocafort and at corner of Sepúlveda, stop to speak to young man we shall call Curly, 29 or 30, 5′ 6″, dark complexion, black hair, thick and curly. In a while, Blue appears and they all go to Mariola bar. Come out after 10 minutes, head toward El Pichi bar. Curly leaves them and goes to Avenida José Antonio, lost to surveillance because of importance of discovering Gorilla's new home. Gorilla, Blue, and Gypsy go to La Habana bar, on Calle Diputación. Blue disappears at corner of Villamarí; Gypsy takes bus with package and Gorilla takes streetcar to MZA station. 1 P.M. *Ten minutes later he takes train to Masnou and at 2:30* P.M. *goes into Grackle's house.*

Like Antonio's father but without his quick resolution, you had also been stalked by the temptation of suicide.

The view irresistibly brings back the educational prints in the out-of-date school encyclopedia that had been your favorite reading during the anemic and extended limbo of your bourgeois adolescence. From the protective grille on the rue de l'Aqueduc, you have at your feet in the foreground the industrial panorama of the Gare du Nord with all the elements that make it up, brought together like a minute and detailed toy station: platform, crane, containers, clearance gauge, tracks, signals, crossing-guard's hut, water tower, pylon, electric cable, rotating sign, scaffolding; at your level, eight hundred feet away, the bridge of the Boulevard de la Chapelle with its heavy traffic of trucks, cars, motorcycles, three-wheelers; and, down the middle of the boulevard, in the background of the picture, an elevated train, with its fantastic and unreal coaches outlined against a cold and windy sky, discolored by a sun of pure whiteness. The whole picture seems specially set up for the studious scholar there is in you and, on more than one occasion, during your wanderings through the area, the image of schoolboy classes and their secret corollary of humiliation, fear, and punishment blooms unpleasantly in your memory and revives for use against that universe, a liberating and cathartic hatred from your vanished youth.

Five months before, on a surly and foggy March Sunday, you had wandered for hours on end, your hands stuck into the pockets of your overcoat and your gaze fixed on the tips of your shoes, alien to the life that was going on around you, with the clear feeling that reality was breaking up between your fingers and in a slow but irreversible way you were beginning the process of liquidation and ruin that was to lead you, as it did everyone, to the ominous end. You had with you the hundred-times-corrected first draft of the letter you had never sent to Dolores and a short note from her written in the days when, in love with each other, you had both proceeded to the sweet and slow exploration of your bodies, both of you young and undamaged, like two strangers who were groping and searching for each other, before penetrating her with your desire. You reread them as you walked, with the harsh certainty that in the future you would never be happy again, and when you emerged, after a long walk, onto the Place de la Bastille, a bit foggy from the Ricards you had drunk during your stroll, you blankly contemplated the slim angel on the column that was foreshortened by the mist and the carnival set up on the sidewalk between the subway entrance and the canal. Violent, imperious, the idea of destruction burst out in you like a revelation.

You crossed the square, dodging the wild traffic. Shooting galleries, wheels of fortune, fortune-tellers' carts, candy booths, ferris wheels, merry-go-rounds, boats attracted a noisy and elemental public that was crushing about, people who were testing their fortune, their luck, their skills, their marksmanship. Happy groups of Beatles were waiting their turn to jump into the assault of the little electric cars and the spinning seats of the wild whip. An imprecise nausea engulfed you, like a mixture of honey and cotton.

Madame NADIA
Horoscopes d'après votre
influence planétaire
Boule de Cristal
Cartes—Tarots

IGOR

Regaine d'affection
Réponse à la pensée
Toutes les sciences occultes
Lignes de la main 3 F.

Madame LEONE—Voyante
Vous parlera sur les 3 temps
Passé
Présent
Avenir
Vous conseillera, vous guidera
quelles que soient vos difficultés

A bucolic scene with stags, sleighs, firs, snow-capped hills, shepherds served as the backdrop of a battle of kitchen artillery. A girl was spinning, solitary and happy, on the wings of a resigned and moony swan. The music of the loudspeakers was smothering and confusing the endless babble of the carnival hawkers. You were walking lost among the crowd, when a sign written in red paint suddenly caught your attention.

I Franc le Voyage
Fragiles du Coeur s'abstenir

A barker—an individual with dark skin and curled mustaches—was giving cardboard tickets to the children and young people who were lining up at the entrance: "*Avancez, Messieurdames. . . . Profitez d'un priz exceptionnel pour faire un voyage surprise que vous n'oublierez jamais. . . . Un voyage qui fera battre votre coeur trois fois plus vite que d'ordinaire. . . . Si vous avez le coeur fragile ne montez surtout pas, Messieurdames. . . . Vous risqueriez inutilement un accident et le Tobogan Fou de Malatesta ne serait tenu pour responsable devant aucun tribunal. . . . Avencez, Messieurdames, avancez. . . . Le tout pour le prix incroyable d'un seul Franc.*"

Your temples were pounding, your forehead ached, your heart was palpitating. The bulbous faces of the man attracted and repelled you at the same time. On the top of the memorial column, the angel of the Bastille was skipping with useless elasticity, the hostage of the winter and the mist. Your turn had come and you took a coin out of your pocket.

"*Une place, s'il vous plait,*" you said.

Mon., Nov. 11—We must change plans of surveillance. Gorilla leaves Grackle's at 4:10 P.M.*, takes train to Barcelona, takes taxi to corner of Calabria and Avenida José Antonio and walks to Blue's garage. Comes out in while with Blue and Nikita joins them in El Pichi bar. Three chat although Blue goes out often to check on work at garage. At 6:15* P.M. *Gorilla and Nikita take walk around block across from Pichi bar. Say good-by and Nikita walks away.*

Gorilla returns to Pichi where Gypsy waiting. 6:45 P.M. *They go to Mariola bar, joined by Blue, and stay together until 7:20* P.M. *Gypsy and Blue leave and go their ways. Gorilla stays alone, walks to center of city and is lost in traffic at 7:45* P.M.

Tues., Nov. 12—At 9:50 A.M. *Gorilla takes train to Barcelona.*

Gets on streetcar, gets off at the Plaza de España, goes into Blue's garage. Leaves, goes to Pichi bar, and Blue appears a few minutes later. Go to Escocés bar, stay there for hour and half. Go back to garage and separate at 1:04 P.M.

Gorilla goes downtown, stops for lunch. At 4:35 P.M. *reaches offices of transport company on corner of Diputación and Paseo de Gracia and buys bus ticket to Gerona. At 4:55* P.M. *goes up Vía Layetana. At corner of Pasaje Permanyer, makes contact with an individual we shall call Paws, about 50, 5′ 5″, bushy eyebrows, large hands, ruddy complexion. They go to Las Antillas bar, on corner of Aragón. Have some drinks and talk for 15 minutes. At 5:10* P.M. *they separate. Gorilla walks slowly to Pichi bar and talks with subject we shall call Gray, about 55, 5′ 8″, large nose, graying hair, white streak in middle of head; looks like worker or peasant. Converses with him about 20 minutes, then goes to Mariola bar. At 6:20* P.M. *they meet Gypsy in the Pichi and are there for more than three quarters of an hour. After stopping at a couple of bars, each one goes his own way. Gorilla to Grackle's house, where he arrives at 9:30* P.M., *Gypsy to his home, and Gray to the Barón de Viver project, next to the Santa Coloma bridge.*

Paws has been identified as Felipe Moreno Vázquez, 9 Llagostera, Barcelona, employed in the Orión factory, 131 Lauria. Moreno left the Nationalist zone for the Red zone and enlisted in the Republican army. Sentenced for desertion at end of war, he took up residence in Tarragona and made contacts with elements of the PSUC, arrested in December of same year; on parole since 5/6/54, took up residence in Barcelona.

Wed., Nov. 13—Gorilla takes 10:45 A.M. *train carrying black attaché case. Gets off at MZA station and after short walk through El Borne market, heads for 40 Princesa and goes into Nikita's house. At 3:45* P.M. *comes out with case. Goes to bus station where he was last night and takes seat on bus to Gerona and, before leaving, buys half-dozen newspapers. Bus leaves at 5:30* P.M. *Three agents of Brigade follow.*

Fri., Nov. 15—At 6:30 P.M. *Gorilla picked up again at Blue's garage in company of latter and three individuals who evidently work there. Gorilla and one of them go to El Pichi and return to shop. Gorilla strolls along sidewalk. Blue comes out and two of them go to Roig print shop, 96 Calle Villamarí. After 20 minutes of conversation they go to Cafetería Puerto Rico, but when a patrol car of this Headquarters arrives and two officers go into bar, Gorilla and Blue leave quickly.*

Several peaceful days passed: swimming at El Hornillo, eating at Constancio's bar, the slow translations of books, sitting peacefully with his mother at night. When the month of August was over, the fair closed and the orchestras went away. The days became noticeably shorter and when the drowsiness of midsummer had passed, the nights were soft and cool. On Saturdays, Antonio would go to sign in at the barracks and chat for a while with the lieutenant. The corporal gave him his censored mail: post cards from Ricardo and Artigas, French magazines, *Life en Español.* Uncle Gabriel's answer showed profound disillusionment at his conduct; in view of the failure of his education, he concluded, his wife and he had decided in the future to devote their efforts to the development of religious and missionary vocations. One day the postman brought him a telegram directly. It was from Dolores, and it said simply: GREETINGS ARRIVE FRIDAY.

That night, in the unarmed torpor of insomnia, the memory of his life as a university student tormented him until dawn. A multitude of disparate episodes were being shuffled in disorder in his brain: the escapade in Paris with Enrique, preparing Álvaro's documentary, the stormy trip to Yeste. His attempts at loss of roots and forgetfulness had tumbled down like a house of cards and, while he was making arrangements for Dolores to stay at the hotel and was making plans for her visit, the wait seemed very long to him.

He waited for her all morning leaning against the café by the highway, and when he spotted her, behind the wheel of her red Dauphine, he ran out into the middle of the road and made her slam on her brakes. Dolores looked even younger, with her short hair and her sleeveless blouse, and she looked at him for a few seconds, surprised and happy, before she gave him a hug.

"I didn't recognize you with that beard, I swear. Oh, you gave me such a scare. . . ."

"I'll shave it off if you want."

"No," she said. "It doesn't make any difference. The important thing is that you're out of jail."

The two of them sat down with emotion and, trying to hide it, they avoided looking directly at each other. Antonio had made himself comfortable beside her and he asked about Álvaro.

"He's still in Cuba," Dolores said. "I don't know when he'll be back."

"Does he write to you?"

"Once in a while. You know how he is. Sometimes months go by without a peep."

"Are you going to stay long?"

"No, just passing through. My parents have come back to Spain, did you hear?"

"I reserved a room for you at the hotel."

"That's impossible, Antonio. Mother's been expecting me for ten days. . . . I only stopped to give you a hug and chat for a few minutes."

His disappointment was obvious, because she stopped short and her eyes began to water suddenly.

"I'm sorry. You must think I'm terribly selfish."

"It's been months since I've been able to talk freely to anyone."

"I'm sorry," Dolores put her hand on his and squeezed it hard for a minute. "I'll stay in town overnight. We've got so many things to talk about that I don't know where to begin."

"Me either," Antonio said.

"People are looking at us as if we were dangerous criminals. . . . Where can we go?"

"Wherever you want to, as long as we don't leave town."

"Remember the last time I was here?" she said. "Why don't we go to the fishery?"

They went on down the main street to the port and past the level crossing they took the Cope road.

"My God," Dolores said. "It's been so long."

They had left the gray shacks behind and the engine was humming faintly in the midst of the opaque silence. The sun was shining with obsessive firmness on the slippery haunches of the hills, it was pouring out waves of blond light onto the motionless nape of the mountains. Life suddenly seemed to have withdrawn from the countryside, and as they disappeared into the haze, the knotty trunks of the olive trees, the plain and twisted fig trees, the pita palisades, the prickly pears gave a vague impression of cardboard artificiality. It was a mute and luminous desolation that brought on the idea of death, the death throes of a thirsty animal lost in the bed of a torrent, the hovering of an eagle over his prey, the heavy stench of a corpse rotting in the sun. Only wind, clouds of yellow dust, the twinkle of some dry and wrinkled rut, the muffled protest of the locusts.

They were on an arid and overcooked steppe, thirsty and hermetic, with white cisterns and houses in ruins, mules and water wheels, withered grass, beehives, plucked palm trees. All one had to do was raise his eyes for a moment to feel himself imprisoned between sky and stone, the useless guest of a mineral and empty universe that seemed to be a punishment of God and was the work of man—who had laid out that thankless land, who had opened the mouths of mines that were yawning at the sun with infinite boredom?—that anonymous work of several generations that had been abandoned one day for some obscure reason, already forgotten by the resigned inhabitants: a bald and hollow world without clouds or birds, as if isolated under a glass bell. The road was made of packed earth and the whirlwind of the car wrapped itself around a pair of Civil Guards on bicycles. The barracks house was sitting at the top of a turn, square and firm in the midst of that blurred decrepitude. The road went along the sea at times and, for stretches, the pebbly ground would give off a blinding glare.

Dolores was looking at the countryside with astonishment and at the crossroads of El Cantal, they turned right. The light was skipping across the surface of the water and the beach stretched out lazily between the rocky promontories. When they stopped, some women were coming along Indian file across the stubble fields, protecting themselves from the hot sun with musty and faded umbrellas. They must have been the families of the Civil Guards—some of them had children in their arms—and, when they got to the shore, they went into the water with their clothes on, still under the shade of their umbrellas, shouting and clutching their ample skirts, fearful that the wind would lift them. Dolores got undressed inside the car and Antonio fell face down onto the sand and closed his eyes.

The sun was beating down on the captive land and bouncing off the blue and quiet sea. Dolores swam energetically out toward the rocks and back to the beach again and she told him about her worries over Álvaro's difficult way of life.

"When he resigned from *France Presse* I was glad. I thought that an experience like the one in Cuba might shake him up a little. . . . Now I don't know what to think."

"Why don't the two of you come back to Spain?" Antonio asked.

Since she was silent, he turned his head away and absorbed himself in the examination of the trim, round hills, the remote and calcinated mountains, the colorless glow of the sky.

"What about you? How are you doing?"

"Just what you see," Antonio answered. "One day and then another and another. The calendar goes on but a person doesn't live. Waiting. Always waiting."

The place was a regular oven. Several times they dove into the water and stayed motionless in the light without stopping their conversation. When the sun relented, they went back to the car and on the sticky, burning seats continued on toward the tuna fishery.

The view of the steppe was stretched out again, parched and thirsty: patches of white clay, rocky ground, ocher hills, stony ravines, mountains crouching like animals in wait. The bulk of the cape walled off the horizon on the left and the fishermen's shacks huddled around the base, between the stubble fields and the sea. A rickety wooden float stuck out audaciously into the transparent blue water. The time before, Antonio and Álvaro had spent a week with the tuna fishermen and on Christmas day a post card written from La Calabardina had reached him in his cell in the Modelo prison.

The car went on, dodging the ruts in the road and, as it went along, chickens went scattering away. There were old people and children sitting outdoors and some of the curious got up to look. The ancient misery of the South was still flourishing, with its retinue of naked children, excrement, and flies, and the thought of visiting his friends with empty hands—Would they all die without knowing what it was, the only reason for which they had been born, the possibility they had conquered one day and which had soon been crushed, of being, of living, of finally proclaiming themselves, simply, to be men?—depressed him. But the young men had already recognized him, and when they got out of the car, they formed a circle around them.

"Antonio," a thin boy with dark features was talking to him. "Remember me?"

"Yes," he said, unsure.

"I'm Taranto's son. You were at my house when they were making the movie."

"Now I remember. You had a black dog and you wanted to be an admiral."

"That's right. The animal's not around any more. He went rabid and the sergeant had to put him away with a shot."

They walked toward the float, accompanied by all the children. The boy was walking head down, with his hands in his pockets. He said that the night before, in just one haul, the men had caught more than seventy-five pounds of tuna.

"What's become of our friends?" Antonio asked.

"The young ones have gone to Germany or to work in the fields like me. . . . Only the old men are left on the sea."

"What about your father, is he still with the fishery?"

"Yes. As soon as he finds out you're here, he'll come swimming over. A week doesn't go by but what he mentions you."

"And your mother?"

"The same as ever. Do you want to stop by and see her?"

Dolores answered for him, and they went to the first row of houses. The ever-present unemployed were gathered in the doorways, talking sadly under the shade of the *chambaos*. In the bar, a Civil Guard in shirt sleeves and sandals was playing dominoes with an old man. The children were still around them, watching their slightest movement, and Antonio heard one of them say, "They're the Frenchies who made the movies."

Taranto's wife seemed to know about the visit: she had put a lace scarf over her shoulders to cover her blouse that was soiled and patched and she draped it across coquettishly like a shawl. The children—four, five?—were stubbornly clinging to her skirts and when they came in, they all ran to hide behind a curtain across the bedroom door.

"Lord, what a racket," the woman said. "Can't you be quiet for one second?"

She had them sit down on two wicker chairs, while the boy and she made themselves comfortable on some boxes. On the walls the pictures and advertising calendars gave an unusual note of color. A child with dark skin would stick his head out behind the blanket from time to time and observe them with his white, laughing mouth, malicious and jovial like a mad puppet.

"Come over here this minute," his mother ordered. "Since

you're getting so brave, I'll give you something to be brave about."

The threat had no effect, and all during the conversation the blackened and mocking face would reappear and withdraw at intervals, as if moved by a spring. Unable to help it, Antonio was reliving the hectic preparations for the documentary, the discussions with the men, all those crowded days that had preceded the catastrophic expedition to Yeste. Taranto's wife served them glasses of sugar water and wanted to know if they had eaten.

"I'm not hungry, thanks."

"What about the young lady?"

"I'm not either."

"If you want to go to the fishing grounds we can rent a boat," the boy said. "My father can fry some fish on board."

"What's the sea like?"

"Didn't you notice?"

"My friend gets seasick very easily."

"Don't worry," the boy said. "It's as smooth as oil."

They said good-by to the mother—after promising her that they would stop by again on their way back—and Antonio agreed on a price with the owner of the boat. In the shack on the dock the women were hard at work opening the stomachs of fish and after washing them in a tub, they would put them in boxes of ice. Others were stretching out the roe and the insides in layers on the ground. The flies were buzzing avidly over the caked tuna blood and in the motionless air that seemed impregnated with light, there floated a smell of emptiness and death mixed with the discharge of brine, odors of pitch, and a faint emanation of tar.

Taranto's son had taken the oars, and Dolores and Antonio settled onto the seats. As they left the mooring, the village became reduced and foreshortened and the children waved good-by. The sun above was insistent, multiplied to the point of paroxysm on the serene sea and on the almost imperceptible winks and vibrations of the waves. As the boy rowed toward the cape, they saw the sun flicker on a buoy, dance on the wet sand like an elf: simultaneously it was blinking on a bottle, encircling the restless flight of a bird, unifying the sea with its diffuse reflection, losing its balance and capsizing into the water. With a motion of his chin, Taranto's son indicated the deserted beaches and said that in the fall they were going to start building a hotel for the Germans.

"They come here, and we go to their country. The sergeant says that nobody is ever happy with what he's got."

"The sun isn't worth any money, but with money you can even buy the sun," Antonio answered.

"From La Calabardina alone over ten have left. There's no life for young people on the sea. The day I get my papers, I'm going to grab the first train out and they won't see me for the dust."

"What does your father say?"

"He's old and he's given up already. I don't want to rot away like him. If I can get work in Barcelona, I'll settle down there."

"Have you done your military service?"

"No. It comes up in March." The boy stopped for a few seconds. "If you know somebody with a job to offer, drop him a line. Tell him that if he needs people two years from now, here I am, made to order."

As they went around the cape they saw the fishery boats—squat and black in the sea. Taranto's son was rowing hard, and with every stroke the boat seemed to take on a fresh thrust. With a hoarse voice he told them how some miners from El Cantal had rented a SEAT to go to Hamburg and at the German border the authorities of the Federal Republic had not let them cross because of some business about their papers. The owner of the car was in cahoots with the customs officials and had disappeared without a trace.

"Four thousand pesetas apiece just to come home empty-handed," he exclaimed. "I call somebody like that a bloodsucker."

"Why didn't they turn him in?"

"Guys like that always have good connections and always get off. . . . If it ever happened to me, I'd grab him right there and strangle him like a dog."

The cork floats showed the vertical placement of the nets and, when they got close to the boats, the men stood up to look and wave at them. They were the long-suffering fishermen of the Andalusian coast, dark-skinned and with faces that were wrinkled like old leather, without sou'westers or rubber boots, wearing the same rags their fathers had used, always smiling with peaceful gentleness under their berets and straw hats.

"We're in luck," the boy said. "I think they're going to haul in the nets."

In the head boat, the fishing master—head and shoulders covered with a sack—was scrutinizing the sea, leaning over a glass. The tuna fishermen were waiting expectantly and on a signal from their chief, the men working on the skiffs raised the sluice. Searching for a way back to the Atlantic—their path cut off by the neck of land—the tuna had gone into the successive compartments until they were all penned in the last cage, and as the sailors began to pull on the ropes and rigging attached to the bottom net, the boy backed water alongside the head boat and helped Dolores on board.

Taranto and Joseles along with the other fishermen from the film were repeating the scene that had been shot four years before, a little older and more worn out than at that time, already besieged by a death that was stirring up their features with an imprecise breath, furtive and anonymous, just like their very existence. Dolores and Antonio were at the head of the net, parallel to the sailors on the skiff, who, with concise, quick movements, were hauling in the net with the catch and dropping it back over the other side, slowly advancing toward the head boat. As they got close, some of them jumped into dinghies and also pulled amidst the deafening shouts.

Antonio was watching, absorbed in that picture of death: pulled along by the rising net, the tuna were spinning wildly and striking the surface with quick blows of their tails. Their merry-go-round was producing a noise that sounded like jollity and the water began to take on a timid rosy stain. The fishermen were tugging ceaselessly on their nets and when the bottom of the net emerged, the throes of the dying fish drowned out the guttural shouts of the men and the commands of the master. During the filming of the documentary, Álvaro had taken some shots of Joseles, stripped to the waist, with his face stained with tuna blood. That was how Joseles himself remembered it as he and Dolores sat on a roll of rope and he smoked a cigarette. The afternoon had turned lazy and ripe and all of a sudden everything was red: the tinted clouds, the ruddy hills, the melancholy union of eroded and ocher hills. A hesitant light was hovering in the air and the sky to the west was taking on the glow of a fire. Colored by the blood of the fish, the sun was shining in the sea, round as a copper plate.

"I didn't recognize you at first," Taranto said. "Are you letting your beard grow?"

"I think I'll keep it."

"If it weren't for the young lady, I would have taken you for a German." Taranto was smiling with a confused look on his face.

"We always talked about you at home and my wife used to say, 'That fellow's forgotten about us.' "

"Friends never forget," he replied.

"They told me you were in town, but I didn't believe it. . . . 'If Antonio's here,' I said to myself, 'he'll certainly come and see us . . .' "

"How are you doing?"

"It's always the same thing with poor people. Work and misery, misery and work. Some fine day we'll die and we won't even know it."

With the chore over, the men gathered around them and were interested in Álvaro and what had happened to the film. From what Antonio could gather, they knew about his exile: Gimpy gave him an endearing pat on the back and, after examining him closely, decided that they had treated him well.

"Who?"

"Your dear friends."

"Just acquaintances."

"A paid vacation at the expense of the State, you've got no complaints coming. I bet a lot of people are jealous of you."

"I'd rather be on the sea," Antonio answered.

"The sea?" Gimpy exclaimed. "We don't even know what color it is. In order to look at it, you have to live like a tourist."

The conversation followed the usual course: there were the same voices, the same words, the same bitter expression of a frustrated and useless existence—supposing that his time came one day, who would revive the dead?—. Then, on the way back to La Calabardina, the fishermen were making fun of Fats—the only bachelor in the group—and were making sarcastic remarks about the bad humor shown by Andaluz, as he sat in the prow of the Cooperative's motorboat eating a slice of bread away from the others.

"His wife is having her period and won't let him touch her."

"That's right. My sister-in-law heard them last night."

"When his better half won't have him, he's on the trail of any skirt he can find."

"And you can smell his maleness in his pants."

"Watch out, there are ladies present," Joseles pointed at Dolores.

"Well, you think about her, then, instead of getting me started."

When they reached La Calabardina, the half-light was erasing the colors. The village had come out to receive them with its children, its old people, and the onlookers grouped together on the wharf were watching the preparations for the unloading with obvious disappointment. "Not very much," the master said. "A thousand pounds, counting the *melbas* and bonitos."

Antonio had felt like going back to town right away, but Taranto insisted and they had to go home with him. Without the disguise of the sun, the ominous misery of the South was revealed in all its crudeness; while they were chatting on inside the house, anguish got control of him—a vague but intense feeling of having forgotten something of great importance, of having committed an irreparable and obscure mistake. When nightfall was complete, the first lamps were lit and the fishermen were going about the beach like shadows. A pair of Civil Guards were going along the shore with their lanterns. Dolores seemed as weary as he, and when they managed to take their leave of the family, Antonio clumsily took a bill out of his pocket and, conscious perhaps that his time would never come, Taranto accepted it. When they shook hands, in the brief interval when they dared to look each other in the eye, Antonio realized that they had both blushed from shame.

The way back was sad. Neither Dolores nor he could put their feelings together and, hunched over the wheel, she was driving nervously, shuddering at every pothole, dip, and bump. The Civil Guards stopped them twice to see the registration papers and when they shined their flashlights on them, the corporal recognized Antonio and asked him about the catch.

"Hurry on home," he added. "You shouldn't be driving around at these hours."

"The lieutenant gave me permission."

"If you have an accident, we'll be to blame. We don't want to be responsible."

On the terrace of the beach pavilion, as they had dinner beside the water, Antonio brought her up to date on the gossip about him that was going around Barcelona: one of the ones arrested—later given seven years because of his own confessions—claimed that Antonio had also turned in his companions—in spite of a complete lack of proof—some friends in the group had advised, against all logic, a policy of complete isolation. "Jail is a dangerous disease," he said. "When somebody catches it, everybody is afraid of contagion."

"I could have helped you."

"The only way you can help me is by going to bed with me."

"If you were talking seriously, I'd take you up on it."

"You're stupendous," Antonio said.

He took her warm hand in his and brushed it with his lips for an instant.

"Don't pay any attention to me," he added. "I was kidding when I said it."

Sat., Nov. 16—At 2:35 P.M. *Gorilla arrives in Barcelona, goes to Orión workshop, and reappears a few minutes later with Paws. Go to Las Antillas bar, spend 10 minutes, and go back to workshop. Quarter hour later Gorilla comes out with one we shall call Lambretto and a very young person. Go back to Las Antillas. At 4:40* P.M. *young man leaves them and Gorilla and Lambretto stay there talking a while at Pasaje Permanyer entrance. Finally take taxi and go to El Pichi where Blue is waiting. Separate at 8* P.M. *Gorilla takes streetcar to station and at 10:10* P.M. *is seen for last time in Grackle's house.*

Lambretto is Julio Marrodán López, 90 Calle Miquel y Badía, Barcelona. Native of Alicante, was tried in that city for underground activities on 9/4/56, released in December of same year. Has lived in Barcelona since then.

Sun., Nov. 17—At 3:50 P.M. *Gorilla gets off train and takes taxi to Las Antillas bar to meet Paws. Has coffee with him and after 20 minutes, with pad of paper and briefcase, goes to Blue's garage. Seeing that it is closed, goes to Pichi bar. Gypsy appears after half hour and when they leave bar, Gorilla is not carrying pad or brief case that Paws had given him. After strolling for a few minutes, both go home.*

Mon., Nov. 18—Peugeot 9089 MG 75, owned by Theo Batet Juanico, stops at 3 P.M. *at intersection of highway and Calle General Goded. Driven by its owner, whom we shall call Skimo. Gorilla gets out, goes into Grackle's house, returns to Peugeot, and goes in it to Barcelona, corner of Lauria and Avenida José Antonio. Gorilla walks around for a while, looking at shop windows, goes into leather-goods store and buys small object. At door of Orión workshop, Paws is waiting for him with a 12-year-old boy. Lambretto, Paws, and child accompany him to Las Antillas bar. Four of them stay there hour. When Lambretto leaves, Paws and child go back to workshop and Gorilla takes bus to MZA station. Takes Masnou train and at 8:30* P.M. *arrives Grackle's house.*

You had loved that land with the slow and arduous spasm of a volcano (you the incubus, she submissive, the rich offering of her misery as a precious dowry for you, joined together, you thought, into one single struggle against a ferocious fate).

Several years had passed since then, and if the hopeful and the ragged Yesterday had gone, Tomorrow had not yet arrived. The land is still there, under the identical and inexorable law; you are far away from it, distracted now, without any grief or awareness of your former overwhelming love. Fate has tricked you both. The obese North has laid eyes on it and an infamous swarm of speculators of the sun (the gold, the silver, and the rich lodes of its insides having been successively exhausted; the woods, the irrigated lands, the pastures; rebellion, pride, the love for man's freedom despoiled by the greedy usury of centuries) has fallen upon you (oh, new, baked Alaska) to accumulate and enrich themselves at the expense of your last free gift (the celestial billy goat, exciting and violent), to found colonies, chalets, snack bars, tourist spots, Andalusian taverns, hotels uglying the countryside without bettering its inhabitants: German experts, wise in the business of beaches, solitary fortune hunters, laureled and gray-haired combatants of the Crusade, and even an elegant lady wearing a Hindu turban and gravely reading the *Poem of the Cid* on the uncomfortable hump of a camel (a maiden on the other hump covers her ancestral lust with a faded parasol).

Land still poor and yet profaned; exhausted and parceled out; centuries old and orphaned still. Look at it, contemplate it. Engrave its image in your retina. The love that unites the two of you can only be said to have been. Is the fault yours or hers? Photographs are enough for you, and memory. Sun, mountains, sea, lizards, stone. Nothing else? Nothing. Corrosive pain. Good-by forever, good-by. Your detour takes you along new roads. You already know that you will never tread her soil again.

Tues., Nov. 19—Gorilla arrives Barcelona and goes to Orión workshop. Met by Lambretto, they have coffee in Las Antillas and talk for 30 minutes. Gorilla walks slowly for several blocks and at corner of Rocafort and Aragón makes contact with woman about 40 who is carrying two brown suitcases, weekend bag, and traveling bag filled with something heavy. It is exactly 12 o'clock. They walk along familiarly and Gorilla puts his hand on woman's shoulder five times. Go into bar on corner of Valencia and Avenida Roma, spend 15 minutes there, and separate at Aragón and Calabria. Gorilla lost in traffic. The woman, whom we shall call Gogo, goes to Calle Villadomat, has her hair done in beauty shop, takes taxi to Hotel Falcón.

At 2:45 P.M. *Gorilla picked up again with Gypsy on Calle Entenza. Gogo leaves hotel at 4:20* P.M.*, strolls, being very cautious, is lost and picked up again. Followed to Villadomat, next to beauty parlor where she had been in morning. At 6* P.M. *makes contact with Gorilla in Mariola bar. They reappear after 20 minutes and on sidewalk by slaughterhouses on Calle Villamarí and exchange objects that seem to be envelopes or small packages, something that cannot be ascertained because of dim light. She takes several small items she has bought from her purse and puts them in Gorilla's pocket. They say good-by. Gogo is lost, picked up again, and she walks through streets for over two hours. At 8:45* P.M. *she goes into Hotel Falcón and does not come out again.*

Wed., Nov. 20—Gogo leaves hotel and walks with great caution, turning around constantly, as if trying to make it impossible to be followed. Takes taxi to Museum of Romanic Art in Montjuich and wanders through it for hour or so. Several pictures taken of her. In afternoon strolls with same mistrust; lost and picked up again twice. At 6 P.M. *appears with bag and small suitcase, takes taxi to MZA station, buys first-class ticket to Cerbère. At 8:30* P.M. *takes train, followed by two agents.*

Investigation at Hotel Falcón shows that Gogo registered on Nov. 17 under name of Colette Audiard, native of Amiens, passport no. 671,380, issued in Paris, 9/01/58. Check of records at Police Headquarters shows that Colette Audiard arrived Barcelona 5/4/59 at Hotel Comercio and with same information at Hotel Zurbano, 1/7/60. Registered as Colette Audiard Lévy. Lévy must be maiden name. Possibility that Gogo has taken trips mentioned to make contact with Gorilla or some other delegate of the CC.

Note must be made of interception of letter on 18th addressed to Lucía Soler Villafranca, alias Grackle. Inside was piece of paper that said, "Charles Aurel, 20 Rue Vitrac, Perpignan, P. O., France." Sender was Miss María López, 35 Balién, Barcelona. Investigation revealed that living in house are Javier López Torres and his wife, Gloria Banús Aurel, and daughter María Dulce. As has been stated, it was visited by Gorilla and Grackle on 4th of current month.

The brief appearance of Dolores and her immediate departure suddenly revealed to him the depths of his loneliness. For a few days Antonio remained inert and as if asleep, reliving in an exhaustive way the details of the meeting, drinking the memory of a few intense and now vanished hours to the dregs. The rigid timetable and its rites that he had imposed upon himself could not remove a desolate impression of emptiness and abandonment. The tonic and luminous image of Dolores was an added test of himself, with its obligatory reference to the real world, and yet, in contrast, it pointed up the simple chance of his exile.

Every morning he would take the sun on the Hornillo beach and at noon he would bicycle over to Constancio's bar. After lunch he would go back home and translate, without great desire, a half-dozen pages of a book of verbose and spiritualist philosophy. At night he would dine with his mother and go back to the esplanade by the dock to chat with Fermín or play dominoes with the fishermen. Swimming had given him a tan, and with his full black beard, he had the proud and somewhat disdainful countenance of an extra disguised as an Arab chieftain.

On Saturdays, before he went to the beach, he would go to sign in at the barracks. The corporal would give him his mail and, on occasion, the lieutenant would come out and chat with him for a few minutes. Once he had asked his advice—he wanted to give a present to one of his superiors—and, with an affected casualness, he asked him if he knew of any biography of Admiral Méndez Núñez. Since Antonio had hesitated, he took him by the arm to his room and showed him his library.

"I have an excellent book on Mary Stuart. Do you know it?"

"No."

"A man with problems, like you, should drop by when some of us get together sometimes. The doctor and the teacher are very interested in you, Ramírez. They're open-minded people. You can say anything you want when you're with them."

"That's very kind of you, lieutenant."

"In the Casino I'm just another civilian, understand? The uniform you wear is one thing, but your personal ideas are something else again. When I get home and take off my uniform, I like to do a little thinking of my own," he was stroking the back of a collection of *Selected Lives* and he stopped. "After all, why insist? You know as well as I do that in this fine country there's no such thing as free speech."

The lieutenant was smiling ironically; Antonio was smiling too, and they shook hands. As he crossed the courtyard of the barracks, he made a ball out of the letters, and when he got to the road, he headed toward town and threw it down a sewer.

Autumn had begun to come on cautiously. The number of outsiders was getting smaller, as was obvious, and the ones who lingered rarely left the boundaries of the beach pavilion, or went directly to the coffeehouses on the main street. The Cadillac of the Consul in Alexandria still came to the deserted esplanade and one night, with a great backdrop of secrecy, Constancio revealed to Antonio that Don Gonzalo's family and the Aguileras planned to stay in town until Christmas.

"The Consul's oldest daughter and Gonzalito are involved," he said. "In the Casino there are rumors of a wedding."

"A pair of lovey-dovies, fine for people who have no trouble finding a place to live," Fermín commented.

"Who can tell," the man from the weather station commented. "Maybe they won't be able to find one that suits them."

On one of his nocturnal wanderings, Antonio bumped into the Falange doctor. He was sitting around in the square with a group of friends and when he saw him, he came over and gave him a big hug.

"At last I've got my hands on you, Ramírez," he exclaimed. "How did they ever get you to hide out in such a small place?"

"The world isn't a teacup, doctor."

"You run away as if they were after your head. . . . Have you got something against us?"

Antonio succinctly explained his timetable, and promised to come by the Casino one day, but the doctor protested and laid a hand with rings on his shoulder.

"No, sir. You're not going to get away just like that, you hear? Right this minute you're coming home to dinner with me."

"Thank you very much, but . . ."

"I won't accept any excuses. My wife is dying to meet you. You'll be right at home with us."

"I'm really unpresentable." He showed him his wrinkled jacket, his faded and dirty pants. "If you want, some other time. . . ."

"I'm pretty sloppy myself. I said today, and that's that."

There was no way out. The doctor took his arm and with his free hand he ceremoniously greeted the friends they passed as he lowered his voice and told him about the latest happenings in town and tried to get what he was doing out of him.

"I passed you sometime back, but I didn't want to bother you because you had someone with you. . . ."

"I don't remember, doctor."

"Yes, a dark girl, a real dish. . . . You were getting out of a car, am I right? A Dauphine with French plates. . . ."

"She's the wife of a good friend of mine," Antonio explained. "Her parents live in Málaga and she stopped off on the way to see me."

"Didn't you go to the fishery?"

"How the devil did you know that?"

"I was in La Calabardina yesterday with Don Gonzalo and they told me."

"With Don Gonzalo?"

"He's just bought the controlling shares on the board of the Cooperative. A master stroke, a born speculator. . . . I'll tell you about it some time."

They walked down the Calle Mayor among the compact mass of idlers and a little before the service station, the doctor stopped in front of a two-story house with dormer windows and balcony railings painted black.

"This is your house, Ramírez. I hope that in the future you'll decide to come see us without having to be begged."

Antonio nodded his assent. The doctor had brought him into a parlor off the hallway and went to tell his wife. While he was examining the family portraits under the gaze of rough and rather ghostly pieces of furniture, he heard some whispering followed by the sound of hurried steps. Someone had drawn the curtain along the hallway and the small head of a little girl peeped out for a moment and stared at him. After a few minutes the doctor returned with a silver tray and two glasses. There was a trace of annoyance on his face.

"All we have is a bottle of Malvasia," he said. "Shall I send the maid out to the store?"

"This is fine, doctor."

"Normally we only drink during meals. . . . Or would you rather I got you an apéritif?"

The woman appeared suddenly, white and chubby. After she had shaken hands with Antonio, she settled into a rocking chair and looked at him in silence with an educated curiosity, as if he were an unknown and unclassified species of insect.

"Here's the famous Ramírez. One of the few nonconformists still left in Spain. . . ."

"Excuse the way I look. Your husband made me come this way."

"We're a little bohemian in my family too," the doctor said. "The teacher often says: 'You people live like artists,' isn't that right, sweet?"

"Can I serve you a little wine?" the wife asked.

Antonio smiled in a friendly way, and had a sip of the dark and sticky liquid. Ever since he had come into the house, he felt himself the object of a voluntary confinement and he was sorry that he was not brave enough to fit the spirit and escape, using any old excuse that came to mind. The doctor had brought the conversation around to politics, and while his wife filled Antonio's glass for the second time, he said with a disillusioned tone, that experience and age had made a skeptic out of him.

"The men of my generation aren't cowards, Ramírez. We're cautious because we have reason to be. Life has dealt us many cruel blows, and we've had plenty of experience, understand?"

"Yes."

"Being a redeemer doesn't set things straight. They're stronger than you and I and they always win. Unless you have the vocation of a martyr, you have to jump through the hoop. Pardon me if I'm offending you, but you haven't been very reasonable in your conduct. A person can make the appearance of submitting, like me, but inside he can be free." He vacillated. "I don't know whether I'm making myself clear."

"Perfectly."

"I too, in my youth, wanted to oppose injustice: social conscience and all that. Save your neighbor. . . . Until one day I realized that my neighbor was quite content with his lot, and he didn't care a fig about saving himself. . . . Would you like some more wine?"

"Just a bit, thanks."

"What this country needs is a breed of men with enterprise, ability, and initiative, people who know how to make money flow; let them take good care of it and they'll make it bear fruit. . . . They're the ones who promote the progress of a country, not romantics like you and me. . . . A few minutes ago I was talking to you about Don Gonzalo, remember?"

"Yes."

"He's an example of what I've been talking about. I know very well that jealous people have probably told you a lot of gossip: that his fortune has mysterious origins, that he got rich on the black market. . . . Well, then, even supposing that those tales were true, the fact isn't important, not at all. What counts is the extraordinary businessman we have today: he and nobody else was able to build up an industry in this town, make land more valuable, attract tourists. If people are better off, they owe it to Don Gonzalo before anything else. You can't feed people on words. . . . Do you want some more to drink?"

"Thank you."

"What most attracts my attention in a person of his type is his powerful ability for invention. . . . Are you surprised at what I'm saying? . . . Don Gonzalo is a creator of ideas above all, a man open to every innovation and yearning; a pragmatist who knows how to be at ease in any situation or event. The other day he was speaking about you, no less, and he said to me: 'Let a person be a communist, anarchist, or anything he feels like being, it's all the same to me. What I can't forgive is failure. If I had known Stalin, I'm sure that we would have got along fine. But Stalin is one thing and the people who supported him another. The world belongs and always will belong to the clever.' "

"I see that you like the wine," his wife said as she poured it for him.

"I also think that he's a profoundly human type. The masses, from the outside, judge him harshly, but they're wrong. Those of us who've had the pleasure of dealing with him, know an aspect of his life that the others don't even suspect: that of a father devoted to his wife and children, attentive and hospitable with his guests. . . . On some occasions, I've seen outstanding traits of goodness in him, quite moving. . . . I don't know whether you know it or not, but every month he sends a check to an orphanage in Murcia. His generosity has no limits, believe me."

"My, you really can drink."

When dinner was over, Antonio felt drunk, and the doctor's discourse reached him wrapped in an alcoholic and foggy halo that made it uniform and took the color out of it. The wife continued scrutinizing him with frigid curiosity, and when the three of them got up from the table to have coffee, he invented an important appointment and took his leave.

The air filled his lungs, fresh and restoring, like a caress. The people had gone to bed early and the terraces of the bars were deserted. The town looked to him like a gigantic cemetery, where every window was a tomb, every building the mausoleum of a dream or hope. Days did not pass for the country and they, its children, were terrifyingly fleeting. The syrupy dregs of the wine were confusing his thoughts: where could he go? what could he do? how could he avenge himself? A barbarian and barren homeland, how many generations of his breed would still be frustrated? for how many days, weeks, months, years would it still be uninhabitable? He crossed the square opposite the *Mater Dolorosa* carved by Salcillo. The sad god of his ancestors was watching over the emptiness with his extended dead arms. Insensible and shut off from the pain of men, he was obscenely nourishing himself like a leech on their useless prayers. Antonio started up a steep alley and, after a way, he stopped and asked a young man for the address of a prostitute.

"The second corner on the right, buddy. It's the little house with the lamp."

He knocked at the door and in a while a robust girl with rosy cheeks, chestnut hair, and red-painted lips came out. When she saw him, she had an impulse to laugh and raised her hand to her mouth. When she bolted the door behind them, she lowered her head and looked at the floor, timid and seeming ashamed.

"What's the matter?" Antonio asked.

"Nothing," she stammered. "All of a sudden like that, it gave me a start."

"Because of the beard?"

"I know who you are and why you're in town. . . . The other day I saw you from a distance, with another man. . . . I never thought that . . ."

"What did you think?"

"I don't know. . . . When they told me about you I didn't imagine that one day I'd see you in my house . . ." the girl was smiling, disturbed. "Gosh, it's even hard for me to look at you. . . ."

"I didn't come here for you to look at me."

"No."

"Come on, do a good job at what you're supposed to do, and shut up."

He sat on the edge of the bed and unbuttoned his pants as he drew her toward him brutally and made her kneel at his feet. It was a way of dying too, of losing himself in the night for an instant. The woman's head was rising and falling between his legs with a rhythm that was intense and stupefying at the same time, and Antonio fell backward with his hands under the nape of his neck and his gaze fixed on the strip of flypaper that—like an immense spider that threatened everything—was swinging softly from the ceiling, very softly.

Thurs., Nov. 21—Gorilla picked up at 9:30 A.M. *At 12:30* P.M. *enters Pichi bar, where Gypsy and Blue are already. Three leave at 12:55* P.M. *and on Calle Viladomat, Gypsy stops to speak with person we shall call Himalaya. Separate after five minutes and Himalaya gets into SEAT 600, license B147,201. Gypsy and Blue are lost. Gorilla goes to MZA station and mails letter. Precautions taken to recover it, and in said letter are found some commercially printed matter in name of Carlos Aurel, 20 Rue Vitrac, Perpignan, formerly residing at 8 Almogávares, Premiá de Mar. Agents who trailed Gogo report she crossed border without incident and they were able to photograph her passport.*

Fri., Nov. 22—Gorilla leaves at 9:15 A.M. *and goes to Blue's garage. Go to Pichi bar together. Separate, and Gorilla walks up Entenza toward Infanta Carlota and the Sarriá highway. At 11:45* A.M. *meets Gypsy in Ruedo bar. Both walk along Londres and at the corner of Urgel make contact with someone we shall call Blacky: 35 years old, 5′ 5″, thin, black hair. Go to Colombia bar. Blacky takes piece of paper out of brief case and shows it to Gorilla. Blacky is heard to say: "One's just as good as a whole lot." Split up at 2:30* P.M. *Blacky goes to 390 Travesera de las Corts. Gypsy and Gorilla stay together. Stop for lunch in restaurant. Gorilla gives Gypsy small black brief case. Go slowly down*

Urgel and go to El Pichi. When they go in, Blue is having coffee with Curly. At 5 P.M. *Gorilla and Gypsy leave bar and at 5:15* P.M. *Curly and Blue. Blue goes to his garage, Curly toward Avenida José Antonio. Lost in traffic a few minutes later.*

Tues., Nov. 26—At 8:30 A.M. *Gorilla and Grackle take taxi with several suitcases to 8 Almogávares, Premiá de Mar, former home of Carlos Aurel. Gorilla gets on train two hours later with small, light-colored brief case and on Plaza Palacio takes taxi to Blue's garage. Goes to Pichi bar with latter, come out after five minutes and Gorilla goes to corner of Rocafort and Aragón. As soon as he gets there, a Peugeot, license 4703 RL 5, stops beside him. It is 12:01* P.M. *Man and woman get out of car, first with a foreign look, whom we shall call Cocteau and Escuchi respectively. Escuchi hugs and kisses Gorilla. Cocteau shakes his hand, gets into car and takes out suitcase. The light-colored brief case must have stayed inside, because it is not seen again. Escuchi and Gorilla hail cab and take suitcase to Gypsy's. Cocteau walks around downtown as if he knew city well and has drink in Estudiantil bar after parking car beside El Águila department store.*

At 3:30 P.M. *Gorilla goes to Blue's garage. Cocteau appears and Blue has him bring car into garage and closes metal street door. Gorilla and Cocteau inside for half an hour while Blue keeps watch outside. Then Cocteau and Gorilla leave in car and go toward Plaza España and Paralelo, lost in traffic a little later.*

Wed., Nov. 27—Escuchi identified as Eulalia Miralles Badía, arrested in 1947 and turned over to Special Tribunal for suppression of freemasonry and communism for having done liaison work for PSUC; released in 1951, goes to France two years later. Cocteau is Roger Daniel Halévy, born in Oran, 1916, French nationality, passport No. 847,321, issued Paris, 7/15/56, ascertained he was at Hotel Regina in Barcelona on 4/14/60, making us suppose that his presence in our city even then was for the accomplishment of some underground mission.

With your friends caught up in the turmoil of politics, what were you doing?

The letter of introduction from a well-known South American Maecenas had opened the doors of the Parisian left-wing intelligentsia for you, and the welcome extended by that group of generous men and women had subtly flattered your vanity. You remembered your first meeting with Maurice Tessier (ascetic face, frank look, the modest gestures of a Roman prelate) in the offices of an important publisher on the Left Bank (the floor carpeted with moquette, the bookcases filled with expensively bound volumes, an attractive blond secretary leaning over her Remington), and the feeling that had paralyzed you then as you faced the passionate interest of your interviewer in what you had to say, was being revived by you now (taking advantage of a brief pause in Antonio's detailed account) with an indulgent smile. (The Spanish cause is not as fashionable as before, and Tessier and his friends, you say to yourself, are no doubt working for the rebels in Angola and Vietnam.)

After an extensive conversation, he had given a telephone number to his secretary and was waiting for the girl's signal before picking up his receiver: "*Allô . . . Josette?*" Absorbed, you were examining the tabernacle of that temple of culture, sanctified by the mute presence of many writers whom you had passionately admired in your youth and who, now enthroned in the pantheon of the immortals, were still there, watching over the order and good management of the House, scrutinizing intruders and guests from the austere position of their photographs. "*Oui. C'est un jeune intellectuel de Barcelone. . . . Un garçon tout à fait révolté contre le Régime. . . . Son expérience est des plus intéressante. . . . Oui, il parle français. . . . Nous pouvons lui organiser une rencontre avec les Cazalis. . . .*" Tessier was speaking with a well-modulated voice and the grave faces of the masters' photographs on the wall seemed to be in remote agreement with his words, giving life to their frozen and inert expressions with the fleeting halo of a smile or a satisfied and swift wink of intelligence.

You went out onto the street dizzy with happiness, still overwhelmed by the hypnotic influence of that autonomous and coveted universe, with the glowing feeling that you had the key to the door and a lifetime seat at the banquet. (Your actor's instinct had somewhat seasoned the story of your experience, and listening to the crises of your incipient autobiography, you had fallen into the trap of your own sentimental trick.)

A few days later (it was around the middle of September, the leaves of the trees were already turning yellow), you went up the carpeted stairs that led to the Tessiers' apartment and you rang the bell as your heart pounded. The master of the house had received you with a smile of complicity and had presented you to the guests seated around the dining-room table one by one: Bernard Cazalis and his wife Léone, the critic Robert Nouveau, Marie Pierre Dreyfuss, Gérard Bondy, and others whose names you had forgotten, all related by a vague and subtle family air, most of them tanned, as you found out later, by the sun and sea of their recent vacations in Spain.

"I spoke to Cazalis about you," Tessier whispered in French, taking you discreetly by the arm. "He's an old surrealist; he still is, even though he broke with Breton's group after the war. He also worked in the Party for two years and he's written quite a fine account of that experience. . . . Right now he's especially interested in Oriental philosophy. . . . Have you seen his article on Michaux and the world of drugs?"

"No."

"It's quite a remarkable piece. . . . Last month my friend went to Spain with his wife, and he's come back all upset. He'd like to do something, the way we all would, but we obviously need the help of the Spaniards. . . . What possibilities do you see for outside help for your Resistance movement?"

Eight years had passed since then, but the memory of your dinner in the austere building on the Rue Solferino was still prowling around, precise and neat, in your capricious memory: the rectangular table, the *salade niçoise* and the *canard aux Olives,* your analysis of the intellectual evolution of Spanish youth and the wild consumption of Beaujolais.

"So, according to what you say, communism has a good hold on the new generation of students. . . ."

". . ."

"It's quite normal. I would go even further and say that it's even absolutely necessary. . . . Experience is not inherited. Young people have to learn for themselves, understand?"

". . ."

"Take heart, my dear friend. We've all been along the same path. It's a requirement that none of us has been able to escape. . . ."

Cazalis was speaking in a relaxed way, watching you with his face of a snake charmer, astronomer, or mandarin, as his thin hands delicately raised the glass of wine and his blue eyes closed you in with clinical and implacable precision.

"What can we do for you? . . . You understand, I imagine,

the role of the Popular Front during the Spanish Civil War. . . . A betrayal that we paid for dearly, *hélas!* . . . We all feel a little to blame. . . . The survival of such a regime in 1955 is really unthinkable. It's a scandal in the real meaning of the word and the scandal must come to an end. . . . We saw Franco on the beach at San Sebastián. We were about forty feet away from him and nobody searched us. . . . An assassination seemed quite possible. All that would be needed would be getting together with a group of Spaniards. Maybe you can give us some useful information. . . ."

The people around the table were examining you attentively, and you were trying to explain the objectives and projects of your friends: you spoke of efforts at propaganda, seminars, informative movie clubs. When you had finished your exposition, the bottles of Beaujolais were empty, and Josette Tessier went to get some more from the rack. There was a brief silence.

"If I understand you correctly, you're still in a preparatory stage," Cazalis said softly.

"Oui, c'est ça."

"You're not in contact with any of the more radical groups?"

"Non, pas encore."

"But I'm right in thinking that they do exist, am I not?"

"Sans doute."

"There's the problem. How to contact them? Do you know of any sort of connection to reach them?"

The looks encircled you again, and you explained that the probabilities for the success of such a violent action seemed remote to you. The country was still living under the impact of the Civil War that had been lost and the majority of political groups were adapting their strategy to the attainment of long-range peaceful objectives. They interrupted you, all in French.

"Et les anarchistes?"

"They too."

"During my trip to Spain I was able to ascertain that the working class had not gone beyond the stage of economic demands," Marie Dreyfuss said. "How will you be able to make their protests have a revolutionary content?"

"That's the problem of our times," Tessier said. "Once the inborn urgency of misery is blunted, the proletariat tends to go to sleep. It's easy to see the results of trade-union paternalism in France. We no longer have a working class."

"The working class exists, but it's been hoodwinked," Cazalis said. "Political cadres have been proven incapable of offering them a total revolutionary strategy. That's why the struggle of the Spanish people interests us. Our awakening can only come from you."

"Hundreds of thousands of Frenchmen go to Spain every year. Let's say, using the most conservative estimate, that ten per cent of them are anti-Franco. . . . I'm sure that they would be quite happy to furnish any kind of help to the boys in the Spanish Resistance."

"What kind of help?" Nouveau asked. "Weapons? Propaganda?"

"That's for the Spaniards to tell us."

"I could have brought in a whole arsenal in the trunk of my car," Gérard Bondy said. "The cops didn't even open it."

"Is it easy to get weapons in Spain?"

"All you would have to do would be to ask us for anything you needed, and we could see that you got it. Especially in summer. The only problem then would be to space our vacations."

The wine had run out again. Josette Tessier went back to the supply, while the people at the table wisely loosened their ties and rolled up their shirt sleeves.

"Have you any continuous contact with the Portuguese patriots?"

"My brother was in Estoril last summer. The condition of the peasant masses is even worse, it seems, than in Spain. According to him, a revolutionary awakening could happen during the coming months."

"Marc also told us about an Aid Committee for the Greek Communists. Do you know about it? It might be useful to work out a common plan of action for Spain, Portugal, and Greece. . . ."

"Do you know the Committee's address?"

"I've got it in my wallet. Favre, Colette Marchand, and the Perraults are on it." Cazalis slowly raised his glass of wine and conceded it a grave and intense look. "They're friends with strong intellectual requirements, dedicated above all to the study of the problem of the Third World. There are ex-Catholics, ex-Communists, surrealists, followers of Naville. . . . They've been through all the churches and from that they've maintained an extreme lucidity, a perennial questioning of all values. . . ."

"What we need above all is a general exchange of ideas with other Committees," Robert Nouveau said. "If we want to be effective, we have to find a valid tactic for each one of the Resistance movements without losing sight, of course, of their deeper unity."

"I'll take care of Marc and his Greeks. . . . Álvaro can get in touch with the Spaniards. . . . Who'll take care of contacts with the Portuguese? . . ."

Josette Tessier reappeared with a fresh supply of wine. Across the table Gérard Bondy was praising Chamaco and Marie Dreyfuss was deploring the excessive use of olive oil on the part of Spanish chefs. Cazalis quietly intervened.

"After the rebuff of the Liberation, it's impossible for the revolutionary spirit to come to us from outside. This is the realm of the Left, but what a Left! A suspicious, unstable, composite, inconsistent Left, preyed upon by all sorts of contradictions. . . . A respectable Left. A Left that doesn't dare call itself by name."

"Our vacation in Spain brought us a little hope, a little fresh air. In your country, at least, the word freedom means something quite definite. Here it's lost its meaning. Everyone is thought to be free and we live in the worst kind of alienation."

"You may not realize it, but the fact is undeniable. You others, you Spaniards are luckier than we are. You keep your revolt intact while we, what could we revolt against? It's all of France itself that we dislike."

"Luckily we still have our colonies and the possibility of working for the various Liberation movements. . . . But what can we do, after all? Get into politics? What difference is there really between a Pinay and a Mendès?"

"I spent a few days in Málaga," Gérard Bondy said in a calm voice. "I got the impression that it would only take a few people and very little time to organize an armed uprising against the Regime."

"My wife and I came to the same conclusion in Catalonia. . . . A revolutionary situation going to waste, a popular drive being squandered because there isn't any stronger line of combat. . . ."

"If the Spanish Resistance needs us, tell your friends that we're ready to take up arms again."

"We've kept in touch with some of the former Maquis. Would you like to meet them?"

Still marveling at the cordiality of your reception, you were absorbed in some exquisite enchanted isle, convinced that you had the password and the key to the truth in your hands, the exalted possibility of supporting the noble struggle of your friends from outside, of contributing effectively to the worthy solution of all the ills of Spain: the unconditional help of French intellectuals, a common strategy with other European Resistance movements, the eventuality of a popular armed uprising were still being shuffled in your head a week later when, for the second time, you climbed the carpeted stairway in the building on the Rue Solferino and rang the bell. Robert Nouveau had taken on the responsibility for the exploratory meeting with the Greeks and the Portuguese, and you had sent Antonio a letter in code, filling him in on the progress of your measures and telling him about the creation of an Aid Committee for the acquisition and transport of arms and propaganda.

Tessier courteously shook hands with you and led you into the living room. A black cat was curled up asleep on the sofa. The phonograph was softly playing *La leçon des Ténèbres* by Couperin.

"Robert Nouveau asked me to give you his excuses," he said. "Have you heard the news?"

"What news?"

"The Algerian National Liberation Front has opened up a new terrorist attack against the French forces."

He sat down opposite you in an easy chair and poured two glasses of whisky.

"We were advised the day before yesterday by one of the leaders. . . . We have to organize a campaign supporting their action in the press right away. Nouveau and I have drawn up an appeal to public opinion which Cazalis has at the moment."

The harsh sound of the telephone interrupted him. You got up from your chair and examined the books lined up on the shelves of the bookcase. The tenor's voice was vibrating softly on the other side of the room. Tessier had sat down on an arm of the sofa and was staring out the window.

"An Algerian? . . . Tell him to come to my place. . . . No, I won't budge. . . . The writing? . . . It was mostly Nouveau's work. . . . What do you think of it? . . . Too many adjectives, *n'est-ce pas?* . . . Good, you can send me a copy at home. . . . *D'accord*. . . . Yes, I'll let you know as soon as he gets here."

When he hung up, you went back to your chair and he lit a cigarette and smiled softly at you.

"We've practically had no sleep for forty-eight hours. I've just been telling my wife: I feel a little the way I did when I joined the Resistance. . . ."

The doorbell rang then, and Tessier excused himself with a gesture. After a few minutes he returned in the company of a man and two women whom you did not know. After the introductions there was a long silence.

"You'll have to excuse me, but I have to take up an urgent problem with these friends. If you can wait for a little while . . ."

"Maybe it would be better if I came back another time," you suggested.

"As you wish, my dear friend. All you have to do is call me and I'll set up a meeting with Nouveau for you."

"What date would be best for you?"

"What about next week? You name the day, it doesn't matter which one. I'm home every morning."

He had taken leave of you with an expression that was both absent and weary and, disappointed at the failure of the meeting, you waited voluntarily for a few days before deciding to call. He answered the phone himself, with a surprised and friendly voice and when you reminded him of the projected discussion with the Greeks and the Portuguese, he explained gravely that Nouveau was on a trip to Algeria and would not return to Paris for a few weeks. He said that the Committee of Intellectuals in sympathy with the Algerian people was to meet in Cazalis's home and he promised to let you know the day and time at an opportune moment so that you could come. According to what you thought you remembered, he did not mention Spain.

You telephoned him two other times before you came to the realization that your country's problems had abandoned the sphere of his preoccupations for good. The vicissitudes of the war in Algeria, the dramatic events in Suez, Hungary, and Poland were completely occupying the energies of the group, while the quixotic struggle of Antonio and your friends against Spain's obtuse and reactionary society and its omnipotent guardians was being asphyxiated in the smoke, mud, and lies of your desolate and useless Years of Peace. As for Gérard Bondy—split off from the others because of political and personal reasons—he had gone to spend several months in Málaga without having organized, as he had planned, his armed insurrection with the help of a group of friends. During his stay in the city, he limited himself to writing a commercial novel with metaphysical pretensions and when he returned to Paris he was received in triumph by the bourgeois critics and awarded the Goncourt Prize.

Thurs., Nov. 27—Gorilla leaves at 9:20 A.M. *In Pichi bar meets Gypsy and another individual we shall call Hasdrubal. The three walk along Entenza and as they pass an agent, he hears Gorilla say to the others: "Well, you know I have complete confidence in you." They return to Pichi, Gorilla leaves, goes to Escocés bar, makes contact with another subject who has a package wrapped in a newspaper and whom we shall call Viti. Go to corner of Viladomat and Consejo de Ciento, and Viti is lost. Gorilla returns to Pichi with package, talks with Gypsy and Hasdrubal. Five minutes later leaves with Gypsy and before they separate, gives him package. Gorilla goes to No. 35 Bailén and after hour reappears with Grackle and Escuchi. Grackle leaves them at Plaza de Tetuán. Gorilla and Escuchi look into Paquito bar. Gypsy is at bar with 33⅓ microgroove record he had bought at Belter's. Gives it to Gorilla, pays his bill and leaves. Other two continue walking along San Juan and at the corner of Ronda San Pedro make contact with Viti, who is now carrying large green suitcase that seems quite heavy. Gorilla takes it and gives record to Viti. Latter hails taxi and disappears.*

Hasdrubal identified as Francisco Peiró Colomer, 37 Calle Oficios, Barcelona, no previous record.

Mon., Dec. 1—Gorilla leaves at 9:45 A.M. *and goes to Gypsy's home. Reappears after 10 minutes and takes bus to Orión workshop. Lambretto and Paws accompany him to Las Antillas bar. Spend half-hour there and separate. Gorilla takes streetcar to Entenza, goes into Mariola bar as if looking for someone, stops by Blue's garage. Goes back to Gypsy's house and at 4:10* P.M. *goes with him to Vergara subway entrance of FF.CC. Catalanes. Moments later they make contact with Hannibal and another person we shall call Codeso. Four go up Balmes, walking in the following order: Gorilla with Hannibal and Gypsy with Codeso. Near seminary, Gorilla opens package that Gypsy is carrying and explains contents to Hannibal. Return to Vergara and separate. At 6:40* P.M.*, Gorilla and Gypsy go to Blue's garage and three go to Pichi. Speak for 20 minutes and separate. Gorilla returns to Grackle's.*

Hannibal identified as Justo Marín Gubern, 7 Calle Madrigal,

Sabadell. Is labor union representative and holds passport No. 78,562, issued Feb. 1960.

Tues., Dec. 2—Gorilla leaves home without being seen. Picked up at 12 M. on Rocafort, heading toward place where on previous Tuesdays made contact with Gogo, Cocteau, and Escuchi. Not seeing anyone, goes to Pichi bar where Gypsy and Blue are waiting. Goes back alone to corner of Rocafort and Aragón and keeps on looking at place of previous contacts. In afternoon reappears with Escuchi, and first one, then other goes past corner several times without finding contact. We must add that when Escuchi arrived, she was talking to herself and was heard to say: "Yes, this is the street. . . . Of course it is," and at that moment, to be absolutely sure, she casually asked one of the men who had her under surveillance: "Excuse me, but is this the Calle Rocafort?" At 5 P.M. *they take taxi and go to MZA station. Reach Grackle's at 8:20* P.M. *and surveillance lifted at 9* P.M.

From then on he was able to abandon himself to his ghosts again, swim in the cold waters of El Hornillo, fuck with the prostitute cloistered on the hill, translate pages and pages of grave metaphysics, chat on and on with the fishermen in Constancio's bar. He was moving about in an ambiguous universe where words had lost their primitive meaning and had assumed fleeting and changing intentions, like light clouds blown by the wind. Freedom and imprisonment were mixed together in an imprecise reality and sometimes he thought it impossible to get out from among the gears. Time went on in an undefined way and Antonio prolonged himself with it, with destructive certainty of some useless event—as unjustifiable and empty as any of his fellow countrymen.

The prostitute had forgiven him his brusqueness on that first day, and every night her strong, firm body would receive his with disciplined softness. After a session like all the others, monotonous and repetitious, it was comforting to sink between her thighs and bite the breasts she tamely offered him, forgetting the ticking of the clock for a few minutes. Habits had become rites and when the weather grew worse toward the end of October and he had to give up his swimming, Antonio continued his bicycle trips and, sitting on a promontory across from the island of El Fraile, for hours on end he would contemplate the apprehensive flight of the small birds, the lazy and deserted beaches, the sky and the sea locked in a gray embrace.

On All Saints' Day he had spent the afternoon in Constancio's bar playing dominoes with the fishermen and, after telling his mother, he invited Fermín to have dinner with him.

"How about the beach pavilion?" Antonio asked.

"Anything you say," Fermín replied. "It's all the same to me."

They crossed the Calle Mayor toward the Paseo. The last of the summer people had disappeared weeks before with their nurses and children, and the neon signs were glowing faintly and sadly. The restaurant of the club had not changed since the days of his adventure with Lolita. As they sat in a corner of the room—the customers had not arrived yet and the waiters were drifting about like shadows—Antonio noticed a table with a dozen places set, in the center of which a superb bouquet of flowers was showing itself off. When he took their order, the waiter told them that it had been reserved by Don Gonzalo.

"I'll bet anything it has something to do with an engagement," Fermín said. "This morning the turtledoves went to church and my mother says they were arm in arm like two sweethearts."

"Something's up, yes sir," the waiter said. "Don Gonzalo came by in person to arrange the dinner and he had twelve bottles of champagne put on ice."

"Afterward, the gossips will say that it's a trick on the part of the parents," Fermín sighed. "Good Lord, what a cruel world it is."

The wine was Valdepeñas claret and it allowed itself to be drunk with deceptive ease. Fermín was joking about the fortunes of the respective families and Antonio was listening to him in silence, ready to explode. The beautiful insolence of the flowers exasperated him. When the guests arrived, he had emptied the bottle and he ordered another one.

"Shall we go?" Fermín proposed.

"Wait a few minutes."

Don Gonzalo was there with his wife and son, and the Spanish Consul in Alexandria with his wife and two girls. There were also a half-dozen guests, dressed in white from head to toe, and Antonio spotted the Falange doctor among them, circumspect and pompous, like a happy flower. The waiters were fluttering about the table and at Don Gonzalo's signal, the chef came over with a tray of antipasto.

"They really do know how to live," Fermín muttered.

Antonio was drinking the wine from the second bottle without pause and he decided to stay on. One of the people at the table was telling a funny story and there was a chorus of shouts. "Wonderful, wonderful," a female voice exclaimed. The doctor had sat down with his back to them, a little bit away from Don Gonzalo, and suddenly he leaned over the woman in between them to whisper a secret in his ear.

"Watch out, they're talking about you."

Don Gonzalo looked at him for an instant—a face like that of thousands of others in the country, long-nosed and shaggy-browed—while the doctor smiled and waved at him. Antonio was still on the Valdepeñas and, with surprise, examined the friendly face of the waiter who had come over to them after a brief exchange of words with Don Gonzalo.

"Are you Señor Ramírez?"

"Yes."

"Don Gonzalo has asked me to invite you to join his table."

The doctor turned to look at him with the expression of an accomplice. The waiter was waiting for his answer, stiff as a board. Antonio finished his glass in one swallow.

"Tell the gentlemen that I thank him very much for his invitation, but that I know how to pick my company myself and that I don't like his."

"What?"

"You heard me."

The man was looking at him as if he had suddenly come face to face with a madman. To calm him down, Antonio patted him on the arm and ordered another bottle of claret.

"Very well, just as you say."

He watched him go over to Don Gonzalo and repeat his words to the stupefaction and rage of the people gathered there. It did not take the doctor long to get up and dash over to him.

"What are you trying to do, Ramírez, make enemies with everyone in town?"

"I'm not trying to do anything, doctor."

"Your conduct is boorish and stupid."

"It probably is."

"You're a poor devil, you hear? A rude and irresponsible fool. . . ."

"Don't get excited," he said softly. "You won't be able to digest your lobster."

"You'll be sorry, Ramírez. I can assure you that you'll be sorry."

The doctor turned his back and Antonio felt immensely happy. The people at the table were looking at him with disdainful reprobation and after a few consultations with the waiter, Don Gonzalo began to tell a story, to the devout attention of those at the table.

"Mister Ramírez."

The bartender had come over to his table with a firm step and was looking at him sternly.

"What is it?"

"The management of this establishment requests that you leave at once."

"Can you tell me how much I owe?"

The bartender called the waiter with a wave of his hand.

"The gentleman's check."

"Sixty-three fifty."

"There you are," Antonio left two bills on the table. "Keep the change."

He went out to the street along with Fermín. A thick swarm of clouds was closing in the horns of the moon and after a few moments had covered it completely. A strong wind was blowing from the sea. On the Paseo there was an empty bench and he sat down on it while he drew in a deep breath of the salty and penetrating smell of the water.

"Now you've done it," Fermín said. "Are you feeling all right?"

"It's more than that, much more," Antonio replied. "I feel young again."

The lights on the fishing boats were flickering like fireflies on the horizon of the sea, in the distance someone was singing a melancholy aria. Antonio listened for a long time, carried away by a rapture that could not be described, before he embraced Fermín and said good night to him. When he went to bed, for the first time in many months he fell fast asleep without the need of sleeping pills.

Wed., Dec. 3—Gorilla goes to Pichi bar at 10:40 A.M. *and from there to Mariola bar, where Blue is waiting with a mechanic from the garage. Surveillance is lifted with entry of lottery sellers, friends of Blue, who might know agents by sight.*

Gorilla picked up again at 2:30 P.M. *at Gypsy's. Takes taxi to Orión workshop and walks toward Pasaje Permanyer as if looking for someone. This afternoon it was noted that he was taking precautions: turns his head frequently and retraces his steps, going all around block, returning to starting point.*

Thurs., Dec. 4—Gorilla leaves at 12:30 P.M. *In Plaza de Correos takes subway to Urquinaona and makes contact with Nikita opposite the Transportes La Catalana. In contrast to day before, no sign of unrest in either of them. Walk along Ronda San Pedro and at 2:20* P.M. *break up. Few minutes later Gorilla is lost on Urquinaona.*

Fri., Dec. 5—Gorilla leaves at 3 P.M. *and after wandering through downtown section goes to Blue's garage. Go to Pichi, return to garage, chat for 20 minutes in doorway, look at shopwindows, disappear. Not picked up either in Mariola or Escocés bars. At 4:15* P.M. *spotted on Calabria, where there is an optical store. Walk along together for moment and split up. Blue goes to garage and Gorilla toward Avenida José Antonio with attaché case seen for first time and which he must have picked up in optical store or in nearby apartment entrance. Takes streetcar, then train, and at 8:03* P.M. *he is at Grackle's. Case is approximately 20" long and 15" wide, 5" thick; dark brown, with handles; gives impression of not weighing very much. Investigation is made with no results of connections of owners of optical store and tenants in next building where there is boardinghouse called Pensión Zamora.*

Sat., Dec. 6—At 2 P.M. *Gorilla takes train at Premiá. Lost on Plaza Palacio and picked up at 5* P.M. *in Pichi with Gypsy and Blue. Latter goes to garage and then home. Gypsy and Gorilla stay in bar until 7* P.M. *watching television program about our Crusade for Freedom. Leave, walking very slowly; Gorilla takes out pad and ball-point and seems to be sketching plan; they argue and Gypsy makes another plan; in that way they reached Floridita bar where Gypsy's wife is waiting. Three of them walk together and visit several bars. Then Gorilla takes train and goes to Grackle's. At 10* P.M. *reappears with her, Escuchi, and a girl we shall call Braids. Four of them go to movies. At 1:30* A.M. *return to Almogávares and surveillance lifted.*

Sun., Dec. 7—Gorilla leaves at 11:45 A.M.*, goes to Escocés bar and meets Skimo, Curly, and Nikita. Half-hour later gets into Peugeot 9098 MG 75 with Skimo and they take off in direction of*

Sans, unable to be followed because of lack of necessary vehicle. Curly says good-by to Nikita and walks toward Avenida José Antonio. Turns down Calabria, passes by optical store, goes in next doorway where Pensión Zamora is and does not reappear.

Mon., Dec. 8—Gorilla not seen.

Tues., Dec. 9—Gorilla spotted at 10:35 A.M. *Takes taxi on Plaza Palacio to corner of Entenza and Avenida José Antonio. Looks into Escocés bar and does not find anyone, slowly makes way to corner of Rocafort and Aragón and near place of contacts passes woman walking slowly and exchanges glance with her. 12:01* P.M. *Woman stops at corner. Gorilla watches her closely, goes over to her as if to ask her something and they greet each other warmly. The woman, whom we shall call Piaf, is short, slim, and carries black purse. Go into Escocés bar and leave after 15 minutes. Go into another bar. When they reappear 10 minutes later, Gorilla carrying small package wrapped in blue paper. Explains something to Piaf and they separate. She takes taxi to Hotel Internacional. Gorilla is lost and at 4:40* P.M. *shows up at Pichi. After quarter hour walks around block and heads for Escocés. At 3:55* P.M. *Piaf arrives. Chat animatedly for half-hour and separate; Gorilla now carrying role of paper about 20″ long and package similar to one in morning, but larger. Goes to Pichi bar and contacts Gypsy. Stay together until 5* P.M. *and when he gets up, Gypsy takes package and roll of paper. Piaf strolls through downtown streets, goes back up Ramblas, and at 8:30* P.M. *returns to hotel.*

Wed., Dec. 10—Piaf leaves hotel at 10:15 A.M. *and meets Gorilla opposite Virreina Palace. Go to Plaza Real, sit down on terrace of bar and separate after half-hour. Piaf goes down to docks and takes boat to breakwater. Gorilla meets Gypsy and Blue in Pichi. Piaf identified as Josette Lefevre, 42 bis rue Fayard, Argenteuil, Seine.*

In afternoon Piaf goes back to hotel, packs bags, pays bill, and takes taxi to Rocafort and Aragón. Gets out, takes out baggage, pays taxi. Five minutes later Gorilla and Gypsy appear as she shows signs of impatience and looks at watch. Gorilla and Gypsy argue before going over to Piaf, Gorilla goes first and introduces her to Gypsy. Gypsy takes bag and overnight case, stops taxi, takes them home to Calle de Almansa. Gorilla and Piaf walk toward Plaza de España, go into Exposition grounds, return to Avenida José Antonio. Gypsy and wife are waiting for them at

Mariola with suitcase different from one mentioned before and large, dark brown brief case; suitcase is beige and reinforced on edges. Four converse; stop taxi and Piaf gets in with new baggage and goes to MZA station. Takes Cerbère train, followed by two agents. Several pictures taken of her on docks and passport is photographed when she crosses border.

Thurs., Dec. 11—Curly identified as Antonio Ramírez Trueba, native of Águilas, Murcia, living in Pensión Zamora, 116 Calabria. Law degree and graduate of diplomatic school. Known in university for Marxist leanings; turns out to be friend of Álvaro Mendiola, author of anti-Spanish film on emigration of Spanish workers impounded by Civil Guard in Yeste, Albacete, 8/23/58.

There was not the slightest doubt about it: the police had worked perfectly. Five centuries of vigilance, inquisition, and censorship had slowly configured the moral structure of this unique organism, considered even by its enemies and detractors as a beacon and model of the many sanitary institutions that, taking their inspiration from it, are proliferating throughout the world.

The realm of Twenty-Five Years of Peace was nothing but the refined and visible product of an underground effort of generations, dedicated to the noble and happy mission of maintaining against wind and tide the rigid immobility of principles, the vital respect for the law, the blind and quick obedience to the mysterious norms that govern that human society arranged into categories and social classes (each one of them representing to perfection its role in the illusory theater of life). After such a vast and profitable experience, the people learned by themselves to apply the cathartic designs, and in that spurious summer of 1963, your homeland had become changed into a grim and sleepy country of thirty-odd million non-uniformed police (including the intractable and the rebels). With your inborn optimism, you thought that in a short time agents would no longer be necessary, because in one way or another, the vigilante, the censor, the spy had secretly infiltrated the souls of your fellow countrymen. In every group, under the bossism inherent in the tribe, the inquisition was reappearing with unsuspected disguises: interrogations, accusations, investigations, questionings. Parallel and opposing police were covering the stiff and exhausted country from one end to the other (the leafy harvest of vocations from an earth that was so baked and thirsty). The husband policed the wife and the wife the husband, the father the son and the son the father, the brother the brother, the citizen his neighbor. Bourgeoisie (monopolist or nationalist, rural or urban), proletariat, peasants, middle sectors: policemen all. Just as much a policeman the proudly isolated intellectual as the kindly novelist with a social conscience (for his intimates, at least). The lifelong friend, the companion of difficult times: police too. (And how many times you yourself, Álvaro, had you not made a pact with the conformist environment, censoring yourself in public and in private, hiding from the rest your irreducible truth: a policeman too, even though it hurts you now.)

We're going to make them pay dearly (you said to yourself) for the Civil War that was lost, the twenty half-cropped years, the ominous facility that invades us. All sick with an incurable illness, all frustrated, all mutilated. How can peace, fullness, peacefulness be re-established in their inner hearts? Sad people, sad country, what kind of psychoanalysis can help you to recover? For you, days will never pass and your children succeed themselves, useless at your bosom facing your inertia, your stubbornness, your madness. Will you change someday? Perhaps yes (you said to yourself), when your bones (yours) fertilize the soil (oh, my country) and other and better men (children still today) will placate with their offering that impossible desire presiding over your fate. When you are dead (you say to yourself), whose task will it be to tell the tale?

Official entry: 8:30 A.M.*, Dec. 18, 1960. On orders of the Chief Inspector of the Social Investigation Brigade of this Headquarters, police inspectors Don Eloy Romero Sánchez, Don Mamerto Cuixart López, and Don Eduardo García Barrios, provided with the corresponding judicial order, presented themselves in the Pensión Zamora, located at 116 Calle Calabria, in the room occupied by Antonio Ramírez Trueba to undertake a search. In the presence of the party in question and before the witnesses José Calvo Martínez, owner of the boardinghouse and José María Cortés Berruezo, an employee of the same, the search was undertaken with the following results: a book entitled* Capital, *by Karl Marx,* Principles of Philosophy, *by George Politzer,* Collected Works, *by Rosa Luxemburg,* Letters from Prison, *by Antonio Gramsci,* Stalin, *by Isaac Deutscher,* Intellectuals and the Spanish War, *by Aldo Garo-*

sci, The Thaw, *by Ilya Ehrenburg,* Selected Poems, *by Rafael Alberti,* Los complementarios, *by Antonio Machado,* Theater, *by Bertolt Brecht, issues of* Cuadernos *and* Ibérica *on Spain, several numbers of* Europe *and* Il Contemporaneo, *the reproduction of a dove drawn by Picasso, etc. All of the books and magazines cited are presented with the statement herein drawn up and which forms part of the indictment to be sent to the proper judicial authority.*

The ambiguity had disappeared. Once more he could walk through town like an outlaw, sensing in the mute condemnation of the others the indelible sign that marked him. The illusion of freedom had finally disappeared and the relaxed imprisonment was nothing but imprisonment: an encirclement of vague but real limits, a mechanism wisely disposed to impede the double flight of body and mind. The sea horizon, everything walling in that landscape forgotten by God that had been destroyed by man's bad management was felt less than the emptiness created by mistrust and fear, the suspicious and furtive looks, the greetings that were barely cloaked, the brief and meaningless conversations. A lonely figure in a captive land, more lonely still because his alien presence multiplied the isolation at every instant the same as the barbarous echo of a shout under an immense dome, so that he could relish his exile the same as imprisonment, an imprisonment that was just like a path toward freedom, freedom the same as man's only aim, the only conscious way to be—or at least that was what he thought—among the multitude of fellow countrymen who thought they were free because they sold—and it was a kind of progress—their miserable working strength cheaply, with a decreed holiday once a week, regularly procreating absurd children, arguing with a strange passion about the knee of a soccer player or the wounded thigh of a bullfighter, bulls themselves and not even that, happy tame bulls who spoke with arrogance about what could be talked about and letting themselves condemn what was condemned, sad herd of oxen without bells, eating the fodder of those who took advantage and the cynics, a heroic people in their day—the unfurled red flags, the fierce faces of men with clenched fists, that air of music *qu'on ne pouvait pas entendre sans que le coeur battit et le sang fut en feu,* do you remember?—reduced after twenty-five years—how, my God, how?—to a vain shadow of the past, to a dead jingle, a drowsy body that one day perhaps would wake up.

The reactions provoked by the incident at the beach club were not long in showing: the next day, as Antonio was translating a particularly obscure passage in his philosophy book, two members of the Civil Guard appeared at his house and asked him to report to the barracks with them. Just as on the afternoon of his arrival in town, people stopped to look at him in the street and from the terrace of a café, somebody swore: "Well done. I hope they shoot him."

The frown with which the lieutenant awaited him was not much different from that of the policeman who had hit him at Headquarters a year before, and Antonio felt a sensation of relief at the idea that the comedy they had been playing together was over once and for all.

"Ramírez," he said, "up till now we've bent over backward for you; but our patience has a limit. Your behavior last night overflowed the cup: it was an act of hooliganism that merits the rejection of all wellborn people. If you would only apologize to Don Gonzalo . . ."

"Not for anything in the world, lieutenant."

"In that case, your status is completely changed. From today on, you will come here and sign the registry twice a day and you will not set foot in any bar or public establishment. If you disobey me, you'll be sorry, understand?"

"Yes, lieutenant."

"Next, you get a shave today or I'll do it my way. Spain isn't Cuba and if you want to be cock of the walk, you'll end up worse than Morón's: no crowing and no feathers."

"Yes, lieutenant."

"My men are not going to leave you alone, day or night, so when you feel like acting up, you know already what will be waiting for you. We'll give you such a face that your own mother won't recognize you."

He took leave of him with a brusque gesture, but as Antonio crossed the courtyard of the house that served as a barracks, he had the corporal call him back.

"That's not all, Ramírez. I want you to know that what you did has meaning and the town has judged your attitude severely. If anybody goes after you, we won't be able to intervene."

"Is that a threat?"

"Take it any way you want."

On his way back to town he went into the first barbershop. The beard no longer mattered to him from the moment when jail had again imposed its limits and brought him back to his status of a free man in the middle of that vast and extensive prison. Fermín had received orders not to greet him, and when they passed casually in the street, he limited himself to a smile. Morning and night Antonio went to sign in at the barracks and during the free time his translation left him, he would take his bicycle and go to dream on some beach, happy to lose himself for a few hours with the harsh sound of the waves that attacked the sand with refined and lacelike arabesques.

During one of those aimless wanderings, a little before Christmas, he went along the paths and trails to La Calabardina. Waiting for the tuna that ran along the coast in spring, the fishery had been shut down, and buoys, chains, anchors, grapnels were lying on the wharf and warehouses of the Cooperative, as decorative and as useless as the unemployed men themselves, the grave and mourning women, the dark and sad children. The shrouded winter sun was shining on the fishermen's shacks and, sitting at the water's edge at the opposite end of the gulf, with apprehensive nostalgia, Antonio watched the furrow the fishing boats were plowing on the surface of the sea and, absorbed now in his quiet melancholy, impressed and absent at the same time, he looked at the shells of the boats drawn up on the beach like exhausted, lifeless dolphins. For some unknown reason, his heart was beating strongly and as he got up there were tears in his eyes.

On his way back—along the same paths and short cuts so he could avoid meeting the Civil Guards—his path was cut off by a short person who seemed to be waiting for him at a bend in the trail, half-hidden among the prickly pears.

"Salud, camarada," he said. "Don't you recognize me?"

The gray hair, the eyes like embers, the jutting jaw were vaguely familiar to him. Antonio hesitated before answering:

"I don't know. I'm not sure."

"I'm Morillo, your father's comrade in arms."

A death penalty commuted at the last minute, fifteen years in prison, bitterness and humiliations had made the former chairman of the town Committee into an old and worn-out man, changed, like so many others in the broad Spanish geography, into a poorly drawn shadow of himself.

"I've been waiting to talk to you for a long time, comrade. I wrote you a note to meet me at midnight in the ruins of the castle, but you didn't come."

"I never got it," Antonio said.

"The time for action has come. The whole country is ready to rise up and it's only waiting for our initiative. . . . When we get the word, we patriots will have to climb the mountain with a firm stride, you hear?"

"Yes."

"In every district there's a Committee for the purchase of rifles and machine guns. Last night one of our submarines passed by with a message in code. . . . When the time comes, I'll let you know. In the meantime, silence and, above all, great care."

He left him, abandoned to his somber delirium, and went back to town. There was not much time left on his sentence, and Antonio was restlessly thinking about the ambiguous world that was lying in wait for him when it ended, the tempting solicitations of an apparently profitable and tranquil universe. He might have felt like withdrawing his stake in the gamble, but even though it had been changed, the game was still going on and, just as at the beach club, facing the future Don Gonzalos that he would meet along the way, he knew, and it was a deeply entrenched certainty in his chest like that of a bird of prey, that something stronger than he was obliging him, would always oblige him, to make another bet.

An automobile suddenly burst into the garden. The three of you were sitting on the porch and the typed copies of the surveillance report were covering the reed mat on which a few hours before the maid had served you coffee. Dolores got up with a sigh.

The sunset was crowning the mountain with a reddish glow and the eucalyptus trees were holding their silvery leaves in dazzling stillness. Swift swallows were plowing through the motionless air, skimming the eaves of the roof with their sharp beaks. The blue of the sea was dissolving its sere and diminished vitality into the sky.

The car had stopped next to the lookout, after carefully avoiding the toys strewn about on the driveway, and Ricardo, Paco, and Artigas got out with a unanimous and endless expression of fatigue. They shouted their decision to have a swim. The vestiges of a sleepless night could be seen on their faces and as they came up the path leading to the pool, Paco did a brilliant strip tease. The dogs escorted him barking, elastic and flexible.

Your friends had dived into the green water and their heads came up smiling over the pointed stones on the edge. You waited for Dolores, stretched out in the sun, absorbed in the dense quiet of the sunset. The sun had just disappeared behind the mountain and a last crimson ray was agonizing among the branches of the cork trees.

"It's been hot as the devil in Barcelona," Artigas was saying.

"Ninety in the shade."

"On the Plaza de España they arrested an Englishwoman in her underwear."

"It wasn't an Englishwoman," Paco corrected. "It was an English man."

"You're getting to be a bigger fairy every day."

"I'm not a fairy," he protested. "I'm a hyposexual."

"It's all the same to me," Artigas said. "To be or not to be," he added in English.

"By the way," Antonio cut in. "What happened to the Danish girls?"

"Ricardo invited them to dinner last night. Ask him."

"That's not true. You were the pagan."

"Whichever way it was, in any case, they eat like acid," Dolores said. "Did you see the way they cleaned up their plates?"

"Denmark is an underdeveloped country, didn't you know?" Paco was pointing at Antonio. "You, economist. . . . What have you got to say about the Spanish miracle?"

It was soothing to abandon yourself to the contact with the warm water, stretch out your arms lazily, float with your sight lost in the colorless and cloudless sky. Ricardo, Artigas, and Paco had come to spend the weekend with you and, thanks to their help, you hoped you could take another step forward toward the knowledge and understanding of things that had happened. Your life was now being reduced to a solitary struggle with the ghosts out of the past, and on the outcome of that battle depended—you knew it—the liquidation of the mortgage that was weighing on your narrow and casual future.

Conscious of the danger, you were walking with resolute step toward the disaster against which you were gambling.

V

Whenever he read the headlines in *France-Soir* in Madame Berger's café, Álvaro was amazed by the stubborn references to the yellow peril, and he would take pleasure in imagining ingenious stratagems for infiltration into the innocent and unalerted West—the shipment of miniature agitators by parcel post, the export of astute and smiling butlers for well-to-do families in the Seiziéme Arrondissement, or by means of a Trojan Horse of a peaceful pilgrimage to Lourdes by a million and a half Chinese, catastrophic predictions that he would sprinkle conveniently with quotations from Spengler, Ortega y Gasset, Keyserling, and Denis de Rougemont. After a trip of several weeks through Holland, Belgium, Switzerland, and West Germany in trains and past stations crowded with emigrants from Galicia, Estremadura, Castile, and Andalusia, he had reached the final conclusion that the real danger was not to come from the distant, remote, and invisible Asians, but from the nearby and increasingly numerous, gaudy and identifiable Spaniards.

The illustrious descendants of the discoverers of the Pacific and the expeditionaries up the Orinoco, the victorious warriors of Mexico and the heroes of Alto Peru, they were departing for the conquest and surrender of pagan, virgin, and unexplored Europe, boldly crossing its vast and mysterious geography without shrinking at frontiers or obstacles, emulating Francisco Pizzaro in their bold crossing of the Alps and Orellana in their daring exploration of the Rhine, speleologists in black and bottomless pits in the mining basins of the North, occupying forces in immense industrial complexes on the Rhine that looked like the product of some resurrected Montezuma, adventurers coming from every corner of Spain, carrying the spiritual and historical baggage of a homeland that is the united destiny of that universal and proud parent of seventeen young nations who pray, sing, and express themselves in its language.

Just as in the days before the fall of Rome, these new and crafty invaders were infiltrating the developed nations of the Common Market, insidiously escorted by the warlike army of women who in a gradual and systematic way were taking over the kitchens, wardrobes, and pantries of the diverse non-monopolist national bourgeoisie and imposing *paella* and olive oil, garlic soup and *sangría* everywhere, extending for the first time after an eclipse of several centuries the everyday example of the language of Cervantes in thousands of strange homes, a prodigious effort at cultural irradiation for a country whose per capita income never went beyond the modest figure of twenty thousand pesetas.

Álvaro had seen them eating enormous sausage sandwiches on the platforms of the Haupt-Bahnhof in Frankfurt, walking along the rue Mont-Blanc in Geneva with a suitcase of disquieting proportions, haggling over the prices on the menu in a bar in the Zeedijk in Amsterdam—small, dark, dolichocephalic Spaniards, with the cute wavy hair that is so attractive to Anglo-Saxon women clinging over their brows, and their tight and faded dungarees, challengingly cut to set off their bullfighters' and dancers' rear ends. A member of the shy flock from the steppe, the Emigrant was smiling at the grave Dutch gentleman who was trying to explain about his wonderful vacation on the Costa Brava, telling the Dutchman yes, that in Spain life is better than anywhere else, that he had taken off, as they say, to get around and see the world and that the sun, the girls, and the wine of Andalusia defy description, and that if he, the Dutch gentleman, goes back there some day, he, Francisco López Fernández, 29 Doctor Pastor, Utrera, invites him to come to his house with his wife and children, and there he will see what Andalusian *gazpacho, sopa de migas,* and Moriles wine are like, and if it so happens that the trip coincides with the Seville Fair, both of them, the Dutch gentleman and Francisco López Fernández, will leave their wives and children at 29 Doctor Pastor and go out and have a good time, drinking and mingling with the men, because there is no place in the world happier than the Triana district or girls with such a lovely walk and eyes that are, he, Francisco López Fernández, tells him, like two shots at point-blank range.

Or talking loud and making comments to the girls in the underground galleries of the Paris subway, always with the inevitable large cardboard suitcase, tied prudently with a cord, showing the change-makers a clumsily written paper with the address of a comrade, or trying to figure out the incomprehensible name of the station where two lines crossed, lustful and show-off fellow countrymen who talked like expert Don Juans because they had been closeted for five minutes with a drunken old woman in the washroom of a bar in Les Halles or for ten francs had screwed a toothless prostitute from the Boulevard de la Chapelle: little Spaniards, five feet tall, with twenty-five, thirty, or thirty-five years of hunger and privation behind them, wandering all over the Peninsula looking for work and living in a shack or cave with a number with the right to pay a monthly rent of three hundred pesetas, who maintained spiritual and human contact with the mother country by means of the attentive reading of the results of the national soccer championship in *Marca* or *Vida Deportiva,* suddenly going out on strike in protest against abominable European cooking that did not include chick peas and returning in triumph to the tribe, recounting their phenomenal sexual feats to their stupefied countrymen, conscious of their romantic and adventurous status as emigrants, carrying a German camera or wearing a fine gold watch, symbols of their new wealth.

During his ten years of exile in Paris, Álvaro had come to know all of the ups and downs of an ephemeral and devouring passion. Successively, he had admired, loved, idealized, grown bored with, despised, avoided them; he had had conversations with them in dirty bars or second-class railway compartments, he had photographed their inhospitable shacks and collective dormitories, he had invited them to his studio with the idea of getting into their lives more intimately and appreciating their problems, difficulties, and hopes better before beginning the filming of the frustrated documentary—an invitation to which they responded strongly, first singly and then by entire families, with old people and children, until they filled the room up like the Marx Brothers' cabin in *A Night at the Opera* and brought on the wrath of Dolores, justly tired of those folkloric and absurd meetings that would usually end up in general drunkenness with its inevitable aftermath of cigarette butts, broken glasses, demonstrations of native songs, and angry complaints from the neighbors.

For more than a year, Álvaro had made efforts to solve their problems, piloting them through the corridors of the *Préfecture de*

Police, the *Bureau de la Main d'Oeuvre*, the *Caisse de la Sécurité Sociale*. For some obscure reason, his studio had become the meeting place for maidservants from the Valencia region—women uniformly dressed in mourning who would appear one fine day at his door with the inevitable large suitcase, just off the Gandía bus and for whom he had to find work among his circle of friends or by answering the advertisements in *France-Soir* or *Le Figaro*. Sitting on the garden bench, his gaze fixed on the fires of the shepherds, that were smoking on the other side of the countryside, Álvaro thought about the mornings spent beside his telephone, proposing the services of some Vicenta to elegant ladies of Auteuil and Neuilly who insisted on finding out whether "*cette fille a un bon rendement*," or whether "*elle est propre*," who, when they found out that she was not alone and was looking for a room for her husband, would alter their tone perceptibly and ask whether "*lui a l'air d'un Musulman*," or "*quel métier fait-il*" with such frigid apprehension and delicate horror that Álvaro would end up replying "he looks like an English prince and he's an Attaché at an Embassy" and hang up.

The list of Vicentas and Vicentes seemed to be endless. Little by little, Álvaro had spaced out the meetings, pretending pressing obligations, turning down the warm invitation to share a bottle of Spanish cognac with a courteous but firm smile. His exalted feelings of brotherhood had lasted exactly the time for the filming of the unfinished movie. From that date on, he pretended to be involved in urgent business if they called him on the telephone; he would not answer the bell that their unmistakable footsteps foretold; he would duck out of sight whenever he saw them prowling around his house. It was a difficult job, but the visitors finally understood, and with the same intensity with which he had previously sought out their company, Álvaro had fled from contact with them or their simple physical proximity, wishing to forget about their existence forever and never completely managing to do so—just as on the night when, after an argument with Dolores, he had got into bed loaded with sleeping pills with no other basic objective except to get a few hours of truce in sleep, and in the torpor of his waking moments, he had been startled by a loud voice coming from the rue Vieille de Temple with a solemn and most Castilian "and then I fucked her," which had opened his eyelids up wide, leaving him until dawn sunken in a feverish state of resentment, blind rage, and desolate and infinite anxiety.

Although they had planned to meet at noon, impatience was too strong for them and they came out of the Cataluña subway at ten to eleven. Ricardo and Paco were waiting for them in a coffee shop on the Avenida de la Luz. At that time the gallery was almost deserted and the idlers who were strolling among the columns could be counted on the fingers of one hand. In the bar there were only an old woman devouring pastries and two uniformed railroad workers.

For two days his friends and he had flooded the city with leaflets. Cars with altered license plates had gone through working-class districts throwing out handbills, while during the soccer game and bullfight of the night before, thousands of leaflets had rained down on the spectators. From what could be ascertained, someone had thrown a bundle of them down from the top of the Columbus monument.

The following plan had been worked out by the University Coordinating Committee: while the crowd gathered in front of the newsstand on Canaletas, students would converge in small groups along Santa Ana, Canuda, Buen Suceso, and Tallers. The main march would advance along Pelayo and give the starting signal. Once the demonstrators were gathered together, they would march down the Ramblas to the Calle Fernando and if the police did not stop them, head toward the City Hall and the legislative building.

Ricardo, Paco, and Artigas and his sister left the subway at Vergara. A dozen jeeps were parked at the intersection of Pelayo and Balmes and, next to the movie, two graycoats were silently smoking with their submachine guns slung. The crowd was milling around on the sidewalk opposite along the tailor shops, clothing stores, and shoe stores. The mass of pedestrians going toward the Rambla de los Estudios was somewhat larger than the one heading toward the Plaza Universidad. Ricardo said that in all certainty many people were waiting for a signal to gather in the place assigned.

They mingled with the crowd and wandered about too, trying to distinguish the real demonstrators from those who were just walking around, unaware of the extraordinary meaning of their presence in those parts. For the moment, it was impossible to calculate and they had to be content with presumptions, divinations, hypotheses, and conjectures. Paco pointed at a group of workers and said that in his opinion they were going to protest too.

Opposite the subway entrance on Pelayo there were pairs of graycoats. On the corner, an individual with a hat and dark glasses was quietly observing the coming and going of the people. When they left him behind, Ricardo said that a few months before he had come to interrogate him at home.

"He's a specialist in university problems. If we keep going in this direction you'll see how we'll spot some more corner-watchers."

Small groups of men were chatting beside the fountain. Artigas and his sister went over to listen while Ricardo and Paco stationed themselves at the door of the Canaletas bar. On the main steps, some companions were being curious like them. Those in the groups were arguing in loud voices and, according to what one could deduce, they were commenting on the results of the final elimination match for the Cup of His Excellency the Generalissimo. Artigas said that they were probably doing it to throw people off the track.

They walked down the Ramblas, mingling with the silent mass of pedestrians. From time to time some fellow students from the Faculty would pass them and they would question each other nervously with their eyes. At the corner of Santa Ana and Canuda there were new groups of graycoats. The clock already said twenty minutes to twelve.

They decided to take another look along the Calle Tallers. After a few seconds, Artigas ran into a student friend of Antonio's who was coming along in a hurry in the opposite direction. Very excited—his lips trembled as he spoke—he told them how the police had made several arrests and a group of twenty jeeps were blocking traffic on the Plaza Castilla.

"How's the march coming?"

"I don't know. When I left it, it still hadn't formed."

They went back to the Ramblas. There their companions were walking along the streets like them, pretending to be looking at shopwindows. Two girls from Pharmacy were examining a roll of tourist post cards with feigned interest. Ricardo and Paco had left the Canaletas bar and they looked for them in vain among the groups arguing about soccer. Traffic was apparently normal. The plainclothesman was still motionless at his observation post on the corner.

The number of familiar faces was visibly growing. Artigas recognized in turn the novelist R. B., a married couple who were abstract painters, several employees of the J. M. publishing house.

The main body of demonstrators was difficult to identify in the midst of the crowd of anonymous faces: the gentleman in gray gloves, for example, had he come to protest? The young man in the leather jacket who was making eyes at the girl selling cigars, was he an authentic soccer fan or an agent of the Brigadilla in disguise? His sister beside him, in like manner, ventured versatile and contradictory suppositions.

For a few moments they wandered from one side to the other in order to gain time. The small groups of intellectuals and students were forming and breaking up spontaneously in the shelter of the newsstands and the groups of fans. In none of the places agreed upon were there signs of agitation. The public was moving peacefully along the commercial sidewalk of Pelayo and, on the corner of Canuda and Santa Ana, the graycoats were also waiting expectantly. Seconds later, twelve o'clock sounded on the bells of the church of Belén.

They found Antonio opposite the Capitol in the company of Paco and Ricardo. The three of them had just come back from the Plaza de la Universidad and they told how the police had broken up the march. The students were converging individually toward Canaletas and the police had picked up several identity cards. According to them there had been no arrests.

Once more they circulated through the crowd and distress and uncertainty were reflected on many faces. There were a hundred students and friends going up and down the Ramblas like village boys and girls during their Sunday strolls. In the neighboring cafés and stores, the indecisive ones were waiting in vain for a signal to join them. The fans were still talking soccer and no one was to be seen on the corners.

At twelve-twenty, Enrique came out of the subway entrance with two friends from Economics, members of the Coordinating Committee: with great gestures and raising their voices, they tried to gather the people around them. There was a brief pause, during which the students seemed to vacillate. Finally a handful gathered around the leaders while the rest scattered along the sidewalks on both sides. Almost immediately, someone unfurled a banner.

The rest happened in a matter of seconds: several plainclothesmen jumped on the group and there was a quick exchange of insults, kicks, and blows. The crowd watched the scene without reacting and as he sneaked around among the onlookers, Artigas spotted Enrique, with a bloody mouth and flanked by two policemen. The three got into a jeep parked at the corner of the Plaza de Cataluña and disappeared at full speed in the crowd.

He suddenly felt infinitely lost, immersed in the surge of voices, in the dull traffic noise. The clock said twelve twenty-six. Only when he ran into Antonio and his friends—taking in the stupor in their looks—did he grasp the real meaning of what had happened. He could not get over his surprise and yet there was not the slightest doubt:

The demonstration had been a failure.

The regular customers of the café that Álvaro frequented apparently belonged to a different species. Located halfway between the Pont-Neuf and the Carrefour de l'Odéon, its dirty and resistant walls, adorned with posters and advertisements for Ricard, Suze, Byhrr, Dubonnet, Cinzano, contained and dammed up successive waves of immigrants from the Peninsula who, thrown out all of a sudden by the changes and fortunes of politics, had dodged, as if in some diabolical and ingenious obstacle course, the crowded highways and swamped boats of the defeat of 1939, the barbed wire, the hunger, and the fleas of Saint-Cyprien and Argelés-sur-Mer, the Nazi extermination camps, and the American incendiary bombs until they had finally come up against those walls and ran aground like old beached ships whose waterway was beyond repair, among the tables covered with ash trays and empty glasses, Madame Berger's zinc bar, with its parchment-like and legendary croissants, the asthmatic coffee-maker, the producer of tasteless *café-crèmes,* and the yellowing and wrinkled notice with the complete and unread text of the *Loi de Repression de l'Ivresse Publique.*

According to what Álvaro had been able to observe, the integrating elements of each historical stratum maintained only a superficial contact with individuals from earlier or later layers, obeying an implicit but scrupulously observed rule of seniority. The members of the first group—the one to which Álvaro belonged—were political or intellectual emigrés who, in most cases, had crossed the Pyrenees, with or without a passport, after a fairly long stay in Carabanchel or the Cárcel Modelo, halfway through the decade of the fifties now, as a result of their participation in student movements or in some episodic demonstration of protest, crowned with a seductive halo of youth and recent exile, which those who—like Álvaro—had exiled themselves because of a family quarrel, the loss of a job, or simply in search of new and more pleasant horizons, did not enjoy. The second layer brought together the already graying emigrés of the years 1944–1950, guests of the camps at Albatera or Miranda del Ebro, who had crossed the border clandestinely to join the French Maquis before the abortive attempt to invade the Arán valley, or had fled at full gallop when they saw their heads in jeopardy as a result of the breaking up and liquidation of the FUE by agents of the Political and Social Brigade during those sad years of fear, drought, hunger, and privation. The third stratum contained the fugitives of Perthus and those who had escaped from Alicante, buried for months on end on the sandy beaches of the Languedoc, forced to build the Atlantic Wall, miraculously saved from the gas chambers of Auschwitz, combat veterans of the Civil War that had been lost, who would look at the others over their shoulders the way the heir to an old fortune looks at the black-market operator enriched by the aftermath of the war or the aristocrat of long standing at the businessman ennobled by a pontifical title or in payment for mysterious services rendered the Regime. And, examining these three first and most important layers, the interested geologist could have uncovered the remains of older sedimentations that had come to rest in the unexplored depths of the café after the harsh repression that followed the events in Asturias in 1934, or the struggle against the Dictatorship of General Primo de Rivera, and even, as Álvaro was able to ascertain one day, the vestiges of the social agitations of 1919, and one fossilized specimen, the only one of its kind, coveted by collectors, experts, and investigators: the survivor of the memorable Tragic Week that in 1909 had bloodied the streets of Barcelona, a wrinkled little old man, the friend and disciple of Francisco Ferrer Guardia, who would appear from time to time in Madame Berger's café, severe and disdainful, with his divinity momentarily gone astray amidst a rabble of *arrivistes,* plebeians, and base mortals, emigré by nature, who had brought with him and for all eternity the clue and key to Truth, abandoned to his miserable fate by the millions and millions of Spaniards who with lamentable stubbornness, were living, growing, and multiplying on the arid, spacious, and sterile soil of the homeland that had been cursed a thousand times.

In spite of the natural quarrels that arose from their different positions in the historical pecking order and their rather rich variety of political opinions, however, those harmoniously superimposed levels did have one single and never-ending theme of common conversation, Spain. The illnesses and eventual cures of which the people there thought they knew in direct proportion to the number of years they had been in exile.

The first time they set foot in Madame Berger's café, the elements of the top and most recent layer felt themselves obligated to explain to the others what had happened in the country up to the very moment of their departure before they realized that their stories not only were of no interest to anyone, but that they also constituted a very serious lack of tact, excusable, it is true, in a novice exile, still ignorant of the subtle rules and regulations that governed the rigorous scale of age. Little by little, as their enthusiasm cooled, they learned to be quiet and assume an attentive expression, answering briefly the questions of the old men with the natural modesty of almost illiterate disciples facing the wisdom and knowledge of an illustrious professor, waiting for the moment—weeks, months, or years later—when they in turn could raise their eyebrows or stick a toothpick in their gums or ostentatiously open up the newspaper during a hurried and feverish discourse by a younger expatriate, the uncontested proof of their status as veterans and their well-earned induction into the new order, emigrés with disdainful looks and cracked voices, in full and solemn possession of historical truth and the rational solution for all the ills of Spain, awaiting the approaching day when things would change and they could return in triumph to the country with the treasures of experience they had accumulated during their long and fruitful exile.

The favorable evolution of his feelings and opinions with respect to Spain found for the first time its exact opposite in the progressive and pitiless criticism of France and the French, as if the growing forgetfulness of the defects of a distant and idealized homeland were being compensated for with the discovery of new and unsuspected vices in the real and tangible universe in which they were living, admiration and disdain perfectly parallel and symmetrical, in fecund and strict relation to the personal status of the individual and the number of years of his stay. The new arrivals of the first layer came dazzled by the completely fabricated myth of Paris and the gaudy varnish of the anemic French culture, avid for love affairs, experiences, and readings and, like Álvaro himself when he first met Dolores, they divided their free time among revivals at the Cinémathèque, plays put on by students of the TNP, and lectures on art and literature at the Sorbonne, falling in love with all the blond girls in the Quartier Latin and the Cité Universitaire, happy to be living in a place where love was a possibility, astounded at the wide freedom and independence of French (or German or Scandinavian) women, making an effort to pronounce correctly a language whose classics they devoured in whole series in their desire to fill rapidly the gaps in a narrow, ultra-Catholic upbringing, until the fatal day when they discovered at their own expense the inborn virile pride of the Spanish male, suddenly frightened at the scandalous infidelity of French (or German or Scandinavian) women, who would forget overnight their glowing promises of love and their eternal vows, to fall—something inconceivable—into the arms of an Italian student with a touch of the fairy about him or those of a solid and exceedingly black scholarship student from Togo or Cameroons, leaving them sunken in the depths of jealousy, wounded self-esteem, and spiteful bitterness, and quickly opening their eyes to the true measure of a French (or German or Scandinavian) woman, so different from the gravity and strength characteristic of the Spanish female, a discovery that dragged along with it the demystification of all remaining values and put French society as a whole in the prisoner's dock.

From then on the innocent and Frenchified elements of the first geological stratum began to speak with disdain about the venality, the rudeness, the petit-bourgeois spirit of the French and they would abandon their painfully acquired accents and pronounce their *r*'s the Spanish way and would carefully cultivate a real Iberian appearance with long sideburns, drooping mustaches, and a kind of languor in their looks that permitted them to be identified at first sight in the midst of the depersonalized masses, anonymous and gray, in which they lived. Instead of wasting their precious time at the Cinémathèque, the TNP, or the Sorbonne, they prefered to get together among Spaniards at Madame Berger's ancient place and there, over a cup of terrible French coffee, recall the historic events that had caused their exile or listen to the stories of the emigrés of the second or third sediment about the breakthrough on the Ebro front, the capture of Belchite, or the Italian defeat at Guadalajara, comparing, in their rich and fluid conversations, the bourgeoisization of the French worker, interested only in his Citroën and his upcoming summer vacation, with the untainted nobility and dignity of the long-suffering Spanish worker, or the monotonous opulence of the fertile Norman fields with the bare landscape—dry stream beds, black poplars, stubble fields—of the silent and ascetic countryside of Castile. No one ever mentioned the names of Baudelaire and Rimbaud with youthful euphoria any more or spoke about French (or German or Scandinavian) women except to criticize them and exhibit before the others gathered there a picturesque display of Don Juanesque adventures that proved categorically the well-earned reputation of the manliness of the Spanish male, married in the end to an upright and healthy Spanish emigrée woman, the mother of their future children, explaining pleasantly to the younger exiles the shameful collective breakup of 1940 and the decisive role of the Spaniards in the Maquis, the first obligatory step along a road that would later lead them to unveil to the innocent the clearly Teutonic origins of modern French philosophy or the decisive influence of Wagner's music on the work of Claude Debussy, to condemn the poor manufacture and low quality of some fortified wines, giving thanks to the massive importation of Prioratos and Riojas, and the terrible taste and disagreeable artificiality of the so unjustly celebrated food, and, after nostalgically mentioning Roncales cheese, shoulders and turnip greens, and Cantimpalo sausage, to decree with a unanimity unusual among Spaniards, that pure, cool, and refreshing water like that of the Guadarrama did not exist, no sir, anywhere else in the world.

The water was running down all across his body. He felt an intermittent itching on his side and his temples were paining him.

When he opened his eyes, the two men were sitting next to the files, absorbed in their newspaper reading. The one with a mustache had hung his jacket over the back of the chair, and from time to time he would knock his cigar ashes against the corner of the table. The tall one was mechanically smoothing out the wrinkles on his pants. The floor was covered with cigarette butts and the air stank with smoke.

"Want to wet your whistle?' the tall one said after a few minutes. "It's first-class sherry. Rodríguez brought it over from the commissary yesterday."

The one with the mustache folded his paper in half and brought it close to the lamp. As he read, his lips could be seen following the thread of the sentence.

"Well, all right, just a little bit."

The tall one filled the two glasses up and took a contented whiff of his before drinking it.

"It has a healthy smell."

"Did you see?" The one with the mustache stopped reading and brought the small glass to his lips.

"See what?"

"Luis Miguel got two ears."

"Where?"

"In Alicante."

"I'd like to see him do it in Madrid or in the Maestranza," the tall one was again swirling the contents of his glass an inch away from his nose. "With filed horns and a crowd of foreigners, anybody with a cape looks good."

"Come on, listen to this: 'With the second bull, Luis Miguel did a *faena de casti*go worthy of an established fighter. . . ."

"He must have bought that guy off."

". . . 'He took four or five forward steps that were top-notch and brought off some right-hand turns that were phenomenal. . . .' "

"Give those bullfight writers twenty duros and they'll shit on their own mothers."

". . . 'Then he went to the kill straight, like a lion, leaving his unequaled abilities waving on high like the flag of a master. . . .' "

"All I can say is that a first-rate bullfighter like Ordóñez picks the Maestranza or the Ventas to show it off in."

"Listen to this: 'The crowd, standing, their throats hoarse from so much shouting and their hands sore from clapping, sanctified the marvelous art of our number one bullfighter. The aroma of his *verónicas* will cling to the sands of the ring forever.' "

"That doesn't prove anything," the tall one said, "except that this guy had his palm well greased. When I saw him in Seville, he heard people hoarse from shouting 'balls,' and the next day the papers blamed the animals."

The one with the mustache threw the paper on the floor and blew a tuft of smoke from his cigar.

"This is great sherry. . . . You say it came from the commissary?"

"Rodríguez bought it yesterday and if we don't watch out, he'll drink it all by himself." The tall one was savoring the contents of his glass with delight. "Well, yes, your Luis Miguel is all right for the movies. Real bullfighters are something else again."

"How many times have you seen him?"

"Just once. But I can tell you, that was enough."

"To judge a first-class performer, you have to catch him in a good fight."

"You can spot a good bullfighter as soon as he steps into the ring. Luis Miguel isn't one and he never will be."

"I saw Ordóñez during the Merced holidays and he didn't convince me either."

"A real bullfighter comes out of nowhere and climbs up by his own ability," the tall one raised his voice. "Look at Manolete. He began with his ass in the air, as they say, and when he died he was a millionaire."

"Wait for the next double fight and we'll see who's right."

The one with the mustache had dropped his cigar butt on the floor and, unexpectedly, he changed the position of his chair.

"Hey, you, big boy," he spoke to him. "Do you like bullfights?"

"Me?"

"Yes, you. . . . Who else?"

"I don't know," Enrique had trouble speaking. As he was coming to, the pain in his side was growing sharper and sharper.

"Come on, big boy. Don't tell me you've never been to the bullfights. . . . Didn't your family ever take you to the Monumental?"

"No."

"Come off it, where the hell did they go to have a good time?" The man was examining him attentively. "I bet you've seen Ordóñez and Luis Miguel . . . in the movies or in the newsreels. . . ."

"Yes, in the movies."

"So, in the movies. . . . I knew you were hiding something. . . . You've seen lots of fights in the Nodo, right?"

"Yes."

"Well, that's what we were getting at. Who do you like best, Ordóñez or Luis Miguel?"

"I really don't know."

"Come on, don't be so modest. You paid your own way into the movies, didn't you?"

"Yes."

"You were sitting comfortably in your seat and you watched the Nodo, didn't you?"

"Yes."

"See how easy it is? Nothing to be ashamed of. A bullfight isn't any crime. My friend and I like them a lot, right?"

"Mad about them," the tall one said.

"We're a couple of fans and we're interested in your opinion," the dark eyes of the man were staring at him. "He roots for Ordóñez, and I like Luis Miguel. We've been arguing for years and we've never been able to agree."

The tall one got up and took a noisy stretch. In the light of the lamp, his shadow stood out gigantically against the wall.

"Yes," he said. "Which one do you like best?"

"I don't know," Enrique said. "I can't remember."

"Don't tell us you can't remember, because it's not true," the man with the mustache said persuasively. "You were sitting right there in your seat and you watched them, you were able to compare their styles. . . . Come on, big boy, try a little bit."

"I don't know."

"Of course you know. The trouble is that you're a timid boy and you're afraid to talk. . . . Come on, be a good boy. Think back a little bit."

"Ordóñez or Luis Miguel?" the tall one said.

"Don't try to be brave, big boy. All you've got to do is pick the one you like."

"Ordóñez or Luis Miguel?" The tall one had taken a few steps forward and the tips of his boots were touching his side.

"Come on, think about it," the one with the mustache had squatted down next to him with solicitude. "Whisper it to me, in my ear."

There was a brief pause. Suddenly it seemed that he was falling into a wall, and his eyes filled with sparks.

"Ordóñez," he panted.

"So, you see?" the one with the mustache gave him a loving pat on the shoulder. "I knew all along that you were fooling us," he turned toward the tall one and pointed at Enrique. "How about that? He says he likes Ordóñez."

"Really?" the tall one said.

"Yes," he stammered.

"Well, then, big boy. We'll introduce you to him."

The legs went away again in the direction of the door to the hall, and Enrique could make out the noise of the key as it turned in the lock. The tall one disappeared from the room and returned after a few moments with some new visitors. Making an effort, Enrique turned his head. The handcuffs had dug into his wrists and his hands were bleeding, swollen and livid.

The tall one waited motionless across from him along with two fat men dressed in gym suits. The one on the left was carrying a wet towel over his forearm like a waiter's napkin.

"Didn't you say that you admired him?" the one with the mustache asked, pointing his finger at the man. "Here he is in person, and right now he's going to take charge of you. . . . His friends call him Ordóñez. . . . This other fellow next to him, this other one you don't like. . . . This one we call Luis Miguel."

The first and almost obligatory idea of Spaniards newly arrived at Madame Berger's café, their heads full of illusions and projects and the dust of the Peninsula still clinging to the soles of their shoes, was the creation of a National Association of Intellectuals in Exile, an ambitious and distant objective whose first stage would be the publication and distribution of a magazine of confrontation and dialogue, open to the political, intellectual, and artistic currents of the modern world. Since his arrival in Paris, Álvaro had attended a dozen or more previous sessions during which there had been endless arguments over title, format, editorial board, budget, and contributions. He had broken old friendships, taken part in cruel exclusions, drawn up rough drafts and presentations that had been accumulating little by little in the drawers of his paper-covered desk among the bundles of family letters, clippings from newspapers, and useless scripts of movies that had never been filmed. Painters whose only stamp of glory was the fact that they were cousins of Tapies, ancient professors living off their academic and barren pens, composers who had proclaimed the heroic decision never to write another note until the fall of the Regime, a whole strange crowd of crustaceans, protected in their dogmas like medieval knights in their jointed and shining armor that gathered together in Madame Berger's café to argue, criticize, knock down, debate, pronounce ferocious anathemas, and draw up insulting letters, victims of an incurable megalomania and a violent indigestion of readings that were translated most often into Marxist formulas that were made useless by their multiple and contradictory elements or phrases that invariably began with the first person singular.

Every candidate for the post of future leader of the future parliament of the Spain of the future would unfurl his vast eloquence on those occasions, hammering at the words as if they were nails—"action," "struggles," "masses," "development," "oligarchy," "monopolies," "recrudescence," "advance"—and, dragged along by his own oratory—learned from others like the Lord's Prayer and repeated with ferocity—he would pronounce high-sounding and rotund dogmas, solemn and theatrical sentences that would miraculously grow like Japanese water flowers, would uncoil like a boa constrictor and climb like vines, and when they were about to die from over-consumption, would still scurry along like flexible and agile tendrils, as if they never, Álvaro thought, never would come to an end.

"Things are getting hot, boys," the latest Messiah fresh from Madrid would regularly announce. "The mood in the streets is magnificent."

The table of contents of the first number of the dead and resuscitated magazine was apt to include a prophetic analysis of the catastrophic Spanish situation, some ponderous essay (with references to Engels) in defense of realism, a round (and leaden) table on the duties of the writer, an anthology of crude poems with a fairly well-known signature that (out of pure negligence) Álvaro had kept in his file.

See the house,
the broken door,
the black depths
of the land.

I speak to you as brother,
I tell you of my woes,
of our mother in her misery,
our fearful Spain.

Oh, Miguel, if you could see
the trampled light,
the rending of the oak,
the ruination.

I go naked. Dawn
arrives.
Miguel, your absence hurts,
is heavy in my soul.

My steps ring out
across the square.
A train is heard. A shout
from out the ditches.

When Saint James returns,
and gathers Spain,
then shall your death and my desires
find the land called Home.

Those projects—examined with the perspective of the years—usually had an intense but fleeting life. The person who had conceived the idea of the magazine and his team of future collaborators would work feverishly all through the night, using their free time in useless visits to presses and in sterile petitions for help, until that inevitable instant when, for some mysterious reason, things would bog down, the meetings would grow less frequent without anyone's really knowing why, and boredom, indolence, and fatigue would come into play, causing them, one after the other, to forget about meetings and dates, break off correspondence, postpone indefinitely the decisive and important get-togethers. Then an intermediate period would take over during which in an implicit way the former future editors would avoid meeting each other as much as possible, somewhat ashamed at their own laziness and fearing that the reproaches of the others would oblige them to justify themselves, and after it had passed, a lot of water under the bridge, they would greet each other again in a free and easy way and not say a word about the magazine or show any surprise at the fact that the other one did not bring it up either—as if the project had never really existed—happy to have a chat and argue about the human and the divine, secret accomplices in a frustrated and unconfessed adventure.

In that way—and in a relatively brief lapse of time—Álvaro had belonged, as movie critic, to the editorial board of magazines entitled *Cuadernos de Cultura, Hojas Libres, Futuro de España, Cuadernos Españoles, La Piel del Toro,* and others whose names had already been forgotten and whose essential characteristic consisted in never having been published—despite the initial outpouring of energy and talent—as the result of those imponderables called laziness, discouragement, skepticism, and lack of will that the damp and unhealthy Paris winter secreted—a rock against which the successive waves of youthful Iberian enthusiasm broke and died. Slowly, as the roots that tied him to childhood and the land were broken, Álvaro could feel forming on his skin a scaly crust: the feeling of the uselessness of his exile and, simultaneously, the impossibility of return. The four walls of Madame Berger's café had hemmed him in, like so many other outcasts, to digest him and make of him one more component of the first geological stratum that spoke with nostalgia of Spain, had an atrocious French pronunciation, and discussed for the nth time with friends the historic necessity of a magazine. After a few years, hardened now, like the members of the second and third layers, he had learned to judge with ironic detachment the attempts of the younger emigrés and one day—the memory of which was painfully fresh in his mind on the terrace—as a group of new arrivals were conscientiously working up a new project, he went to his studio and got a folder that contained the previous tables of contents and gave it to them with a smile.

That night, as he was waiting for Dolores in the lobby of the École des Beaux Arts, Álvaro had the intuition, with southern clarity, that he had lost his youth forever.

The three of us had gotten together: Tonet, a short Cordovan who was good at singing soleares, and the one talking to you now, Francisco Olmos Carrasco, always at your service. On the docks, your honor, everything is open and aboveboard, everybody minds their own business, no ideas, no covering up, and night before last, Monday, that is, Tonet, the Cordovan, and yours truly had a good meal with Manolo, a foreman from Tarragona who handles a dozen boats all by himself and has a strong wine he gets from his province that's like the blood of a Mihura; at Manolo's house, I mean when it comes to drinking, people drink and nobody leaves with their stomachs empty, that's why that fellow Gómez Molina, who's a pushy guy, comes up to catch on that there's a party and there he is, large as life, after so mary free drinks, getting the men fighting and putting down the girls, because if you give a person enough rope, he'll never stop talking, your honor, I can swear by that and as I was saying, the night before last, Monday, that is, Tonet, the Cordovan, and yours truly were on our way over to Manolo's just as Manolo himself was getting home, and there we were, the four of us, eating and drinking wine, and the Cordovan gave out with some girls and I did a tango, and everybody was getting along fine the way seafaring people should, when this guy Gómez Molina comes along with that black face of his that's enough to scare the devil himself, and that's when the trouble starts, your honor, all the fault of that bad penny who was needed there about as much as a dog at mass, which is not at all, and he starts telling jokes to one of Manolo's women relatives and starts telling loud stories the way he's used to with his wife, poor woman, he ruined her, and since Manolo is a nice guy and keeps quiet, I get mad for him and I don't want them not to show him any respect when he's with his wife, yours truly, I mean, I stand up and I tell this customer, hold it, blacky, there's ladies present, and even though he cuts it out, he gives me a dirty look and says you come on outside, we've got to have a little talk, but Tonet and Manolo separate us and things go on as if nothing happened, until Manolo and his wife go to bed, and Tonet and the Cordovan and yours truly leave with the individual in question, I mean Gómez Molina, still tagging along, and the man insists on buying us a drink and since we say no, he won't listen and insists on buying a round in a bar in the Barrio Chino and even though I know that this guy is bad medicine and I don't want anything to do with hillbillies, the fellow is stubborn and tells Tonet, you Catalonians are a low bunch, no collons, no nothing, and in order to avoid any trouble, because the thing was getting ugly, the Cordovan hails a cab and there the three of us are, caught with this Gómez Molina guy, who's less than nobody, on our way to District 5, and we're feeling no pain, the way men do, with all that Tarragona wine, which is a corker, your honor, but we end up in a bar full of loafers, all friends, it seems, of that Gómez Molina guy, people who run away from the police as if they were after them, and right there by the Santa Madrona gate we've having a few drinks in peace and quiet, when this guy, I mean Gómez Molina, feels like singing, and the waitress, who's a whore and hasn't got any hair on her tongue, shows him a sign that says no singing or dancing allowed, but the guy starts up with some tarantas again, and the woman insults him, and Gómez Molina passes a remark about

Catalonian mothers, and the man who must be the owner tells us, that's it, you get the hell out of here, you bunch of bastards, he says, you're nothing but a bunch of hick bastards, I mean, begging your honor's pardon; well, the thing got to the point of put up or shut up, and to avoid trouble, I go out onto the street with Tonet when who comes out behind us but Gómez Molina and he starts on the Catalonians again, honor and collons, I'm not sure if I'm making myself clear, and I look him in the eye and tell him to shut up or I'll smack him so hard his own father won't recognize him, and that's where we are when the guy opens out like a fan, holding a knife about this long, and yours truly happens to have a bottle of beer and I break off the bottom so I can defend myself, and before I have a chance to touch a hair on the guy's head, I swear to you, I hear the watchman with his whistle and two graycoats come tearing at me and they beat me with their clubs, a beating that almost killed me, your honor, even though I tell them with all respect due to the Law, no, not me, I'm innocent, it's Gómez Molina you want, the bastard who was shitting on Catalonian mothers. . . . And when I come to I don't see the Gómez Molina guy, or the Cordovan who was good at soleares, or Tonet, and what I do see are three poor guys like me, locked up in the cell with me, what's the matter with you, damn it, I say, well, wait a few hours, because this is only the beginning, they gave me such a going over last year that I couldn't move for a week, I'm innocent, I tell them, it's all the fault of a son of a bitch who was insulting Catalonian mothers, but nobody will listen to me and since the three of them are quiet, you, why are you here, I ask one of them, and the guy says they caught me with a package of pot on the Calle San Rafael, how about you, me, a blond fellow tells me, for being with two Frenchwomen, I was going with two pimps and a guy from the secret police caught me without papers and brought me here, the third one, if he isn't a fairy, I'll eat my hat, doesn't answer me, and when I ask him again, he says, I haven't done anything, it must be some mix-up, you're the one who's mixed up, the pot guy says, because I've seen you standing in line for the movies more than you've seen your mother's cunt, and while I'm cursing my luck, somebody unlocks the door and a guy comes in even more messed up than me, en cago en Deu y la seva Mare, *he says, yes,* en cago en Deu, le mare que els va parir, pero que m'han fotut, cony, que m'han fotut, *they tie your balls around your neck like a necktie, that's what they do to you, I was sleeping on a bench on the Ramblas, not doing anything, and the bastards hit me with their clubs, that'll teach you to sleep it off here like any mother's son, the pot guy says, can't you see that guys who sleep on the streets make a bad impression on the tourists, because we're Europeans now, you fucking peasant, and one of these days they'll even let us into the Common Market, the common cunt's where they ought to let you in, the wounded guy says, and the door opens again and a gypsy drunk as a lord comes in with his clothes all covered with vomit, I want to speak to the captain, the young guy says, he told me to see him in a little while, tell him it's important, don't worry, sweety, the pot guy says, you just take it easy and fix your hair and put some make-up on, because they're going to take your picture, full-face and profile, for the Nodo, if they haven't already got you on file from the other times, faggy, and when the young guy starts to cry, the one with the pot sneaks up behind him and moves backward and forward, flapping his elbows, as if he was cornholing him, leave me alone, the young guy says, I want to see the captain, how long are they going to keep us here the guy with the French girls says, no one answers him, and the young guy beats on the door with his fists and the pot guy says that at nine o'clock they'll put us in a truck and take us to headquarters, why headquarters, for booking the pot one says, first they take your picture, then they make you play the piano. . . . When I wake up again, it's after nine and my whole body aches, and the guard opens the door and they bring us down to the street handcuffed together, the wagon is full of people and when we get in, the ones inside complain and curse our mothers, and a guy with a painted face and a flower in his buttonhole points at the young guy, hey, he says, look who's here, it's Fabiola, and as soon as the truck starts up, we all start to sway, bumping into each other because we're packed in like sardines, and the handcuffs are cutting into my wrists, and every so often, more people get in and the air gets stuffy, stop shoving, you bastards, the pot guy says, and at headquarters they line us up by threes in the back of the room and take away our ball-points, our shoelaces, our watches, our belts, and our wallets, the captain, where's the captain, the young guy says, and when we go down to the basement, we pass a kid who can barely drag himself along, held up by a pair of graycoats, good lord, look what they've done to him, he must be a hoodlum, no, the pot guy says, he's a student, day before yesterday they caught some of them in front of the Canaletas bar, and the guard shoves us inside the cell and I grab the bars, I'm innocent, I say, the guilty one is that guy Gómez Molina who was drunk and shitting on Catalonian mothers. . . .*

On one of his first visits to Madame Berger's café, Álvaro was invited to a meeting sponsored by the old Republican parties, the objective of which, from what he could gather from a modest mimeographed pamphlet, was the "development of a policy of agreement and common action which would put an end, once and for all, to the fatal internal divisions brought on by exile." The invitation bore the endorsement of some twenty personalities with names that were remotely familiar and who represented in turn such groupings as *Izquierda Republicana, Partido Republicano Federal, Unión Republicana, Esquerra Catalana, Partido Republicano Gallego,* and even am *Alianza Democrática Valenciana Sección Exterior* (a piece of information that led one to imagine the unsuspected existence of complex, subtle, and mysterious branches of the organization in the interior of that province).

For several hours, Álvaro had been wandering from one end of the Quartier Latin to the other in the company of a *onírica* and foggy little Dutch girl with a passion for Norman alcohol, Negro art, and occult sciences, whom he had met quite casually while standing in line at the Foyer de Sainte-Geneviève and who, between endless drinks of *p'tit calva* and with a more or less incomprehensible language, had dragged him in turn to the Cinémathèque on the rue d'Ulm (just as the box office was closing), to a lecture at the Club de 4 Vents on the theme "*La cybernétique et l'homme moderne*" (during which the girl had a fortunate snooze and then started clapping when she woke up, interrupting the speaker in the middle of his talk), and to a meeting organized by the UNEF to protest against the inadequate meals in student restaurants (a demonstration broken up by the *Préfecture de Police* with blows, stone-throwing, and clubbing, that had the virtue of shaking her out of her torpor) before she deposited him in a curious literary salon filled with pale young men with gazelle eyes, disappearing finally in a brusque and definite way, leaving him facing a fearsome matron in her sixties with false eyebrows and dyed blond hair who, after a forced exchange of smiles and the vain attempt to "*Et vous écrivez aussi, sans doute,"* had clutched at the fact of his nationality with an entranced and surprising *"Ah, c'est bien d'être Espagnol,"* which had suddenly and hopelessly sunk him into a desolating pit of despair, confusion, and perplexity.

Everything else—the obligatory visit to Madame Berger's café and his subsequent attendance at the political meeting of the Republican parties—had been the logical consequence of an afternoon that had started with such dire prospects. Without really knowing how—his body still warmed by the effects of the *p'tits calvas*—Alvaro woke up at the door of a building that belonged to the Académie des Sciences de Paris, where in the lobby there was on display a dusty bust of a gentleman with a frock coat and wig and the inscription: *Georges Louis de Buffon, Montbard 1707—Paris 1788*. Other Spaniards wrapped in frayed topcoats and raincoats seemed to be waiting for the arrival of reinforcements before deciding to enter the uninviting and cold lecture hall, which had been decorated for the occasion with the red, yellow, and purple flag of the Republic of 1931.

Álvaro settled down in one of the empty seats toward the front and looked around. The people there—a hundred, perhaps more —had passed the limits of mature age, and Álvaro calculated their vital mean to be within the sixties. He knew some of them by sight from having run into them in Madame Berger's café: old Colonel Carrasco, who kept a careful account of his salary since April, 1939, revised in accordance with the progressive increase in the cost of living due to the devaluation of the peseta and with his promotion to brigadier general in accordance with normal promotions in the table of organization, for the day when Republican legality would finally be re-established; a former Minister of Merchant Marine of the Government-in-Exile to whom gossips in the café attributed the possession of a superb flotilla of toy boats with which he solemnly played as he took a bath; two Aragonese anarchists, childhood friends of Durruti. When they recognized him, they gave him a nod. The social origin and profession of the others were difficult to establish. The two gentlemen in the front row were dressed with the careful elegance of two businessmen. Next to Álvaro, an old man was wiping his nose with a piece of red cloth. There were also a dozen women and a young man wearing a corduroy jacket.

When the lights on stage were turned on, somebody in the back threw out a bunch of handbills that rained down on the small audience and, taking advantage of the confusion, the guilty party slipped out the exit. Álvaro grabbed one of the sheets as it floated down and read: NO DIVISIVE MANEUVERS. At the same time, there was the sound of hurried steps, and several of those present got up and ran after the fugitive, while someone with a strong voice climbed up onto the stage with an agility not proper for his years, and exhorted the audience to be calm: "Ladies and gentlemen, friends, we urge you to excuse this regrettable invasion, which, unfortunately, is not the work of an isolated individual, but that of a group of cheap politicians who have been threatened in their comfortable position of waiting and inaction by our initiative in restoring the original spirit of agreement and friendship among the most genuine forces of those of us in exile." There was some applause—very strong, as if to compensate for the small number of people—and Álvaro's neighbor stood up on his chair and repeated several times: "This provocation is intolerable." Colonel Carrasco was perorating animatedly in the midst of a circle of ladies and was menacing the author of the act with the handle of his cane. The ex-minister and the Aragonese anarchists had joined the nucleus of pursuers and returned after a moment, very agitated and gesticulating and shouting to each other. "We must be calm, gentlemen, we must be calm," the man on the platform was insisting. "The act of vandalism you have just witnessed must not upset the calmness of our spirits or incite us to answer violence with violence. The reasons behind our presence in this auditorium are based upon our desire to break the vicious circle of hate and quarreling that has paralyzed the political forces in exile, so that we can offer the heroic Spanish people what they have been expecting from us for twenty years, a unified platform that will exclude the divisive elements that live off the blood and suffering of the masses in order to . . ."

The loud applause of the people there prevented him from going on. A small man had appeared on the platform. He was bald, wearing glasses, and was escorted by two other old men wearing dark suits like him and, as the final late arrivals trailed furtively in from the lobby, the man with the powerful voice turned smiling toward the trio and announced: "We have with us one of the great authors of the Constitution of 1931, a firm champion of the invincible cause of the Republic, a noted debater famous throughout the world, Dr. Carnero." The applause broke out with renewed energy, and Dr. Carnero bowed left and right before sitting down behind the table and taking a sheaf of papers out of the inside of his jacket. The man with the powerful voice waited until it was quiet, and proceeded to the introduction of the speaker. He began by stating that the speaker needed no introduction, for it was a question of a person who was loved and admired by all for the nobility of his spirit and the blinding clarity of his ideas. Dr. Carnero, born into the bosom of a very humble family in Orense, had been familiar since childhood with the suffering and injustices imposed upon the various Spanish nationalities by an obscurantist and retrograde monarchy. Dr. Carnero had worked the land between the ages of eight and fifteen in order to relieve his parents' critical situation, and he had learned to read and write thanks to the solicitude and help of Eliseo Sánchez, a country schoolteacher who subscribed to libertarian ideas and who, when young Rafael had not even reached the age of twelve, had put into his hands a book by the unforgettable Bakunin, the reading of which was a real revelation for the boy, an episode masterfully described by Dr. Carnero himself in his memoirs, *The Forging of a Fighter*, published in Mexico and distributed in any number of countries. From that day on, Dr. Carnero, with great tenacity, had plunged into the works of the most important revolutionary authors and polemicists, equipping himself intellectually for the combat that was to guide his future life. At the age of eighteen, having just arrived in Madrid, with no other baggage but his calloused hands of a worker and his generous heart of a patriot, he comes to know the dismal Bourbon dungeons for the first time. Dr. Carnero dreams of a Spain free of chains and, in spite of the crude threats of Maura's hirelings, he puts in opposition his integrity of a virile and complete opponent, a glorious scene described in the first volume of his memoirs, which everyone present must remember. At the age of twenty-three Dr. Carnero publishes in the newspaper *La Batalla* a courageous article in which he implacably denounces the crimes perpetrated by the Church against the cause of the Spanish people and from that time on his private life and his fertile activity as a journalist merge into one single existence that is dedicated to the triumph of republican and libertarian ideals. Everything else, his struggle against the Juntas of Defense and the Dictatorship of Primo de Rivera, his outstanding role in the Republic of 1931, his tireless struggle against the praetorian uprising of 1936, first in the trenches and later on in exile, are now in the public domain, because Dr. Carnero's glory knows no limits or frontiers, and the author has described it, as a guide and example for future generations, in that work of his that was so highly praised by the most demanding critics the world over, *Spain's Dark Night*. Therefore, the presence in this hall of Dr. Carnero is a symbol in itself. A symbol of the ardent and fraternal Spain that will, without a doubt, be the Spain of tomorrow on that day when the forces in exile decide to unite in order to free the Spanish nationalities from the despotic and bloody dictatorship that holds them in subjection.

There was a new and nourished burst of applause, and Dr. Carnero greeted the audience with a slight nod of his head, carefully adjusted his glasses on his nose, and straightened out the papers he had laid on the table.

"Ladies and gentlemen," he said it in such a strong voice that, for a moment, Álvaro had the impression that he was speaking into a microphone. "The chroniclers say that when he was very old, Michelangelo was found going through the streets of Rome on a certain January morning, hugging the walls. They asked him where he was going, shaking with age and the cold; and he answered quite naturally: 'I'm going to school to see if I can learn something.' Joaquín Costa, the divine Teacher, already in his sixties and crippled with myelitis, was invited to come to Madrid to speak to the Chamber of Deputies against one of the infamous laws concocted by untamed Maurism. Right from the railroad station, and even before going to his hotel to wash up, that sublime invalid made them take him to the Ateneo, where his friends found him later on, up to his neck in books . . ." After the first moment of surprise had passed, Álvaro peeped out of the corner of his eye to get the reaction of those present, still lulled by the effects of fatigue and the aftertaste of the *p'tits calvas*. The one who had given the introduction and Dr. Carnero's two companions were sitting on the right of the platform and were receiving the slow flow of the speech with an expression of enraptured peace. Beside Álvaro, the old man with the piece of red cloth was smiling with delight in the same way. Colonel Carrasco was listening, turned to stone with attention, his hands resting on the head of his sword stick. The two women next to him were nodding approval and, at intervals, would exchange a tender look of complicity. Feeling himself left out of that fraternal communion, Álvaro spotted the enraptured face of the former

Minister of Merchant Marine, the respectful looks of the Aragonese anarchists, the beatific rictus of the young man in the corduroy jacket. The silence in the shabby hall was seraphic, almost eucharistic, and Dr. Carnero's hoarse voice was vibrating in the air, successively melodic, incisive, grave, dramatic, jocular: " 'You do not have a delicate intelligence,' a finicky reader who looked like a pupil of the Loyolas once said to Luis Bonafoux. To which the grand Puerto Rican, from the island of the Antilles and the café of the same name on the Puerta del Sol, replied: 'What's important to me is to have a brain that is strong in breadth of vision and in the ability to penetrate. I don't lose any sleep over anything else. Everything else one can easily get or receive as a gratuity.' Julio Ferry used to say that when one has genius, he is always bad-tempered, a genial quality. Inertia and apathy are not paths to goodness, but to renunciation and retreat; that is, denying one's self and fleeing from others; dodging morality like a bullfighter and having no respect for what is around one. The political writer must possess the temperament of a gothic flamboyant and a tropical jungle. He must have thought and feeling forever fused in mortal embrace. And work based on that attitude is a militia, a militancy. Beautiful aping ways, affected niceties are fine for a tearoom, a beauty parlor, or a gathering of pretty painted girls. They are out of place in the arena or the ring where the problems are aired upon which at times the fate of a century or of a country and now, even, the whole zoo brought out of Noah's Ark depend . . ." The audience was listening with ecstasy, and Álvaro examined once more the three men on the podium, Colonel Carrasco, the little old man with the red handkerchief, the former Minister of Merchant Marine, the Aragonese anarchists, and the young man with the corduroy jacket, before rolling his eyes in turn and abandoning himself to the magnetic outpouring of the speech, tremendously happy about that unexpected chance to integrate himself in an incomprehensible but real universe after his unsuccessful raids on the line at the movies, the lecture on cybernetics, the student meeting of the UNEF, and the extravagant literary salon, with his stomach, forehead and eyes impregnated with *p'tits calvas,* on the same wave length as those admiring men and women, respectful and attentive, who were smiling mysteriously, nodding approval, and looking at each other like accomplices, cradled by the well-modulated and varying voice of the speaker: "The correct and sure road to reach the place where

Claret wanted to go is not that one. The contemplative Brahman, setting out to redeem myriads of beings fascinated with their navels was mistaken in his method. The path that moves the progress of History is the reaction of nerve, not prayers. About a quarter of a century ago, a half-dozen eager men tried to repeat the miracle of Moses in Spain, striking the hostile rock with the magic wand that all sorcerers have to make a stream of living water pour forth. More than prophets and palmists, those Spaniards where characters from Meunier. They started from the concept that the word is a seed; that speaking is a significant act, and that writing is doing. With the baggage of that decalogue, the innovators to whom we refer embarked upon the difficult task of twisting the course of history in our country. The panorama that surrounded them was not inspiring, however: the ground was a glacier; the sky a petrified fog; the air their chests took in the emissary of pneumonia. Those who had worked at previous attempts, who, tired of fighting against the ungrateful land, had stuck their hoes into the earth and had fallen into the furrow . . ." The miracle had finally been produced, and with his eyes opened to his inexpressible inner happiness, Álvaro felt lulled and rocked, penetrated and possessed, literally wrapped up in Dr. Carnero's persuasive voice, with the intimate and intoxicating certainty of knowing that he was a part of a human collectivity fastened together in a pact that was not less firm because it was not known, sorry only that the foggy Dutch girl was not there to cap that celebration of peace, friendship, and camaraderie with the support of her presence, healthy and diaphanous, vegetable and restoring. "A Monarchy bursting with soothing promises," the voice went on, "restored in some new Saguntum without the complete, free, clear, and meditated answer of the electoral body, of the complete population of voting age and of both sexes, that is, is purely and simply inadmissible. That would be a mockery that the average Spaniard, after everything he has suffered in his dignity as a man and a citizen, could never tolerate. That is why it is better to keep on with today's obstruction which, with its obvious evils, will bring on internal unrest and external help that can accelerate the cure. But the other plan, as it maintained a substantially identical political situation, would contribute, both inside and outside the country, the paralyzing disorder of a swindle. It would be the coup de grâce for all hope of any authentic and democratic normality. And we Republicans are already doing enough as, on the altars of peace, with limitless obeisance to the will of the Nation, with scrupulous respect for the democratic and libertarian idea, we renounce the absolute priority that corresponds to us in principle, and accept the appearance, under conditions of parity with a different regime, before the constituent court of the Nation, so that we may obtain from the same, as we hope, the confirmation of our firm rights . . ." At that point, it was no longer necessary to open his eyes and glance about the auditorium, so sure as he was that he would make out the devout and fervent faces of the three men on the platform, the old man with the red cloth, and the former Minister of Merchant Marine, completely captivated too by the melodious singsong that was pouring from the lips of the speaker, like a neophyte observer at a ritual initiation or a play in an unfamiliar language, satisfied at having ended the day with an unforgettable brotherhood, in spite of the bitter taste of the *p'tits calvas* and the unfortunate absence of the Dutch girl, whom he would have liked to have hugged passionately as Dr. Carnero, accompanying himself with vehement gestures, tirelessly went on with his elevated and celestial speech: "If something must be re-established immediately, it is our pure and beloved Republic. If that is impossible, due to outside pressures, then, before the country decides calmly, nothing should be restored. But, on the other hand, since it is impossible to continue facing the tragic alternative between the people's abject state and their despair, we must get out of this blind alley as soon as possible. Which way? you are probably asking. . . . Toward a situation that, unable to be either Monarchy or Republic at the moment, unable to have a precise institutional form, must, therefore, be interim, transitory, dedicated exclusively to the re-establishment of an essential and generic democratic order at the end of which the people, peacefully, consciously, freely, will elect, under any institutional form they prefer, the representatives who will outline it, articulate it, and install it solidly and forever in the sight of and with the consensus of the whole Nation . . ."

Transported to divine heights—Seraphim, Cherubim, Throne, Dominion, Prince, Power, and Virtue—Álvaro had not paid attention to the repeated pounding on the door—with his eyes closed and the aftertaste of the *p'tits calvas* in his mouth—until the strength and repetition of the kicks took on an alarming intensity and, along with the other spectators, he turned his head around to discover with indignant surprise a group of individuals who, shouting such phrases as "Down with the divisionists" and "Mummies back to the museum," were attempting to open a path to the platform where Dr. Carnero was speaking and could not be heard. They knocked over chairs and threw out handfuls of leaflets which were falling on the audience in the midst of a deafening gabble of shrieks, insults, shoves, and punches.

"Step down!"

"This is an outrage."

"Divisionists!"

"Shame! Shame!"

"Back to the museum!"

The hubbub of voices grew and, caught up in the tide of combatants, Álvaro caught a glimpse of the majestic figure of Colonel Carrasco, who, with the noble bearing of an officer recently graduated from the Academy, was gallantly brandishing his slim cane at the enemy. The public formed a barrier in the aisle and, giving up their objective of occupying the podium, the invaders slowly withdrew toward the exit. The old man with the red cloth had grabbed one of them by the back of the neck and was scratching him fiercely with his thin and parchment-like hands. At the door there was a final exchange of blows and insults, followed by a new and heavier rain of handbills. Before disappearing for good, someone threw a rotten egg that landed with sacrilegious accuracy, after describing a perfect parabola, on the sheaf of papers that covered the severe and almost liturgical speaker's table.

Dr. Carnero lowered his head as if overwhelmed by the magnitude of that peaceful disaster. When the aggressors had been expelled, the audience shouted and argued without paying attention to the pacifying words of the man who had introduced him, who, with pathetic gestures and invocations, was exhorting them to be calm.

"Comrades. . . . The spirit of concord that animates this great gathering of . . ."

"The Constitution of 1931 is a dead letter," shouted the former Minister of Merchant Marine, standing on a chair. "If we want to be reborn out of the ashes of the past . . ."

"The Spanish people have the floor."

"Our mistakes oblige us to . . ."

"Only national unity will permit us to overthrow . . ."

The tumult was growing with every moment, and several speakers intervened with shouts, gravely raising their arms and expounding diverse and contradictory political programs from their improvised platforms. The man who had made the introduction was clapping his hands in a last and desperate effort to make himself heard, and he took advantage of a moment of truce to proclaim in a dramatic voice:

"Let us be frank. . . . The emigration has not had leaders of stature who have been able to unite around them the disoriented and dispersed forces that . . ."

"What do you mean, no leaders?"

The interruption broke like a thunderclap, and Álvaro saw a gentlemen in his sixties who, standing in turn on another chair, was showing his indignation with a rapid series of gestures and expressions characteristic of a man used to expressing himself easily in public.

"What about me?"

They were all silent, obeying the imperative tone of his voice, and with his hazy sight, Álvaro looked at his clenched fist and the swollen blue veins on his forehead.

"Me. In the elections to the Cortes in 1933, in my district of Manzanares, I obtained a plurality of sixty-five hundred votes over the reactionary candidate supported by . . ."

A belch of *p'tit calva* stronger than the previous ones obliged him to run out into the hallway and, with no time to reach the bathroom, Álvaro vomited at length and copiously, his forehead leaning on the base that held the bust of *Georges Louis Leclerc de Buffon, Montbard 1707—Paris 1788* under the compassionate gaze of an old woman dressed in black who looked like a member of the *Armée du Salut* and who—after having gone into the auditorium of the Académie de Sciences by chance, had retreated immediately, startled by the incomprehensible and noisy spectacle—patted him lovingly on the shoulder, saying with an unmistakable Russian accent: "*Alors, jeune homme, ça ne va pas?*"

They had agreed to meet at the café on the corner, a hundred feet away from the lawyer's house. When Artigas and Paco arrived, Antonio was pacing on the opposite sidewalk, impatiently smoking a cigarette. When he spotted them, he waved and crossed the street. His dark raincoat and the brief case gave him the caricature air of a conspirator.

"If I belonged to the cops, I'd arrest you on suspicion at once," Paco said. "Couldn't you wear something else?"

"What the fuck do you want me to wear?"

"You could have got a haircut at least. . . . Someday that look of a Murcian bandit of yours is going to get us all in a mess."

"I'm completely antiseptic," Antonio said. "Two graycoats were sitting next to me on the bus and I had fun taking the list of signatures out of my briefcase right under their noses."

"You just keep on fooling around and you'll see what'll happen. Someday they'll grab you and scrape the hide off your ass."

"Anything new on Enrique?" Artigas asked.

"No, nothing."

"My sister went to see his mother and you know what the old girl came out with?" Artigas was staring directly at him. "She said it was all your fault."

"Mine?"

"That's right. She gave her a lecture that lasted over three hours about bad company and bad books. . . . My sister said she was ready to climb the walls when she left."

They leaned on the bar and Paco ordered three coffees.

"Have you got the typewriter back?"

"Yes."

"We have to turn out more copies. If anyone else signs, we can add him later."

"I've got a date with Gasparini at one o'clock."

"I'll send a copy to Álvaro, for the French papers."

"Alvarito . . ." Antonio said. "I'd like to know where the hell he is. . . . Since he started traveling, you can't keep track of him."

"He doesn't even want to see the face of his own father," Artigas said. "A guy from the University went to visit him at home and he says he's always drunk as a lord."

"One drink has the same effect as a hundred now," Paco said. "Paris has turned him into a bum."

"Oh, leave him alone. . . . What do the two of you know?"

"You don't believe it?" Artigas said. "Letters can say something. Paco was there when the guy told me, right?"

"O.K., O.K. . . . What are we here for, to see that guy or to criticize Álvaro?"

"Yeah," Artigas said. "Let's shake it a little, or we'll be late."

Paco paid for the three coffees, and when they got onto the street, he pointed at a wooden bench.

"I'll wait for you there," he said.

"Why?"

"We look like a delegation. Two's plenty."

"You're always trying to get out of things," Artigas said.

"If you want to stay, go ahead. I'll go up with Antonio."

"No. Artigas and I'll go. You wait for us down here."

He followed them with his eyes until they disappeared through the entrance. People were coming and going peacefully along the sidewalk and a traffic policeman at the corner was up on his platform directing the slight traffic and solemn and theatrical gestures. Paco examined in turn a nurse with a baby carriage, two ladies with missals and mantillas who were whispering secrets into each other's ear on their way home from church, a handsomely dressed old man with a silver-topped cane. The people seemed to be happy to be alive, with that tranquil assurance of those who felt protected from any surprise, the inhabitants of a world without beginning or end that was perpetually being repeated to infinity. After a few seconds of hesitation, he sat down on the bench and lit a Rumbo. Next to him, a small man in a frayed trench coat was attentively going over the headlines of his paper: "Manolo Cuevas and Carlos Ribero awarded ears in San Sebastián de los Reyes." He imagined Tusquets's face, restless and sorrowful at the same time, when he discovered the purpose of the visit: "There's no way out for us Spaniards, believe me." Along the opposite sidewalk, a woman with a touch of the common about her was leading a blond boy dressed up like a figurine by the hand. At a signal from the policeman, the cars coming down in the direction of Plaza Cataluña yielded to two taxis coming from the left. The little man was still wrapped up in his reading of the paper. "Manolo Ears and Carlos Reyes awarded riberos in San Sebastián de las Cuevas." A pair of lovers, a boy with a carton of bottles, another nurse in uniform pushing a carriage. The common woman had disappeared into a notions shop with the child. On the platform at the intersection, the policeman was moving with the rigidity of a puppet. "Sebastián Cuevas and Manolo Ribero awarded reyes in San Carlos de las Ears." Sprawling in his easy chair, with a glass of Carlos I in his hand, the lawyer was meditating upon the sad fate of his compatriots: "It's all of no use, my friends. . . . Poor Spain!" The two armed police patrolmen guarding the entrance of the banking establishment—"Capital 2,000,000,000 pesetas, entirely disbursed"—went over to chat with the woman selling newspapers. "Sebastián Riberto and Reyes Ears awarded cuevas in San Manolo de los Carlos." The cigarette tasted bad and he threw it away and lit another. The Barcelonans were passing by along the sidewalk, satisfied, conscious of having lived another day exactly like the rest, one with no hostile upsets or disagreeable changes. What had been going on in the cells at Headquarters was just a stupid accident, the bothersome interference of a parasite in a perfectly synchronized program, melodious and pleasing to the ear. "Sebastián Ears and Ribero Reyes awarded carlos in San Cuevas de los Manolos." The two nurses were chatting animatedly beside their carriages. The common woman appeared again with the child and stopped in front of the newsstand. Upstairs, the former leader of Estat Catalá was talking, talking in a tireless way: "Every country gets the government it deserves. . . ." Life would never change, the firm hand of a most prudent pilot was guiding the ship away from the dangers of any unforeseen contingency. The nurses, the children, the lovers, the shopgirls could sleep peacefully, walk sleepfully, dream walkfully, live in dreams, the happy meshing of a machine that had no phallus, as immortal as the order that watched over the exact and repeated symmetry of their gestures. "Manolo Cuevas and Sebastián Reyes awarded manolos in San Ears de los Ribero." The little man caught his twisted look and folded up the paper with annoyance.

Almost at the same time, Antonio and Artigas came out onto the street. The two of them seemed all worked up and when he spotted him, Antonio stopped and hit his fist against his other hand.

"The bastard, oh, that bastard."

"What happened?" Paco asked. "Did you get his signature?"

"The motherfucker." Antonio was looking up angrily at the row of balconies where the lawyer lived, and he spat in anger on the ground. "The chicken son of a bitch wouldn't sign it."

Madame Berger's café was square in shape and covered a raw surface of eighty-six square yards. Its furniture consisted of nine tables, two side-benches, and a variable number of chairs, between thirty and thirty-five. The lights were neon and the walls were decorated with mirrors, posters, calendars, empty bottles, and the indispensable text of the *Loi de Repression de l'Ivresse Publique*.

Although the make-up of the clientele would change with some regularity, anyone who left Paris for a few years could still return with the calm assurance that on his return he would find an appreciable majority of familiar faces. The elements that constituted the different geological strata would be continuing their tireless monologues on Spain and Spaniards, never listening to the soliloquies of the others, like radios with worn and raspy speakers that at alternating intervals rebroadcast different programs. The repertory of anecdotes and stories was the same as always, and the traveler would have the curious feeling that time had come to a halt.

Without needing to set foot in Madame Berger's café—on afternoons when inertia took control of him and he stayed in bed, waiting for Dolores to come home, his gaze fixed on the rundown and propped-up houses of the Faubourg du Temple—Álvaro could reconstruct the conversations of the people gathered there with the complete assurance of an actual witness.

"In my case, Besteiro's proclamation caught me on the Albacete front and the day the Moors surrounded the town, I hid in the house of a friend who had a sister in the Falange . . ."

"That reminds me of something that happened to me just before the Figols uprising, during Azaña's second ministry . . ."

". . . I intended to escape from there and get to Alicante, when I heard about the fall of Madrid and the Fascist victory on the radio . . ."

". . . I'd been sent from Barcelona by the Union to discuss with representatives of management . . ."

". . . The house was right next door to the Welfare mess hall, and since I didn't want to compromise my friend, I climbed out the window one night without telling him . . ."

". . . And when I get to the station, I see a detachment of Civil Guards on the platform, under the command of a lieutenant they called Fire-Face . . ."

". . . and I crossed the whole province on foot along with two other soldiers from my division, both of them Communists . . ."

". . . a mean fellow, with a scar this long on his forehead that Abd-el-Krim's rebels had given him . . ."

". . . when we got to a town called Madrigueras, we heard an order to halt . . ."

". . . who was later shot at the start of the war . . ."

". . . and my buddies and I started to run as fast as we could, thinking they were Falangists . . ."

". . . As soon as I get off the train, the Civil Guards point their guns at me . . ."

". . . until all at once, I recognize the voice of a commissar from my brigade who had somehow got ahold of a Legion uniform . . ."

". . . and Fire-Face says to me: 'You're coming with us right now, you son of a bitch' . . ."

"I went through something like that in Argelés . . ."

". . . a man named Pedro Oliveira, who was in jail with me in Albatera and later got away to Mexico . . ."

". . . Since I knew the kind of tricks the cutey played on UGT people . . ."

". . . two Senegalese wanted to get a gold watch away from me . . ."

". . . Yes indeed, yes, the commissar of the Fifth. An Estremaduran, very dark; he looked like a Gypsy . . ."

". . . I thought, this guy, what he wants to do is enforce the law of 'shot while trying to escape' . . ."

". . . that was a gift from Sánchez Pascual, the *Izquierda Republicana* deputy . . ."

". . . Well, as I was saying, Oliveira had got ahold of a Legion uniform . . ."

". . . and put the blame on the CNT, the way they did with poor Pepito Blanco . . ."

". . . that he had given to me when he was dying in the military hospital in Tarragona, a month before the Fascists got there . . ."

"That's like what happened to me in Miranda de Ebro with a Frenchman who was a strong Gaullist and . . ."

". . . and Oliveira tells me . . ."

". . . when I passed a patrol of Assault Guards on the street . . ."

". . . The two Senegalese were waiting for me when I came out of the showers . . ."

". . . he'd crossed the Pyrenees to get to North Africa . . ."

". . . I've got a friend in Mazarrón who's got a motor boat the four of us can use to escape in . . ."

". . . under the command of a Republican sergeant, a man called González Miret . . ."

". . . *Eh, tua, Español, fe vuar ta montre* . . ."

". . . who became a friend of yours truly, because the only one in the barracks who could get along in his language . . ."

"Say, what happened to me once, in Brunete . . ."

. . . Days, weeks, months, years used up in recalling, arguing, pontificating, not listening, saying terrible things about France, dusting off memories of the war and announcing the imminent fall of the Regime, all of which, back in his native country, Álvaro was reliving, just as during the time he had lain by the window of his studio as the sunset slowly brought out the perspective of gray roofs and Carpaccio chimneys, saying to himself over and over again with infinite bitterness, we Spaniards, carry self-centeredness, envy, and rancor in our blood; if Spanish society is intolerant, it is due above all to the fact that there is some hidden Manichee in the heart of every Spaniard, and—isolated now, in the middle of the night, useless, unjustifiable, and rootless—he would conclude with a mixture of grim stupor and horrified joy that the land of all you cannot be taken in like breath because none of you yourselves can be taken in like breath.

"They had gone too far this time everybody agreed they had gone too far it did not seem possible that it was possible especially since it was a question of boys from good families the sons of martyrs or victim of sickness contracted during the Red terror all having had a Christian education in private schools some of them especially dedicated to the Immaculate Heart of Mary and beneficiaries of the divine promise in respect to the practice of the First Fridays of the Month boys who had appeared later on in neat tuxedos in the boxes of the Liceo and had been active members of Musical Youth rubbing elbows with the elite with the best circles of Barcelona society future members of the Equestrian Club or appearing on the fields of the Royal Polo Club there where the beautiful and modest girls from good families our daughters have chaste fun in the company of perfectly raised young men like them future famous doctors well-known lawyers career diplomats worthy heirs to daddy's fabric factory or flourishing and prosperous silk looms in spite of the ups and downs of the Stabilization Plan and the terrible restriction of bank credit the source of so many anxieties tears and troubles regulars at the Palau and chamber theaters and movie clubs sighing perhaps over the quiet chaste and innocent graduates of Asunción or José María our daughters innocently exposed to the influence of a noxious contact with those amoral worms raised in the pulpy heart of the fruit serpents nesting in our warm breasts ravens ready to tear out our eyes spendthrifts and wasters of the capital of virtue the capital of firmness the capital of honesty the capital of good name and the capital-capital of refined and well-descended families with famous names enriched in Cuba and the Philippines or in the Universal Exposition of 1888 or the one in 1929 threatened in their existence and their goods by gunmen of the FAI and the Russian Chekas and their following of traitors and pouncing wolves in sheep's clothing of the Generalitat and the accursed Republic of 1931 dancers of the *sardana* with Catalonian berets on Sunday and *salves* to the *Mare de Deu* of Montserrat before the yearned-for trip to the France of the *Front Populaire* the first obligatory step on the road to the Burgos headquarters and the triumphal return with Moors and Christians arm in arm in the heady air brought on at that time by the ardent partisans of a German victory and Wagner's music sustenance of the expeditionary heroes of the Blue Division in its noble task of extirpating the cancer of Communism forever from long-suffering Russia regular readers of the magazine *Signal* and the Ufa newsreels before subscribing in 1945 to the bulletin of the American Embassy and the pretty Spanish edition of *Life* in colors disillusioned by the well-intentioned but ill-fated mistakes of Adolf Hitler terrified by the brutal murder of Mussolini and happy that the provident action of an unconquered leader the supreme peacemaker and the lasting guarantee that in his hands order will not only be broken but will never suffer the slightest shadow of upset had saved them from the unforeseen contingencies of the glass-breaking fate of the Instituto Británico during the withdrawal of embassies proud of the ferocious Iberian particularism that distinguishes us from the other corrupt and decadent peoples the enthusiastic spectators at the great demonstrations of support and at the healthful admonitory parades satisfied with the fortunate conclusion of the Spanish-American agreements and the concordat with Pius XII Pastor Angelicus of the Marian dogma lover of lambs and children future saint venerated on altars the prelude to triumphal admission into NATO and with the protective tariffs needed in the Europe of the Common Market Europeans in short with the bikini finally permitted on the beaches and risqué French movies and even clandestine sessions of strip tease and we were all trembling in horror at the unsuspected depths of the evil knowing all the time that God had not wanted it and it could have attacked with equal strength any of our wandering children drawn away by evil books and neorealist films and contact with disguised agents just as those parents ashamed in their comprehensible but vain attempt to whitewash those lost souls assuring left and right with tears in their eyes that they did not know anything that they had fought without realizing that they were unaware of the real thrust of their maneuver and its ramifications abroad and the vociferous legions on the other side of the Pyrenees and the discredited political parties a gang of common criminals who from abroad were plotting against Spaniard order with the small but infamous collaboration of the schemers of the traitors and of the resentful ones inside the country that they the nodding parents had belonged to in their youth to the Somatén and had supported the *coup d'état* of Primo de Rivera and had been victims of hateful persecutions during the Republic before joining the Movement of salvation in Burgos San Sebastián or Salamanca germanophiles until the death of Hitler americanophiles after that of Roosevelt members of honorable civilian bodies and supporters of many priestly vocations and religious missionary orders and pious works and we all put on circumstantial faces pretending not to believe the unbelievable pitying ourselves really who would have thought of coming to this evil that this was the will of God mentally placing ourselves in their role of humiliated parents whose offspring have irretrievably stained the sacrosanct family name and we mediated frightened at the extent of the virus and on the perverse tricks of the enemy since it is a question of an enemy and the proofs gathered by a police force especially dedicated to the Archangel Gabriel do not allow doubts of any kind since it is a model organization and the celestial messenger of the Lord exercises over it his influence and guidance in its work of preserving the people from the dangers that lie in wait for them so that society can rest in confidence thanks to their constant watch their spirit of sacrifice and their permanent vigilance and even though in truth we have never been completely out of danger and scandal has more than once touched some religious and well-established family in the shape of cuckoldry by a best friend from an even better family or the heir who is hopelessly homosexual or their slip of an inexperienced girl and the subsequent hurried trip to Switzerland were all minor sins over which it is prudent to throw the veil of forgetfulness exposed as we all are by our weak natures to the solicitations of the flesh and unable to say beforehand I will not drink of this water forgetfulness that covered even the most spicy stories even if they were the main fare at gatherings and made our innocent and pious women quiver with startling pleasure like that startling film taken by the impotent husband of his wife a girl from a good family in the company of two Negroes superbly endowed with virile attributes two sexually overdeveloped Senegalese according to the happy and privileged viewers of the film as is common among economically underdeveloped countries an insolent paradox that challenges the cheapest doctrine or scientific explanation of the world from the time of Aristotle to Karl Marx but that disgrace was a kind that no attempt at penitence or regeneration would ever be able to erase being as it was the case of young people from excellent families beneficiaries of a happy and unanimous peace such as we or our parents or our grandparents had never seen a peace so thorough that to the new generation it must seem natural when in reality it is not a natural product but the precious work of culture thanks to the vigilance of a man who is always in his place tireless watchman's eye and perennial sentinel of the defense of the essential postulates of public order certain that our ethnic criticism leaves us often dissatisfied and we like to ask for pears from an elm or look for artichokes in the gulf but it is also true that the last thing that breaks in us is hope and hope when it is accompanied by faith and by love is a stock that can be quoted on the market of the spirit and youth as demanding as it may be still has the common vertex of that magic name that all across the broad skin of the bull resounds like an homage of fervor and raised up with its invincible sword is the semaphore that watches day and night and marks our route along new and sage paths far from the black and stormy waters of parliamentarianism and freedom of the press unhurriedly waiting for the tender fruit of a centennial dynasty to mature in its cocoon lovingly woven to insure that on some distant day very distant the continuity and survival of the peace we know that youth is a synonym for generosity and that enthusiasm when mistaken is proper in a race that has given glorious examples of its spirit of initiative in the field of overseas commerce and the textile industry in the Exchange and Insurance Companies but on occasion youth good upbringing and wealth are no excuse but rather aggravation and these young fellows agitating in the streets perverse propagators of false tales rumors absurdities and lies who could have been our sons or the future husbands of our pure and virtuous daughters and who are not and never will be now thanks be to God in spite of all the sympathy we feel for their most honorable parents whose grief we sincerely share deserve a final and exemplary punishment for their rash attempt to open the gates of our country once more to that immense swarm of soulless fanatics who want to drag us into the most bloody and spurious slavery punishment yes for those who forget the elementary duties of recognition and gratitude and were trying again to throw us into the abyss of inorganic democracy into a repulsively plebeian universe scratching out the spiritual values of an age-old civilization that is the torch of our History an ecumenical civilization that discovered and populated worlds where they brought the cross and the church bell the book and the plow wheat and the ballad and within every Spanish breast an incorruptible racial feeling of dignity and independence upsetting peace not only in its negative concept of not fighting but also a new peace made powerful by its revolutionary vision of man as a creature of God therefore it is necessary for us to renew our vigilance the necessary hygienic prophylactic of the virus we who were born as they say on that sublime date that now seems to us to be the dividing summit of the two historical slopes and all on this side breaks away from the hill like a torrent fed by miraculous springs of heroism and we do not shrink from speaking of a miracle when from the very pit of death one returns to the mercy of life and the spirit aided by the supernatural with one single prodigy of will gets up and revives gloriously and this is what happened then by the works and the grace of God and the Most Holy Virgin on that unforgettable and happy day to be remembered *per omnia secula seculorum.*"

The daily visits to Madame Berger's café often held some surprises. Normally, the monotonous exhumation of the war years would be followed by the inevitable diagnosis of the ills of Spain: the people gathered there would comment on the latest happenings in the Peninsula—the abortive demonstration by university students, the letter of the Falangist malcontents, the spectacular drop in the price of olives, or a declaration by Don Juan's Privy Council—with brief and lapidary comments such as "The Regime has entered its final phase of decomposition and decay." "The desperate attempts of the Dictatorship show its increasing incapacity when it has to face the united action of the masses of the people," "The Spanish economy is a ship without a rudder," or "Internal contradictions are getting sharper"—opinions that vibrated like a chanted magical conjuration in the atmosphere that was thick with smoke, as Madame Berger's black cat slept curled up on the trap door of the bar and the pair of *clochards* who lived in the subway ventilator on the rue de l'Ancienne Comédie once more caressed their old dispute, with threats of separation, mutual accusations, and tender and unexpected reconciliations. From time to time, however, elements of the younger strata would abandon, without anyone's knowing why, the well-plowed furrows of politics to tote up—and inform the people in the café along the way—a variegated collection of adventures that lent credence in a patent sort of way to the innate possession on the part of the party involved of a sexual temperament so rich as to be envied. On one of those exceptional occasions—with no reference to the ills of Spain or the painful and well-known remembrances—Álvaro was invited to take part in a spree.

It had all happened a little after Enrique's arrival and the authors of the invitations were two students from Madrid at the Cité Universitaire whom Enrique had met in the prison yard at Carabanchel a few weeks before he was released. The taller one spoke about the studio of a Norwegian nymphomaniac painter and marijuana user, the key to which, he affirmed, had been given to him by its owner because of some obscure incident with a dope pusher. All they had to do, he said, was to call up a few chicks and organize a pajama party so that things would get hot and come to their logical conclusion. It seems there was a phonograph and a stack of records and enough wine to get a regiment drunk.

While the tall one went to get the key, Álvaro and his friends walked toward the Rhûmerie Martiniquaise with their heads full of confused projects, erotic, happy, and sensual, like a bunch of schoolboys on the town for the first time. The Paris sky was misty and vague and in the market on the Rue Buci, the vendors were hawking their merchandise.

"Where are you going?" Enrique asked.

"I want to get some cigarettes and call Michèle. She likes this kind of party."

"O.K. We'll wait for you on the terrace."

Álvaro turned down the Boulevard Saint Germain to the Old Navy and in the telephone booth he dialed the number on the rue de Belleville.

"*Allô.*"

Michèle's voice sounded melancholy, soft, soothing, and a little sleepy next to his ear.

"*C'est moi.*"

"*Je suis fatiguée*. I've spent over four hours looking at the ceiling light without closing my eyes. It's got me bugged. . . . I don't know whether I can keep it up until the end."

"Why are you looking at it?"

"I don't know."

"*Dis-moi*. What are you doing this afternoon?"

"I already told you, looking at the light."

"No, stop kidding. Are you free tonight?"

"Why do you ask?"

"I'm with some friends. I want to invite you to a friend's studio to have some drinks and listen to some records."

"I'm so hot. I don't think I can move."

"I'll borrow a fan for you."

"You will?"

"I promise."

"*Merde*. I stopped looking at the light. It's all your fault, understand?"

"I'll meet you at the Rhûmerie Martiniquaise."

"Who are your friends?"

"Some guys I met in the café."

"Spaniards?"

"Yes."

"I don't like Spaniards. I don't like people from any underdeveloped country. They're all so short and so horribly dirty."

"My friends are tall and very proper."

"You think there'll be some Miles Davis records?"

"*Certainement*."

"And will I be able to strip bareass?"

"You can do whatever you want to."

"*Bon*. In that case I'll come."

Álvaro came out of the sticky booth onto the Boulevard Saint Germain. The vacation exodus had already begun and traffic on the strip was noticeably diminished. Across from La Pérgola some bearded students had parked an old car painted like a checkerboard. Enrique, Soler, Baró and the other Spaniards were occupying two corner tables on the terrace of the Rhûmerie.

"Did you get her?"

"She'll be right along."

"I know a chick who's a ballbuster," the other one from Madrid said. He felt in his pockets, looking for his wallet, and when he found it, he opened it and took out a picture. "How do you like that?"

"Is she French?"

"No, German. She's got one of those temperaments that, what the hell, why should I tell you guys. . . ."

"Hey," Baró said. "Why don't you invite her to come along?"

"She's not in Paris. Yesterday she went to visit her family in Frankfurt."

"Son of a bitch. We need some chicks like that."

"I've been fucking a Danish girl too. . . . That other blonde in the raincoat. . . . I took the picture myself in the Parc Monceau. Let's see if she's home."

The student from Madrid got up to telephone and the picture of the Danish girl passed from hand to hand. After the inspection, Soler brought out the contents of his wallet.

"Mine doesn't suck her thumb either. . . Take a look."

"Is she the one you met in line at the Cinémathèque?"

"No. I dropped that one a couple of months ago. . . . I like this one better."

"Where's she from?"

"Argentina, but her parents are English. Her family sent her to Paris to study ceramics."

"Go ahead, tell her to come along. We'll give her some free lessons at the studio."

"She can't."

"Why not?"

"Yesterday she ate something that didn't agree with her and she's in bed. . . . This morning I had to call a doctor."

"Take a look at that!" Soler exclaimed. "Good enough to eat!" Along the sidewalk, a mulatto girl was walking, swaying lazily. She must have been only sixteen, but she had the body of a woman. She was wearing a very tight red silk skirt and an off-the-shoulder blouse. "*Voulez-vous boire quelque chose, mademoiselle?*"

"*On vous offre un verre.*"

"*Arretez-vous. Soyez gentille.*"

"Damned whore. . . . Did you see the way she wiggled her ass? . . . Hey, mademoiselle!"

"What are you doing?"

"I'm going after her. . . ."

"If you can convince her, we'll give you first prize."

"No harm in trying."

Soler ran off in the direction of the church of Saint Germain des Prés until he got alongside the mulatto girl next to the gardens. From his observation post on the terrace, Álvaro watched him whispering mysterious compliments, with all the solemnity of ancient seducers. The girl was looking straight ahead and stepped up her pace.

"She's not home," the boy from Madrid explained, coming back from the telephone. "Her landlady said she'd gone out."

"Why don't you try in the Cluny?"

"It's not worth it. It looks as if she's gone to the movies with her sister."

Soler and the mulatto girl had disappeared into the crowd. A girl in a shirt and dungarees was coming along the sidewalk.

"*Mademoiselle, s'il vous plait . . .*"

"*Voulez-vous vous asseoir avec nous?*"

"What about Luis?" the one from Madrid asked.

"I don't know. He hasn't come yet. . . ."

The blonde went off toward the Odéon. One of the group, with an Andalusian accent, was talking about a married Frenchwoman who worked in a travel agency with whom he went to bed regularly. Stifling a yawn, Enrique suggested inviting her to the studio. The Andalusian said that she wasn't free.

"Her husband is beginning to get suspicious and waits for her after work."

"How do you work it, then?"

"I pick her up at lunch time and we go to a hotel."

"Say," Baró said. "Is that why you're so skinny?"

"The best part of it is that she isn't the only one I've been laying."

"No?"

"I've also been screwing an Italian girl."

"You better take some peppermint. They say it's an aphrodisiac."

"They're all aphrodisiacs for me," the Andalusian said. "Even mineral water."

A chestnut-haired beauty passed by on the sidewalk, holding the arm of a Negro. At the crosswalk, a convertible with a load of blonde girls was waiting for the green light. The student from Madrid gave a whistle.

"Five females like that and we'll have a real time. . . . What I can't understand is what's keeping Luis. . . . Where did he say he had the key?"

"Hey, I think they're calling you," Baró interrupted.

"Me?"

"Yes, the waiter."

"Monsieur Alonso?"

"Yes, you're right. . . . I wonder who it is?"

"Probably the Dane."

"*C'est vous monsieur Alonso?*"

"*Oui.*"

"*On vous appele au téléphone.*"

The Madrid student disappeared inside the bar. Instants later Soler reappeared from among the passers-by with a triumphant smile on his face. The mulatto girl was not with him.

"What's up?"

"What happened, did she tell you to go to hell?"

"To hell?" Soler took a piece of paper out of his pocket. "What do you say about that?"

He exhibited it for a few seconds and after folding it carefully, put it back.

"What is it?"

"Her address. I'm going to call her tomorrow at eleven."

"Come on, let's see it."

"So you can take down the number and call her yourself? Uh, uh, chum, uh, uh. . . ."

"Tell somebody else, because I don't buy it. . . . I bet you're making it up."

"You can bet any amount you like, baby, because this one is all signed up. . . . I've got her name and address right here, boy. . . ."

"If you've got her all won over," Baró asked, "why didn't you bring her back with you?"

"She had to meet a girl friend and I didn't want to push it. . . . But I can tell you that we've got a date or I'm Swiss and my name is William Tell."

"Where are you going to take her?"

"That's between her and me."

The one from Madrid came back, making his way among the tables. His face showed his annoyance.

"Was it the Dane?"

"No, it was Luis."

"What's up?"

"He says he can't find the key. . . . He'd evidently given it to the *concierge* to clean up the studio and her place is closed."

"Hell," Enrique said. "What do we do now?"

"He told me he was going to look for her at a bar she usually goes to in the afternoon and that he'll call back."

"Oh, shit," Baró said. "And here I was all worked up to screw her. . . . Do you think he's telling the truth?"

"About what?"

"About the key. It sounds like a dodge to me."

"No," the one from Madrid said. "I know the Norwegian girl, her name is Inge. . . . Besides, I was there once with Luis, at the studio. . . ."

"What's it like?"

"For a screwing session, terrific. . . . There are at least four couches and a closet this size full of wine. . . ."

"We ought to try to get some chicks."

"Look, here comes one. . . . Mademoiselle!"

"*Voulez-vous boire un verre?*"

The girl passed beside them, climbed the steps to the terrace, and stood in front of the group with a delightful expression of fatigue and boredom, equally infinite.

"*Salut,*" she said, facing Álvaro.

"Oh, do you know her?"

"*Les copains dont je t'avais parlé*. My friend Michèle."

There was a chorus of courteous replies followed by a brief and admiring silence. Michèle was wearing an old pair of summer slacks and a blouse cut off at the ribs. Her navel stood out delicately against the dark skin of her abdomen.

"Sit down."

"I'm beat," she said. "What should I have to drink?"

"I don't know. How about a rum?"

"I already went through half a bottle at home."

"Well, then, have some coffee."

"A double rum with lots of ice," she ordered. "Oh, don't get so close, please. . . . It's so hot. . . . I wish I could be completely naked. . . ."

"Wait'll we get to the studio."

"In the taxi on the way over I decided that I was going to marry an Eskimo. It must be wild making love on the ice, don't you think?"

"I never tried it."

"You ought to. I'm sure that there must be places in Paris where people can screw in a refrigerated room. Safe and sound."

"I'm not sure that cold is good for a man, at least on that level."

"Quite the contrary, it's exciting, look . . . it's a well-known fact . . . cold hardens the organ . . . it's heat that makes it soft."

Two exquisitely dressed girls were slipping past the terrace, softly swinging their hips. Following the looks of the group, Michèle looked at them with indifference.

"Son of a bitch. We ought to have a few chicks like that for the studio. . . ."

"Since we haven't got the key . . ."

"He said he'd call back."

"You can trust the bastard if you want. . . . The other day he was supposed to meet me in the Mabillon to see the Ivens movie and the guy never showed up."

The waiter appeared with the double rum. Michèle drank it down in one swallow, with restless eagerness, and ordered another.

"I'd like it with more ice, please."

"Look at the bitch," Baró said in Spanish. "Did you see her toss it down?"

"What did he say?"

"Nothing," Álvaro said.

"That's not true," Michèle was looking at Baró with calm irritation. "He was talking about me."

"He was surprised at the way you drink."

"I don't like to have people look at me that way. I detest looks of scorn from people from underdeveloped countries. Tell him that I'm a Lesbian."

"She says that she's a dike."

"The other day I had an Algerian after me all day. He followed me everywhere, he tried to feel me up. . . . He stuck so close that he ended up wearing me out. . . ."

"Did you make it with him?"

"I'll never work for African independence again."

The waiter came with a second double rum. This time Michèle drank half of it in one sip.

"Well," she said. "What are we doing here?"

"We're waiting for the guy with the keys to the studio."

"He ought to be along any minute," the one from Madrid said.

"I'm hot. I'd like to strip bareass."

"Why doesn't someone go look for him?" the Andalusian said.

"You, for example," said Enrique.

"We're losing time here like a bunch of imbeciles," Soler said. "Where did you say the studio was?"

"On the rue Saint André des Arts."

"Telephone for Monsieur Alonso."

"Go ahead. It's Luis."

Michèle finished what was in the glass and called the waiter.

"More of the same."

"You're going to get stoned."

"I don't care. I'm sick of waiting."

"We'll be going right away," Álvaro said.

"You promised me a fan and some Miles Davis records."

"Be patient for just another second."

"Hey, look at that chick. . . ." the Andalusian said.

"Can't you see she's got someone with her?"

"The guy looks like a fag."

"Fag or not, the son of a bitch has got her in tow."

The student from Madrid came back with his head down. Michèle was examining him closely.

"What's up?" Soler said.

"Nothing. He hasn't found the key."

"Didn't I tell you?" Baró said. "The guy was putting us on."

"He said he'd call back again."

"I'm not waiting around any more," Enrique said.

"Where can we go?"

The waiter served the third double rum. Michèle closed her eyes and tossed it down as if it were a laxative.

"What's happening now?" she asked in a sticky voice.

"The key's lost," Álvaro said.

"You Spaniards are a bunch of shitheads. . . . You're no good for anything."

"It's the fault of the *concierge,*" Soler said. "She had the key and she's gone."

"You're all a bunch of backward and incapable people." Her tongue was heavy as she spoke.

"What if we get a locksmith?" the Andalusian said.

"Underdeveloped," Michèle was repeating. "Now I can see why you lost the Civil War."

An hour later they were still on the terrace of the Rhûmerie Martiniquaise and Michèle was drinking more double rums on ice and looking at them with flaming eyes. Then Enrique proposed making the rounds of the bars along the Rue de la Huchette and the group slowly broke up. Álvaro's friends were maneuvering around Michèle like tempting sentimental drones and ended up singing folk songs together and inviting her in turn to their homes in Andalusia, Castile, Catalonia, and Estremadura.

"If you come to Almodóvar with me, you'll see the most beautiful place in the world."

In the taxi on the way back to the rue de Belleville, Michèle crumpled up the piece of paper with their addresses and tossed it out the window.

"*Ah, mon chèri,*" she sobbed. "Do you understand?"

In the passing light from a shop window, Álvaro glimpsed her beautiful eyes filled with a flow of alcoholic tears—shining and uncontainable.

"I wonder what's true in you. . . . In any case, love is beautiful and it's still a myth."

They appeared in the hotel room—the fourth floor of a solid building with a modern elevator and a red-carpeted staircase—at ten twenty-three in the morning. The maid had come up a few minutes earlier with the breakfast tray and the cup of coffee was still steaming on the night table. A half-dozen clean shirts were piled on the open suitcase next to the airline ticket—Barcelona-Milan via Nice—and the camera. Through the half-open door of the bathroom, the dull sound of water running in the bathtub could be heard.

"Mister Gasparini?"

The first one was wearing a brown trench coat with the belt tied tightly, and he stepped aside to make way for the other one —a bald man in his forties wearing a navy-blue suit.

"Police," he said simply.

He showed a rectangular card with his number and his picture, but he put it back in his pocket without giving him much time to read it. Gasparini instinctively buttoned up his pajamas.

"Why am I honored with this visit . . . ?"

"A formality," the bald one said. "Our informants have told us of your presence in the city and we wanted to exchange some impressions with you." He put his hand into his pocket and took out a pack of filter cigarettes. "Would you like a smoke?"

"I just finished one, thanks."

"Our original aim was to see you immediately so that we could collaborate with you and inform you of the means at our command, but our work load prevented us," he traced a smile. "I hope you'll forgive us."

"You're very kind. Really, I'm here on vacation, you know. . . ."

"The weather hasn't been too good lately. . . . Five solid days of rain, rather unusual for May. . . ."

"Maybe you came to have a rest, Mister Gasparini."

"Yes, as a tourist."

"Every foreigner tells us the same thing. Modern life, the noise, they upset the nervous system. People are looking for a little peace, a little calm . . ." the bald one took in the room with a circular look. "You've seen our city, I imagine."

"Yes, I have."

"I'm glad," he said. "Countries that have something to hide close their doors to foreigners, prevent them from moving about freely. . . . Not us. Here, whoever wants to come can come, he can walk around as if he were back home in his own house and do whatever he feels like doing, as long as he obeys the local laws. . . . You, for example, did we put any obstacle in your path to stop you coming to Spain?"

"No, none at all."

"The tourist business is our best propaganda, believe me. You yourself have probably been able to appreciate the social peace, the public order. . . . On the other hand, we have a bad press abroad, do you know why?"

"No."

"Because so many journalists who visit us, instead of reporting what they see with their own eyes, close themselves up in their hotel rooms and write a string of exaggerations and lies." The voice of the bald one had become noticeably firmer. "What do you have to say about that, Mister Gasparini? Does it seem honest to you?"

"Excuse me a moment. The faucet in the bathtub is on and the water will overflow."

He opened the door to the bathroom, and as he passed by the mirror he looked at himself for a couple of seconds. His rumpled hair and his day-old beard made him look old before his time. He turned off the faucet, he tore up Antonio's post card and threw it into the toilet, and he pulled the chain. In front of the mirror again, he wet his face and quickly combed his hair. In the bedroom, the man in the trench coat was calmly going through his luggage.

"Naturally, the same as in any country in the world, we have our malcontents," the bald one said. "Some out of ignorance and others because they like to fish in muddy waters. But they're just a handful, and socially they don't represent anyone, understand?"

"That man . . ."

"Oh, don't worry," the bald one was smiling. "My partner is a little curious and he likes to stick his nose in everywhere," he turned toward the dresser and thoughtfully examined the airline ticket. "Are you leaving today?"

"Yes."

"What time do you have to be at the airport?"

"Two o'clock, I think. . . . It must be written on the envelope."

"If we don't watch out, you'll go back to your country without having the pleasure of knowing us. . . . It would be a great pity, I assure you. . . . That camera, is it German?"

"Yes."

"Are you a good photographer?"

"Just an amateur."

"I love photography," the bald one looked the Leica over for a few moments and inspected the upper pocket in the suitcase. "It's a shame that cameras are so expensive. . . . If I get to Germany someday, I'll buy one. They say you can get one there at half the price." His hand suddenly emerged with an envelope of photographs and negatives. "May I?"

"Do you have a search warrant?"

"Oh, please, I beg you," the bald one took the photographs out of the envelope and began to look at them one by one. "I'm just curious, as I told you. I also do some photography in my spare time. Last week my brother-in-law loaned me his Kodak and I took pictures of my kids at the zoo. . . . Thirty-six pictures. I'll show them to you some time."

The one in the trench coat had found the date book. Without saying a word, he ran through the telephone numbers and stopped at the calendar part where appointments are written.

"When did you arrive in our city, Mister Gasparini?"

"It'll be a week on Friday."

"Yes, so I see. . . . *Arrivo a Barcellona,* you have a very clear hand. . . ."

"Did you have a good trip?"

"With what right? . . ."

"No matter what they say, the airplane is the most comfortable and efficient means of transportation. . . ." The one with the trenchcoat was smiling deferentially. "I see here, *lunedi nuove maggio,* a date with a certain Antonio. . . . Do you remember?"

"Antonio?"

"Yes, Monday the ninth. In your book you've written 'Antonio, twelve o'clock.' Take a look."

"You don't have his address?"

"No. I happened to strike up a conversation with him and we became friendly. . . . I don't even know his last name."

"He didn't give you his telephone number, of course."

"No."

There was a brief silence, and the one in the trench coat lit a cigarette. His partner was looking at the pictures with an intent expression.

"Do you know someone called Enrique López Rojas . . . ?" the one in the trench coat asked.

"Did you say Enrique López Rojas?"

"That's right."

"No. I've never met anybody by that name."

"Not in Italy either?"

"No."

"Are you quite sure, Mister Gasparini?"

"Absolutely."

"That's strange. When we picked him up he had your address written in his book. . . . Don't you live at 15 Via del Torchio in Milan?"

"Yes."

"During the interrogation, he confessed that he knew you. He said that you and a professor from the University of Bologna . . ."

"I tell you I don't know who he is."

"In that case, let me fill you in a little. . . . This boy belongs to a fine family. His father was murdered by the Reds during the war and his mother's brother died fighting on our side with the Nuestra Señora de Monserrat Regiment. . . . Here's a picture of him, do you recognize him now?"

"I told you already that I don't know who you're talking about."

"Last summer he spent a few weeks in Italy, and when he came back, he brought with him instructions on how to organize strikes and student demonstrations. . . . He got mixed up here with a handful of undesirables. When we caught him, we were able to prove that he had fallen even lower: obscene pictures, drawings, marijuana cigarettes. . . . A real debasement. By the way, do you know what he said about you?"

"I don't know and I'm not interested. I already told you . . ."

"Whatever you say, Mister Gasparini. I just wanted to give you an idea of his moral character. . . ."

"His activities bordered on common crimes," the bald one said.

"His poor mother couldn't believe at first that her son was dragging down his name without remorse or shame. . . . We're human like everyone else, Mister Gasparini. I can swear to you that it was very hard on her when we told her the truth. . . ."

"Are these pictures yours?" the bald one suddenly asked.

"Yes."

"Did you take them yourself?"

"Yes."

"Would you allow me to make a comment, Mister Gasparini? . . . The opinion of a simple Spanish amateur."

"Of course."

The bald one lit another cigarette and slowly breathed in its aroma.

"I don't think you've done a good job on capturing the reality of our country. . . . Why do you insist on photographing unfortunate children and run-down shacks? Do you really think that's Spain? No. They've given you a bum steer."

"No one has steered me at all," he protested.

"What would you say if we went to your country and, instead of photographing its beauties and accomplishments, we looked for the most miserable and sordid things and came back to Spain saying: 'Look, gentlemen, this is Italy.' You'd be offended, Mister Gasparini. Like any good patriot, you'd consider yourself insulted by our conduct. . . . When did you say you were leaving?"

"One o'clock."

"Let's see," the bald one looked at his watch. "Right now it's ten to eleven. All I need is an hour and a half to convince you of your error. . . . Would you be so kind as to get dressed?"

"Get dressed?"

"We're going to take a drive and, on the way, we'll take some pictures. . . . I see that you have two rolls of film left in your suitcase."

"Is that an order?"

"It's a friendly invitation, Mister Gasparini. I would be very sad if you were to leave Spain without having learned a whole series of elementary things. . . . Our country is very beautiful and the people live peacefully and happily. I want to show you the cafés of El Ensanche, the Victory Monument, our professional schools. . . . There you will see a reality that you haven't been aware of: happy men and women, laughing children. . . . These pictures you've taken aren't too good artistically. There are too many shadows, they're monotonous. That's why, if you don't mind, I'm going to get rid of them. . . . I wouldn't want them to think badly of you in your own country, Mister Gasparini. . . . If we still have good light for a while, we can take some better ones."

On occasion, Madame Berger's café would receive the visit of some illustrious traveler. During his ten years of exile in Paris, along with the flock of political exiles and lazy students—for whom the simple fact of wandering around the Quartier Latin served as the justification of an existence that would have been considered useless in any other part of the world—Álvaro had run into a dozen artists and writers who had been summoned to the difficult conquest of Paris, ephemeral representatives of the genius and shape of Spain in the salons and literary circles of the Rive Gauche, whom the glowing reception given by the French intellectuals of the Left had led to believe for a moment that the time of their triumph and elevation finally and forever had arrived.

Invitations to meetings and banquets rained upon the newly arrived Spaniard with long sideburns and deep dark eyes, women looked at him intensely and men listened to him with an almost mystical attention: he was the figure of the day, the glorious heir of the combatants of the Civil War, the innocent victim of a Regime imposed by Hitler and Mussolini with the ignoble complicity of the western democracies. "*Qu'est-ce que nous pouvons faire pour vous?*" his devoted and stirred admirers would ask, and all that was necessary then was to put on a long-suffering and grave expression and wrap himself in a disdainful and haughty silence, so that the collective masochism would release itself and his hosts would furiously accuse themselves of all the evils and misfortunes that had befallen Spain, *c'est de notre faute, nous sommes tous des coupables,* while he would drink that unique and exquisite instant down to the dregs, the unexpected end of a career of genius in its infancy, the living incarnation of the drama of an unconquerable people, sold and turned over to exploiters and rapists from now till eternity—respect and veneration that one fateful day, obeying the irresistible magnetism of the headlines in *France-Soir,* would be transferred to Hungarian refugees or Tibetan rebels with the consequent searching out and discovery of new heroes who would be converted overnight into the center of attraction at soirees and meetings, wined and dined with the same enthusiasm with which, weeks before, had fallen upon him, making him suddenly feel despoiled of his flighty halo, like a dethroned and conquered king who is invited out of mere pity, and as if giving him to understand that in the future he will have to use and not abuse such courtesy.

Álvaro knew a few of those heroes of the moment who had still not recovered from the stupor of their fall, reliving their splendorous past in Madame Berger's café, dissolved now into the anonymous mass of students and political emigrés, waiting for the moment when a new and ambitious volunteer would climb up onto the tightrope and tumble down to the ground. Stretched out on the couch, by the light of the porch windows, he recalled the afternoon that Soler had shown up at the café with the recent winner of the Planeta Prize, an individual named Fernández, who had come up to Paris with a half-dozen novels that had been best sellers in Spain and which, after careful reflection, he had decided to entrust to the publisher who had translated Hemingway into French. His appearance had worked the miracle of silencing conversations, and the expatriates of the various geological layers slowly gathered around him to listen to the luminous cultural message that was coming to them from the Peninsula.

"Why, precisely, Hemingway's publisher?"

"I would like to see *Lives Without Aim* published in the same collection as *The Old Man and the Sea.*"

"Do you like William Faulkner?"

"He's a fraud. My favorite writers are Maugham and Vicki Baum."

"Are you familiar with Sartre's work?"

"My wife thumbed through one of his books and she says he writes about filth."

"And Kafka?"

"I've never read him."

"What do you think of Robbe-Grillet?"

"Who did you say?"

"Are you a follower of the *nouveau roman?*"

"Neither my wife nor I can handle French. Spanish is more than enough for us."

"How long did it take you to write your last novel?"

"Eight days."

"Do you rewrite?"

"Never. What's gained in niceties is lost in a lack of spontaneity."

"What narrative technique do you prefer?"

"Technique is another fraud. Cervantes didn't know anything about theories when he wrote *Don Quixote*."

"Are you working on something new?"

"Yes. I have in mind a novel about the battle of the generations, between fathers and sons, and I'm going to set it in Harlem."

"Oh, you've been to the United States?"

"No, this is the first time I've ever been out of Spain."

"Do you like Paris?"

"Why, yes. Very much. Except that the food is awful and there are too many monuments. At the hotel, nothing but a mess of sauces and all that stuff, very little that's solid. Me, I just don't go for sauces. I like to eat solid things, none of your cheeses or butter. . . . I spent three days in Germany eating nothing but sausages. You ought to see how they drink, and then they say they're so civilized."

The ring had closed in around the novelist, and Madame Berger herself seemed absorbed in the jargon, leaning on the bar, while the cat stretched in the croissant basket and carefully examined the dusty text of the *Loi de Repression de l'Ivresse Publique*.

". . . And just to think that there's a restaurant in Gracia where they give you a roast shoulder of lamb for thirty-two pesetas . . . and for ten *duros* you can have Codorniu, not like here, where we ordered a bottle of champagne and couldn't even finish it. . . . Everything is yogurt and jam here, and when the time to pay comes, hold on tight! . . . When I think that in the Casa Agut they give you a steak and French fries for twenty-four pesetas . . . would you believe it, twenty-four pesetas! . . . And the chicken and potatoes in El Abrevadero? . . . And the thing they call *terrina de liebre* in El Canario? . . . Four pesetas for a portion of small birds and beer!"

"What impresses you most about Paris?"

"The lovers. The way they carry on in the street without anyone saying anything, even in front of Notre Dame. . . ."

"Have you been inside the church?"

"Yes, yesterday I went to mass with my wife. . . . Of course, just a while back, I read a book on the private life of that devil Victor Hugo. . . . Gilbert Cesbron says that he had children by every single one of his maidservants! . . ."

"Getting back to novels, what do you think about censorship?"

"What happens with books is that the publishers are getting tired of losing money and are taking a positive stand. I mean that they only publish what they know will obviously sell. . . . Me, for example, they do a printing of fifty thousand. In the bookstore in my town, the only books that sell are mine."

"Have your books got good reviews?"

"I can't complain. Some writers call me the Spanish Balzac."

"That's very interesting," Baró said smoothly. "Here they call Balzac the French Fernández."

There was a tense silence. The novelist let the observation pass.

"In any case, I'm more interested in my readers than in the critics," he added.

"What do you see for the future of Spanish culture?"

"Magnificent. Back there you have the group on the magazine *Índice*. . . . In the last number they took care of Karl Marx."

"Are you going to stay in Paris long?"

"No. Just long enough to get my translations arranged. . . . I'd rather be in Barcelona or on my farm in Cáceres."

. . . The conversation went on for several hours, and at nightfall, the novelist had taken leave of the people gathered around with the expression of regret of a man who cannot give freely of his time: "I'm sorry, but my wife is waiting for me back at the hotel. We want to go see one of those reviews with naked gals. . . . They've told me that some of them are married gals who do it to earn a little change. What I can't understand is how their husbands . . ."

After he had left—Álvaro was smiling as he remembered it, his gaze lost on the disk of the moon that was crowning the summit of the mountains—Baró waited a few seconds with an enigmatic smile and showed the gathering in the café the leather binding of a passport that was lying on the ragged oilcloth of the bench.

"Whose is it?"

"Look." The novelist had a very serious expression in the identity photograph. "The son of a bitch left it behind."

"Why didn't you tell him? Do you want him to get into trouble?"

"Trouble?"

Baró laughed until he cried. Without warning, he grabbed the passport in both hands and tore it in two.

"What are you doing!" the proclamation broke out simultaneously from several corners of the café.

"You've seen. Fuck it."

"What about the guy?"

Baró dried his eyes and answered simply:

"It doesn't matter. Just another exile."

A few months after the abortive student demonstration—public order and social peace happily re-established—Ricardo and Artigas went to Madrid one weekend with the object of seeing Enrique and his comrades on the Coordinating Committee, who had been transferred to the provincial prison in Carabanchel. The meeting took place in a room set up like a bird cage, through two sets of wire separated by a narrow passageway along which a guard kept walking. To be heard, it was necessary to shout, and prisoners and visitors looked at each other, mutually annoyed by the common sound of the voices, trying to clarify with gestures and expressions their chaotic, twisted, and inconclusive sentences. For the university students from Barcelona, the enforced rest seemed to have been good, and pressing up against the metallic mesh like orangutans in the zoo, they accepted their repeated attempts at conversation with an ironic smile. There was no shadow of reproach in their eyes. After a half-hour of gibberish, a bell rang and, without giving them time to react, the prisoners retired, surrounded by their guards. Ricardo and Artigas found themselves on the street, disoriented and confused, lost in the silent line of friends and relatives who were heading toward the bus stop, back to the city that was hostile, spread out, and anonymous, stretching out before their eyes like an overwhelming nightmare.

A few hours later, before boarding the plane that was to take them to Barcelona, a group of friends drove them to the nearby town of Paracuellos del Jarama. There, at the foot of a few ocher hills, naked of all vegetation, is a cemetery where Nationalists shot during the war years were buried. The graves of soldiers, priests, and other people fallen for God and for Spain are lined up, half-hidden in the weeds, with their crosses, mortuary wreaths, and epitaphs that recalled past deeds and distant glories, decorations and titles obtained during the uprising in Asturias, the events at Jaca, or the war against the rebels of Abd-el-Krim. The panorama is splendid, and spring had transformed the plain into an immense and red-tinted poppy field.

The old caretaker was sitting beside the gate waiting for closing time, and when they came out, he smiled sadly at them: "At first," he said, "lots of people used to come: widows, parents, friends, visitors. . . . Everything was kept neat and the graves were well cared for. . . . Not now. . . . People have lost their respect for the dead. . . . They come here on Sunday to picnic and have a good time. . . . The other day I had to throw out a couple who were dancing among the crosses, listening to a transistor. . . . Others lay down with their sweethearts or do their business. . . . It's something that makes your soul shrink up. . . . In my day they didn't do things like that, believe me. . . ."

On the plane, fifteen thousand feet above the dark and invisible Castilian plateau, Artigas and Ricardo had remembered the caretaker's words, and they had repeated them a hundred and one times in the intermittent drowsiness of their vigil, wondering when, oh Lord, after how many days, weeks, months, or years, would the Regime and its people disappear into indifference and forgetfulness as distant and absurd as those sad names engraved on the stones of that profaned and withered cemetery.

Hours on end were spent in reconstructing the existence of those years, the one lived by Álvaro and the one that had gone on without him after the already remote date of his departure, thanks to interminable conversations with Artigas, Ricardo, or some other survivor of the group in the nocturnal coolness of the terrace: time seemed to float away as they attempted to grasp it, offering them nothing but a mix-up of isolated images, truncated scenes, colorless and hazy memories, the residue of a period against which they had fought without success, from which they had tried to flee and which had ended up devouring them.

. . . Like that afternoon—reassembled with Dolores's help—when, coming out of Madame Berger's café, they had wandered through the neighborhood of the rue Mouffetard, stopping to drink anise in Arab coffee shops and in a tiny bar on the Passage des Patriarches that had a bowl of colored fish and a bronze statue of Saint Genevieve of Paris as decoration, and you had got into a conversation with a pair of bearded *clochards* who were leaning on the zinc counter and strongly criticizing the trashmen and their disloyal collections, and you had invited them to share their troubles with you.

"We were playing pinball," Dolores said. "You kept on winning and I was furious with you, remember?"

The anise had warmed their spirits and the two of them felt unexpectedly happy, with a desire to laugh and communicate with their neighbors.

"*Mademoiselle est Italienne?*"

"*Non, Espagnole.*"

The older *clochard* stroked his beard and looked at them with pride.

"*Ah, l'Espagne. . . . Teruel, Belchite. . . . Je connais.*"

His eyes were like two globes, blue and reddish. Dolores had emptied her glass with one drink and was staring at him.

"How long since you were there?"

"Oh, ho." The *clochard* made an imprecise gesture. "It was during the war. . . . Boom, boom, boom. . . ."

"You lived in Spain?"

"Me?" The *clochard* shook his head no. "I went to join up, I did. . . . Oh, what a country. . . ."

"A volunteer?" Álvaro asked.

"Yes, sir."

"On which side?"

The question seemed to have caught him off guard. The *clochard* examined Álvaro suspiciously and made a visible effort at concentration.

"The good side," he finally said.

"What did you call the good side?"

"*Vive la République,*" the *clochard* clenched his fist and raised his hand. "I'm a Republican, I am."

"Ah, good."

"My general was Queipo de Llano."

"What?"

"Queipo de Llano," the *clochard* came to attention. "Ah, those were the good old days."

"Then you were with the Fascists," Álvaro said.

"With the Fascists?" the *clochard* was looking at him with mistrust again. "I'm a patriot, I am. . . . I was in Panama and I left."

"Queipo de Llano was on Franco's side."

"Franco's?" the *clochard's* face showed real stupor. "Oh, no."

"Oh, yes," Álvaro said. "If you were with him, that means you were fighting against the Republic."

"Never in my life. I fought for the Republic, I did. I was wounded here," he brought his hand to his fly and made a move as if to unbutton it. "Begging Mademoiselle's pardon."

"I tell you that Queipo de Llano was a Fascist," Álvaro said.

"I was a Republican and a patriot."

"And you were with Queipo?"

"*Oui, Monsieur.*"

"You're mistaken, let's see. If you were a Republican, you were fighting against Queipo. And if you were fighting with Queipo, you were not a Republican."

The *clochard* was looking at them alternately with an expression of disbelief. Finally he turned to his companion.

"What the hell. It's all a mess."

"You're full of shit," the other one said.

"I can't remember," the *clochard* said. "I was wounded three times, but I can't remember."

"Come on," Álvaro said. "Make an effort."

The *clochard* drank down his wine and slapped his forehead.

"I can't remember anything any more," he said with a gesture of excusing himself.

"Then I asked him what anthem they sang, the *Himno de Riego* or *Cara al Sol*. . . ."

Dolores had hummed a stanza of each, and both times the *clochard* had accompanied her with a hoarse voice and had waved his arms, grasping an imaginary baton.

"Yes, that's the one. . . ."

"But which of the two?"

"Me, I used to sing one that went like this.

Ah, mon chéri
oui joue moi s'en
de la trompette
de la trompette . . .

"You're full of shit," the other one said.

"Shut your face."

"You've got your wars mixed up," the younger one insisted.

"That was against the Algerians."

"I can't remember. . . . It was so long ago. . . ."

"Well . . ." Álvaro said.

"*Putain de bordel de merde*. I can't remember any more."

Dolores and Álvaro had not been able to hold back a touch of laughter as the *clochard* scratched his head and looked around with an absorbed expression.

"The guy solved the Spanish problem once and for all. Everybody should follow his example. . . . Erase it and start all over again."

"I wish my father could have heard him," Dolores said with her cheeks flushed. "He and all the other exiles in Mexico and their cherished memories. . . ."

"And my uncles, parroting the newspaper lies. . . . The everlasting Civil War. . . . What difference does it make to us?"

Escorted by the *clochards* they had gone along the rue Mouffetard singing and laughing like children, so you don't remember anything at all, nothing at all, he's made it, you see, let's do like him, it was so long ago, all of that. . . .

"That night we went to bed for the second time," Álvaro said. "We got a taxi on the Contrescarpe and I took you to my studio."

"You'd been drinking and you didn't even touch me," Dolores said.

"I was afraid."

"Everything began the next day, remember?"

"No," Álvaro said. "When I finally did make love to you, I was drunk too."

VI

Grandiloquent and pompous clouds, the kind that could announce the opening of an opera, were drifting off toward the sea beyond the naked green of the trees. The heat of the afternoon had abated somewhat, and a pleasant breeze was making the pine needles and the tiny sprouts on the acacias tremble. The frogs were spacing their croaks in the pond. The maid had forgotten the children's book of maps at the foot of the chaise longue and Dolores leaned over to pick it up and was looking at it attentively.

It was an English atlas from before World War II, and the dominions, protectorates, and possessions of the British Commonwealth were in different colors from those of other countries: Nazi aggression had not yet come about, and the political balance established by the Locarno agreements and the tutelage of the League of Nations seemed to guarantee a serene and lasting order, protected from revolutions and subversive threats, a comical and feeble security, you thought now, like that of the Holy Alliance among the monarchs of that fabulous and distant period of the Austro-Hungarian Empire.

Ten years previously, some time before you had fallen in love, you had abandoned your families with the idea of traveling and getting to know a life that was different from that of the Spanish nucleus in which you had been raised (the Barcelona society that had been reconstituted after the fears and frights of the war for you; the gregarious and anachronistic universe of the Republican exiles in Mexico in her case): opening the geography book and turning the pages was, therefore, an evasion, a flight, a dream, the free and easy soaring of some fakir on the yearned-for magic carpet. During the war and the postwar years, the project seemed utopian, and going to any of the countries that you were avidly examining on the map meant running up against difficulties and sudden and impassable barriers: applications that were refused, distant visas, long and useless lines before stony functionaries with faces of inquisitors (good-conduct certificates, passes, endorsements, stamps, seals all demanded *ad infinitum,* like a demented burlesque scene from Menotti's *The Consul*).

When you finally got away (anticipating by a few years the wave of pioneers and *conquistadores* who were emulating Magellan, Cortés, and Pizarro) in their discovery and exploration of a new world (the Quartier Latin and Saint Germain, Soviet movies and literature, banned in Spain), you were overwhelmed by a deep and savage happiness. The dream that you had fondled for so long was taking shape, and Dolores had settled into it harmoniously, channeling your life toward other horizons, far from your country and its fauna. Little by little (without your being aware of it), your desires were being fulfilled with disconcerting ease (the slightest remorse of recompense obtained without merit or effort): the filming of the documentary on emigration first, and your professional obligations later, took both of you in turn to places you had been yearning to know during your youth, substituting for childhood imagination and adolescent myth, in that way, the ambiguous, contradictory, and complex reality of a memory lived over again, of experience gained all at once. Monte Carlo, Switzerland, Venice, Hamburg, Holland ceased being just names with the aura of the memory of tales and stories that you had read about them, and became the beacons and landmarks of your common history with Dolores (the encounter with Europe juxtaposed upon the mutual revelation of your bodies, the unsuccessful insertion of urban industrial civilization into the ups and downs and incidents of the measureless passion that you both shared).

The frontiers and limits that had kept you imprisoned before had suddenly been erased, and as you looked at the atlas during that unpleasant summer of 1963, one by one, you brought back the pages of your amorous dossier from the time you had met by chance in a boardinghouse on the rue Chomel, until that day when, after all means of salvation and ransom for a union that was being undermined every day by avaricious and vengeful time had been exhausted, you lay down next to her in the darkness and said: "There's nothing we can do for each other any more." (With that proverbial Hispanic extremism, the Regime was driving out of the country hundreds of thousands of Spaniards who had been held back previously by the impassable wall of the Pyrenees.

During your recent convalescence on the Côte d'Azur, you had struck up a friendship with one of them on the docks of Monaco: a man in his thirties, simple and rough, a sailor on a yacht belonging to a famous singer.

"Señor Álvaro, the government we have in Spain, is it good or bad?"

You looked at him: his frank face, his open expression, a peaceful question in his eyes. At his age, it would have been cruel to despoil him of so many illusions, and you patted him on the shoulder.

"Not just good, fellow. Very good.")

The clouds are moving off, suddenly scattering. Sea and sky are blending their tones into an imprecise blue band. A blackbird flies along the ground and goes up to roost on the ridge of the roof. From the opposite slopes across the valley the echo sends back the measured and rhythmical chopping of the woodcutters.

The contents of the atlas are an integral part of your lives, and as you lean over it, time past comes to life again.

Elliptical, tangled, its course follows right along the sinuous meandering of memory.

The voices of recall are speaking.

Listen.

A run-down bourgeois neighborhood, silent and somber. A gray building on a gray street, the gray work of some gray architect of funereal inspiration. A staircase that has seen better days and some old crystal chandeliers, a threadbare carpet, stained-glass windows, plush love seats. A heavy door with an illegible plaque.

EDMONDE MARIE DE HEREDIA

SOLFÈGE—CHANT—DICTION

A city: Paris. And a date: 1954.

Your first meeting with Dolores.

(When, a few weeks before your fainting spell, you passed by the teacher's building, scaffolding and canvas covered the outside. The painters had touched up the façade, cornices, window frames, piers, and the stone Venus that supported the main balcony was the object of a careful cleaning by an Italian peasant: after having spent a long time scrubbing her breasts, stomach, and thighs, he carefully touched up the dark triangle of her neglected sex and her haunches with such careful application that the others laughed at him. The Venus was bearing that outrage with frigid dignity, and as you continued on toward the rue de Varennes, you wished you could have caught the scene with your Kodak.)

She was a distant relative of the poet, *d'une ligne colatérale,* she would add, pointing a bony finger at the faded photograph on top of the piano, "he knew me when I was quite small; my mother always told me that he would pick me up in his arms for hours on end": you tried to remember what the author of the *Trophées* was to her, as, with mustache and sideburns, he left his solemn reception into the French Academy, dressed in the handsome and garish uniform of the immortals. Around him, dozens of photographs, faded too, taken in different poses, hair styles, and dresses, one single model: Madame Edmonde Marie de Heredia, photographed, still in her adolescence, beside a Doric column on the day of her debut; years later, wearing an extravagant feathered hat, on the day of her entry into the Paris Conservatory; in the Salle Pleyel, in the company of Nadia Boulanger, during a benefit performance for the victims of the Tokyo earthquake of 1923. "*La belle époque,*" she would say, taking in with a wave of her hand the memories stacked along the walls, the windows, the bureaus, and the sideboards in that dark and ancient parlor. "Art, in those days, was a religion, with its gods, its priests, its faithful, its temples, not the vulgar commercial enterprise it has become today, when any *parvenu* at all without the first notions of *solfège* can allow himself the privilege of giving recitals without anyone's, I really mean that, without anyone's being aware that he's an imposter." Her powdered face protected and made hazy by the shadows, Madame de Heredia sat upright on the sofa, her mind far away, it might be said, in some marvelous and distant dream. The heavy curtains softened the sullen gray sky, and at dusk, the lighted lamps in the corners seemed to be watching over votive offerings or relics: the veronica, arms of Christs, and heads of saints that would have filled you with fear and guilt during your poisoned Spanish adolescence

"*Bon. Recommencez.*"

and the student whose turn it was (a myopic and timid Canadian, or the pedantic Argentinian who broke you both up with laughter when he announced emphatically in French: "Madame, I would like to be penetrated from head to toe by French culture"), after the obligatory and rich pause for personal memories was over, would recite again

Comme un vol de gerfauts hors du charnier natal under the haughty vigilance of the teacher, as the other boarders in the grubby place would pretend that they were taking notes and reviewing the *solfège* lessons that Madame de Heredia regularly postponed under new pretexts that were contradictory and absurd.

"No, not that way. This isn't the Berlitz School or the Alliance Française. A little more spirit, a little more fire. We'll get back to it tomorrow."

(The pupils would retire to their rooms and she would recall for her favorite one the memorable scene when she was decorated by General Pershing, or incidents during her artistic tour of Portugal. A black cat was sleeping, curled up on her lap, and Madame de Heredia would pet it mechanically as her gaze became lost among the tufts of the carpet.)

Maybe you had passed each other in the hall without noticing, foreign to the bonds that would unite you in the future, still unaware of the hidden desire and of the evidence that one now was (existed) for (by) the other. You could only remember her fleeting silhouette outlined in the doorway as she turned out the light and sank into the darkness of the hall, almost scurrying past Madame de Heredia's parlor and the conclave of guests gathered there. You knew that her family was in Mexico, that she had come to Paris to study French and drawing, that she owed two months' rent. Her face?—you had been unable to describe it. You had run into her on the line at the Foyer de Sainte Genéviève, and when she smiled at you, it took you a few seconds to recognize her, as if, by guessing the future strength of your passion, you said to yourself, you had drawn back, startled, had tried to close your eyes.

"The poor thing has troubles," Madame de Heredia whispered in one of the autobiographical parentheses that she interspersed in her lessons, "she's had a fight with her family and they haven't sent her a penny." The pupils turned their heads toward the hallway through which the guilty party had just sped past, and Madame de Heredia raised her voice and imposed silence with an energetic movement of her hand.

"*Bon soir, mademoiselle*. Have you been thinking about me?"

"*Oui, Madame.*"

"That's what you said last week, *ma petite.*"

"I cabled my parents."

The story had begun to fascinate you. A mute solidarity joined you to Dolores, to the slim silhouette of Dolores as she dodged the presence of Madame de Heredia and her severe court of pupils. On more than one occasion, during one of your frequent spells of insomnia, you had heard her returning early in the morning, walking on tiptoes, and getting into bed without turning on the light. A mild impulse instigated you to follow her when, taking advantage of the teacher's morning toilet, she quietly left the apartment and, wrapped up in her white parka, she lost herself in the drabness and the melancholy of the Paris winter. You followed her at a discreet distance to the Bureau de la Main d'Oeuvre Étrangère, where she often went with the hope of finding work, without having made up your mind to speak to her yet, sensing perhaps the intensity of the love that was to grow up between you, holding back with selfish delight the moment when you could show it to her.

Were you aware at that time how serious her lack of funds was? Most likely not, absorbed as you were in the certainty of your inclination toward her, in the joyous preamble of what was to be your common history. Dolores also seemed withdrawn, and spying on her without raising her suspicions was child's play for you, already used to things like that. One day you saw her talking to a stranger in the middle of the street and suddenly doubt seized you. Were you jealous of her? It was absurd on your part, you, who up till then had made no effort to win her and would have fled from her if you had chanced to bump into each other on the stairs. When they separated and she went on her way, a strange unhappiness came over you, and as you searched for a higher court to which to appeal, the incident seemed so miraculous to you that you gave thanks to God.

Some days later, as she distributed the mail to the rooms, Madame de Heredia had knocked on her door: "Nothing for you yet, *ma petite*. Do you really expect that money order?"

"*Oui, Madame.*"

"You've kept me waiting for two months already. I can't let you have the room indefinitely."

"I expect an answer today."

"Are you sure?"

"I hope so."

"*Bon*. We'll talk about it again tomorrow."

You followed her through the Quartier Latin toward the center for student aid on the rue Soufflot. Dolores had bought a paper at a stand on the Boulevard Saint-Michel, and was reading the want ads with an absent and urgent expression. Several times you saw her take a pencil from the pocket of her parka and quietly circle some address. As she disappeared through the door of the building, you went into a nearby café and had a cup of tea. Dolores came out a few minutes later, crossed the boulevard, and went into the Luxembourg gardens. December had undressed the branches on the trees, children were running about wrapped up like little elves. The sun was a white disk, devoid of brightness or of heat. She sat down on a bench opposite the flower beds and tossed the newspaper into a trash basket. Her eyes were wild as she looked at the wintry desolation of the garden. Without warning, she hid her face in her hands and began to weep.

You went away confused. A retrospective sense of blame was working on you along with the firm intention to assume your responsibilities right there, accept with pleasure the unhoped-for offer of that love. When you got back to the teacher's apartment, Madame de Heredia had finished her laborious morning coiffure.

"*Excusez-moi, Madame*. Did you speak to Dolores?"

"*Oui, mon petit*. I told her this morning that I can't let her keep the room any more. She's a fine girl, no doubt, but what else can I do? The Centre d'Accueil sends me new students every day. I have to honor my commitments."

"How much does she owe you?"

"Two months rent, besides the lessons."

"Eighty thousand?"

"Exactly."

"I just ran into her by the PTT, and she asked me to give you this money." You held out the bunch of bills and Madame de Heredia watched you with disbelief. "You can count them."

"Did she get her money order?"

"It was held up in the mails for a long time."

"Poor thing. Where is she now?"

"She went to class."

"I have to call the Centre d'Accueil right away and tell them that the room isn't available. When will she be back?"

"I don't know."

"I'd like to surprise her. Buy her a bouquet of flowers."

"You're too kind, Madame."

That was all there was to it: her destiny sealed behind her back, irremediably decided in a few seconds by that sudden, naked act of love. (Perhaps Dolores was still on the bench in the Luxembourg, without suspecting the change in direction, still separated by a few hours from that life that she was to share with you in the future, from the reciprocal desire that, by its breadth and depth, year after year, would be impossible for the two of you to placate.)

When she finally did come home, Madame de Heredia had finished her lessons and the parlor was empty. You were smoking in your room, stretched out on the old rose comforter, and the almost imperceptible sound of her steps startled you. You heard her go down the hall past your door, put her key in the lock. Then the loud voice of the teacher, her startled silence that was filled with both happiness and anxiety. You opened up an IDHEC notebook and pretended to be absorbed in its reading. For a few moments the beating of your heart was keeping time to the dialogue. Madame de Heredia was assuring her that she would never again doubt her word, and Dolores was silent with enigmatic complicity. When they separated, the clock said ten. A few seconds later, there was a knock on your door.

"*Entrez.*" (Had you said it in Spanish or in French?)

Dolores appeared in the doorway and paused a few seconds on the threshold, impassive and seeming previously resigned to your presence, with an angry and strange expression that would never be erased from your memory. She was wearing tight black slacks and a thick knit sweater. Her short hair, combed over her forehead, gave her the ambiguous (fortunate) look of a boy.

"Madame de Heredia told me that you . . ." her voice sounded extremely harsh.

"Yes."

"Why did you do it?"

"I don't know," you stammered.

She took a cigarette from her pocket and lit it with a brusque gesture. You had got up from the bed and were standing next to her, not daring to look at her.

"I knew that you were having trouble."

"You were very kind."

"I didn't want you . . ."

"Please. Turn around while I get undressed."

You turned your back without understanding her intentions as yet, and you looked with fear at the greenish light of the lamp shade, the heavy drapes on the window. A blond shepherdess with the expression of an accomplice was smiling at you, framed in an oval of garlands and clover leaves. The wrinkled unmade bed was a coarse invitation to love. Suddenly your eyes watered.

"No," you said. "No, no, no."

Dolores had taken off the sweater and was looking at you with her unbuttoned blouse and her slacks half down, intercepted suddenly (the inner spring had snapped) in their abrupt (harmonious) challenging movement.

"For God's sake, no."

You looked at each other then for the first time. The expression of rage had disappeared from her face, and her loneliness had merged with yours, both of them joined in one very long arpeggio.

"What's the matter?"

"I don't know."

"Forgive me," she said.

Her voice broke too. Her bright eyes opposite yours were sinking.

"I thought that you . . ."

"No."

"I didn't want to hurt you."

"I know."

"Don't look at me like that."

You closed your eyes and her hand stroked you, the anesthesia of salvation. "My love. My love," with a thin, magnetic voice that you seemed to be hearing for the first time.

That night you went to bed together but you did not penetrate her. The union of your tears had preceded that of your bodies by a few days, and the salty and tender nuptials in that anachronistic boardinghouse bedroom had completely wiped out your past, making out of you and her the blind instruments of a common moral adventure that not even the implacable and strict human time would be able completely to destroy. The daily erosion (or was it a mirage of yours?) could not prevail against what there was between you of the precious, the unique, the irreplaceable. Only death (you knew) and its calm destruction. But with both of you swept away (you said to yourself), who would there be to care about the disaster?

In the Venetian mirror on the garret-like wall of the studio on the rue Vieille de Temple, you were following the synchronized movements of your bodies as you made love, and when you were sated, you would often silently assay that singular perfection of hers. Especially created for you, made to order for you, Dolores was fused into it in a delicate synthesis, beauty and grace, strength and tenderness. Pleasing and pleasant to be seen, cordial and receptive to the touch, was she, as you sometimes wondered with pride, a simple and tangible projection of your soul? Her understanding and your alienation were mutually complementary, and all the gold in the world would not have been enough to liquidate the debt you had assumed at that time. Your avid mouth on her burning lips, your sex delaying in hers, the truce that came after so many gray years of loneliness and boredom, did they have a price? Her smile afterward, and her sad gesture when she would painfully separate from you, how could you pay for that? Now that the precepts and codes imposed on you by your teachers had been exorcised, your way of life and the quick pleasure of your incubus accepted, Dolores had wisely disciplined your impulses, had satisfied, over the years, your growing need for love. Your union was built on a pre-established harmony: no chance, no contingency between you and her. As if beforehand, you concluded, someone, devil or angel, had been watching out for you in advance.

When the sun went down behind the gray roofs and the red chimneys, with black cats and white doves subtly modifying the proportions of strong and weak shades that in their way constituted one of the great delights of the picture, the light of the sunset would shorten the lines and curves of your bodies as they were reflected in the mirror and give back to you, little by little, to you and to her, your remote and displaced identities. Dolores was impassive, absorbed in some secret thought, and you were coming to in the calm of night, telling yourself over and over again, as you tell yourself now, in this apathetic and indolent summer of 1963, the day when everything shall be forgotten and our bones will rot far from one another, perhaps, our love will still seem indispensable and the exact opposite of the fate and chance of others, always fortuitous, always eventual, unforeseen, absurd, left to fortune, arbitrary, useless, always a gamble.

Dolores had gone inside for a few minutes, and as you waited for her to return, you recalled with a smile Madame de Heredia's face, perpetually powdered, the black cat curled up in her lap, the group of pupils gathered around the Elizabethan sofa. Trophies and mementos of her artistic career were mixed up and void there in the shadows, and an imprecise feeling of unreality infected the atmosphere as if, far-removed from the laws of physics, the cushiony universe of the boardinghouse was floating outside of time and space, subject to some special and autonomous system that strangely found its justification in itself, *vous voyez la photo, c'est lui,* Frédéric, a man in his fifties, graying, elegant, photographed in a simple linen shirt and light pants, standing in front of some noble ruins, most likely Paestum or Pompeii, *un être extraordinaire, Monsieur,* a real music-lover, we've known each other for a long time, and Madame de Heredia would sigh before she went on with the lesson and placed her thin, yellowish hand on the piano keys. On several occasions, during that innovating and stimulating autumn of 1954, you had passed him several times, preceded by the ecstatic figure of Madame de Heredia, as he went to the parlor, with the severe and rigorous dress of a stockbroker. Then the teacher would suspend her classes and, with a quick glance, make her pupils understand that their presence was not needed, because she, Madame de Heredia, was going to listen alone with Frédéric to some inspired work by Schubert, perhaps the sonatas of Scarlatti, that he would pluck for her note by note with melancholy and distinguished simplicity. The teacher would carefully close the door and, all through the afternoon, the melodious notes from the piano would follow, one after the other, in the half-darkness, interpolated by brief periods of silence that were acute, electric, and paralyzing. Madame de Heredia would sit motionless on the sofa, a cup of tea in her hand, and, when he had finished his delicate interpretation of the score, Frédéric would change the position of the stool and modestly accept the deep sigh of thanks that she gave him, an artist of refined sensibility, Monsieur, an incomparable critic of music, happy as she was at not having to share so much delight with anyone, drinking down to the dregs those fleeting hours of intimate and exquisite communion. We both have the same tastes and a mutual love for beautiful things, Mozart, Beethoven, Schubert, Mendelssohn, and you thought about the two of them, conversing without the necessity of words, transported by his serene and luminous music, the inhabitants of a world that was perfect and passionless, the spotless and dynamic creation of their spirit. Autumn passed slowly, and twice a week Madame la Heredia would brush off her old evening dresses to go with Frédéric to the rue Gaveau or the Champs Elysées theater, often accompanied by Sébastien, the eighteen-year-old son that she had had from her husband some months before the yearned-for divorce, desired by her because of her husband's grossness and vulgarity, I was afraid to bring him out at first, but he was immediately touched by his youth and now he loves him almost as much as if he were his own son, and the teacher would then go on at length about the common and plebeian character of Sébastien's father, interested only in material things and appetites, contrasting him to Frédéric's nobility and loftiness, the pure lover of ideal and bodiless pleasures, the alert and agile seeker after beauty. He's too pure for these times, Madame de Heredia would murmur, we live, he and I, like two exiles, and in the opportune silence of the sunset, just right for secrets, she would confess to you that their reciprocal friendship had slowly grown into love, not physical love, she hastened to say immediately, at least for the moment, still platonic and almost angelic, but of such an intensity and violence that she, *ma parole*, had never known before: sometimes, as he plays Schubert, he will look at me and his eyes will fill with tears, his mother died when he was ten years old and he's never gotten over it. You would listen to her without a word, and Madame de Heredia would fill the vases and the bowls in the parlor with the roses that Frédéric had sent to her along with a card written in his own hand, distracted from the study and recitation of the lessons by that absorbing love. *Bon, recommençons,* she would sigh, but her thoughts, you knew, were lightly flying off elsewhere, toward the rooms where Frédéric, fulfilling his worldly obligations, was arguing with some other music-lover about the last magnificent concert of the Stuttgart Chamber Orchestra or was destroying with one incisive phrase the mediocre recital given by Schwarzkopf, surrounded by exceptional beings like himself, innocent, smiling, poetic, unpredictable. During the three months that they had been going out together, Frédéric had not declared his love or revealed his real feelings, but did that really matter? His looks were enough, and the deep silences that would inevitably follow his fascinating interpretation of a score, he loved her, yes, he loved her, and she loved him too, although, unlike that prosaic and brutish husband of hateful memory, Frédéric did not seek her body or even to kiss her, and he had limited himself to squeezing her hand forcefully between his own and looking at her as he stroked her with his velvety, doelike eyes. Up to now he's been living so withdrawn from love that he doesn't dare believe in it. Monsieur, our tale is like a dream to him, and, right on time to bear her out, Frédéric would appear in the apartment, with his austere City dress and the usual bouquet of flowers, virginal and perfect, with that quintessential and impalpable distinction that, according to the teacher, was the unmistakable stamp of a gentleman. You would go back to your room, leaving them to their tender backwater of love and happiness, and you would wait with curiosity for the moment when the first chord on the piano would inaugurate the esoteric dialogue between the two and Frédéric would look intensely into her eyes and squeeze her hand passionately, as if through osmosis it were possible for him to pass on to her the indescribable and intact love that there was in him. No, nothing yet, he has a sensibility on the surface of his skin, and I don't want to treat things too harshly, Madame de Heredia would say after the visit, women frightened him, no doubt, in his youth he had probably experienced some bitter sentimental deceptions, or, perhaps, like that distant cousin whom she had outlined on a biographical occasion, he was still emotionally tied to his mother and had sworn to be faithful to her unto death, *l'amour, alors, est une profanation, vous comprenez?* and you agreed, in silence, with that little cram course in the ideas of Stekel, Marcelle Segal, and Monsignor Fulton J. Sheen, deep in the submarine half-shadow of the parlor, as the teacher's stern black cat rested in her lap. Frédéric would make an almost daily appearance in the apartment with his bunch of roses, and Madame de Heredia was something to be seen then, hurrying off to fix her hair, appearing a few minutes later with her face powdered and an aggressive smell of perfume, rejuvenated and vibrant, having regained the worldly aplomb of her triumphal finery and her yellowing photographs. The piano would sound again, docile under the light and winged magic of Frédéric's hands, and you would imagine the tense and receptive face of the teacher during the transparent and concise interpretation of the Adagio in B minor by Mozart: you play better than Gieseking, he's too cold for me, sometimes he misses the tragic echoes of the piece. Frédéric would receive the compliments with devout humility, and, putting your IDHEC textbooks aside, you would apply your ear to the cursed door that was between your room and the parlor and would try to guess from the intensity of Madame de Heredia's sigh, whether Frédéric had sat down next to her, and, since it was now *de rigueur* between them, was softly holding her hand. Nothing, nothing yet, the teacher said afterward, Frédéric was too timid, the close presence of the boarders worried him, an excess of respect toward the fair sex, the result of the cruel and premature death of his mother inhibited his natural impulses and kept him imprisoned in a sublime adoration of womankind, immaterial and distant. Great tact would be necessary, a good deal of patience and tenderness, so as not to wound his delicate sensibility, to overcome his exquisite bashfulness little by little, imperceptibly to transform that love, which up till then had been ethereal, into a physical relationship that, with feminine intuition, she could foresee quite strongly as something impetuous and volcanic. Madame de Heredia was counting on a trip to the country for that, a good lunch on the grass, the caresses of the lazy autumn sun, the discreet aid of a well-seasoned meal, and an insidious bottle of wine. Sébastien would go with them and, at a sign from his mother, he would disappear into the woods, leaving the two of them in the solitude of accomplices, disturbing, almost shameful. He'll declare his love for me out there, he's still afraid, but since I understand him, and the teacher would reveal to you some ancient stories about famous men whose exemplary existences had been destroyed one day by some terrible, unscrupulous adventuress, but she would assure Frédéric, the ideal, persevering, and assiduous presence of Frédéric, of her unmeasurable desire for love, her vast comprehension, her deep and palpitating tenderness. Sébastien would often stop by to see them of late, and the paternal affection that Frédéric showed him was a source of beatitude and wonder on the part of Madame de Heredia, he feels lonely, *vous comprenez?* He feels the need to integrate himself into a family and, forgetting once more the *solfège* lesson of one of her students, she would tell you with all the luxury of details about the concert that the three of them had attended the night before, emphasizing, with her beautiful soprano voice, the generous solicitude of Frédéric, the singular care that he was taking with Sébastien's aural education, with the formation and refinement of his artistic tastes. *Il m'aime, oui, il m'aime,* he's going to tell me soon, I can sense it: Madame de Heredia would go on by herself in the darkness of the parlor, and the cat would agree tacitly with a voluptuous stretch, *ce soir, peut-être demain.* The roses followed every day, and the calming interpretations of Brahms, and the charming silences, nothing yet today, *patientons,* in between evenings of music at the Salle Pleyel and instructive visits to Debussy's birthplace or the town house where Mozart had lived, during which Frédéric would show the boy the precious treasure of his erudition, of his thoughtful and grave opinions, of his rich and varied culture. Nothing, nothing yet: but with his bashfulness, was there really any cause for alarm? Frédéric was not familiar with that base and vulgar form of love, his realm existed only in the superior domains of the spirit. She understood him, ah, how she understood him: born into a simoniacal and soullèss century, where advantage, concupiscence, and profit were corrupting the very essence of Art, was there anything more natural and more logical than his fervent withdrawal? She was satisfied with his peaceful look, the wonderful contact with his hands, the diligent attention that, out of love for her, he scrupulously showed her child. His roses in the afternoon, weren't they sufficient proof of love? And the warm little notes that came with them, did they not reveal, perhaps, in an equal way, the breadth of his tenderness? If he would only speak at last, if he would say something to me at least; but no, foolishness, his circumspection was more eloquent than speeches, the long silences between them played the same harmonious role as pauses in music. Then why worry? Maybe Frédéric had no other means of communication, and tonal language, neat and clear, took the place, by his inner law, of the utilitarian, commercialized, and equivocal language of other people. However, oh, however, when Madame de Heredia, with prudent astuteness, would allude in passing to the necessity of establishing a home, of establishing a family, Frédéric would retreat into a cautious silence, would perceptibly soften the pressure of his fingers, would look anxiously at the door. After a certain number of attempts, she had not insisted again. Frédéric loved her, no doubt, with a pure and celestial love, but how could she explain, then, his repugnance to regularize their situation publicly? An unconsummated marriage, it's all the same to me, all she asked for was the mystical enchantment with which he interpreted Schubert's sonatas, the exchange of looks that tempered and clothed the magnitude of the silences, the subtle and delicate touching of their hands. Sébastien was with them: from your room you could hear the Rondo in G major, opus 51, by Beethoven, the sonorous and dynamic progression with no change in tempo that gave the theme its perfect continuity, its articulated and robust brilliance. For some days, Madame de Heredia had been showing signs of nervousness, and when she reviewed the *solfège* lessons of her pupils, she would stop in the middle of a sentence and give a lost look at the carmine-colored roses emerging from the porcelain vases and pitchers: *il faut qu'il se décide,* she would say to you before she left with her son for the usual Thursday concert, I can't take any more of this hide-and-seek. You heard her return downcast, and you would selfishly turn out the light in your room so as to avoid her litany of lamentations. To each one of her frontal attacks, Frédéric would respond with new evasions, and things would be right back where they were at the start, ground zero, in spite of her use of schemes and stratagems. At certain moments, Madame de Heredia would imagine that Frédéric had stopped loving her, she thought she had spotted a metallic and hard glow in his eyes. Imagination, delirium, he's going to drive me crazy, she would say, it's today or never. And once more the ritual of the flowers, his lover's notes, the evocative and suggestive music, the deep and interminable silences. It's the last time, we're not going on like this for ten years just because Monsieur is timid, and once more the gamuts, the chromatic scales, the octaves, the chords, the trills of a virtuoso, and a baroque interpretation that would plunge the entire house into a receptive and sensuous atmosphere, a state of loving trance, exalted and rhythmical. I should have made him understand from the beginning, he's a coward: Madame de Heredia was speaking to the hazy image of herself reflected in the mirror, and an immense pity for her fate had clouded her eyes with tears. And yet, I do love him, *oui, je l'aime, mon Dieu,* what a mess. The taxi was waiting for her at the door with Frédéric and the boy, and the latter's soothing presence and the former's tender care comforted her again, made her doubts miraculously vanish. After all, Monsieur, *à mon âge*, what can one ask of life? and still the round of flowers, musical evenings, furtive touches, emotional silences, the oh, *non,* this time it's all over, once and for all, from here on I won't go any more, until that memorable night when he did not appear and did not send her a bouquet of roses or a fiery card, and she called him a hundred times without getting him in, without being able to throw her reproaches and offenses into his face like a handful of confetti, her threats and insults, resolved to forget everything a half-hour later with just the sound of his voice and listening to his reasonable excuses, imagining in her wakeful delirium, his soft and soothing voice as it whispered words of love as old as the world itself, *je t'aime,* Edmonde, I love you, *pardon, pardon encore,* my sweet, my lovely, my tender love. You had finally gone to sleep, lulled by the sound of her steps and the echo of her demented soliloquy, *oui, c'est ça,* he has a mistress and he's afraid to confess it to me, but I forgive him, his presence is all I need, and, when you woke up, the apartment seemed to have been shaken by a violent explosion, and Madame de Heredia was storming back and forth shaking a rectangular envelope in her hand, angry and disheveled in the midst of that oppressive décor of dead photographs, roses that had withered forever, sublime evenings that would never again be, *mon Dieu, oh, mon Dieu,* brought back to unpleasant old age and harsh reality, the prisoner of precarious time and the gift of life, Monsieur, do you understand? sobbing, as she handed you the letter, that swine has run off with my son.

The two of you were sitting in a corner of the garden, and you were both weaving and unweaving with the humble tenacity of Penelope the slow and delicate mesh of the imaginary dialogue.

"Do you love me?"

"Yes."

"You've only known me for a week. You hardly know who I am."

"I've known you forever."

"Kiss me."

"I'm falling in love with you."

"Give me a kiss."

"You're different from other people, and so am I. We were made for each other."

"Why don't you go to bed with me?"

"I'm afraid."

"Do other women make you afraid?"

"You make me afraid."

"Let me cuddle you."

"You don't exist. I invited you into existence."

"We've been in love for six months. Do I still interest you?"

"An infinite 'still.' "

"Do you like my body?"

"I don't know it. I'll never know it completely."

"I put yours together again too. Every day. Every second."

"I'm lost in you. In your sex. In your eyes."

"My love."

"You're the only woman for me."

"Are you getting used to me?"

"I'll never get used to you."

"A year. It's been a year now that we've been living together."

"Leave time alone."

"That's what's left us alone."

"The past doesn't count. You're the only one who counts."

"Do you miss what there was before?"

"There's no before with you. I was born with you. I begin with you."

"Do you remember when you were afraid of me?"

"I'm still afraid of you."

"My body belongs to you."

"I can't possess you. You're the air I breathe. The water that runs through my fingers."

"Don't you get tired?"

"I drink and I'm still thirsty."

"I have to know that you love me. Every minute. At this very moment."

"Two years of peace and forgetfulness. I was born just two years ago."

"Time doesn't exist."

"You're my past. My marks of identity are false."

"Do you love me?"

"I still don't know your body. I haven't got to the bottom."

"Why were you drinking yesterday?"

"It's something stronger than me. At first I was able to accept the idea of your looking at another man. Now I can't."

"Why didn't you tell me?"

"I didn't want to butt in. You're a free person."

"I'm not free and neither are you."

"Jealousy disgusts me."

"You're too secretive. We've been together for three years, and sometimes I think I don't know anything about you."

"I'm not secretive, I'm bashful."

"I never keep things inside me. When something bothers me, I tell you."

"You're stronger than I."

"I've been noticing changes in you for some time now."

"I'm getting old."

"You look at me and you seem to be thinking about something else."

"I'm bored with my work."

"Give it up. Go back to Spain."

"Spain's all over for me."

"Take a trip."

"Trips don't solve anything."

"You drink too much."

"Tell me what else I can do."

"Aren't I any help to you?"

"I didn't say that."

"When I feel that you're sad, I get sad too."

"It's not your fault."

"I'm horrified with the idea of hurting you. I love you. I'm in love with you."

"So am I. But we can't do anything for each other."

"Why do you say that?"

"You know what I'm like."

"It doesn't matter. I'm proud of you."

"We'll never be able to find each other."

"Don't you like my body?"

"I can drown in it."

"Five years together, do you realize it?"

"Lately I think you've been sad too."

"It's because of you. When you do things you don't like to. When you drink. When I guess the desire I can't fight against."

"Character is fate."

"Sometimes I don't know whether you love me."

"I do love you."

"I can feel your jealousy, but I can't feel your love."

"Why are you crying?"

"Female reasons."

"Was that why you felt so sick yesterday?"

"I'm afraid so."

"You were brilliant."

"Don't worry about it. We'll fix it up."

"I don't want to force you."

"I'm forcing myself."

"I don't want to leave anything behind me, understand?"

"You won't leave anything, either in me or in anybody else."

"That's the only freedom I've got."

"You've made me pay a lot for it."

"Forget about it."

"I can't. I can see him leaning over me. His dirty face. His dirty hands."

"There's a gleam in your eyes that I don't know."

"I still haven't digested Geneva."

"It's still too soon. You'll forget it someday."

"It's sticking in me like a knife. That's why I went with Enrique."

"Don't mention his name."

"You dirtied me. I had to get even."

"There are some things I can't talk about. My life's story is full of gaps."

"I would have moved heaven and earth to purify myself. To bury once and for all that part of my memory where you are."

"Shut up. Don't make me any worse than I am."

"If you were only happy."

"You can see the result."

"Why did you do it?"

"I went on the roller coaster and when I got off I fainted."

"Do you feel like finishing?"

"Yes."

"I wish I were dead."

"Don't cry."

"I thought that you'd find yourself again in Cuba."

"I've lost my country and I've lost my people."

"What do you plan on doing?"

"I can't do anything. I don't even know who I am."

"What about your friends?"

"I don't have any friends."

"Nothing matters as long as you want to keep going forward."

"I want to keep going forward."

"What are you looking for here?"

"I don't know."

"Do you love me?"

"I was born to love you and to suffer for you."

(The images of past time vanish in the air behind the ghostly round of people captured in the family album, in that same garden where you are resting now, in the shade of the same eucalyptus trees: the crisscross and agile ballet of forgotten steps and dead voices. the tranquil and bloodless hecatomb of intense and now exhausted moments; the slippery passage of days that erodes and corrupts everything. You and she alone, in precarious balance, safe from and at the mercy of the inevitable shipwreck.)

A familiar scene goes round and round in your memory: you are in that busy part of Paris near the Saint Martin canal, and a late winter sun is shining on the water.

You are walking slowly. The Arab has abandoned his contemplation of the hoists and starts walking, careful and suspicious, with his hands in his pockets. Sixty feet away from you, you can easily observe his rubber boots, his coarse blue denim pants, his leather jacket with fleece lapels, the wool cap tight on his head. His discreet presence governs the street. When he reaches the small, naked gardens of the square, he turns in the direction of the boulevard, waits for the green signal without turning, crosses the street, and, just as you figured, continues walking toward La Chapelle under the rusty roof of the elevated. You imitate him.

The wind has driven away the *clochards* who are usually flopping on the wooden benches, and with the exception of a few busy and absorbed passers-by, in the middle there is only a small circle of bystanders and a pair of inveterate *pétanque* players. The Arab stops to look with an absent expression. When you come up and follow his example, he examines you for a few seconds with deep black eyes. He has taken his right hand out of the pocket of his jacket, and, in a mechanical way, he strokes his mustache with his thumb and index finger.

The train hums past above and its roar brutally shakes the ground. Suddenly removed from space and time, you remember that one day, in a shabby hotel nearby, you had made love (with whom?) on the run (it was late, you had an appointment at *France Presse*), and your ejaculation had coincided exactly with the trembling brought on by the passing of the train. (The logical consequence of the noise or pure chance?) Since then, you think nostalgically, you haven't ever tried it again.

Children dressed up as Sioux Indians run past in front of you, shooting off their toy pistols. The Arab walks slowly and attentively scrutinizes the shops and stores along the sidewalk. Two women of the *Armée du Salut* are going toward Barbés, withdrawn and silent, with the inept grace of God painted on their faces. The squalid sun seems to be unpeeling the moldering fronts of the buildings and is reflected on the windows without any flicker.

(As a necessary horizon for you, the face of Jerónimo, of the successive reincarnations of Jerónimo in some delicate and masterful face, dreaming and violent, had watched like a hallmark over the ups and downs of your passion for Dolores with the magnetic and brusque force with which it had struck you the first time. When you separated, he left without giving you his address or asking for yours. He had two women, six children, and you never did find out his name.)

You were slowly going through the pages of the atlas, and each colored print of the accidental and changeable political geography of Europe brought to your memory some image that, as accusation or purge, was added to the dossier of your common history with Dolores and, in a subtle way, it modified it. Since you had joined *France Presse,* the editors had been sending you all over the world to photograph the idyll of sad princesses (fatuous Rubén Darío promoted to the position of editor-in-chief of *France Dimanche*), or the talked-about divorce of a famous actress ("*J'ai surpris Annette dans les bras de Sacha*") and, for a while, your agitated existence as a *paparazzo* had consoled you for the unsuccessful and irreparable ruin of the projected documentary on emigration. Dolores was traveling with you, and the nostalgia for Spain had been disappearing little by little, as if the roots that had joined you to the tribe had been drying up, one after the other, as a consequence for your long expatriation and of the reciprocal indifference. An amputated branch of the native trunk, a plant growing in the air, expelled like so many others, now and always, by the jealous guardians of your century-old heritage.

Resting in the garden, where the inconsistent child that you had been had vegetated and lounged with his people until the sudden revelation of his passion for Jerónimo, you were lazily remembering Amsterdam and its canals, the phosphorescent shopwindows of Zeedijk, with its seductive prostitutes, like captive mermaids in an aquarium, the Mascotte bar and the robot orchestra that played calypso tunes as sparks came out of their fierce eyes, the oil stains from the ships that were floating like rafts or gigantic drowned butterflies, the line of sailors waiting to be tattooed in Sint Olofs Steeg, the dance hall where Dolores flirted with a West Indian and, after one of your scenes, the two of you had kissed until you had lost your breath.

She was looking with you at the small city map that was beside the map of Holland, and forgotten moments of your walks and remote shreds of your conversations came up like bubbles in your memory, dissolving immediately in a sudden succession of images projected, one might say, in a kaleidoscope. (As in other places in Flanders and the Low Countries, Spanish culture, asphyxiated by the inhospitable dryness of the steppe and the proverbial intolerance of its inhabitants, had taken root under the protection of the Protestant Reformation and its generous breadth of thought, taking shape in a multitude of works with an inspiration that was just and free, serene and lasting. A seed scattered by the wind, the intelligence of your people had fallen on arable land, and after many centuries the fruits were evidence of an innovating and rebellious impulse that you thought deserved better luck. That errant Spain, that vagabond Spain, substituted in your heart for the official Spain that was taught to serfs and masters, the one for the boorish people of hood and sackcloths, the bullfight pens and the Holy Week processions.

In Hamburg you both had visited, until you were exhausted, the bars in Reeperbahn and St. Paoli (the Rattenkeller, the Katakombe, the Rote Katze, the Mustapha, the Venus), and in Bruges you had witnessed an unusual scene (do you remember, Dolores?): severe Flemish children who seemed to have emerged from some baroque painting had organized a ring-around-a-rosy and were impassively watching the meritorious efforts of a half-dozen little old women who, obeying the referee's whistle, were spinning and spinning, smiling and docile, around an artificial pond with white water lilies in it. Little by little, to the blind admiration of the first months, there had followed an ambiguous attitude *vis-à-vis* the new and frozen industrial religion of the Europeans: the backdrop of cranes, scaffolding, bulldozers, smokestacks that you had seen in the Ruhr valley during your trips had made you understand suddenly that you were fighting for a world that would be uninhabitable for you. Under a deceptive appearance of comfort, the conditions of life were hard, feelings tended to disappear, human relations became commercialized. Your rebellion would not find a place there either, and it was nothing but a prolongation, you said to yourself, of your pre-capitalist and feudal Spanish world, today on the road to liquidation and demolition without the necessity of your participation or of that of your friends, without nobility, without morality, without justice, by the narrow and simple dynamics of the economic process.

Every page of the atlas brought back some memory of yours, and Dolores figured in all of them, successively distant, hostile, passionate, loving: a sun devoured by its own glow was being reflected in her wide and undirected eyes opposite the cliffs of Marina Piccola; strolling through the streets of Rome, she seemed to adjust her movements to the rules of a harmonious and unforeseeable law; absorbed, she contemplated the admirable "Regents of the Almshouse" by Hals, the prodigious play of light and shadow, the thick and rhythmical musicality of the painting.

There was a pause, during which the clouds that were floating off toward the southeast took on a dull, opaque shade. In the distance one could hear the automobile horns and the sick panting of the locomotive along the railroad.

Dolores had gone to the kitchen to get some ice, and she put a bottle in the pail to chill. It was a few minutes before the Angelus and Dr. d'Asnières's bitter drops. The locusts were chorusing their strident sounds in the woods, and you opened up the atlas in the middle.

MONACO, a small principality in Europe, located in the French Dept. of the Maritime Alps; ½ sq. mi.; (Monagasques); Cap. *Monaco*. Port on a promontory of the Mediterranean Sea. Famous for its Casino. Beaches.

The last time you had been there, weeks after the fainting spell that had hit you on the Boulevard Richard Lenoir, you had occasionally gone to sessions of small groups of twist, rock, and Madison with wild names, and the mystical delirium that had overcome the audience and the state of trance into which some of the young people had fallen, worked the miracle of shaking you out of your torpor.

On what strange planet were you living?

. . . In 1956, still young and undamaged. Dolores and you had visited the gambling parlors where your Uncle Néstor had dissipated his fortune, and after you tried your luck in vain, you both went out onto the terrace that stands out in the shadow of the Hotel de Paris over the La Condamine section. It was growing dark: a sleepwalking glow was arising out of the gray waters of the harbor, and the red lights of the buoys and the white neon beacons were making a useless effort at becoming pale. Life was smiling down on the two of you, and in the fullness a passion that you thought you would never be able to satiate assailed you suddenly, violently, the intuition of time and its clandestine work of erosion, the irremedial death of feelings, and the very decrepitude of the both of you: long before you, Uncle Néstor and his Irish girl friend had passed through the same places, equally absorbed in the joy of their lovers' crises; since the cause for which they had been fighting had been recognized, a clear future was opening up before their eyes, and no force in the world, they thought, innocently perhaps, would ever be able to undermine their union. Eternal, intact, their adventure was being strung out peacefully along with them, as if it never, you said to yourself, had any end.

Three decades had suddenly been erased and fate was shuffling its cards. Little by little, you remembered, the rocky promontory of the palace was being dissolved in the half-light. A lulling quietude was paralyzing the life of the port. A tern was coming from the other side of the cape, and when it got close, it veered off out to sea again.

The couple that was observing that insomniac panorama, was it you or was it they?

When the question was repeated, seven years later, you think now, you did not think you could answer it.

The distant shouts of the children startled you.

Aunt Dolores
waaah
a wasp
waaaah
Aunt Dolores

waaaaah waaaaaah
Aunt Dolores
four years before
a few months after the failure of the peaceful national strike and the second wave of imprisonments
with your sight lost on the sleepwalking swans of the lake in Geneva you were crossing the Pont du Montblanc in the midst of a delegation of delegates joined together there no doubt for some altruistic end that was practical and beneficial
one of those magnanimous congresses against war hunger unemployment sickness underdevelopment invented by the prosperous Swiss hotel industry
(I wonder why there are no Congresses
you said to yourself
for the ruination and perdition of the human species sponsored by the most notorious criminals of the century
Landru Petiot Giuliano Al Capone Dillinger)
and the child was walking along the railing of the bridge and was examining the sad Swiss panorama that was like a Swiss post card with a critical and censorious look
why are we here
Dolores has to see a man
what man
a friend
I'm tired
look at the lake
I don't like it
do you want to take a boat ride
I want to go back to Paris
it was here that your Uncle Néstor had hanged himself before you were born in his room at the Bel-Air sanitarium and his revolt against the Spanish society of his time died with him just as yours will die no doubt if you don't give it a concrete and precise form and if you do not succeed in channeling it first *do you want some ice cream* he had looked out over the icebox countryside of water firs mountain snow *no I don't want any* the Nordic whiteness of the air the stiff and gloomy sun as he tied his silk scarf to the knob on the window and reread for the last time the letter he had written to your grandmother *what do you feel like doing then* the letter that she kept with her until her death and which your mother refused

to show you *go home* all of its potential rebellion buried in nothingness digested in their memory a simple useless name in the moribund family tree *where's Aunty* you want to be an epilogue and not a beginning their mistake must end with you *we're going to see her now* what comes from you ought to be buried *where?* reparation and forgetfulness *near here* in the bottom of a Swiss lake mixed with semen and the residue of all the sewers

buy me a Mickey Mouse book

as she sat opposite you you examined her knees with almost painful attention the refined and almost perfect curve that disappeared underneath the hem of her skirt *what can we do* the admirable legs that you had learned every inch of with the ample slowness and breadth of passion *I don't know it's so unexpected* brutally interrupted by the fold of the plaid blanket *what are you thinking about* there was a spark of anger in her eyes just as on the day she came to your room in Madame de Heredia's house and began to get undressed as a challenge *well you already know what I think but if you want* you turned your glance toward the hem of her checkered skirt *I didn't say that I'm only interested in your opinion* to the convex line of her thighs that pointed the hidden and desired sex *if you're afraid of* again the unusual glow in her eyes furtively seeking yours *no I'm not afraid* with a bashful expression she pulled her skirt down over her knees *if you think there's any danger at all* she lit a cigarette and nervously thumbed through an illustrated magazine *nothing ever happens don't worry it's female business I'll take care of it*

the two of you had a date in a café on the Place Bourg-du-Four where students from the school of architecture went the child was walking along momentarily absorbed in his

reading of Mickey Mouse and new delegations with emblems and pennants poured out of the hotels on the Place Longemalle

Americans who looked like cowboys Protestant ministers with white clerical collars folkloric groups from some African country virtuous women with frozen and toothpasty smiles

Uncle Néstor tested the strength of the scarf before tying it around the window knob and looked out over the firs in the Bel-Air garden the dark and motionless waters of Lake Léman meditating perhaps on how vain a rebellion condemned to disappear with him was

where are we going
to wait for Dolores
I'm tired
it's right here
his photograph does not appear in the family album and the one that had been on your mother's dresser disappeared after her death you can scarcely remember an insolent and romantic face that attracted the maternal instinct in women completely forgotten after thirty years as if he had never existed
you sat down at the first empty table in the café opposite the door through which Dolores would come
what do you want
immersed in the reading of Mickey Mouse
an orangeade with lots of sugar
no one could have picked a better place to end it all here on the shore of the lake where your Uncle Néstor had hanged himself as if a fatality hung over the family by the same Swiss lake looking out at the neurasthenic countryside
you got up and stopped your examination of the colored prints in the atlas that represented the Helvetian Confederation physical political economic linguistic simultaneous with the running about of the maidservant who was frightened by the child's shrieks and the serene voice of Dolores
bring me some cotton and the bottle of formol, please
in one of the drawers in the desk there was a letter from Uncle Néstor written from the Bel-Air sanitarium dated a few months before his suicide
you looked for it in the folder religiously kept by your mother with the rough drafts of his translations of Yeats and the notes for a future anthology of Irish poetry
if you don't want to send any more money don't bother anyway I am not coming back to Barcelona
I didn't pick you people and you didn't pick me nobody is to blame
dying for Ireland would have been an exaggeration I'm better off in this watch shop
I shall die from dislike of Switzerland far from your churches and your priests all his will save you the expenses of my funeral and burial
you went back to the garden
Dolores had suddenly appeared in the doorway and you studied her face trying to guess her feelings

the smooth stomach the slim legs Italian shoes with a daring and elegant line
un café s'il vous plait
Aunt Dolores
she took a cigarette out of her case lit it slowly exhaled the smoke
what did he say
four o'clock this afternoon
Aunt Dolores
sweety
when are we going to leave
she pours her frustrated maternity out on the child she makes an effort to attempt at tenderness as if she would never be able to repeat them
you think it's dangerous
at the point we've reached it makes no difference to me
within four hours you will be free again without ties that bind you to life the master of a thick nothingness like Uncle Néstor
if you want to try the other address
for heaven's sake be quiet
the two of you were waiting lying down in the hotel room without your knowing what was going on inside alien to one another like two strangers after a casual and accidental meeting
the child was putting a fleet of paper boats in the bathtub he was having wars naval battles aerial bombardments submarine encounters atomic explosions as Dolores lit one cigarette with the butt of another and was absorbed in the flowered wallpaper
recalling the somber building of the Bel-Air sanitarium that you visited on your first trip to Switzerland still inhabited after thirty-five years by the wandering ghost of your Uncle Néstor
the frozen and windy air the oblique rain the damp and sad garden that had brought back to your memory that of the convent where you had seen your grandmother for the last time
like him you wanted to break with everything that you had received as a loan just as much without your asking that they had given to you
god religion morality laws fortune
trying to imagine his lonely walks along the shores of Lake Léman through that sanitarium of rich foreigners with flower beds paths arbors ponds built in the early part of the century to shelter the delusions of grandeur of some Russian aristocrat

the meager inheritance that he had left behind the translations and poems lost during the war dead without punishment or glory in a Swiss rest home
saying to yourself
you're not here by chance today's agony is a warning
how long will it be before you extinguish yourself
the unsuccessful author of a documentary on the Spanish flock expelled from their land by oppression unemployment hunger injustice
your rebellion is emptied out here your rebellion will die with you
with superstitious solemnity Dolores was going through the motions of a bullfighter who looks over his costume before going to the ring and once more you admired her pained and unfortunate body made for love and tenderness
are you angry with me
no
a watermelon sliced in two the knife sinks into the juicy heart of the fruit
you went toward her and took her clumsily by the waist
swear to me
when he wrote his farewell letter it was toward the end of autumn and a shrouded and apprehensive sun perhaps was lighting up the snow on the mountains
let me go I'll be late
he tied the scarf around his neck and let himself drop
I'll go with you
I'd rather go by myself
the fleet of paper boats was resting on the bottom of the tub and on the child's face an implacable boredom could be seen
where are you going
I have to do an errand
what about Uncle
he'll take you for a walk
we'll go to the park
I don't want to
what do you want to do
go back to Paris
perfumed and dressed as if for a wedding ceremony the bloody seed dissolved forever in the obscene waters of the lake
you could have held her back even hugged her begging her not to go to the appointment

I'll wait for you in the bar across the street
anything you say
I won't budge from the terrace
you went over to the window opened the blinds and spied on her as she crossed the street in the midst of the disciplined Swiss crowd
what are you looking at
nothing
there's nothing to do
let's go out
the two of you went down the red-carpeted stairs you left the key at the desk you bought a copy of *La Tribune*
the millions of Indians dying of hunger the oppressed racial minorities the victims of atomic radiation served as a pretext for the incessant parade of commissions sub-commissions committees delegations secretariats
a completely slippery and cold group metallic and modern exclusively dedicated
that was what it said
for the good of their fellow man and the salvation of humanity
nuns with white hoods flapping like butterflies Hindus with faces as tight and as heavy as the head of a cane Scandinavian tourists with wet and strawlike faces mixing in with the big-bellied and peaceful watchmaking people Italian laborers with calloused hands and strong sculptured features circles of Spanish women catapulted out of the villages on the plateau with their inevitable black dresses and cardboard suitcases
Geneva is a station at the end of the line no one can live there with impunity and Uncle Néstor could not have picked a better place to end his days or Dolores to destroy the germ of that hated seed
pardon vous désirez quelque chose
thank you Madame I was taking a walk
you smiled
someone in my family died here a long time ago you understand
no she did not understand
in her eyes there was clear suspicion and without going to the portico where two ladies of advanced age seemed to be enjoying the softness of the drizzle you went back along the path lined with fir trees toward the rusty gate that opened onto the street
CLINIQUE DU BEL-AIR
you were on the terrace again with your gaze fixed on the map

of the Helvetian Confederation and the child's moans were dully filtering out from inside the house

I want to go to the movies

MONKEY BUSINESS with the Marx Brothers dubbed in French

an hour later on the Boulevard des Tranchées on the terrace of the café opposite the doorway

deux places s'il vous plait

Álvaro always confuses Marx (Karl) with Marx (Brothers) and Monroe (President) with Monroe (Marilyn)

the audience was laughing loudly and you followed the usher's flashlight down to two empty seats in the first row

I can't see very good

ssh

I want to sit farther back

be quiet

the images vaguely reminded you of some movie that you had seen with your mother on a Thursday afternoon in the remote limbo of your childhood

what the devil was its title in Spanish

you see this gat

it's very cute did Santa Claus give it to you

he gave me a locomotive

listen you fool do you know who I am

don't tell me animal, vegetable, or mineral

aagh

animal

listen I'm Alky Briggs

and I'm the guy who's been dying to meet you

have you got any last questions before I bump you off

yes

go ahead

do you really think a girl should let a boy kiss her on the first date

four o'clock by the lighted clock on the wall the man's dirty hands manipulating the instruments

why doesn't he shoot

Dolores came out from the porch leading Luisito by the hand and his face was innocent and happy again

a wasp stung him

does it hurt

yes

eleven-year-old boys don't cry

she was probably lying on the bed who knows whether he might try to take advantage of her *why is he hiding* to dilate you understand *oh look what they're doing* his slimy lips on her skin *are they good men or bad men* the depressing room in the Bel-Air clinic the firs the Swiss panorama of the lake *who's the fat man* the scarf tied to the knob the accursed seed *he's trying to escape isn't he* everything has been useless it was written that it was to end in Switzerland in some dirty sewer at the bottom of Lake Léman

after I got my marriage license I led a dog's life

maybe it was a dog license

the theater was laughing and stamping

you got up

let's go

it isn't over yet

Dolores is waiting for us

Geneva again international and provincial shapeless and profuse abandoning yourself to the desolate inventory of your heritage and your gifts

Dolores had sat down beside you with her legs crossed and was examining in her turn the map of the Helvetian Confederation

we never got to Saas-Fee

you rolled your eyes

you remembered the precise moment when she had appeared hesitantly on the sidewalk of the Boulevard des Tranchées and the child ran merrily to meet her while you ran frightened to the nearest taxi stand

pale disheveled hollow-eyed still confused by the morphine

what's the matter

nothing love

why are you crying

the terrible dash to the Place Longemalle her hands clutched together over her skirt her waxen face her absent look

Uncle Álvaro and I saw a funny movie

it was fun

I like the one who doesn't talk the best

the lobby of the hotel with its delegations and conventioneers the endless carpeted corridor the antiquated double bed the obsessive wallpaper

the features of her face made thinner by the pain the

goddamn it to hell

repeated in a soft voice as she bled and you went out again with the child to get some tranquilizers at the drugstore scheduled to be open through the streets of that Geneva that you still hate and want to forget forever

like Néstor just like Uncle Néstor

the sun was flaming through the branches of the eucalyptus trees the wind shakes their silvery leaves the frogs croak in the pond hidden among the cork trees a blackbird can be heard singing

three years have passed since then and the memory of the weekend dissolves and is annulled in the certainty of your clear and silky armistice

Dolores has uncorked the bottle chilling in the ice bucket she fills two glasses to the brim drinks half of hers in one sip turns the page in the atlas

I'd rather forget she says

her hand lingers on yours for an instant and when she turns to face you

(the sun softly colors her face and in the pupils of her eyes there are the reflections of mica)

the past seems suddenly abolished and she looks at you as if she had just invented looking

He had arrived unexpectedly, a few weeks after receiving his conditional freedom, and he came to your studio on the rue Vieille du Temple without giving you any explanations about the trip and making you understand by the intonation of his voice that you should not ask for any either. He looked the same as ten years before: a little fatter, perhaps, and with a beginning of baldness that he carefully hid by combing a lock of hair forward. His personality had not changed since then, and the harsh experiences he had undergone in the past few years had not left any mark on him. He spoke about his imprisonment as if it had been a common cold, and he referred to the interrogations he had been put through with the same ironical detachment as he would have about the extraction of a molar in a dentist's office: something routine and bothersome, of course, but which, even though it does hurt people, when all was said and done had not killed anybody. The tale of his tortures and the protests that it raised abroad brought a smile from him: exaggerations, he seemed to be saying, nowadays even women can stand up under it. A romantic halo encircled him and he rejected it with modesty and disdain. His struggle and that of his companions occupied him completely, and exiled in Paris, he continued living in Spain. The city for him was the branch lines, stations, and exits of the subway where he had his dates; the movies, the sessions where they showed films and documentaries about the Civil War; the press, the small item in the paper or press-service reports that spoke about the policies of the Spanish Regime. A thick and invisible veil separated him from the rest of the community where he was living physically: like so many other thousands of fellow countrymen, fugitives of the war enclosed in their shells, obliged to resist for days, weeks, months, years, the assault of a reality that for them was alien and hostile, with all the love and sadness, tenderness and hope put into a land where one unlucky day, you said to yourself, they had expiated the curse of having been born.

Several months had passed since his arrival, and in his free time he would come to visit the two of you in the studio on the rue Vieille du Temple, and with that paticnt condescension of his toward those who did not think like him, he would explain to you the real situation in the country and the already foreseeable unfolding of events. You heard him mention the names of Marx and Lenin with the same ardor that he had previously used when he mentioned those of José Antonio and Ramiro de Maeztu, and you were moved by his sincerity. Dolores would also listen to him attentively and, sometimes, when you would argue, she would take his side against your agnosticism.

It was a winter afternoon—do you remember?: transparent and diaphanous—: the three of you had a date in Saint-Germain and you were walking, late as usual, when you spotted them at a distance on the covered terrace of the café, side by side, waiting for you. He was talking with his habitual vehemence, content and sure of himself, and Dolores was looking at him with an intensity that, until then, she had reserved for you, her cheeks flushed and her eyes aglow. The unfathomable creature that she had been since your trip to Geneva was smiling brightly again, absorbed. You had the sudden feeling that you were intruding.

The countryside changed. Objects took on an autonomous, impenetrable existence. Nothingness opened up at your feet. Pedestrians and cars were circulating chaotically, deprived of finality and substance. The world was a stranger to you and you were a stranger to the world. The contact between the both of you had broken. Irremediably alone.

It was an unusual, hazy, and foggy Venice, completely different from the one that Dolores and you had known when *France Presse* had sent you to photograph pretty and silly starlets as they walked along in bikinis on the sad nineteenth-century beach of the Lido, or fed the pigeons and smiled with over-white teeth alongside the Doge's palace and, at regular intervals, the *vaporetti* coming from the Grand Canal would deposit on the floating docks by the Captaincy and all along the Riva degli Schiavoni a load of tourists craving for Wiener schnitzel and Halles Bier, dressed, without distinction as to sex or age, in elk skin or velvet shorts, and who, owning one or several cameras, would burst forth in compact groups toward the disciplined and delicate perspective of the square, possessed by the unhealthy urge to record for posterity their passage through those parts, recording for the family album the dull image of a child surrounded by pigeons or a fat wife profiled against the reliefs of the Logetta, while at the various-colored tables of the Quadri or the Florian, other tourists with identical velvet shorts and Tyrolean hats would be writing dozens and dozens of post cards with greetings and astonished comments, as if the real object of the trip for all of them had been the post cards and the family albums and not the admirable view of Saint Mark's, with its Byzantine palaces and the columns, statues, marbles, and mosaics of a richly beautiful church, dominant and intact in spite of the small orchestras sitting up on platforms in the cafés and contaminating the sticky and damp atmosphere with the strains of *The Blue Danube,* the *Turkish March,* the *Polovetsian Dances* from *Prince Igor, Carnival in Venice,* Schubert's *Military March, O Sole Mio, Granada, Ciao, Ciao Bambino,* melding the scattered polyglot confusion of the conversations, the historical résumés of the guides, the names of inns that are not *espansif,* the pimps and hawkers, the inarticulate voices of children, the discreet cooing of the doves.

The cold had swept away the tourists with their knapsacks, the multicolored tables of the cafés, the platforms with musicians, and, erased by the morning mist, the square looked to you just as it had been painted by Bellini four centuries ago, with the slightly asymmetrical façades of the Procuratie Vecchie and the Procuratie

Nuove, the clock tower with the Virgin, the Magi, and the signs of the Zodiac, the Campanile, the cathedral. Some natives went by with a quick step, almost hidden under their wrappings, and, absolute masters of the place, the pigeons were flying about impatiently and awaiting the firing of the cannons to take flight in a deafening whirl toward the eaves and cupolas, waiting for the joyous outpouring of the people in charge of feeding them. Behind the windows, the plush easy chairs at the Florian were caring for their ornamental and showy clientele. Dolores was walking in silence underneath the arcades, and when she breathed, her breath would form a small frozen globe that floated for a few seconds in the air before disappearing mysteriously into the cold.

It was pleasant to come out onto the Piazzetta with her and, sitting underneath the Lion of Saint Mark's or the marble statue of Saint Theodore, to look at the dirty and choppy water of the lagoon, the noisy rocking of the gondolas among the mooring posts, the gulls as they dove after their prey, the white wake of a motor launch as it rose and fell quickly against the waves, and, still farther away, the posts of the buoys lined up like a game of bowls and the bell towers of the churches of San Giorgio Maggiore and La Giudecca, hazy, almost dissolved in the mist, or to lose one's self in a labyrinth of alleys with strange names, Ramo de Cá Raspi, Rio Terrá San Aponal, Sestier de Castelo, Boca de Piazza, Fondamenta delle Osmarin, Pescaria de Canaregio, Rugheta del Ravano, Sottoportego del Spiron d'Oro, Mazzarietta Due Aprile, Corte Saracina, Barbaria della Tole, Campiello de San Quero, or Calle di Mezzo de la Vida and come out unexpectedly opposite the Scuola de San Rocco or the Campo de Santa Maria Formosa with your feet cold inside your shoes and your hands stiff inside your gloves, to drink a cup of bitter and burning coffee before continuing on toward San Giorgio degli Schiavoni and stopping to drink in once more the perfection of *San Trifone ammansa il basilisco* or the *Funerali di San Gerolamo* by Carpaccio, eating an eel *alla barcarola con polenta* in a *trattoria* and drinking a bottle of good Merlot.

You had both spent so many waking nights uselessly trying to figure out the crisis of your feelings and the deterioration of your relations, possessed by an unmeasurable necessity for balance and a goad of sincerity that bordered on exhibitionism in the vast inventory of your unfaithfulness that was real or desired, adventures and histories, that it had made two strangers out of Dolores and you, each one surprised at his lack of knowledge of the life of the other, somewhat unsheltered too by the collapse of all your plans, dreams, and illusions—so that your looks would rub each other only as if they were afraid to wound, and your conversation had been reduced to the indispensable minimum of words, a simple commentary, generally, about a view, a painting, or the strength or smoothness of a wine, not recovered yet from the surprise of your new, vast, and disoriented freedom, and suspicious that some small incident or an observation outside of time would bring about the final break that in some obscure but instinctive way, you knew was irreparable.

That surly and cold Venice, sumptuously unreal in the mist, reflected you in your perpendicular loneliness like a mirror made of cloudy quicksilver when, half-frozen after your daily aimless walk through the streets, you let yourselves down onto the soft cushions of the seats in Harry's Bar alongside a Bloody Mary or a cocktail exquisitely prepared by a photogenic bartender with agile and flexible hands, wrapped up in the buzz of the conversations of a clientele made up of American women in Persian lamb coats and gentlemen with small gold chains on their wrists and blond-dyed hair—or if, abandoning Dolores in one of the innumerable souvenir shops on the Salizzada San Moisé or the Calle Larga San Marco, you would wander for hours, wherever your legs wanted to take you, getting lost in *cuppi di sacco* and narrow alleys, carrying the fixed idea of your seven years of life together, unable to admit, in your obstinate negation of the evidence, the real magnitude of the failure of both of you, recomposing the elements from the file as if it were a puzzle, and taking them apart again, perpetually dissatisfied with yourself since that instant you relived the time the two of you had made your first visit during the film festival, when you had not yet lost your like of travel, and you would savor every discovery, a wine, a Veronese painting, a bead necklace, a Murano lamp as a logical projection of your love, and you would forge plans for the not too distant day when things would change in Spain, and you would be able to take free advantage of your destiny, with the absurd hope of rescuing the hypothetical remains of the shipwreck and humbly begin a new life again, leaning your elbows, you did not know how, on the railing of the Fondamenta Nuova, across from the foggy island of melancholy communal commentary, the buoys and poles that mark the way to Torcello, and the spread-out, motionless, and dead-appearing waters of the lagoon.

Entire days of solitary wandering through that dense and distilled labyrinth, looking for each other vaguely in the neighborhood of the Pescheria or the shops in the Jewish quarter, until you ran into each other in some small hidden courtyard or over the zinc counter in a shop, and continuing on your way like two accidental and occasional lovers who stop to admire the fountain of the Campo di Santos Giovanni e Paolo, or the Gothic façade of the Foscari palace, before plunging voraciously as one being in between the warm and welcome sheets in some small hotel—or, as on the afternoon that you spotted Dolores in the distance and you amused yourself by following her without her knowing it, spying on her as if she were a stranger, a game that you suddenly abandoned when you discovered that, as a matter of fact, she was, and you gradually began to feel like a supplanted rival or a detective hired to get evidence against yourself, haunted by the terrifying possibility of her meeting another man, and really spying on her finally, as if you were seeing her for the first time in your life.

The glacial and imprecise Venice of the Via Garibaldi, with its street market and booths and stands and its taverns frequented by hardened *grappa* drinkers, where you came across the trio, two men and a woman, who were slowly walking toward the Fondamenta di Santa Anna, and something in the irate look on the face of the taller man and the beautiful and mournful face of the woman made you sense that a drama was near at hand, and you slowed down and tuned your ear, just at the moment when he faced her and said some incomprehensible words, trembling with hate, and the other man intervened to calm him down and only managed to excite him all the more, making him speak almost in shouts, *no, non sono frottole, te dico e ti repeto che ci sono testimoni, hai capito,* and the woman was saying Piero, Piero, with her eyes red, and she used the sleeve of her coat to wipe them, and you pretended that you were scrutinizing the contents of a marine-supply store, and they kept on walking toward the bridge and he insulted her again, seizing her violently by the lapels, *maladetto quel giorno hai capito, maladetto quel giorno,* and like an automaton she repeated Piero, Piero, and the other man was looking back cautiously and was trying to separate them, and you looked at the dark water of the desolate canal of San

Pietro, with the miserable houses huddling along the bank and the corroded walls of the old arsenal, *ti giuro che non é vero, Piero, ti giuro, ti giuro,* and the trio went forward again with you following, along the double row of gray houses on the Campazzo Quintavalle, and the wind brought snatches of sentences to your ears that came out of their lips along the frozen tufts of smoke, and you ran into each other unexpectedly at sunset on the deserted Campo di San Pietro, and the trio was taking refuge under the church to argue, and on the way back to the hotel, you tried to imagine the depths of the passion that existed among them and the oaths of love and the reciprocal search of their bodies before the obligatory and sad ending, asking yourself with bitterness how that insidious degeneration had been possible, and as you thought about Dolores, about the serene provocation of Dolores's sex, her breasts, and her lips, you heard the slow tolling of the death knell on the bells and you wept silently to yourself.

As you came around the curve, you could make out several groups of people going up the side of the hill toward the *plante*. The rhythmical sound of the *enkomos* could be heard, faint in the distance, and a circle of people accompanied the twisting and turning of an *íreme* around his *nkrikamo* with their chants. The *diablito* was wearing a hood made out of a bag, a velvet hat, and a red pompom; from his sleeves, short skirts, and leggings, gaudy trim of hemp was hanging, and with every movement of his body, he would make the bells tied around his waist ring. The *íreme* was shaking his *itón,* twisting as if he were drunk, while the *lazarillo* led him to the *fambá*. After an obstinate resistance, he rubbed his small brush across the forehead of an old *Iyamba* and peaceably went up the path behind the *erikundé* of his *nkrikamo.*

You parked next to the bus stop, and when you got out, the children surrounded you and asked if you were Russian. A paved path led up the hill toward the small flat square where the faithful were gathering. The chapel was a modest building, one story high, and as they entered, the *abakuás* took off their hats and carefully closed the door. A rudimentary staircase went up to the top of the hill. Along the way, small houses proliferated like toadstools, with their colored roofs, their colonial doorways, and their ungainly television antennas. The two sides of the hill converged on the small square like a set built especially to emphasize the pomp of the ceremony.

When you got there, the faithful were playing the *enkomos*, the *ekón*, and the *tumbadora*, backing up the monotonous recitation of the *moruá*: *Eforí mañene forí Eforí manenecum eforí Sesé aporitán Becura Ibondá awanaribe Efor eforí*. A mulatto with a short-sleeved shirt and a red silk kerchief tied around his neck was emptying a bottle of rum into a coconut shell and passing it around among those present. Instants later, you heard the roar of *Ekué* in the interior of the *fambá*. The onlookers awaited the appearance of the *mpego* at the entrance to the chapel, and one after the other, the *indísimes* took off their shirts and rolled up their pants, forming a line, barefoot and bare chested, while the sponsors stood behind them and put their hands on their shoulders.

You watched the *amalogrí* with fascination. The *mpego*—a huge Negro—had come out with the *mokuba*, the incense burner, the bottles of cane liquor and wine, and the faithful gathered around the novices. When the purification began, they sang in a hoarse voice *Anamabó, anamabó*, while the *mpego* cleansed the *indísimes* with the magic plant and drew yellow crosses on their chests, arms, legs, and backs, to the sound of shouts of *nkomo aquerebá, nkomo aquerebá*, which were followed by those of *Unarobia apanga robia* as the operation was repeated with white chalk. The musicians were beating the drums in an obsessive way. A militiaman was playing the *ekón* with a small stick. Little by little, the fever was growing and the *abakuás* marked the rhythm, wiggling their bodies with delicate and quick tremors. *Mimba, mimba, barori*, the faithful chanted and the *mpego*, as he sprinkled the chests, faces, backs of the novices with cane alcohol, *acaransé, acaransé*, and the wine expelled from his mouth sprinkled the dark skin of the future *obonékue*, ready to be joined by the work and the grace of the *mokuba* and the roars of the Voice to the sacred spirits of *Sikán* and *Tánze;* the *enkomos* sounded violently, the stick ran furiously over the *ekón*, and the *ñáñigos* repeated, as if possessed, *Umón Abasí, Umón Abasí, at* the same time as the *mpego*, who with the basil dipped in holy water was washing the unclean bodies of the *indísimes; Camio Abasó Quesongo, Camio Abasó Quesongo*, he perfumed them one by one with the incense burner, *Tafitá nanumbre*, he put a blindfold of red silk over their eyes and they knelt blinded with the palms of their hands on the ground in front of the sponsors who stood by to comfort them. The *ekón* and the drums were hammering rhythmically on everyone's ears, conjuring up the presence of the *eribangandó* hidden in the secret *fambá,* a red-and-black little devil who twisted and danced with a jingling of bells as he went toward the prostrated novices, *Indísime Isón Paraguao Quende Yayomá,* and slipped his legs over them, *Indísime Isón Paraguao Quende Yayomá,* that all the faithful chorused in unison, like a mad prayer, like a psalm, *Indísime Isón Paraguao Quende Yayomá,* the brotherhood and love from which only he was excluded.

For a long time you just followed wherever your feet took you. Your head was empty and your heart was beating like a clock. A steep path wound down among the small wooden houses and suddenly emerged on an automobile graveyard. The old Fords, Cadillacs, Chevrolets, DeSotos were slowly decomposing on the flat, the rusty and broken-down witnesses of a time that had disappeared. No windows, no wheels, no engines, the bodies showed their hungry jaws, opened in a dark and painful yawn. The mangy buzzards were tracing spirals over the automobile skeletons, and you flopped down on your back in a clearing and stared up at the sky. A smell of death and putrefaction sharply penetrated the countryside. The sun was beating down strongly and the air was stagnant.

You lost all sense of time. Three black dots were flying from the coast toward the military objectives on the bay. Indifferent, you waited for the wail of the sirens and the sound of the explosions. Little by little, as sleep came over you, you had the feeling that you were growing roots and were being joined permanently to the earth. Making an effort, you opened your eyes one last time. A woman was singing in the distance and you tuned in your hearing, as if her words might contain some message expressly destined for you. The three specks were still cutting through the air. Autumn had begun ahead of time and all around you life was continuing.

March, 1963. Remember it.

The monarchy was decapitated there, the ominous symbol of its power taken by assault, the transgressor of unjust laws rotting in the age-old fortress was freed of his chains by the iconoclast mob. Look at it, surrounded by the sun, blotted out by haze, dampened by drizzle. The column rises up in the middle, robust and sturdy, topped by a slim and weightless angel. Bars, cafés, restaurants, movies surround it with a glowing ring of luminous signs. Beautiful and sprightly, run-down and uncomfortable, several centuries of agitated and confused history converge on it and form it. The merry-go-rounds, the bump-cars, the shooting galleries that take refuge on their platforms give it the curious look of a Texas town. A stream of automobiles covers it during rush hour; at dawn, the deserted cobblestones seem to miss the audacious people who had torn them up, and seem to be dreaming sadly about a better fate. On the waters of the canal, a few modern buildings reflect their obtuse forms. Streets, boulevards, avenues make dates on it, drawing the assiduous clientele out of the bars, the painted women of Balajo and Bousca, the toughs and pimps of the rue de Lappe. The carnival goes on night and day, baroque, indifferent. Sometimes the distant echo of an accordion supplies the muted background for an absurd drunken argument.

During the endless gray hours, all roads led there (to the roller coaster and the fainting spell), as if nothing (you tell yourself now), absolutely nothing could placate (oh Place de la Bastille) your heavy hunger for death.

Life had magnanimously ransomed you.

The ward in the Saint Antoine hospital was spinning and spinning around you, and Dolores was softly holding your hand and spinning the same way, luminous and agile, with an adult expression of love that you had not known on her. Ancient prayers came back to your memory, the ruinous vestiges of some remote dream, Christ and Changó as one, the Most Benign Sovereign Jesus my Love of First Fridays and the visit to the Most Holy and Most Indian Ison Paraguao Quende Yayomá in the Cuban *ñáñigo* cult and Lucumí ceremonies in Regla: therefore I give You thanks and promise to flee all occasions of danger and build my house forever in your Divine Sex from which I hope for the help to love you until the end sobeit, with a three-hundred-day indulgence and even plenary if it is recited frequently during life and, furthermore, one is confessed and has received communion or is contrite at least, invoking the Most Holy Name of Ekué, with the mouth if possible, if not, with the heart, and accepting with patience the hand of death from the Lord as an expiation for our sins. Your head ached, your body ached, and the ghostly spectacle of the ward anticipated in your eyes the fate that just fortune was reserving for you: to die far from your country and from its timid phalanx of subjects, immersed in the vast stream of human suffering, equitably purged by the mistakes of others and also by your own.

The old men who were dying without families, the workers maimed by their own tools, the Arabs and Negroes who, *allah yaouddi,* moaned in a language you did not understand, had shown you the path along which, some day or other, you would have to pass if you wanted to give back clean to the earth what in purity belonged to it. You should look for your salvation there, in them and in their obscure universe, just as instinctive and without anyone's apprenticeship, close beside them, you had looked for love: breaking away, little by little, from everything that you had received as a loan; the privileges and facilities with which your people had attempted to win you since your child hood. Nakedness, then, such richness. Their virtuous disdain, then, such a gift. The open pit between you and them: such was the broad margin of your freedom.

In that anonymous hospital in the anonymous and spread-out city, during long waking nights and the silence broken by coughs and moaning, you had returned to life free of past as well as future, strange and alien to yourself, ductile, malleable, without a homeland, without a home, without friends, pure uncertain present, born at your age of thirty-two, simply Álvaro Mendiola, with no marks of identity.

You closed the atlas and you examined the last picture you had taken of Spain with your Linhof ten years before
on the open avenue over the rubble of Santa Madrona and the Arco del Teatro Los Gambriles and the legendary Cirolla
next to the ragged walls of houses being torn down and the chimney of a factory in ruins
something like an involuntary Tower of Pisa that was crippled and decrepit
about thirty yards away from the Calle Conde de Asalto that looked like something reduced in price
a charity raffle draws a motley and flowery audience of American sailors tourists local people idlers, children
a characteristic model from the Castilian plain announces the prizes

over the loud-speaker and the looks of the curious converge toward the platform where there is a monkey with lively eyes and a restless expression
irregular fur spotted with open patches and bald spots short arms and an aggressively red ass
he listens to the spiel of the auctioneer moves about spins around the post to which he is tied climbs up to the ceiling destroys a cardboard box slides down sits
suddenly a Flamenco-like *cuplé* takes the place of the dying voice of the loud-speaker
a dizzy synthesis of the matter of the Spain of brass bands and tambourines secrecy and sacristy
of moans from a sexiloquacious female with window grating balconies carnations mantillas combs
the whole ancient arsenal of a second-rate Mérimée
deafens the ears with its heavy volume
the monkey listens puzzled bites the remnants of the cardboard box with fury tries to get away from the overwhelming nightmare climbs the pole angrily shakes his chain
the Hispanic female follows him with her vaginal sighs
panic seizes the animal his eyes show an opaque terror
the castanets the guitar the *olés* the yelps fall on him
they attack cruelly
they drive him mad
they make him jump slip away leap
the American sailors are still there with the tourists
the local people
the idlers
the children
on the card you now have in front of you there is no background of sound but its eloquence makes the astounding vocal exhibition unnecessary
the photograph was taken against the light and might serve as an illustration
you think
a half-century after it was written
in this bastard and simoniacal year of 1963
for the famous
up-to-date
and never contradicted
poem by Machado.

VII

"On this point there is unanimous agreement the standard of living has been rising visibly until it has spread across the Peninsula from one end to the other the high-sounding geography of imperial names Madrigal de las Atlas Torres Puente del Arzobispo Villarreal de los Infantes Egea de los Caballeros Motilla del Palancar as a Herr Schmidt or a Monsieur Dupont anyone at all behind the wheel of his Citroën or his Volkswagen could note over the years the slow but very solid take-off of a country that had been poor for many centuries propelled today thanks to twenty-five years of peace and social order along the magnificent and broad path of industry and progress because for almost three decades now we have the privilege of a beneficent system that our fathers and our grandfathers and our great-grandfathers never had the privilege of enjoying a system that imperturbably resisted a world war that was at its gates and desolated half of Europe on the moral side even more than on the material and put the other half into captivity a peace that precisely because it was absolute now seems natural to us and it is not natural because it is not something that is given spontaneously by nature the way she gives rain or sun dawn and sunset day and night this peace that we enjoy the origin and source of current progress and well-being is the work of one man and a Regime that by disciplining ordering rising above purging our natural propensity to fraternal fights and turmoil was able to invent for the glory and example of future generations and even though peace is desirable for the whole country and its organism suffers when peace is disturbed people less glandular than ours can tolerate upset and disorder without bringing on the fatal consequences but not the Spanish people among us when peace is altered the consequences are instantaneous and severe and the menacing shadow of Cain darkens as Fray Luis would say 'this sad and spacious Spain' so that as it fades away toward the distant horizon of the past the invariable date of the first of April we see its unique significance more clearly like a huge mountain that can only be viewed from afar that is why although to many fancy-dressed youths and gentlemen of today who did not know the sorrows of the war or the pleasure of having won it and find themselves with the table all set it seems useless to remember what they want to forget forever we the combatants of that time products of the present well-being thanks to this peace will tell those forgetful and memory-lacking gentlemen you are gentlemen and potentates and you are peacefully sitting on the sidewalk and you have good color and take care of your skin the light came forth one April first in the fullness of a spring that on sky earth and sea was longed for announced in the heroic proposal and in the secure hope of the liberating hymn and since then we have passed through a long period of difficulties and combat we have had to maintain energetically our direction in the face of misunderstanding the hate and the blindness of the liberal States of invertebrate and inorganic democracy but after those years of hunger and privation the result of the blockade and the droughts this thing that many call the Spanish miracle has been our common work that of all Spaniards who gave their efforts and discipline to get through such a difficult and fundamental period and now that with our economic plan the evolution is obvious the betterment notable and the means at hand for the nation infinitely superior it is enough to see the neuter and empty looks of Herr Schmidt or Monsieur Dupont one of the twelve million or more who according to official estimates will visit our country this year attracted by the warmth of the sun the lovely walk of the women the deceptive wines the virile emotions of the bullring the monkish beauty of the countryside low prices to appreciate the improvement in highways and railroads the multiplication of hotels and restaurants the proliferation of vehicles and television stations clear signs of the prodigious and opportune take-off no one can deny in public now that the consumer market is growing and the country is industrialized between 1935 and this year basic production has grown spectacularly 72% of all Spaniards use cotton underwear as compared to 37% during the Republic shoes are gradually replacing humble canvas sandals those who used to walk to work ride bicycles today former bicyclists ride motorcycles former motorcyclists ride triumphantly through town in a SEAT 600 or a Renault 4CV instead of the uninviting and sad single plate restaurants display complete menus conveniently translated into several languages the working population consumes milk and eggs and sometimes even chicken on Sundays in the summertime the result is that it is impossible to distinguish the worker from his employer the bookkeeper smokes light tobacco and buys a television set and a refrigerator on time the peasant woman wears lipstick and uses stockings just like those of the distinguished lady if the inevitable centers of misery survive it is generally a matter of isolated cases to which the Spaniard's innate racial generosity gives aid and if we still publish in our press 'Help for unfortunate family with small child mother very ill father unemployed' 'Food and help for sick peasant family with six children under age of ten mother died in childbirth' or 'Orthopedic leg for single woman of 53 without family or means' we do it because we are sure that thanks to the quick intervention of magnanimous and charitable souls the little ones will be able to satisfy their hunger completely the unemployed will find the means to obtain a ticket to Germany or Switzerland and the unprotected single woman will obtain the desired limb the peace prosperity radiant progress in which we walk today having arrived are the obvious fruit of our policy of the service of a man for a nation opposite us there rises up the voice of our dead the firmness of those who gave us their will the heritage of those who gave us their blood the will of those who are no longer among us and that will that testament and that mandate we must sustain with arms in our hands it is not enough that the battle has ended the battle may end but no one can rest we know it quite well because our chests are covered with medals our bodies are covered with scars our hearts heavy with grief and we know that after the battle when it seems that it is time to pick the fruits of victory one still must keep vigil over his arms this is the hardest part the guard the sentinel the reserves the service the caring of some for the dreams of others and this is our permanent mission which we will never abdicate watching over the peace the dream the order the work the advance for we have been recognized now as part of the free world the anchor and the guide for the naive and forgetful West."

That was what the official spokesmen were saying, jubilantly as the uncontainable waves of tourists, bearing prodigality and benefits, injected new and unworried blood into the ancient country, ran across its entranced countryside and its dead cities: a rich transfusion of dollars that circulated by railroad, airplane, ship, highway; the unexpected but saving plague for a condemned and barren homeland, covered now, as if with balm, with inns and with hotels, service stations and restaurants, souvenir shops and snack bars, maids and pimps, male prostitutes and guides, flamenco singers and *bailaoras*. Modernization had arrived, alien to morality and justice, and the economic take-off threatened to anesthetize forever a people who had not recovered after twenty-five years from the long and thick dream in which they had lethargically remained after their military defeat during the war. Statistics do not lie, however, and for anyone who had known the stifling atmosphere of those years of persecution and punishment, hunger and privation—the obligatory pass to go from Madrid to Getafe, the meager ration card—the visible betterment of recent times or the simple possibility of obtaining the coveted passport was for most people a happy break with the asphyxia and immobility of before. Little by little, thanks to the two-way flow of foreigners and emigrants, expatriates and tourists, into Spain and out of it, the Spaniard was learning, for the first time in history, to work, to eat, to travel, to exploit commercially his virtues and defects, to assimilate the economic values of industrial societies, to commercialize himself, to prostitute himself and all of it—an extreme paradox in a land singularly rich in ferocious and bloody contrasts—under a system that was primitive and originally created to impede it: a flag unfurled one day to justify the horrible slaughter, abandoned afterward like a worn-out suit or an old shoe; a sacred cause—those were their words—for which the phalanxes of youths with generous hearts and narrow minds had offered up their lives. Some of the dead were rotting right now, useless and absurd, devoured, even in memory, by the work of capricious history, not only indifferent, but allergic to the virtues of immolation and sacrifice.

But while every day the press exhibited the indices and graphs of a take-off arrived at, among other reasons, because of the strict military discipline imposed on the working class and the maintenance of the archaic and inhuman means of production in the agricultural sector, who would evoke on the other hand the memory of those who, at the price of their blood, sweat, and tears, had been its real builders and its victims, equally anonymous? The sad, silent humanity who had borne on its shoulders the weight of that necessary accumulation, who remembered it? Under the bright veneer of figures and the insolent unfolding of comparisons there was a dark course of suffering, an immense and bottomless sea where no ray of light had ever come or would come: the barefoot, empty-handed, and broken life of millions and millions of fellow countrymen, frustrated in their own and personal essence, relegated, humiliated, sold; the painful mass of beings who had come into the world with no logic; a tool for work in the shape of a man, subject to the laws of supply and demand like a poor and worn-out piece of merchandise. That cesspool of injustices, offenses, sicknesses, death, into which their pain was distilled, drop by drop, through a crude and secret retort, their sand castles perpetually being washed away by time, their modest and invisible work, like that of coral, the support and basis of the lazy and futile life of the others, would they serve, at least, as fertilizer and manure, food and sustenance? Those of whom the son of God had said: "Ye are the salt of the earth," would they fertilize one day the arid and ungrateful soil of their severe and immortal Stepmother?

Transcribed during the preparations for the filming of the abortive documentary, the biographies of the emigrants—the first wave of a sea in perpetual motion—rose up in the midst of the peaceful and pleasant rural countryside like a grave and imperishable accusation, all of the slow apprenticeship in pain, shame, and astuteness, the injustice and humiliations of those years jotted down on narrow and brief pages, rigorous and strict, that no progress, no well-being, no modernization—and it was a consoling certainty for you—would ever be able to erase.

This chair and the wicker basket there on top of it are worth more to me than all the friends in the world and have been more faithful because when this basket comes back through the prison bars it always has something to eat in it and this chair is the same one that the Falangists made me sit in before they put me in jail and when I was in jail the wicker basket that is on top of the chair would bring me all the miserable things it could and every day I was glad when it came to see me this chair and this basket do not have to thank anybody for anything because many former Republicans were walking by out on the street and the basket did not get even a penny from them

this basket that went out to beg from door to door to bring me something to eat and this chair where they tied me up in front of my wife say all of this is true the chair where they hit me with a whip and the basket that my wife took begging

it is a shame this chair and this basket say that they evicted you from your house taking advantage of the fact that I was in jail the judge had sent the court order but I could not leave jail so the landlord came with the judge and the city police and told the people there to get out into the street

and they put the furniture out onto the sidewalk and my wife had the child in her arms and she did not know where to go and when after a week they came to the jail to give me a kiss and tell me a couple of words the words my wife told me made me very sad they said they've taken away our house Im in the street and when she told me what was going on I couldn't sleep and I vomited the little bit I had eaten

and this chair and this basket know that everything Im saying is the real truth because they remember when they whipped me and the small amount of bread my wife would get from house to house and after a year they transferred me from the jail to the hospital and from there they released me with a piece of paper that said José Bernabeu had been arrested for being a Red . . .

On one of those misty sunsets in that slow and unpleasant Paris winter, shut up in your studio on the rue Vieille du Temple, with a bottle of Beaujolais and a half pack of Gitanes filters on the night table, you had relived the twenty-five years of your shrunken existence, and the desolation and emptiness you found in them had left you in terror. Álvaro, you said to yourself, it can't go on like this, you exiled yourself to Paris under the pretext of studying movie directing and, apart from going to the Cinémathèque on the rue d'Ulm, you still haven't passed your exams at the IDHEC, you haven't finished the shooting script of your brilliant future film, you haven't made the slightest effort to get a job as the assistant to one of the "sacred cows." You got out of Spain (abandoning your friends in the midst of a difficult and uncertain political struggle) to complete the work that you were carrying (or thought you were carrying) inside yourself, and in those two years of bohemian life in Paris, what have you done?: sleep, eat, smoke, get drunk, kill time in conversation and listless arguments with veteran exiled fellow countrymen in Madame Berger's ancient café. Are you proud of the results? You abandoned action to become an artist, and when it's all said and done, what are you?: a voluntary exile who sleeps (twelve hours a day), smokes (a pack and a half of Gitanes filters), eats (once a day, in the dark Foyer de Sainte Genéviève), drinks (a quart or a quart and a half of red wine, depending on how things are), goes to the movies (Eisenstein, Pudovkin, Visconti, Lang, Welles; always the same ones).

You looked out of the dormer window over the beautiful sight of roofs and chimneys in the form of a truncated cone that inevitably brought back the memory of the perspective of *Il miracolo della reliquia della Santa Croce* that you had admired in Venice, and you looked at the uncertain and skittish Paris sky as the neighbors in the courtyard were once more repeating for you (it might be said) their daily skirmish over the pigeons (fed by the old man on the second floor and chased by the widow on the third with buckets of water).

Old Man: God is watching you, Madame.

Widow: I am a believer too, Monsieur.

Old Man: You've done a wicked thing.

Widow: My conscience is the one to tell me that, my dear sir.

Old Man: They're nothing but poor, innocent creatures.

Widow: Innocent, perhaps, but also dirty.

Old Man: They don't hurt anyone.

Widow: They get everything dirty.

Old Man: You too, you have to take care of your needs, Madame.

Widow: In any case, you can be sure that I don't do it out my window, my dear sir.

A few hours before, on the freezing platform of the Gare d'Austerlitz, while you were waiting for the Barcelona train that Antonio was supposed to be on, sent to collect funds for the newly created student movement, you had watched for the first time the arrival of an expedition of Spaniards, contracted, no doubt, by some Paris industrial enterprise, and as you examined the lost and almost drowned faces of your fellow countrymen as they viewed the spectacle of that silent and disciplined crowd, so unusual for them, so different from the vociferous and chaotic Spanish crowds, you had an anguished feeling of stupor and you were sorry you had not brought along your 16 mm camera. Driven out by unemployment, hunger, underdevelopment into countries with a cold and efficient civilization, what would happen later on, you thought, to those men who were bound to tribal values and customs that had long since disappeared from the rest of the Continent? Would they adapt to modern urban and industrial civilization, or would they react against it with the Iberian and proverbial indigenous impermeability of all of you?

The idea of a sociological documentary about the reasons for their emigration, the filmed exposition of their painful odyssey (the slow and difficult flight from misery that had begun with their peasant origins) suddenly caught hold of your conscience as an enterprise that was not only impassioned but (because of the rebellion against your common fate of a Spaniard, heir to the situation created as a result of the Civil War that it implied) strictly necessary. The image of the workers wrapped up in their old sheepskin jackets, wearing their berets and miserable canvas shoes had been associated in your memory since then with the panorama of roofs and chimneys by Carpaccio that you had envisioned during that vast and melancholy sunset.

Old Man: Have a care, God will punish you some day.

Widow: The good Lord has better things to do than worrying about your pigeons.

Old Man: Don't be too sure about that, my dear lady.

You took a drink of Beaujolais in order to slow down the dizzy succession of ideas that were coming to your mind. Hazy in the fog in the distance, the ungainly outline of the Eiffel Tower could be made out. Antonio was to come for dinner with you, and as the neighbors carried on their metaphysical guerrilla warfare over the kindness that should be shown to doves, you flopped down to rest on the couch and you observed, abstractedly, the changeable and ephemeral reflection of the light on the ceiling of the dormer-window casement in your studio.

We spent three days that were very cold and after the three days at six o'clock in the morning they take my mother to the hospital half-dead from underneath the railroad bridge and I was left with my father and since my father is too ashamed to beg he dictated a letter to me saying what was happening and the first place I went to was the parish of San Pedro and the priest at San Pedro's gave us 0.10 pesetas and my father told him that God would repay him and I asked him to give me back the paper because my father did not know how to write and with the 10 céntimos we did not have enough to buy food and that since I was small I could beg for bread and that my father had nothing and from there we went to the Calle Topete and in a house my father gave them the letter and they gave him 10 pesetas and the barber who is across from the police station gave me 5 pesetas from there we went to the Carmen parish and the priest at the Carmen after reading the letter said that he could not give us anything that my father had brought the trouble on himself that he should have left his family home and that God could not do anything for us and I went away from there very sad and we went to Cruz Grande, No. 1, and the maidservant came out and my father handed her the letter and she said that the gentleman of the house would see about it and my father told her that at least she could give us a little bread for the child who was crying and when we were leaving the good gentleman came out and asked him young as he was why he was begging but when he read the letter we went to the hospital and the doctor said they were operating on my mother right then and then he saw that everything was true and he said for us to burn everything we had from the bridge that he would take care of everything and in the courtyard he gave us something to eat and I was very small and I was so hungry that with the kindness and the love that good gentleman showed me I will always remember him and never forget him and then he washed me as if I was his own son changed all my clothes and took me by the hand and we went to the hospital and he said that my mother would be all right and we would have everything we needed.

You were on your way back from filming typical scenes of the tribe (the tin huts, the mangy dogs, the naked children with distended bellies) in the vanished shanty towns of La Barceloneta (subsequently converted into the elegant Paseo Marítimo of a flourishing city in full development, with blue-painted parking spaces, modern lighting, private industrial polygons, and directional signs in several languages) and the surprise that came over you at that time when you came face to face with the fatalistic resignation of your flock (the same flock which, expelled from the downtown districts, had reappeared in the suburbs with a tenacious and disconcerting drive) came back to you now (in the lazy and hot dusk, two days after Professor Ayuso's burial) with a pious and bitter feeling of irony.

. . . Your first contact with the South had been through its men. Ever since childhood you had been able to distinguish them by their accents and manner of speaking, so different from those of the Catalonians. You heard them singing on the scaffolds, cursing in Public Works excavations, arguing as they swept the streets, chatting in the sun in their uniforms, the three-cornered hats, the carbines, the green tunics of the Civil Guard. Their faces too were different from the people around you: somewhat darker—Arab perhaps—rough and elegant at the same time, with a vivacity that always surprised you. In public offices they would sign documents by dipping their thumbs in ink and placing it at the bottom of the page. You knew that they were poorer than the rest and you thought less intelligent therefore. Since they did the hardest jobs, you took it for granted that they had been born to toil. Later on, during your military service, the daily contact with Murcians and Andalusians revealed a surprising fact to you: the families huddled together in the suburbs were fleeing from something. The Barcelona shanty towns were an escape from another even worse poverty, cruel and inhuman. This discovery inspired in you the desire to travel through the South. Your friends spoke about Lubrín, Totana, Adra, Guadix. When you finally did cross the frontier of the Segura river with Dolores and Antonio, the severity of the countryside captivated you. The blue sky, the ocher and rosy color of the earth, the yellow of the wheat fields, all tempted you with their unusual beauty. As you neared Almería and were looking at its lunar mountains, its bleak countryside, its white clay, the revelation changed to love. In Sorbas you stopped to have a drink at a roadside café and you said to Dolores: "This is the most beautiful place in the world." The owner was working behind the bar and he looked at you with raised eyebrows. His voice still buzzes in your ears with his reply: "For us, sir, this is a cursed land. . . ."

The heat was slowly abating and you got up out of the chaise longue. The maid had left the transistor on and, undecided whether to take a stroll through the woods as you had planned when you got up, you went over to the table and listened to the news bulletin that was faintly coming from the radio.

". . . for the new director of the regional syndicate, Señor Tusquets . . ." (could it be the same one?)

You went back to your biographies and with a finger, you brusquely erased the Voice.

And after six months in Tarrasa my wife had a daughter who was born ahead of time and we looked for some help because we didnt have any money to bury her with and nobody paid any attention to us and we kept her like that in a basket for three days which is what makes me saddest of all in my life because nobody has ever seen such a thing in the whole world as having to carry her in a basket to the funeral parlor this is justice this is dignity having to carry this child as if she was a dog to the funeral parlor wrapped up in rags in the bottom of a basket

and then I asked for justice not only for me but for my poor children and I explained how we had come all muddy and freezing with the cold the local Director of Public Health came to see us and he himself saw with his own eyes how we were but what did it matter to him with lights in his house and a good roof over it and heat because after he came and promised lots of things if I ever saw him again I cant remember

then I went to the radio station and asked him to let me speak and tell people what was happening to us so that the town would know in that way and charitable people could help us but they told me that in order to speak I would have to have a good education and that I didnt know how to express myself and to be patient my good man and the gentleman at the station gave me 5 pesetas

and I went back to the Town Hall in Tarrasa again and I asked them to please come for a moment and they would see what our conditions were like and they told me that the people there were very busy and that I would have to make a request in writing and not to forget the stamp and the 4.50 pesetas fee

and I told them Im not asking for anything else in the world except lights and a roof for my house so that my son will grow up and not die young and waiting for the answer from the Town Hall we were still in that shack for more than three years

You interrupt your reading for a few minutes. The panorama slowly passes by, the eroded and naked hills follow one after the other, as if in a lunar landscape, the vegetation becomes sparser, the sun dominates everything: it sparkles on the stony bottoms of dry gulches, it palliates the withered yellow of a fig tree, it makes the exhausted variety of colors uniform. You are in the heart of arid Andalusia: the white houses of the town huddling beneath the bulk of the church seem as unreal as the belfry that shelters them, as if they had come forth out of some remote mirage, the sudden creatures of your delirious imagination.

You go into the town, you park your car by the square, you risk a glance around, ready to leave with the same speed with which you arrived. (You are traveling through the country collecting the necessary testimonials for the filming of your future documentary, and the memories of Enrique, of the arrest and tortures suffered by Enrique plague and torment you.)

The sun is beating down on the whitewashed fronts of the buildings: a food store, a bar crowded with heavy-browed and dark men, a beauty parlor. On the corner of the main street a faded sign suddenly attracts your attention

PUBLIC LIBRARY

(Who the devil did any reading on this steppe?)

The building has two stories, with a round balcony held up by carved stone brackets. The blinds are drawn. The front door is closed. You pound the knocker uselessly.

"There's nobody there," a person says.

"What time do they open?"

"There's no set time."

The man is picking his gums with a toothpick and he looks you over with mild curiosity.

"Are you the new schoolteacher?"

"No, I'm not."

"Since we were expecting him next week . . ."

"I was just passing through and when I saw the sign I thought it was open."

"They almost never open," the man says. "But if you want to take a look, I know who has the key."

"I don't want to bother you."

"Not at all. She's a relative of mine. She lives close by."

Several children were looking at you as they drooled. The man turned to them and put his hand on the head of the tallest one.

"Do you know where Julia lives?"

"Which Julia?"

"The one who has the sandal shop in the entrance way."

"Yes, sir."

"Run tell her to give you the key to the library, that there's a gentleman here who wants to take a look at it."

The boy runs off. You thank the man with a smile.

"Julia's daughter is the one who cleans up, dusts, opens the windows . . ."

"Every day?"

"Ho, ho. On Christmas and in the summer. . . . When the provincial inspector comes by."

"Don't they open it up any other time?"

"No, unless someone comes from outside like yourself." The man seems to be thinking. "Last year a student came from Madrid."

Eight or ten children surround the two of you now, following the conversation. Some of them whisper to each other and go to tell the people in the bar. The boy with the message comes back in a few moments.

"Julia's gone. She went to Granada and she won't be back till Tuesday."

"What about her daughter?"

"She's not there either."

"Who'd you talk to?"

"Perico."

The man folds his arms. Some onlookers have come over to listen and watch the scene in silence.

"Julia's daughter's with her sister-in-law," one of them says. "I saw them together half an hour ago."

"Whereabouts?"

"At the grain warehouse."

"Go see her," the man says to the boy. "Tell her to give you the key."

"It's not worth all the trouble," you protest.

"Not at all, sir, no trouble at all. The boy'll be right back."

When the child leaves, the number of onlookers grows even larger. Soon there are twenty, twenty-five, thirty. The children say "he's a Frenchy," the adults look at you as if they expected a speech. A priest in a dirty cassock crosses the square and looks at you out of the corner of his eye. Before he disappears from your field of vision, you see him having a few words with one of the children and, from the direction of his looks, you guess that they are talking about you.

"Where are you from, if you don't mind?" the man asks.

"Barcelona."

"That car, is it French?"

"Yes."

"I thought so from the 'F' on the license. . . ."

The men slowly come in closer. The word France goes from mouth to mouth. Some ask if there is any work there. (The same old story and in spite of the custom, the color rises in your face.)

The child comes panting back.

"She says her mother's got the key."

"Didn't you say she went to Granada?"

"Yes."

"What about the key?"

"She took it with her."

There is a silence. The onlookers remain there expectantly, waiting for your reaction. There are forty of them now, perhaps fifty. The new arrivals ask what's going on and you hear whispers of "Barcelona," "library," "France."

"What's going on here?"

The voice is categorical and the gathering makes way for a member of the Civil Guard: mustache, dark glasses, three-cornered hat, dirty tunic, patched pants.

"Nothing," the man says. "This gentleman wanted to see the library, and since Julia's not here, I sent the kid for the key."

"Who wants to see the library, you?"

"Yes."

"Your identity card, please."

The audience seems to have stopped breathing, hanging on your movements. The sun is beating down on you.

"I don't have a card, I have a passport."

"Are you a foreigner?"

"No."

"Then how come you don't have a card?"

"I live abroad."

"And why do you live abroad?"

"Personal reasons."

"Let's see your passport."

The Guard examines it suspiciously and turns the pages one by one with cautious slowness.

"This stamp, where's it from?"

"Germany."

"What about this other one?"

"Holland."

"What's your profession?"

"I'm a photographer."

"How long have you been in Spain this time?"

"See . . . . right here. Police Headquarters, La Junquera . . . August 2."

"Oh, yes. . . . Do you have any family in these parts?"

"No."

"Tourist?"

"Yes, a tourist."

"And you say you want to see the library?"

"I was just curious."

"It's closed."

"So they tell me."

The Guard gives you back your passport. His rough features contract until they force out a smile.

"Just routine questions, you understand."

The men follow your lips. Your silence has doubtless cheated them.

"We have to be very careful, do I make myself clear? We don't know what kind of people come from outside or what brings them here. . . ." His expression is cordial now: "Well, you understand. . . . Fine, you can go now."

"Thank you."

"Have a good trip."

When the Guard leaves, the group breaks up little by little. The children go back to their games. The men retreat to the bar.

You cross the square and you go back to your car. The sun is still shining down strongly on the whitewashed houses of the town. A swallow cuts through space with agility and, with slender indolence, hides under the tiled eaves of the public library.

(The library was probably still closed and the sociological comments were sleeping in your files as a consequence of the interrupted filming of the documentary and the confiscation of the film by the authorities in Yeste. Enrique was living the fervor and the drama of the Revolution in Cuba and, as in the past, you were lazily dreaming in that diffuse afternoon, stretched out on a chaise longue in the garden in the pleasant shade of the trees.)

and that's how it went until 1950 when we left Tarrasa and how we went through some calamities until we got to Gerona and the child that was born in Tarrasa went with us to Gerona where we got passports to go to France and when we reached Figueras the poor thing got sick and a doctor looked at him and told us that it wasnt anything so the next morning we took the bus and got off at the first French capital the one called Perpignan and we went right to the migration depot and the child was looked at by a French doctor very good and very kind and very intelligent and when he looked at him this doctor said there was no cure

and then we went to the Spanish Console and the secretary said Ill pay for your trip and you take him back to Spain but the company wouldnt sell us a ticket because the child was in no condition to travel and from the station we went back to the migration depot

and then I went back to the Spanish Console and the secretary when he saw how the child was suffering said that he couldnt do anything but just then the Console General who had just come from the United States came out and said right off that the child should get papers to get into the hospital right away and that this injustice will not happen again because I am a Spaniard and I have been Console in America for 20 years and that the child should have a cup of broth right away but when we got to the hospital he turned black on me all of a sudden and an hour later the poor child died we went back to the Console and cursed his father and his mother we were so upset over our only son who was from Tarrasa and we had to leave him in Perpignan and the Console said patience in the name of your son because this Console knows how to take care of sons of the Homeland

and he gave him as fine a burial as there was and Ill never forget Perpignan because neither the armed forces nor the

French authorities missed doing everything they could for us and with that respect and that love that is good for us we left giving a warm embrace to Perpignan and to all of the people who lived there

Evoke (transcribe) this scene so that it will not die with you.

Coming back from Switzerland with some other people from the agency, you had stopped in central France for a few days, following one of the gastronomical itineraries recommended by the *Guide Michelin* (Valence, Villefort, Chateau de la Muse, Millau, Saint-Affrique, Lacaune, Castres) and you found yourself on an inhospitable station in Toulouse, waiting for the express that would take you to Paris (a little fatigued from overindulgence in the liquids of St-Péray, Cornas, St-Saturnin, Gaillac, rosy, generous, and exquisite), when you noticed her on the platform: she was a woman a little over thirty, beautiful, dark, somewhat shabby, wrapped in an imitation Persian lamb coat, who was walking back and forth in the opposite direction from you, passing you continually, with a violent and uncontrollable agitation.

"*Pardon, Monsieur.* Is the train from Cerbère late?"

The employee of the SNCF had nodded negatively, and from the woman's accent (similar in a certain way to Dolores's when she was waking up or when she was sleepy), you deduced that it was a question of a fellow countrywoman with several years of residence in France (hairdresser, seamstress, or something like that). When the express arrived between the two central platforms (the panting of the locomotive intertwined with the incomprehensible gabble of the loud-speaker and the demanding bell of the sandwich cart), you saw her running along past the coaches, anxiously scrutinizing the faces of the passengers in the windows until she came to an old woman dressed in mourning whose frightened head was emerging, you thought, like that of a bird just taken from its nest.

"*Mamá,*" the woman shouted. "*Mamá.*"

You got into the coach after her and you went to her second-class compartment (the mother's baggage consisted of two large wicker baskets covered with cloth and a half-dozen cardboard boxes tied with string). The two women were crying in each other's arms and, as you pretended to be digging in your traveling bag, you spied on them at your leisure out of the corner of your eye: the mother, a peasant woman dressed in black, with her coarse kerchief over her head, her rustic coat, her humble household slippers; the daughter, with her imitation Persian lamb coat, Italian shoes of elegant design, a silk scarf around her neck; the old woman, with the misery and poverty of her native steppe still clinging to her yellow, withered skin; the young woman, attractive and composed, urbane and sophisticated; both of them embracing, both of them weeping, kissing and almost sucking, clinging to each other, happy and silent.

"Sixteen years, my God. Sixteen years."

The three of you were there in the compartment and as the train sped through the invisible (nocturnal) French countryside, the lost mother and the recovered daughter, the lost daughter and the recovered mother were caressing each other after their long and anguished separation (exodus, German occupation, bombing raids, for the one; hunger, blockade, closed frontier, for the other) as if the both of them had just discovered love, as if both of them had just invented love; with a handkerchief dampened in cologne, the daughter had wet the forehead, cheeks, lips of the mother (as if to cleanse her, you said to yourself, of the poverty and pain of those sixteen years); she had taken the coarse kerchief off her head and put her own on her; she had exchanged her slippers for some dark and modest shoes; she had taken off the coat that had worn down to the weave, and with a maternal gesture (she, the daughter) had wrapped her in her imitation Persian coat. The mother was letting her do it, dazzled by her happiness, and with her daughter's every gesture, with her daughter's every movement, a tear (a new tear) would form, precious and pure, in her eyes and would flow down across her wrinkled cheek, shining like a pearl.

When human despair crushed you more strongly than usual (which was happening lately with a certain frequency), the memory of the mother and daughter, of the meeting of the mother and daughter in a second-class compartment (on their way to Paris across a darkened France) would cure you and comfort you in the midst of the sadness and melancholy that (through your own fault, perhaps) was your daily fare. Facing the irreparable disaster of a death that, since the fainting spell on the Boulevard Richard Lenoir, you knew was certain, it pained you that their memory might disappear with you, and sitting in the garden under the moving and uncertain shade of the trees, you could feel a violent and useless rebellion against avaricious fate growing in your inner self. A fate that condemned it forever just as it was condemning you (it seemed impossible, you still felt young, vigorous sap still coursed through your body) to hard, harsh, insatiable forgetfulness.

With the gentlemans address we went to his house and when we went to his house that good gentleman told us that he had hired someone else because there was a law that said you could not give work to any Spanish worker and then I asked him why he had us come from Spain and he answered me that the one in charge in this town is me and I answered him youve put one over on me and you tricked me and then I went to the town hall and the workers in this French town took a look at my contract and gave us something to eat and told me not to let myself be taken that French workers were the friends of Spanish workers and that because he had broken French laws and had tricked us and tricked others this good gentleman would have it rough because France would let him know what it means to trick a workingman and that I should go as soon as possible to the Ministry of Labor in Narbonne because there that landowner would never trick another worker because when he found out how my child had died that good gentleman would remember what a working man was worth

and then they told me to get a lawyer as soon as I could and my lawyer was a woman called Marisa Carreras the daughter of a Catalonian father and from there we went right to an inn and the lady lawyer was very good and kind to us and paid our bill at the inn and gave us a thousand francs for the trip back because here there is nothing for Bernabeu to do that good gentleman has everything sewed up

and back in Gerona my wife was about to have another child who is the second one we have alive and she went into the hospital after two weeks and since I hadnt found any work I went to the Town Hall so they would give me a pass to the mess hall but after three days they got tired because they thought I was a loafer and then I said they should give me work until she gets out and they said you get out of here right now and I said I havent got any place to eat or sleep there isnt any law or justice here and because I said those things out loud they put me in jail for the second time

During your frequent trips across the vast and unworthy geography of your homeland, as you crossed the naked hills of the Andalusian steppe or the linear countryside of the montonous plains of La Mancha, you would often stop in some white-and-yellow settlement or a primitive and forgotten fishing village, and in the tavern, the market, or the inn, according to where you were, you would chat with the inhabitants and skillfully strike up a friendship with them. Since you were safe from need, thanks to the chance of fate that had rewarded you with being born into a rich cradle, you would listen to them talk for hours on end about their lives, their families, their work, their privations, their hopes, with an impassioned interest that your interlocutors candidly took to be pure brotherhood, but which you alone knew in your heart, although you did not recognize it at the moment, was dictated by the sordid aim of finishing your coveted documentary on emigration. In that way, with a bottle of Jumilla or some glasses of Moriles as fuel, you forged intense and ephemeral friendships with ox drivers from Lubrín, woodcutters from Siles, mule drivers from Totana, masons from Cuevas with fallacious promises of visits, the exchange of addresses, and promises to answer their letters with periodic regularity. When you said good-by to them, the emotion of their rough embrace or handshake would fill you with an ambiguous feeling of cynicism and guilt. You had the feeling that when you offered them your friendship, you were deceiving them and you were unfortunately deceiving yourself, because once the fleeting atmosphere created by your presence had been dissipated, you would forget them at once and you would never see them again. What was a simple chance meeting for you, could have been an important event for them. Obliged to repeat the scene time and again because of the needs of the filming, you had reached the painful conclusion that the brotherhood with which you had deceived yourself at first did not really exist nor could it exist, because when you separated, you would continue on with your mobile destiny and, without any intervening miracles, they would go on with their obscure and vegetative lives until they gave their poor bones back to the land in some flower-laden and bright Southern cemetery.

Their letters and post cards, written in a clumsy country hand, had come to rest on the distant desk in your studio on the rue Vieille du Temple like pathetic messages for help found inside a bottle after its long and hazardous crossing, after, a long time after the intervention of the authorities in Yeste had brought the filming of the documentary to an end. Greetings on your name day, Christmas cards, autographed family portraits piled up year after year on your files and books until that day when, wishing to break once and for all with your past and motivated by the itch to put a little order into your papers, you threw them into the fire without rereading them.

That night (it was winter, it was cold, it was even snowing) as you sat beside the peaceful and unprotected body of Dolores, meditating on the clean and deceived love of the men who, believing in you (with difficulty), had written them, you had appraised (with a thick and lucid horror) the decrepit basis of your privileged and unjust status.

This chair says José Bernabeu the chair here stayed home saying poor Bernabeu I stay here with sorrow this chair said I see that you are a working and an honorable man and you have had to go out this Sunday all day long to earn something to eat this chair promises you that some day you will have your reward because this chair is for all the boys and girls who love Catalonia and the boys and girls of the whole world because this chair carries the four bars and the shield of the Catalonian nation

this chair loves all boys and girls who have been abandoned by you this chair says that here have sat the true Catalonians and the true people of legal Spain that we have suffered miseries and imprisonment while you are taking advantage and treat us like slaves

this is being said by this chair that will be called Companys and then Freedom by name because José Bernabeu has baptized it in the name of the fallen ones of our Catalonia beloved by all the men of our legal Spain

and this chair was very sad because the chair had heard the words that people were saying some said Im going to Sitges for the summer others Im going to Majorca and this chair was listening to the shamelessness of the boorgeoisie and of the leaders of the Falange Española

this chair says madam boorgeoisie of Barcelona leaders of the

Syndicate who go together this chair asks the family of José Bernabeu what do they have to eat and this chair answers that you cant answer

well Ill answer soon you already see that Im a chair you well connected you were those revolutionaries who wanted to change everything and now you yourselves are exploiting the poor people this chair says that the people are cowed but one day theyll ask for a reckoning from you

that you the four leaders have no mercy because no one who is not of your thinking doesnt find bread or work

this chair says that its been ten years since you put the people into an inquisition but that one day ours will come too

because you have deceived Catalonia and our legal Spain in order to take advantage and make money

because the evils that you have done this chair has seen and has registered

because this chair has the four Catalonian bars and the right of legal Spain

and you in this chair that is named Companys with Freedom for a second name

in this chair baptized by José Bernabeu

in this chair I say

you will never be able to sit.

In the peaceful backwater of summer, as the dying sun equalized the hills planted with vineyards and carob beans, it was pleasant to abandon your reading and let your eyes wander across the bleeding sunset, examining things one by one, as if it were the first time and your past had suddenly been abolished, while Dolores, beside you, was reading the typed notebooks that you had left on the table and was nervously lighting one cigarette with the butt of another. The time for the injection and the ominous drops prescribed by Dr. d'Asnières was drawing near and you thought, to comfort yourself, about the coming visit of your friends, about the severe chords of the *Requiem,* about the rosy and caressing color of the new brand of wine. The shadow of Companys's old elector had disappeared into the clear air, and all that remained was you in that beautiful and undisciplined garden, listening to the measured beats of your heart, your hand stretched out on Dolores's thin hand. The compact silence was the result of an infinity of tiny sounds—the frogs' slow croaking in the pond, the buzzing of the locusts, the soft melody of the wind among the leaves of the eucalyptus trees—and, at intervals, the ax blows of the woodcutters, or the distant puffing of the locomotive made you raise your eyes and follow the concise, tight flight of the birds for a few moments across the half-awake light. Dolores had finished her reading and her look crossed yours, still intact and blue, as objects slowly dissolved into the aggressive red of the afternoon.

"Have you heard anything about him?" she asked you.

"Once in a while." You were speaking and it was as if someone else, a stranger, were answering for you. "It seems he found work in a tile factory and stayed in Tarrasa."

"What about his son? Do you remember when he came to borrow some books from us?"

You recalled his rough face, with thick lips and heavy eyebrows, while he leaned on the table in your studio on the rue Vieille du Temple and dusted off the story of his father with his gaze fixed on his shoes.

"Didn't I ever tell you?"

Dolores was asking you with her eyes, her beautiful hair hanging in locks over her forehead.

"No."

"He went back to Spain and he got into trouble."

His image floated before you again, serene and serious in the uncertain light, the same as the day when he came to say good-by to the both of you and he shook your hand for the last time.

"What kind of trouble?"

"They caught him with propaganda and they arrested him."

A blackbird had lighted on the eaves. Simultaneously the caretaker's daughter came out onto the terrace with the glass of water and the drops.

"Where is he?"

"In jail."

Your temples were suddenly pounding and, crouching in the depths of your breast, you felt a restless and dull afterpain.

"For a long time?"

"I don't know."

The drops lazily dissolved in the glass of water and in spite of your efforts, the boy's face stuck in your memory, obstinate and pugnacious, like a mute reproach.

"Who told you?" Dolores had got up from the chaise longue and was gracefully holding out the glass to you.

"Antonio." The afternoon was slowly sinking and you were speaking again. "They elected him union go-between and he got caught in the haul that followed."

VIII

It dawned without your noticing
the sun is coming up now behind the hill like a round skullcap a spherical buoy a half orange
there is peace and quiet in the garden
the birds are chirping in the branches of the eucalpytus trees the swallows are infinitely subtle an unknown serenity beautifies the countryside
up on the porch
the ash trays full of butts the empty bottles the glasses the needle tired out from so much repetition of the *Requiem* the sofa with the bundles of letters addressed to your great-grandfather the yellowed volume of *La Illustración Española y Americana*
are the tangible proofs of your night on watch
the minute exploration of your recent past
the family myth that had resided over the fate of your remote childhood
sleepiness is conquered and a dizzy lucidity possesses you
you do not want to rest go to bed forget what you have managed with so much difficulty in those short hours snatched away from sleep an impulse stronger than you turns you toward the hill where Professor Ayuso is resting
Dolores is sleeping
everybody is sleeping
you go out into the garden
you start the car
and getting ahead of the demented caravan of vehicles that is crossing the country from one side to the other
you too head toward Barcelona

By changing the direction of the telescope you could distinguish in turn

the green plain of El Prat the sea muddied by the recent outflow of the river the solitary lighthouse attacked by the bites of the waves from the new jetty under construction for the free port the oil tanks at La Campsa the cypresses and niches of the Southwest cemetery the black piles of coal in El Morrot a fleet of boats with their sails unfurled according to the rules of a mysterious and decorative strategy the sea gulls milling around the sewer mouths the lighthouse stuck into the steep and stony flank of the hill the railroad tracks with their locomotives and freight cars the ships anchored outside the harbor waiting for the pilot's signal to unload

new oil tanks modern sheds piles of soft coal the construction work on a gigantic silo the crane working on the extension of the jetty an American speedboat a launch packed with tourists the mussel beds more cranes gray black white ships the wharves inside the harbor coal trains on sidings among the piles scaffolding the towers of the aerial lift the main docks more cranes more sheds more ships . .

the lower terrace of the castle with its moats cannons visitors cars the terraced gardens of Miramar the Puerta de la Paz with its minute balanced discoverer La Barceloneta made hazy by the heat the thick smoke from the factories of Pueblo Nuevo the chaotic geometry of the city the diffuse steam of the hot season the haughty and voluptuous flight of a bird the proud chimneys of La Cefsa the gardens again

the hazy mountains that walled off the horizon belfries and steeples of churches somber baroque buildings smoke powerful banks that emerge from the anonymity like giraffe necks or menacing periscopes the towers of Sagrada Familia cupolas sordid skyscrapers a city spread out like an immense hive an infinity of houses cells hives flat hills mist the sinister Tibidabo with its church its gigantic arm its miniature airplane its terraces

the residential districts the hazy mountains smoke factories the bull ring the fairgrounds blear-eyed buildings gardens cypresses the remains of shacks bulldozers brigades of workers the park the old towers of the useless stadium the aged palace of the Exposition shacks in ruin new huts beacons silvery avenues the country the suburbs more smoke more chimneys more factories . . .

The telescopes were gray-green in color about four feet long on a fixed metal support and a spinning adjustable disk that even a short Spaniard from the plateau could work easily thanks to a step on the base that was a foot off the ground
to start them all that was necessary was to follow the instructions written on the right and on the left of the eyepieces

1 PESETA
INTRODUZCA LA MONEDA
INTRODUISEZ LA MONNAIE
INSERT COIN
GELDSTUCK EINWERFEN
APRIETE EL BOTÓN A FONDO
POUSSEZ LE BOUTON À FOND
PUSH BUTTON COMPLETELY DOWN
KNOPF VOLLSTADING EINDRUCKEN

and with your eyebrows close to the circular ring of the lens you can scrutinize point by point the rich and complex panorama of the city described as follows in the booklet in four languages profusely distributed to tourist cars as they arrive
Situated at 2 degrees 9 minutes longitude East of the Greenwich meridian and at 41 degrees 21 minutes North latitude, Barcelona is spread out on a plain between the rivers Besós and Llobregat that gradually descends from the amphitheater formed by the surrounding mountains that protect it from northerly winds to the ancient Mare Nostrum. Our city enjoys a temperate climate whose limits rarely exceed 85°F. or go below 32°F., resulting in an ideal mean temperature, which for the past five years has been 61°F. During the same period, the barometric pressure varied between 28.4 and 29.9 inches. Humidity, perhaps the most unpleasant element in our climate, has averaged 70% over the same period.
Not counting the suburbs surrounding it (one municipality of which has a population of 100,000), Barcelona, within the city limits, an area of 35.28 sq. mi., includes a population of

over a million and a half, giving it a mean of 44,060 inhabitants per square mile, the densest in Spain. The demographic development of the city is quite high, the result of a death rate that is lower than the birth rate and of the continuous migration from the province and from the rest of Spain, notably from the South.

The amphitheater of mountains surrounding Barcelona on the north has been almost completely reforested with a park. The highest point, the peak of Tibidabo (1720 ft. above sea level) is an ideal point from which to view the City, an easily accessible tourist spot where the still unfinished church of Sagrado Corazón stands, begun by San Juan Bosco. Another lookout over the provincial capital is the summit and hillside of Montjuich, the hill where its history began, crowned by the fortress that was returned to the city as a museum after a long military history.

Every June, Barcelona puts on one of the most important International Expositions. Products of Barcelona are exported to all countries of the world. International sporting events are celebrated, and every year there is an opera season in the great Liceo Theater. The Museum of Ancient Art is the finest in the world for Romantic art; the Pueblo Español offers a curious and brief model of architecture from all over Spain. Besides these universally recognized values, Barcelona has others of unknown character, since they come from ancient traditions. In winter, the fair of the mangers surrounds the neighborhood of the cathedral, and there is the turkey fair, and the parade of the Tres Tombs *marches through the City with their top hats and richly liveried horses. And in springtime, in honor of Saint George, the old Provincial Palace is filled with roses, on the Rambla de Cataluña the palms announce Palm Sunday and the age-old Calle del Hospital draws the visitor with the aroma of honey and the aromatic medicinal plants of the fair of San Ponç.*

On Corpus Christi day, the cloister of the Cathedral is decorated with l'ou com ball *over the fountain, and the solemn procession emerges with floats and the giants who dance to the music of flute and tambourine, those giants whom Chesterton, deeply moved, followed along the streets like a small child. And in the summer there are the* Fiestas Mayores *with their noisy happiness.*

This is our City; a city with all the defects of large cities and those of the peculiarities of its inhabitants; but a city that works, that lives happily under a usually blue sky, and that tries to be for visitors what it was when Don Quixote saw it more than three hundred years ago.

You imagined the knight Don Quixote with his lance his helmet and armor cooking in the sun of that lazy August morning of 1963 in the midst of the barbarian caravans of Huns Goths Suevians Vandals Alani who with dark glasses shorts straw hats wine bottles cameras castanets sandals peasant shoes *banderillas* nylon blouses Tyrolean shorts print shirts were looking at the view of the city gathered around the telescopes under the watchful eyes of the guides and the bus drivers who were making comments in Catalan
regarde comme c'est beau
c'est magnifique
mais oui c'est Christophe Colomb
it's so wonderful
qu'est-ce que c'est que ça
can you see the boat
guarda il mare
what country are they from
formidable
look at the cathedral
Danes
à gauche
ça c'est la Sagrada Familia
also welch hereliche Anssicht
look at that little one
c'est extraordinaire
là-bas près du port
guarda amore
cette brume de chaleur
it's so nice
tu as vu les oiseaux
unglanblicht die Boote der Hafen
ce sont des mouettes
è un barco americano
où est-il notre hôtel
look at the birds

look at that chick
guarda amore
c'est sublime
how about those teats
passe-moi la Retina
that one looks like Bardot
il giorno più caldo de
regarde le portavions
las Ramblas c'est plus bas
darling isn't it beautiful
man what an ass
je vois à droite
that's a nice twosome
non vedo il albergo
I'd like to roll around with her
n'oublie pas de mettre le filtre
dove andiamo mangiare

The cable had arrived unexpectedly and after the family conclave in your Uncle César's gloomy dining room the discussions went on all during the week
he must be the son of Florita Ernesto's cousin
no Mercedes Antoñito died in California
when Adelaída was widowed she married a Fornet but she had a son by
they're from the Cienfuegos branch
Aunt Lucía's little boy was named Alejandro
there are only a few minutes left before the ship is to dock and the contagion of the others' excitation has taken hold of you
the word Cuba still brings back to your mind the countryside Uncle Eulogio described so many times the fortune carefully preserved by your distant relatives the peaceful and consoling refuge in the face of the gloomy menace of the Kirghiz and their fabulous women who give birth on horseback
an unknown anxiety possesses you as the transatlantic liner slowly comes into the dock and the passengers on deck wave their handkerchiefs at you
everyone is there
Uncle César Aunt Mercedes Jorge the girl cousins

solemnly dressed as the occasion demands for such an outstanding event happy at restoring the links that had been broken over long years of blockade and uninterrupted war satisfied at finding at last other Mendiolas richer than they were after a quarter of a century of separation anxieties bitterness suffering death
waving their handkerchiefs too from the terrace of the second level of the wharf scrutinizing the now close faces of the passengers and emigrants who had boarded in Havana
that one
no that one
that man
the one with the hat on
no not that one
the one in back
conjecturing
conspiring
you were separated by a distance of seventy feet and as the passengers came down the gangplank to go through immigration and customs Uncle César used his pass as adviser to Congress and you all went into the place of honor reserved for distinguished guests
the passengers were coming through a glass door and the appearance of each one of them stirred you all up not that one not that one either or that one or that one
until the number of those still lined up grew small and the girl cousins began to count them on their fingers
a blond gentleman
a young couple
two old women who looked like old maids
a family group
a single girl
a cripple
a Negro
no one fit the one who had sent the cable or seemed to have the characteristics they expected
the stigmas
of the formerly magnificent and prosperous
and then devout and stingy
family
because he's not there

he hasn't come
maybe the blond man
no
not him either
he's going away too
I don't understand
without your noticing the Negro had come over and timidly asked
Mendiola
yes Mendiola
and that wealthy descendant of some Kaffir slave of your remote great-grandfather put out his hand
excuse me he said
I think we're relatives
there were no effusive ceremonies parties banquets and the outraged Aunt Mercedes wrinkled up her ample nose
that night
it was during that skinny meager year of 1946
a melancholy Negro dined alone in an expensive restaurant in Barcelona

The city you were looking at, was it yours
the flock of tourists had disappeared behind the guide and following the instructions written to the right and left of the telescope you put another coin into the slot and pushed the button all the way down
you examined in turn
the mausoleums and funeral monuments of Pedralbes Sarriá Bonanova constructed like residential villas or summer houses
the wild Gaudí-like and "modern-style" pantheons that could be distinguished from the prosaic and spread-out Ensanche
the blocks of niches in the modern city with its heavy traffic of funeral processions and walking dead
the cells sockets and urns of the immense slum beehive
the shacks and huts condemned like their precarious owners to the inevitable fate of potters field
the cemetery was outside your city was the cemetery
you left the scope of the instrument
the haze softened the reflection of the sun and mixed in with the

vapor from the chimneys the smoke from the factories the silent exhaust of the vehicles the panting of a million and a half inhabitants crowded into this hot day who were eating working drinking walking without really knowing
you asked yourself
whether their life was or was not
as your classic writers had thought
a hazy ephemeral rubbed-out and inconsistent dream

You continued unhurriedly on your way
bombards culverins gun carriages cannons that in remote and now forgotten times had guarded the military security of the Spaniards of your caste were now the target of the lenses of improvised photographers a part of family group shots arms over shoulders hands together looks smiles
dozens of cars with foreign licenses were in the parking lot at the lookout and the ones still arriving endlessly had to go along the austere walls of the castle cross the bridge again in the opposite direction and look for a spot in the outside parking lot
a little way from the telescopes two sentries in dress uniform were watching the coming and going of the public with the stupefied and servile look of two intruders in a gala family reunion
you walked along the side terrace behind a group of Germans who were in ecstasy over the view of the sea the harmonious unfurling of the sails the aircraft carriers of the American Sixth Fleet the small and agile gulls
the gardens stretched out beyond the castle with their trees flowers shrubs trash baskets benches
with a rapid glance you took in the well-lined paths the grass borders the anti-aircraft guns friendly ornamental senile
you went through an open postern in the curtain of the façade and along an indirectly lighted corridor you came out into what had been the drill yard of the retired military fortress
the ground was cobblestone the four galleries formed a cloister with severe stone arches and at the corners there were flower pots vases and even a well with the pulley held up by forged iron
in the center

in the middle of a square of grass marked off by four stones
a somber base held up the equestrian statue of a bronze warrior the gift of the City
the plaque said so
to its Liberator and Caudillo
you took refuge in the shade of the porticos
the tourists were going through in compact groups toward the Army museum they were photographing the equestrian statue they were clustered around the souvenir stands they were turning the card racks they were going into the shop with Antiques Heraldic Material Lead Soldiers

ENTRADA LIBRE
ENTRÉ LIBRE
ENTRANCE FREE
EINTRITT FREI

the bullfight poster suddenly drew your attention

SOUVENIR SOUVENIR
OF SPAIN OF SPAIN
Monumental Bullring
Great Bullfight
6 Beautiful and Brave Bulls 6
with the pink and green colors
of the famous ranch of
Don Baltasar Iban of Madrid
for the great bullfighters
LUIS MIGUEL DOMINGUÍN
ICI VOTRE NOM—YOUR NAME . HERE—HIER, IHRE NAMEN
ANTONIO ORDÓÑEZ
with their respective teams
music furnished by the Band of
"La Popular Sansense"

you passed by quickly
a crowd of curious people was examining the photographic compositions in which a bullfighter (headless) was placing (with the stamp of a master) a pair of *banderillas* and a Gypsy woman (also headless) was fanning herself (very flashy she was) opposite a mock-up of the Giralda

in a devilish Esperanto a characteristic example of a little Spaniard from the steppe was explaining that it was a matter of a cut-off image with which the señoras y caballeros messieurs et dames ladies and gentlemen here present could surprise their friends and acquaintances dressed as bullfighters and Gypsies when they returned to sus respectivos países leur pays d'origine your native countries and afirmar así su personalidad affirmer leur personalité show your personality with the story of your adventuras españolas aventures espagnoles Spanish adventures

SU FOTO EN 20 MINUTOS
VOTRE PHOTO EN 20 MINUTES
YOUR PICTURE IN 20 MINUTES
IHR FOTO IN 20 MINUTEN

(in the morning paper you had read the chilling news of a student of philosophy from Madrid who was paying for his education by having his picture taken with tourists dressed as a bullfighter in a famous and typical bar in Palma de Mallorca
what kind of philosophical system would he conceive
you asked yourself
this future and unique genius this Erasmus from Atocha)
you climbed the stairs to the broad naked terraces of the castle
the empty sentry boxes at the corners stood up like the rocks of a broken-down chess set
with the military prison closed the paving blocks eroded by the wind the broken-down observation posts were surviving with a resigned and quiet nostalgia
away from the groups of tourists who with their hats dark glasses cameras were adventuring about the brilliant desolation of the bricks you sat down on an abutment of the wall and watched the unreal flight of the birds the hot and violent courtyard the vague blue sky the fanatical sun that seemed to be burning everything up
light solitude emptiness silence death
the ancestral limits of the jail were reconstituted in a treacherous and subtle way under the polished stone the plastering carefully brought out the rejuvenated and clean façades the conscience whitewashed by the absolution and forgetfulness of History
blinded by the abrupt reflection you closed your eyes for a moment

Nevertheless
in this same environment of burned earth remote sky impossible birds obsessive light
during the reign of the Twenty-Five Years of Peace recognized and celebrated by all right-thinking people in the world
armed men had beaten defenseless fellow countrymen with whips lashes clubs had vent their fury on them with rifle butts ropes boots guns
men whose only crime had been to take up arms in defense of their legal government fulfill their oath of allegiance to the Republic proclaim their right to a just and noble existence believe in the free will of a human being write the word FREEDOM on walls fences sidewalks buildings
they had counted a thousand and one times the columns in the cloister calculated the exact number of paving stones on the ground mentally measured the avaricious and strict confines that held them in
chasing a miserable ball made out of rags staring at the infinite blue square of the sky spying on the free and generous flight of the birds
beating their heads against the wall spitting blood
running lightly until they lost consciousness obeying in silence the call of the bugle waiting their turn before the dirty common pot lining up in ragged overalls after mass
sleeping in dark and damp dungeons shivering with cold on winter nights dreaming about inaccessible and beautiful women listening for the rough sound of the boots that would announce the changing of the guard
they had knelt on Sundays during the elevation of the Holy Host masturbated in the thick and propitious den of the evil-smelling mats opened their veins in a sudden attack of alienation and madness
condemned to death
they looked for the last time at the sky the clouds the birds all that in one way or another represented life for them
they spent the agitated vigil that precedes execution they wrote their farewell letters to father mother wife sweetheart children they ate the last plate of lentils they avidly drank the last cup of coffee they walked to the execution wall under guard surrounded pushed held up by their executioners
they faced the rifles with serenity wept bravely asked permission

to give the command to fire begged for their lives made peace with God refused the solace of the priest shouted laughed howled pissed from fear
they fell cut down by the bullets
they gave up their last sigh

The climate is magnificent
the place is located in the subtropical zone and the benign action of the ocean currents make its winters brief and mild its summers stimulating and cool an ideal country in short for rheumatics and people suffering from gout
its flora is splendid generous wild
immense fruit trees of varying colors huge and exotic
the wild animals wander freely through the fields fight off destructive plagues are friends and allies of man
your house crowns the height of a hill surrounded by blue sea coral reefs white sand beaches clumps of coconut palms
the round sun shines down on the treetops and there is not a single cloud in the sky
from your window you take in the crops of coffee cacao vanilla sugar cane copra
baobabs palms ceibas sequoias figs
smokestacks of the plantations where your peasants and workers are hard at work
the awning the pond the arbor the gardens
the foremen came over to meet you awaiting your orders
you gave them quickly
like a self-made Texan severe and silent
terse with words and brusque in appearance
but discreet and noble in your heart
while your wife and children swing in their hammocks surrounded by exquisitely dressed guests
Latin-American ladies with fans necklaces *moiré* skirts satin slippers
gentlemen in top hats
agile greyhounds slender cats showy parrots decorative children
the dance is about to start
you open it with the prettiest girl turning and turning under the gaudy decorations on the ceilings
an old waltz from the Austro-Hungarian Empire

lighted by candlesticks held by liveried servants
with a glass of champagne in your hand
you go to the stables
an Anglo-Arabian horse called Johnny
you saddle him
you leave at a gallop
the Negroes wave lovingly
their food consists of cane sugar wild flowers aromatic herbs
without your having to resort to punishment they admire you they respect you they love you
their personality is soft and they are Catholics
you call them all by name
Bobó
Sesé
Arará
just as in novels by Emilio Salgari
and they ask your blessing kneel kiss your hand
you spend a long time riding over your lands to see that everything is in order
your property your real estate your animals your income
the peasants take off their hats as they greet you
the old men smile at you
the children gather around
the animals of the jungle escort you
briars and orchids incline as you pass and they seem to be doing you homage
you think you are safe
enthroned in your position now and forever
and when you wake up a few seconds later
you come to in your room in the country house with the *Geography of Cuba* of your Uncle Eulogio under your pillow
no scepter
no crown
no underlings
no kingdom
a conscientious reader of Spengler and Keyserling in a menopausal country of the Old Continent condemned to disappear because of your soft life and the slow degeneration of the race
with the serious abandonment of your thirteen years
unarmed
overcome by fear

at the mercy of the carnivorous Kirghiz
and their fabulous women who give birth on horseback

You opened your eyes again brought back by the hot summer sun
without knowing for certain whether the recent past of your country was real
or whether it was simply a question
as everything led you to believe on that suffocating day in August in the Year of Our Lord 1963 and as happened with certain frequency in your latitudes
just one month after your return to Spain
forty-eight hours after Ayuso's burial
in your exploratory sentimental journey
of a hallucination
a bad dream
a drunkard's characteristic hangover
the prosaic and vulgar phenomenon of a mirage

Forward then
you went down to the courtyard you passed by the doors of the cells changed into souvenir shops you dodged new groups of tourists fresh off the buses you went into the corridor through which those condemned to death were led to the wall you went out into the open air you retrod the path of those who had been shot
a path several feet wide that led along a tunnel to the mythical moats of the castle
the door was wide open and from the opening a visitor could take in a section of the well-kept garden with borders of grass trees cypresses climbing vines
foreigners and natives were walking slowly along the paths
they would stop to admire the begonia pots take pictures of the walls that had been the scenes of the vengeful executions
brigades of workers had carefully erased the bullet marks and opened to the indiscreet looks of the curious the place seemed to proclaim to the four winds its innocence deny the legends and fables invented by envious and resentful people deny for future generations of Spaniards its presumed blame

Although there was no plaque that said so the President of the abrogated Generalitat de Catalunya had lived in Montjuich during the last moments of his life
turned over by the Nazis after the fall of France the politician feted one day by the crowds in Barcelona went down into the moat of the castle escorted by the soldiers' bayonets
he thought with pain and nostalgia about his beloved city
he breathed in the pure wild air of the mountain
he looked at the clear blue sky for the last time
you gave a twenty-duro bill to the caretaker of the garden and without having to ask the question
your intent had been so obvious
the man guided you toward the left pointed at a blank part of the wall and said lowering his voice
here is
sir
where they shot Companys

They had told you when you were a child and you had believed it
obliged to free his slaves by decree of the Colonial Government
your great-grandfather had brought his Negroes together in the plantation sugar mill and with tears in his eyes
because of course he loved them
he declared them free
suffering beings like everyone else
with no protection over them at all
abandoned to cruel fate
with no owner
with no master
with no protection
and when they heard him
the Negroes wept in turn
because your great-grandfather was a good man
he did not whip them
he fed them
he protected them
and in their own
rustic and primitive
savage way

they
the Negroes
loved him too
but it was all a lie
his protection
the food
the pretended love that joined them all together
the pain of the separation
the speeches
the tears
you know now
since you too have freed yourself from them and are sailing on alone
saying to yourself
blessed be my deviation
everything that separates me from all of you and brings me closer to the pariahs
the accursed
the Negroes
my intelligence
my heart
my instinct
blessed be they
thanks be given to god
infinite thanks
now and forevermore

On the right an iron grating protected the redoubt dedicated to the memory of those Fallen for God and for Spain
it was an evocative corner a peaceful silent retreat
with an altar of simple lines a bronze statue a rustic garden through which lizards played to their hearts' content with visible and slow sensuality
a guide was informing the tourists of what had happened in Barcelona between July 1936 and January 1939
and just like a Monsieur Dupont Mister Brown Herr Schmidt of the ten or so million who were honoring you all with a visit that summer you went over to listen to his explanations
ici messieurs dames c'est l'endroit où fûrent fusillés par les Rouges pendant notre guerre de Libération de nombreux hauts officiers

de l'Armée de prêtres de personnalités relevantes de la vie sociale de notre ville
the foreigners were listening with an intent expression and you went away from them
an unconquerable nausea came over you
prend-moi une photo
regarde c'est le Monument aux Morts
ladies and gentlemen
mon Dieu quelle chaleur
can it be possible
you said to yourself
that this is the end
that you all must respect as something definite
the injustice imposed by the force of arms
to make what had once existed never exist
a feasible undertaking for those skillful puppet masters of the idea existence and attributes of God
tu te rappelles l'année dernière
look here my darling
c'est extraordinaire l'impression de paix
de quelle guerre s'agit-il
you had returned to Spain after ten years of waiting taken up in plans projects dreams speculations utopias
and just like the Limping Devil from the vantage point of the lookouts
you were spying on your native city
tired
ill
without strength
on the brink of suicide
listening to the beats of a fragile heart that
just as on the Boulevard Richard Lenoir six months before
was foretelling
was already announcing
the necessary farewell
an old man dressed in a seersucker suit was fanning himself in the shadow of the wall indifferent and as if removed from the chatter of his transistor
you leaned on the railing of the lookout and you opened the tourist folder written in four languages
SHORT HISTORY OF OUR CITY

on the ruins of an Iberian village inhabited by the Layetans the Roman colony Faventia Julia Augusta Pia Barcino was founded
in Hispania Citerior whose capital was Tarraco
telling yourself
nothing worthwhile can come out of you or out of the human stew in which you live or out of these sad times
better to shut up
shut your mouth
not prolong as routine the laughable farce of the intellectual who thinks he is suffering and obscenely proclaims it
for his country for its people
going down the Spain and all that shit
with your gaze lost on the sea the jetty the American Sixth Fleet the coal piles the oil tanks the sailboats the gulls the sewers
get away from your flock your detour honors you
cultivate everything that separates you from them
glorify whatever in you bothers them
the strict and absolute negation of their order that is what you are
as the old man fans himself relaxed and happy
and the transistor goes on tirelessly
under King Ataulfus it became the capital of the Visigothic Empire which in the fifth century extended through Hispania and Gallia when the capital was transferred to Toledo Barcelona lost its importance
thinking about the history of your country a history that was yours only for moments
in its past which was nothing but that
a past
and it was lucky to have been so because no clean present poured forth from it
in the deeds of its people
because you had to call them something
even though they were as sterile in their results as the barren and avaricious soil of its steppe
a demonstration *ad absurdum* of a battle kept up century after century against inner ghosts and demons a fight of brother against lucid brother whose memory neither time nor death respected
the Spanish civil war
là-bas vers la droite

assassinés par les Rouges
it suffered the vicissitudes of the Christian kingdoms invaded by the Moslems in the eighth century it was reconquered by the Franks under the command of Louis the Pious in the year 801
soul of Ochún sanctify me
body of Changó save me
blood of the way of Yemayá intoxicate me
the green plain of El Prat the solitary lighthouse attacked by the waves the new breakwater under construction in the free port
crying out
everything has been futile
oh my country
my birth among yours and the deep love that
without your asking
for years I have obstinately offered you
let us part like good friends while there still is time
nothing joins us except your beautiful language stained today by sophistry lies angelic hypotheses apparent truths
phrases empty as hollow shells
distilled syllogisms
good words
then it became the capital of the Spanish March against the Mohammedan Empire Wilfred the Hairy declared the title Count of Barcelona hereditary in 897
rambling
better to live among foreigners who express themselves in a strange tongue than in the midst of countrymen who prostitute yours every day
they lower their heads
what can you do they say
faced with the brutal order that denies them and despoils them of their precious and irreplaceable essence
modern scaffolding piles of soft coal a launch loaded with tourists mussel beds gray black white ships docks cranes
after those invasions Barcelona emerged as the capital of an independent State the former March was now Catalonia
asking yourself
your present despair is it a triumph for them
he conquers who after sowing harvests only useless strife and parched death

regarde mon chéri
do you really like that
là-bas c'est Majorque
from Ramón Berenguer I on it acquired more and more importance it annexed the territories conquered from the Moslems and extended its domains into what is today part of France
listening to the chorus of the Voices that attack you like the premonitory witches in the first act of *Macbeth*
think about it there's still time
our firmness is unmovable no effort of yours will be able to undermine it
we are stone and stone we will remain
don't insist any more go away
look toward other horizons turn your back on all of us
forget about us and we will forget you
your passion was a mistake
heed it
SALIDA
SORTIE
EXIT
AUSGANG
tout le monde est partie
come here my darling
the towers of the aerial lift the docks more cranes more sheds more ships
with James I the Conqueror a new policy of expansion began across the Mediterranean
violent and sumptuous sex of Changó refresh me
maternal Yemayá receive me
hide me in your uterus
do not let them drag me out of you
the Puerta de la Paz La Barceloneta the thick smoke from the factories
but no
that is not their victory
and if a fate that is harsh for you as it was for the others takes you away
without your wishing
before you see the life of your country and its men restored
leave evidence at least of this time do not forget what happened there do not be silent

the chaotic geometry of the city the three chimneys of La Cefsa
belfries and spires of churches gardens
on va rater le car
tu te rends compte
perhaps someone will understand later
what order you tried to resist and what your crime was
INTRODUZCA LA MONEDA
INTRODUISEZ LA MONNAIE
INSERT COIN
GELDSTUCK EINWARFEN

Havana–Paris–Saint-Tropez–Tangier
Autumn 1962–Spring 1966